James Pomerantz

THE FLATHEAD SALOON AND CATHOUSE

AmErica House
BALTIMORE

First printing

ISBN: 1-893162-13-3
PUBLISHED BY AMERICA HOUSE BOOK PUBLISHERS
www.ericahouse.com
Baltimore

Printed in Canada

THAT WHICH COMES TO US IN LIFE MUST BE EARNED

OR IT HAS NO VALUE.

WHAT COMES TO US BY CHANCE IS OUR CHARACTER,

OUR ULTIMATE VALUE.

SUCCESS WILL NOT BE A MEASURE OF QUANTITY,

IT IS SIMPLY THE CONSTITUTION OF THE PATH

AND THE DIRECTION OF THE HEART.

This book is dedicated to my wife, Mary, and our four children. They have shared my frustrations, tolerated my hours, and supported my varied endeavors. As a writer, it is ironic when I have few words to describe those most important in my life. I love them unconditionally.

Many thanks to:

Frank and Shirley Lockridge	Lakeside, Montana
Pete Rolfing	Somers, Montana
Sheriff James R. Dupont	Flathead County Sheriff's Office
Job Hernandez	Tactical Unit, Chicago Police Department
James Howard	Attorney at Law, Lakeside, Montana
Kathleen Burch	Rehabilitation Institute of Chicago
Dr. Richard Pomerantz	Ann Arbor, Michigan
Hugo Ralli	Gibson's Steakhouse, Chicago, Illinois
Jim O'Conner	Chicago, Illinois
Richard Gayle	Attorney, Chicago, Illinois
Steve Balmes	Chicago, Illinois
Ray and Toni Tonelli	Northbrook, Illinois

The residents of Lakeside, Big Fork, and Somers, Montana

E. S.--Thank you, from my heart and my family.

My parents, in so many ways.

THEY CALL SOMEPLACE PARADISE,

I DON'T KNOW WHY.

YOU CALL SOMEPLACE PARADISE

KISS IT GOODBYE.

DON HENLEY   GLENN FREY

CHAPTER ONE

"Hello." She picked the telephone up on the second ring.

"May I speak to Marvin Tracy, please?" Mickey Baine asked.

"Who is this?" Her voice was sultry.

"My name is Garett Baine. I'm calling from the Dean Witter office in Chicago."

"Do you know my husband?"

"No, ma'am. I'm calling to introduce myself and provide some information about Dean Witter.

I'm not selling anything, today. This call is to provide information on the services that Dean

Witter can provide."

"Why didn't you introduce yourself to me?" The woman asked.

"Excuse me." Baine noted the rising inflection in her voice.

"Why did you assume, Mr. Garett, that my husband controls the money at this house?"

"I didn't assume anything, ma'am. Should I be speaking to you?"

"Do women scare you, Mr. Garett?"

"I'll have to admit that sometimes they do, ma'am." Baine chuckled.

"Women with money shouldn't scare you, Mr. Garett. I buy municipal bonds. We never purchase less than five hundred at a crack. Have you ever landed a $500,000 hit on a cold call, Mr. Garett?"

"Not that I recall."

"It won't happen today, either. I'm not much in the mood for business."

"I'm sorry to disturb you, ma'am. What day would be more convenient to speak to you about our bond inventory?" Baine's grip tightened on the phone.

"Pity about today. These calls creep up the inside of my thighs like wet sand on a warm holiday. Would you like to know what I'm wearing, Mr. Garett?"

"Ma'am?"

7

"Not much, at all. I enjoy walking around a large house on Sheridan Road wearing nothing. I like my body, Mr. Garett. It's my finest asset You search to uncover assets, don't you?"

"Investable assets, ma'am." Baine was tired of this game.

"Precisely, Mr. Garett. I have an investable asset. So far, the returns have been phenomenal. Can you suggest any new positions for my assets? I enjoy risk, Mr. Garett."

"Let me get back to you on that one." Garett Baine placed the receiver down, abruptly ending the call.

Garett Baine sat at his desk in the bullpen area at Dean Witter Reynolds in Chicago. He was not quite sure of how he ended up at this particular vocation. Garett Baine had been an account executive at Dean Witter for nearly two years. Sexual torment had not been a topic of discussion during sales training.

"R.J." Garett yelled across the bullpen floor.

"What, Garett?"

"Does your mother still live on Sheridan Road?"

The bullpen at a major brokerage house is the area where new brokers and broker trainees conduct all of their business. Polo shirts and silk ties rarely leave the confined quarters of the bullpen. Private offices are only given to those reaching certain specific financial plateaus. They must achieve specific numbers in assets gathered, accounts opened, and gross production. Gross production is another phrase for commissions generated. Garett Baine had made a career change at the age of forty. Now forty-two, Garett fit like a square peg in a round hole. At five feet ten inches tall, he carried a stocky frame. Garett played outside linebacker for two years at Indiana, before tiring of his practice dummy status. A one hundred and ninety pound walk-on doesn't win a job in the Big Ten. His days now, lead him to the free weights and heavy bags. There are no low impact machines or aerobics classes. Bruce Carson, Dean Witter's Branch Manager at the Loop office, hired Garett for his entrepreneurial background and not his unorthodox appearance. While the company stopped short of specific policies on hair length and facial hair, Carson made clear his misgivings. Garett Baine wore a closely trimmed full beard, and his blond hair had grown darker over the past ten years. Garett's hair was swept back in layers and reached the top of his thick shoulders. Ties and jackets were mandatory, but the alligator boots were unique. Ann Volker, the lone female broker in the bullpen, gave Garett a sign for his desk not long after he arrived. The sign read, "Jimmy Buffet meets Warren Buffet."

Garett was in the middle of his daily cold-calling. This practice is commonly referred to as telemarketing annoyance. New brokers are strictly monitored, and calls are counted on a daily basis. Branch managers publish a monthly newsletter ranking the bullpen brokers by the number of calls made. In this office, two-hundred dials per day is a good day. Out of those two hundred calls, a broker may get to speak to forty people, or 'buying units'. He may have mild interest from ten. Out of the mildly interested ten, he may meet one. The inability to deal with rejection will destroy most new brokers. A new broker must interrupt people during dinner. He must disturb their weekends. Success is taught as a numbers game. To be successful, a broker must understand that he is a salesman before he ever becomes a financial planner. The new broker must travel through the pages of every local telephone book. He must invent new ways to disturb families and invade their private hours. The new broker must rehearse plausible twenty second sound bites to limit the initial hang-up response. The profession breeds futility, while self analysis surpasses despicable. Garett was forty-two years old, married to Lindsay and father to four children.

"My name is Garett Baine and I work for Dean Witter, here in Chicago. The reason for my call sir, is to see if you have any interest in an 8.5% Preferred Stock from Commonwealth Edison, non-callable for five years. It is a new issue, so there is no commission paid on your end. The price is $25.00 per share. Does this sound like something you would be interested in adding to your portfolio?"

"How did you get my name?"

"Dean Witter uses a number of marketing sources for names."

"Well, take me off this god damn list. I do not do business over the phone..." Click, the phone was already hung up before the man could finish his last sentence. Garett could never get used to cold-calling. He knew it was necessary, but despised every thought and picture of himself doing it. During his first week of training, Garett Baine noticed an unusual sense of futility throughout the bullpen. Unlimited potential could never produce the present moral. Garett vowed to make his new career different.

"Hello, my name is Garett Baine and I work for Dean Witter..." The routine was the same.

"Did you want to speak to Mr. Villa?"

"Yes, is he in?"

"No, he has been dead for three years. Do you think someone could cross his name off these lists? I seriously doubt he will be buying many stocks. "

"Sorry, ma'am. We'll take care of this problem right away." Garett was lying. There would be nothing done about the man's name coming up time and time again. The list was from an outside source and there were simply too many names that didn't belong. Marketing lists were rarely updated. Do Not Call Lists existed in training sessions. Garett had never seen one.

"Hey, Sunshine. Are you still putting any prospects or clients into Putnam New Opportunities?"

"Shit, yes. The fucker is up 29% with no Dean Witter, five percent back end bullshit."

"What about the trailers?"

"Fuck the trailers. I'll worry about the trailers when my book is well over $10 million. I need the accounts, now."

Sunshine was Ken Grady, a one year broker from the Lincoln Park section of Chicago. Ken complained about everything. In this light he was not much different than most of the new brokers at the Dean Witter downtown office. Ken was unique because he constantly vocalized his complaints. He would ramble on about how one could not sink much lower than their current vocation. Many brokers coming into the securities business having achieved some degree of success in other businesses. Garett had owned four restaurants during the eighties. At one time, he had over one-hundred employees. Ken had worked for Yves Saint Laurent, and at one point was making in excess of $200,000 per year as a sales rep. Companies began to downsize and realize that they were paying their sales people too much money. Now, they were both destined to earn less than forty-thousand dollars for their second year in the brokerage business. This compensation proved hardly a figure worth enduring almost constant rejection. The upside potential slipped further and further away; there are no limits on the potential income of a broker. Simply gather fifty to one-hundred million dollars in assets managed and a broker can relax. A broker's job is the hardest job to earn thirty thousand dollars and the easiest job to earn a quarter million dollars. At most major firms, eighty percent of new brokers are out of the business in less than two years.

At any given time of the day or evening, the noise in the bullpen was distracting at best and overwhelming more often than not. Chaos is fourteen to twenty brokers calling residential numbers until eight-thirty p.m. in an open office. Small nerf footballs fly from one cubicle to the next. Arguments on the previous day's college hoops action and who's giving how many points tonight are raging. This is the backdrop to "qualified individuals " making sales presentations concerning an individual's retirement income or life savings.

"Shit, that God damn lady thought I was selling real estate." one broker blurted out. "I tell her I'm from Dean Witter and she thanks me for calling but they have no desire to sell their home. At that point, I just tell her to keep us in mind when she is ready."

"Hey Jake, are you selling any Trexon these days? It dumped a point yesterday and New York put it on the restricted list. Christ, Spencer and his clients must own the company by now."

"I have beaten that horse to death and I'm still swinging the stick. I haven't sold two lousy shares in the last two weeks. That story line is spent. The stock's been flat for a year. They can restrict it all they want. The son of a bitch has no more legs. Where's the rest of that list we split?"

"We finished that thing last week."

Jake is thirty-nine years old, married with two daughters. As a salesman for a candy company in the Pittsburgh area, he did very well until he was laid off in another company downsizing. His wife works as the public relations director to a major manufacturing company. She was offered a job in the Chicago area at a salary of over $100,000 per year. They have lived in Chicago for three years. Matt Hipple is a twenty-four year old recent graduate of the University of Illinois. Matt looks like he is eighteen, and is talented, aggressive, and smart. He has to stay on the phones. Once people see Matt, they are more inclined to adopt him than turn over their life savings. It is a difficult sale at twenty four years old, to convince a couple ready for retirement that you can handle what took them a life time to attain. Shaving seems to be a requirement most clients have for their male brokers.

Garett Baine hated his predicament. He understood that sacrifice could lead to the future for his family that the restaurant business did not provide. He felt that this business might take three to five years to build to a satisfactory level. Twenty months into the profession, three to five years would not bring him anywhere close to a satisfactory level. Garett began another call.

"Hello, my name is Garett Baine with Dean Witter here in Chicago..."

"Wait a minute, wait a minute," came the voice on the other end. "Do I know you?"

"No, but..."

"But what? I don't know you, we've never met. Yet, you guys call me constantly trying to shove some form of investment down my throat. I don't want people calling my house who don't know me. Can you comprehend that, asshole? You guys are all low rent dirt bags."

With that the gentleman hung up. Garett softly placed the receiver back, and turned his head towards Sunshine.

"Tell me again why we do this. Take this number and call this prick back for me. Tell him you are representing the Low Rent Dirt Bags of America and we take umbrage to his disparaging remarks. Tell him we are proud to be Low Rent Dirt Bags and on behalf of Low Rent Dirt Bags everywhere, we will carry on." Ken took the number and dialed. There was no answer.

11

The brokers in the bullpen at Dean Witter in Chicago choreographed the practice of retaliation.

Dean Witter is located in the heart of Chicago's Loop. This company generates over five billion dollars in revenue annually. The Chicago office is one of two flagship offices for the firm, the other being located at the World Trade Center in New York City. Garett Baine is one of nearly nine-thousand brokers nationwide for Dean Witter. The downtown Chicago office is home to well over one-hundred of these brokers. Garett takes the escalator down to Monroe Street, where he hustles past the throngs of the disenchanted. He wonders which one of the delinquent acts from his rebellious youth condemned him to this uncivilized version of speed dial humiliation. Located four blocks from the office, the International Parking Garage sits at the gateway to Grant Park. This structure houses twelve floors for parking, roughly fifteen hundred cars. Monthly fees start at two-hundred dollars. The owners of this venture decided that extracting large sums of money from its customers was simply not enough, and added ethnic musical identification to each floor.

Five years ago, Garett Baine owned two restaurants. He had over one-hundred employees and a combined gross volume of over two million dollars. His income had averaged $125,000 during the eighties. Every decision made at his businesses would ultimately come down to him. He had no partners. Now, five years later, Garett's commissions totaled less than forty-thousand for the previous twelve months. He spent his day cold-calling seniors. Evenings would be spent cold-calling homes in search of the pension rollover or the fortune sitting in money market. Long gone, were the proceeds from the sale of Garett's last restaurant. He was barely meeting his monthly expenses. This foray into the world of financial investments had become a ten year apprenticeship that he wanted no part of. Garett Baine simply didn't handle humiliation as well as some. Now, each day he stood in the lobby of this parking garage known as "The International Garage", where each floor was named after a different country. One was the U.S. Two was Spain. Three was England. And so on. As the elevator reached each floor the doors would open to the music of that particular country. Parking every day on Mexico required a stroll to his car accompanied by the Mexican Hat Dance music. Walking to his Blazer, Garett realized humiliation had no boundaries.

Leaving the city of Chicago during rush hour is an ordeal consisting of daily gridlock. Parking lots masquerade as expressways. The nightmare of Garett's position included the commuter shuffle, complete with a twelve step program on road rage. Eyes forward, never tail gate, never display the middle finger, etc., etc. The urban landscape crept along with the constant scramble to find the faster lane. Wives were waiting at home to remind the highway jockeys of how the geek next door was exercising his stock options, planning the new addition, or making reservations for Cancun. Career frustrations seemed to bring up the success level of the neighborhood. Garett was driving a 1989 Chevy Blazer with 77,000 miles on it. The outside finish was down to the primer and the vehicle was covered with nicks and scratches.. During the eighties Garett had owned three different BMW's, a Porsche 911, a Mitsubishi 3000GT, and a Nissan 300ZX. Each night in traffic, Garett watched as the cars of his youth gleamed beside his Blazer. Personalized plates spoke of wealthy traders and yuppie lawyers. The miles wore on like a parade of sarcasm, scratching the blackboard of Garett's existence.

Garett and Lindsay Baine live in Sheridan Shores, a wealthy suburb north of Chicago and located along Lake Michigan. They bought their house in early 1983 and watched property values skyrocket through the eighties. Their four children range in ages from ten to three. The house is a Victorian design, built somewhere around the turn of the century. There are no records on exactly what year the house was built, and during construction of a new addition in 1987, they found a train schedule from 1903 in one of the walls they took down. Lindsay had looked at this house once and told Garett that she had found the house of their dreams. Actually, it was the house of her dreams. Over the years the price of real estate in Sheridan Shores has reached a level of absurdity. There is not a lot or a bungalow in this small community priced under a quarter of a million dollars, and the average price of a home is over one million dollars. Garett could never afford this community today. Taxes in Sheridan Shores are astronomical. The schools are nationally ranked. The number of clubs, organizations, silent auctions, travel agencies, real estate offices, and grade school aged children in therapy is implausible. Garett Baine needed a take home income in excess of $70,000 to remain in Sheridan Shores. With their savings depleted, the inevitable would have to be addressed.

Garett was greeted in the usual manner as he arrived home. Conner and Christopher, ages 5 and 3, attempted to tackle their father each night. Jake, age 10, was at basketball practice and Maggie, age 9, was at Irish Dance lessons.

"Garett, your father called and wants you to call him as soon as you get home. He said it was important, but wouldn't say anything more." Lindsay kissed him on the cheek as she relayed the message. She has always hated the restaurant business because of the hours, but these days those hours didn't seem so bad considering the money they have given up. Lindsay was constantly frustrated when Garett was in the bar business because they could never do anything with their neighbors and friends.

13

Garett always worked on Friday and Saturday nights. Now they could finally go out, and they didn't have the money.

"Dad, it's me. What's going on?"

"Garett, I just got word on your grandfather. He passed away a couple of weeks ago. You know I haven't heard from him in over a year. I didn't even know where he was living. I just knew it somewhere near Kalispell, Montana. He has lived there for the last twenty years or so, but we never stayed in touch. I think you have had more contact with him than I have. He always sent the kids presents and they never met him. All your kids have known is that they have had a great-grandfather living in the Northwest somewhere. They never knew that the most important part of his life always centered on a bottle of Jack Daniels and a pack of Camels. The man's skin was like leather and at the age of eighty, he looked one-hundred and ten. He would be ninety this year. Anyway, the coroner's office called from Kalispell. Seems like Randolf Baine died in his sleep two weeks ago. They need someone to identify the body and there is some sort of will that needs to be read out there, according to his instructions. Can you go out there and take care of this for me. Your mother and I would prefer not to go. You know, I never understood why he didn't attend my mother's funeral twenty years ago."

"I'll go, dad. Don't worry, I'll take care of everything."

"Thanks, Garett."

*   *   *

Lindsay and Garett have been married for thirteen years. The four children were a blessing, but Garett was feeling the pressure of raising them in the lifestyle they have been used to. Losing a position paying over one-hundred thousand dollars per year and starting from scratch again had begun to take a toll on Garett's marriage. Young vows of undying love, love that would not be affected by the ravages of material wealth, had somewhat grown accustomed to the amenities of living in Sheridan Shores along Chicago's affluent North Shore. Lindsay never listened to Garett when he spoke of how insecure the restaurant business was. She never imagined that they would be without an income. Garett, apparently, never took himself too seriously because they spent every dime they made. He was an ambitious and hard working individual, but it is ironic that he wound up in the securities business. The business of planning for the financial future of other individuals. Four or five days in Montana would not be a bitter pill to swallow for either Garett or Lindsay. In fact, they had been getting on each other's nerves so much lately, neither would admit to the relief in the knowledge that Garett would be leaving for a few days. They played the martyr role very well.

"Lindsay, I've got to go out to Montana for a few days. My grandfather died near Kalispell, Montana. He died a couple of weeks ago and they just notified my father. You know what kind of relationship they had. Anyway, he asked me to go out there for him and take care of the arrangements for bringing his body back here and the reading of his will. He left instructions that his will be read in Kalispell. This is not a good time for me to be leaving work, but I promised my father I would do this." Garett was lying. He was thrilled to be getting out of Chicago for a few days and having someone else pick up the tab. He had never been to Montana, but the location was not important.

"Great Garett. I think it is a very generous gesture for you to tell your father that this is not a problem. We have four kids and you are home sparingly as it is. Now, you're going to Montana to take care of the infamous Randolf Baine's funeral arrangements. Your father is retired. His responsibilities consist of golfing, checking out the men's department sale at Bloomingdale's, or where to have lunch with his buddies. Do what you want. God knows your business won't be affected by your absence. Hell, it might even improve." Lindsay made her stand, careful not to hammer too hard. The quips were digs not designed to actually induce Garett to cancel his plans. She couldn't let him leave without injecting what a hardship he would be creating. They still loved each other. It simply used to be easier and more fun. Money and respect in their community had become indistinguishable. Wealth garnered respect. Morality had no address. Garett had grown tired of being judged by the size of his financial portfolio. Meteoric shifts in personal income continue to inspire the introspective return to spirituality. The search for something more in life is often ignited by the acquisition of something less. Garett called and made arrangements to leave for Kalispell the next day.

*   *   *

15

CHAPTER TWO

Flying out of O'Hare International Airport in the middle of the winter is crowded and congested on a good day. On a bad day, when the weather roars in Chicago, the airline schedules across the country are affected. Luckily, this day was a benign January day in the Midwest. The sky was overcast and gray, temperature in the high teens, and Garett Baine's flight left on time. The Delta flight would make a stop in Salt Lake City and then proceed to stops in Kalispell and Missoula. He really hadn't thought about his grandfather much, until recently. When he left the restaurant business, Garett often thought of his grandfather and his precious independence. The notion of Randolf's lifetime of rebellion, had become folklore within the family. Randolf Baine was a retired dentist, and the meanest son of a bitch that controlled a drill in the country. Technology was not his style. Garett remembered visits to his grandparents' house when he was very young. These visits would always include a dental check-up. Garett got lucky because he had good teeth; he never felt the wrath of Grandpa's drill. His brother and sister were never quite so lucky. They would go kicking and screaming, as each visit would reveal sizable decay and numerous cavities. Randolf Baine would explain to his frightened grandchildren why they didn't need novocaine. The dental office was attached to the family home, and the screaming would rattle the walls as Grandpa made his point.

Randolf Baine never warmed up to his grandchildren. He tolerated them politely. Randolf didn't have many friends and didn't care. Here was a man that epitomized rough around the edges. Those edges were the softer side. After being diagnosed with emphysema, his doctors were informed that he had no intention of quitting smoking or drinking. He barked at them, refusing to give up the things in life he enjoyed. At his age, he rationalized that his habits were his existence and therefore he would not cease. That man dared his disease to kill him, and it never progressed from that initial visit. He spit in the face of his medical advice and never said another word about it. Neither did his doctors. Randolf had only one soft side and that was with his wife, Lexi. He could be as mean and rude as the day was long, but he treated that woman with a reverence no one understood. He was a wandering soul during the early years of his marriage. There were affairs, and they divorced and remarried, twice. Lexi never made threats or raised her voice. She knew what kind of man she married, and she never asked him to change. Over the years, he did change, and grew to love and respect every minute they had together. Garett always got the feeling that family visits were an intrusion into his life and his time with Lexi. She was the only person he ever wanted to please. He loved his children, but Lexi raised them, and when she died, he took off. He had his attorney sell the house and business. Randolf did not attend his wife's funeral. He was gone. No one knew where. He settled in Montana, where he remained for the last twenty years. Loners gravitate to no one. The inherent absence of any need for approval is what frustrates the majority of those spending a lifetime seeking the approval of others. Garett Baine sat on this Delta flight and thought about his grandfather, a man he barely knew. Garett thought about this man he envied.

The Delta flight finally emerged from the thick cloud cover and softly touched down on the narrow runway of Glacier Park International Airport. Nestled in next to the Swan Range Mountains at the foothills of the Canadian Rockies, Glacier Park International Airport services the northwestern portion of Montana, including Flathead County. Kalispell is the county seat for Flathead County. It is located roughly twelve miles from the airport. Flathead County is home to Glacier National Park, Big Mountain Ski Resort, Hungry Horse Dam, Whitefish, Big Fork, Columbia Falls, and Flathead Lake. Advertised as America's most beautiful lake, Flathead Lake is thirty-seven miles long and the largest fresh water lake west of the Mississippi. Garett rented a Jeep and managed to listen for some directions, not really paying too much attention to what the girl was saying. Highway 2 south to Highway 93 would bring him through Kalispell and into Lakeside and Big Fork, his destination. The red Jeep Cherokee was an expensive vehicle to rent, but the terrain and the lack of knowledge about his destination deemed the expense necessary. On the congested expressways of our big cities, one out of every two vehicles is a four wheel drive sport utility vehicle such as a Cherokee or the Land Cruiser. Garett always questioned the need for suburban housewives to own vehicles designed to ascend the slopes of Kilimanjaro. Garett Baine grabbed his bags and headed outside for the car. The airport sits in a small valley surrounded by the misty peaks of the Canadian Rockies. Garett pulled away from the airport and headed south on Highway 2, unimpressed by the terrain. The mountains in the distance were grand monuments cluttered with a low sky. The roadside

17

viewing while driving into Kalispell left him a bit surprised and disappointed. Trailer parks, auto repair businesses, farm equipment sales lots, and dilapidated businesses of all sorts scattered the highway leading into Kalispell. K-Marts, Value-Marts and the concrete spread of northern Illinois had apparently reached the Pacific Northwest. The fast-food cancer and the retail mentality of complete overkill had not been selective in its pursuit to ruin the entire country.

The Cherokee rolled through Kalispell, a city of nearly 12,000. The five thousand square miles of Flathead County had a total population estimated to be more than 70,000. Garett picked up Highway 93 in Kalispell and would take that another twenty miles to Lakeside and Big Fork. Kalispell is the largest city in the county and it seemed to be having a difficult time blending the traditional and the modern. The influx of mass marketing and chain outlets were gradually erasing the character this community had retained for years. The road south was covered with a white haze and gravel, used to buffer the ice buildup on the roads. Garett wasn't shy about his speed. He wanted to see where he was headed before the light of day disappeared. Suddenly the city was gone, as clearing the hill in front of him and leaving Kalispell in the rear view mirror, Montana appeared on the horizon.

The twenty mile trip from Kalispell to Lakeside was a pleasure. Each mile brought him closer to what Randolf Baine had found. The world had slowed down and for the first time in years, Garett wanted to stop and take a look. Highway 93 forged a rolling and scenic path towards Flathead Lake. The soft hills and the mountains in the distance crept up quickly and the Cherokee became engulfed in postcard beauty as the road led them through a series of sharp curves and steep drops. Although the lake was not visible yet, the terrain was changing with every minute. The mountains were closing in on the road, their rocky terraces now suddenly spilling gravel onto the two-lane highway. A faint mist began creeping along the pavement. Ahead, there was a deserted road stop for fisherman. During the summertime this area was teeming with vehicles pulling boat trailers and packed with gear. Garett pulled the car into the deserted boat loading strip. The Cherokee door opened as one foot slid to the ground before the vehicle reached a complete stop. The quiet was commonplace on Flathead Lake. The air hung still. The mountains formed a wind block, and consequently, the lake rarely froze. Garett Baine walked a few steps toward the edge of the water. What lay in front of him took his breath away. This muscular body of water covered with a gentle mist rising slightly from a glasslike surface, had carved a home in the Mission Ranges of the Canadian Rockies. Garett Baine cast his tired eyes on nature's finest child. A child as beautiful as anything he had ever seen before. The lake was flanked by Big Fork and Lakeside. These two communities were mirrored historically amid the wooded banks of the mammoth lake. Here, Garett stopped wondering what Randolf Baine had been looking for. He sat there for awhile. The door to the Cherokee was still open. It was January in Montana, cloudy and the temperature had dropped to ten degrees. Garett felt at home in a place he'd never been.

Garett spent the night at a small strip motel in Lakeside. This community is made up of a limited number of businesses all bunched together along Highway 93. The residents of Lakeside live along Flathead Lake and the surrounding hills. This a tiny community in the winter and a haven for the summer migration of Southern California. Hollywood had recently discovered Flathead Lake, and some very influential producers and directors had purchased homes along the lake. This property was selling for upwards of one-half million dollars per acre. A small branch of Montana Federal Bank was located at the flashing yellow light that marked the entire business district. Michael Ramirez had an office in the bank building. Michael had been born in Mexico and grew up in Los Angeles. He went to Crenshaw High School and later graduated from the University of California at Santa Barbara and the University of Montana Law School. Michael was thirty-five years old, married with one small daughter. He was the only attorney in Lakeside and one of his clients was Randolf Baine.

There were no secretaries in this office and Michael came out to greet Garett as he heard the door open.

"You must be Garett Baine. I hope you had no trouble in getting here. It appears that my instructions over the phone worked. You're here. Please sit down. How was the weather in Chicago when you left?"

"It is nice to meet you, Mr. Ramirez. I don't remember what the weather was in Chicago when I left. I guarantee you, it was shitty. Take my word for it. Chicago has crappy weather from November through March. Let's hear about Randolf Baine. My grandfather was not a role model for the Waltons. He seemed to be bothered by family functions and had certainly divorced himself from our lives completely when my grandmother died. Hell, he didn't even come to the funeral. So here I am. I flew a couple of thousand miles to listen to a will because my own father didn't feel like coming. Let's get to it, Michael Ramirez. Why did Randolf Baine need someone to be here for the reading of his will?"

"Well, Mr. Baine, it seems as though Randolf's personality is a genetic quality that has survived a couple of generations. Randolf Baine left a will with me. In this state, there is a personal representative appointed by the deceased. In Illinois, this person would be the executor. Randolf knew your father would not come to handle this. He held no bad

19

feelings toward his son and understood the distance created between them was his doing. His personal representative for his will and estate is you. I have a copy of his will, but he left an audio tape for you to hear. Shall I play it now?"

"By all means."

Michael Ramirez pulled a small cassette recorder from his desk and placed it in front of Garett. The tape began.

"How do you like Montana, Garett? Beats the hell out of Chicago, huh? Whether you like it or not, it sure beats the hell out of where I am. Garett, I am sure you are wondering why I had you come out here for this occasion. Your father did not want to come here and the last thing I ever wanted him to do, was to come here because no one else would. He has never forgiven me for not attending your grandmother's funeral. We were on shaky ground before that. I was never much for raising my children, a task wonderfully accomplished by my wife. I paid for my family and although I did not travel for a living, I might as well have. I was not there for my kids. I did not hold myself in the highest regard, so I kept my distance. I made no apologies for my life during my life, but I make them now."

"Your father has made himself very successful. He has learned an independence and developed a determination that I was always very proud of. I left after your grandmother died because I wanted to leave. Your father thinks that I was too self-centered and selfish to attend her funeral. He's right about the self-centered and selfish part, but he's wrong about why I didn't come to my own wife's funeral. Lexi asked me to meet her after she died. She asked me to go to a place that touched the clouds and get as close as I could to her. She never asked much of me because I was there and that made her feel safe. She told me right before she died that she was afraid of being alone, not dying. She wanted me to think of a place where we could be as close as possible. Wherever that place turned out to be, I had to go there. She knew I would be there and she would feel safe again. Garett, I never skipped your grandmother's funeral. I went to be with her one last time. I knew of a place called Going to the Sun Road in Glacier National Park, about fifty miles north of here. This is a place where the sun gets so close it burns the hair on your arms. When she died, I came here. I told her not to be afraid and as the clouds surrounded me and I felt her one more time. I knew I would stay close. I have remained here in Montana since she died. I wish I had brought her here long before she died. We spent most of our lives missing what was really important or at least I did. She knew."

"Your father is sixty-nine years old now. He is happy spending the money he took his lifetime to acquire. I didn't give him much when I was here, but I can give him something special now. I can give his son an opportunity to change the quality of his life. Make a difference for your kids. Do not build that wall of ambition to achieve your financial success. This will isolate you from your family during the time of their lives they really need you. Quit spending your time on this planet doing something you despise doing. I am giving your father the chance to see his son and his grandchildren happy. This has to do with ass–move yours and quit kissing everyone else's. I own a home on Flathead Lake. The land is nearly an acre and a half with full lake frontage. The home is fairly new, but needs work. I rebuilt the existing structure after I purchased the property. the place is big. Four or five bedrooms. It's been a long time since I checked. There is a fifty foot pier and two boat houses, but no boats. I was too old to bother. This property is yours. I didn't leave much cash, maybe a few thousand dollars. Use it on the house. The house sits about thirty feet above the lake level on the edge of the Rockies that rise right out of the water. Every room looks out over a masterpiece. Bring your family here, Garett. You couldn't earn in a lifetime what you'll wake up to every morning. You're not a follower, Garett. There's enough of them. I'm giving you the ride. Now, go find the road."

Michael Ramirez leaned over and turned off the recorder. Garett began to squirm a bit in his chair. In the back of his mind he imagined Randolf leaving an undetermined sum of money, but never did he expect much to go to him.

"Mr. Ramirez," Garett began, "I don't know what to say. My grandfather has been estranged from our family for years. My kids would receive an occasional gift, but he has been somewhat of an enigma for the last two decades. Tell me about his property. Are you familiar with where it is? He probably left me some kind of a shack, run down, beat to hell, right?"

"Garett, your grandfather left you one of the most beautiful lots in the state of Montana. I am very familiar with his property and his home. The combined value of his home and land is in excess of one million dollars. There are no more buildable lots on Flathead Lake and your grandfather's lot possesses the view of a lifetime. His home might need some work, but he has kept the structure immaculate. It is a sprawling ranch design, built above the lake level. Randolf leveled the small house on the lot when he purchased the property in 1975. He had his home built that same year. I believe he never thought he would live as long as he did. The home was never for him. He always looked at himself as a temporary tenant."

Garett stood up and walked to the window in Michael Ramirez' office. Through the towering pine trees he could see the outlines of the Swan and Mission Ranges of the Rocky Mountains.

"We never knew. We never knew why he skipped my grandmother's funeral. We never knew him at all, did we?"

"No one really did Garett, except Lexi and she's been gone for twenty years. He came out here and settled. People left him alone and he was happy that way. He spent most of his time fishing or working on one project or another on his property. Sit down Garett. This chapter isn't over, yet." Michael Ramirez took a folder from his desk and began to review some papers.

"Your grandfather kept to himself most of the time. People around here aren't quite as quick to judge someone. Randolf developed one close relationship during his years in Flathead County. Sitting at the north end of the lake, a couple miles outside of Lakeside, is a restaurant and tavern called The Flathead Saloon And Cathouse. It is actually in Somers, a tiny town situated at the very northern tip of Flathead Lake. Originally, The Flathead Saloon And Cathouse was a stage coach docking point during the late 1800's and the early Twentieth Century. Obviously, this stop provided more than food and drink. With the advent of the railroads, patrons became scarce. The diminished threat from the Indian Nations and elimination of the stage coach forced the location to be transformed into a full time restaurant and saloon. The ownership changed hands a couple of times between the wars. After World War II, The Flathead Saloon And Cathouse had fallen into complete disrepair and was actually closed for almost five years in the late forties. Kenton Gabel bought the property in 1949 for almost nothing. He owned it for forty-seven years. He completely rebuilt the structure into one of the areas top historical landmarks. The last renovation was the most extensive. Convoys of logging trucks from the north converged on Somers to complete the new structure. Mr. Gabel erected a magnificent tavern of rough logs from the lumber country of Western Canada. Expansive windows cris-crossed the support trusses while the cathedral ceilings were climbing to well over twenty feet high. The bar was a time warp of the wilderness never to be lost from Montana. Mounted grizzly, black bear, mountain lions, and many other species indigenous to the Northwest adorned the walls. Kenton Gabel and your grandfather became close friends. Some say they were the only ones that could understand the other or wanted to. Kenton was a World War II veteran who came to Flathead County from the war. He had no family and never got married. He was a cranky bastard, but he owned the most incredible tavern west of the Mississippi. People put up with his grizzled attitude because his place was to die for. The Flathead Saloon And Cathouse was the gateway to the 117,760 acres of Flathead Lake and from the right seat at the bar, you could see every acre of water. Your grandfather spent much of his twenty years in Montana at The Flathead Saloon And

Cathouse with Kenton Gabel. Mr. Gabel died two weeks before your grandfather died. He suffered a heart attack as he was closing one night and passed away the next day. The Flathead Saloon And Cathouse has been closed since. Kenton had no family that we ever knew about. His only relationship was with your grandfather. When he died, he left his property to Randolf Baine. Randolf never knew. He got sick almost immediately after Kenton died. By the time we were notified of Mr. Gabel's wishes, your grandfather was gone. This will all create some paper trails from one lawyer to another, but the bottom line Garett is simple. You are the sole heir to Randolf Baine's estate. Therefore, not only do you own his home and property as per his instructions. You now own The Flathead Saloon And Cathouse because Randolf's will specified you to take all of his possessions. I had a real estate appraiser give me an estimate on what The Flathead Saloon And Cathouse is worth, the property and the building. He owned over ten acres of lakefront. The estimate was over five million dollars. Montana probate is approximately four months. There will be some ads placed in the local papers announcing this transition. If there are no claims on the estate during this period, it is yours. The same will be true for your grandfather's home. In the meantime, you are free to take possession. Any claims against the estates would have to be decided in court. You may not open The Flathead Saloon And Cathouse until the estate has settled. Licenses cannot be transferred for a business in probate. I anticipate no challenges to either estate. Mr Gabel and Mr. Baine spent a great deal of time together at that establishment. My guess is that Mr. Gabel knew quite a bit about you and Randolf's plan to see you come out here. Why else would he leave his business to a ninety-year old man? Word got around that some doctors told your grandfather, years ago, that he would die from emphysema if he didn't quit smoking. The son of a bitch was smoking until the day he died. It wouldn't surprise me if he dictated where and when he died. Welcome to Montana, Garett."

Garett Baine was stunned. He came to Montana to get away from his profession. After passing six different licensing exams to become a stock broker, he was sentenced to three to five years of cold-calling, the twentieth century vehicle of unsolicited intrusion. This trip was supposed to be an expense paid time-out from the nightmare on Monroe Street. Lindsay and Garett needed time to find some common ground on which to weather these years of building a client base in the brokerage business. At this moment, all of his thoughts were centered on never picking up the telephone again to utter those redundant pitches in search of clients. The enormity of what was given to him had not registered completely. He felt the weight of the world lift from his shoulders. In that instance, he was happy again.

"Can I use your phone? I would like to call my wife. I have a sneaking suspicion this news may cheer her up."

"Be my guest, I'll leave you alone in my office." With that, Michael Ramirez walked out of the room. Garett Baine dialed his home.

When Lindsay answered the phone, Garett began to relay the developments of the day. He initiated the conversation by talking about his grandfather, his reasons for leaving the way he did, his feelings toward his own son and his aspirations for our family. Lindsay never said a word as she was informed of the lakefront home on Flathead Lake. Garett told her about the mist from the lake and the grandeur of the Canadian Rockies. He talked about how the view would just suck the air out of you. Lindsay listened to the history behind The Flathead Saloon And Cathouse and the unique relationship between Kenton Gabel and Randolf Baine. He told her that they had been given a magnificent opportunity and some of the most sought after property in the western United States. As he spoke to his wife, he couldn't help thinking about visiting his new acquisitions as soon as the call had ended. Garett explained how this would be an experience most children could only dream about.

"Lindsay, I could go on endlessly. After running into so many brick walls over the last few years, this is unbelievable. I knew I liked that old man for some reason. He was an independent son of a bitch and died with the clearest view of life, I have ever seen or heard. Your mother used to tell me to be careful about what I wished for because it might come true. Those two have to be looking down on us and smiling. They began to understand that if it takes a lifetime to grasp how to live it, then it was time to speed up the process. I haven't had much of a chance to digest all of this. I'm still waiting to wake up."

"Garett, I don't know what to say. All of the problems that we have gone through over the past three or four years seem to have been a test. I can't believe a man you hardly knew, left you everything. Explain this to me. Does this lawyer give you the value of those properties? Does the estate sell the properties? Is there a time table? How long will you have to stay out there?"

"I'm not sure of the logistics involved." Garett replied, certain of one thing. "I'll call you back when I learn more about the steps we need to take."

"This must be how people feel when they win the lottery. Six million dollars, Garett. Have you talked to the attorney about how long before the property could be put on the market?"

"No, I haven't had a chance to ask him. He is waiting here to go over some other aspects of the settlement. I'll call you later. I love you and kiss the kids for me." Garett slowly put the receiver back. Michael Ramirez had left. Garett Baine had no intention of selling anything. As soon as things became final, they would be moving to Montana. The images of leaving the congested mayhem of Chicago for a terrific business and a beautiful home in a place they write songs about were real. He would bring his family here. This would not be an issue.

*   *   *

CHAPTER THREE

As the Delta DC-10 knifed through the clouds back to Chicago, Garett Baine sat deliberating the property he had inherited. Windows of opportunity open seldom. Garett had no intention of focusing on the reasons. There was something guiding these events, and whatever it was, Garett would not put them up for auction. Garett had spent much of the morning, prior to his departure, at Randolf's home on Flathead Lake. Its sprawling design fit the terrain instinctively. Located high above the water line, the home was constructed of mammoth cedar logs stacked in perfect geometric wedges. The cedar shake roof line rose and fell with each room. The family room peaked at eighteen feet. Garett sat spellbound in this room of glass. He became a visitor in a novel that could find no words to describe the expanse he possessed. The kitchen boasted of two large institutional ranges and two Sub-Zero refrigerators. The island butcher block table measured seven feet in length. The table was shadowed high above by wrought iron fixtures adorned with numerous hanging copper pots and pans. Skylights and long windows engulfed the kitchen. Montana's Mission and Swan Ranges painted the mural of reflecting colors dancing through the glass. Reasoning had to be the transparent manifestation to fear change. Change had come calling, and Garett welcomed the new visitor.

He made arrangements with Michael Ramirez to proceed with the probate filings. Michael would make sure the restaurant was not neglected. He would keep the heat to a minimum and pay all of the on going bills from the cash left in the restaurant account. Garett had gone to The Flathead Saloon And Cathouse with Michael on the day after the wills were read. There he made a list of all perishable items and instructed Michael which ones to throw out. He wasn't sure about exactly when he would be returning, so the list was extensive. The coolers were to be shut down, cleaned, and left with the doors open. Beer lines should be disconnected and cleaned. All produce would be tossed and any vacuum sealed meat should be frozen. All bakery items were expendable, as were all dairy items. Garett's years in the restaurant business made this task very easy and enjoyable. Michael had to make arrangements for these tasks to be completed. He would be paid a fee, which he insisted was not necessary. The Flathead Saloon And Cathouse was a splendid structure dripping in character. This place had been Kenton Gabel's only family. He watched it grow as a parent watched his children grow. The double fourteen foot doors were made of rough cut Canadian timber. Each door required some serious effort to pull open, partly due to the excess size and weight coupled with the over-sized springs pulling it back shut. There were no vestibules here. A full dose of the Montana air would spill into the main bar area and dining room each time the doors were opened. Inside and out, the structure was immaculate. The decor sketched the Northwest. It was timeless. The support structures were all rough cut timber framing the expansive glass that enveloped all four sides of the building. The main cathedral ceiling rose nearly twenty-five feet to crest at the center of the main dining room. Bolted crossing beams surrounded a circular fireplace that rose like a great stone pyramid from the center of the room. From every vantage point in the restaurant and bar area, the view was spectacular. An open air deck running the length of the building overlooked Flathead Lake and the mountains that framed it. In the summer, this deck was full of patrons dining and watching the fishing boats launch from the docking station directly across the highway. The Flathead Saloon And Cathouse was guarded by the eyes of all those animals adorning the walls. Garett felt good that they were there. He thought about sitting on that deck and downing a couple of Molsons as his flight was in final approach to Chicago.

Lindsay Baine sat at the airport waiting for Garett's plane to arrive. She was forty years old and still knock down gorgeous. Her high cheekbones and slight build spoke model from day one. She had dabbled in modeling during college, but couldn't stand the slimy men associated with that business. Her long blonde hair had recently given way to a stylish shorter cut that framed her Donna Karan sportcoat and brushed the top of her shoulders. Lindsay grew up in the Sauganash section of Chicago, a strict Irish Catholic neighborhood and home to a majority of the politically influential Democratic Party operatives. Lindsay's mother went to mass seven days a week. Her father worked for the city parks department. Her grandfather, Dan Nolan, grew up with Richard Daley Sr. and became Chief of Detectives for the Chicago Police Department in the fifties and sixties. Lindsay lived her upbringing. Her wedding night was her first time, a decision she has never regretted. Their four children and one lost through miscarriage, would have easily been more if she was the only vote. The last few years have been tough on Garett, financially. She had a hard time moving backward and thought some of Garett's decisions were poor judgment. She still loved him, though. He had something she could not let go of. Lindsay had parked the Plymouth Voyager on the upper departure level at O'Hare. She and the kids would wait for Garett there. They could avoid the congestion of the lower level and Garett had no need to check any bags. As he approached the vehicle, the sliding door flew open with the force of the old stockyard gates used to hustle cattle to the meat houses. Four young screaming individuals of varying sizes converged on Garett Baine.

"Daaaaaaaddy!" Each child positioned some part of the body as his or hers to latch onto. Jake, the oldest, had just recently grown out of this stage. He simply put his arms around Garett's waist and squeezed as hard as he could. "I missed you, Dad." The group finally made their way back to the van and Garett put his arms around his wife as he slid into the drivers seat. The embrace was long. With her face buried in his shoulder, Lindsay kept repeating how she couldn't believe what had transpired on his trip. Garett pulled the van out of the concourse and headed for the tollway. He began relating the events of his meeting with Michael Ramirez. They had inherited property worth in excess of six million dollars. The legal proceedings would take four to six months, but these were merely formalities. Challenges to the estate of either man seemed unlikely.

The drive to Sheridan Shores took thirty minutes. It was late and time to put the kids to bed, a task Garett had missed even though he was gone for a short time. Separation from his children proved hard for Garett. He took Conner and Christopher upstairs to bed. Christopher snuggled under his blankets and never moved. Conner bounced in and out of bed from a mysterious source of nocturnal energy. Conner never quit out of fear or intimidation, but finally fell asleep from exhaustion.

"You know that I have had to spend so much time at work lately. Well, do you know why every night, Mommy has you say an extra prayer for me and my new job?"

"Because you hate it?" Christopher asked with a little voice.

"That's not the reason, but it could be." Garett laughed. "The reason is God listens to little boys and their wishes."

"Don't you have to go to work anymore?" Christopher asked.

"I still have to go to work, but I think I'll be getting a new job pretty soon. And you know what I'll be able to do on this new job?"

"Bring us with?" Christopher tried to follow, but didn't have a clue.

"You bet!" Garett responded as he pulled the blankets up on both of his young sons. "I'm pretty tired of spending all day at work and not seeing you guys." He kissed them both and smiled knowing what their future held. "You guys get some sleep and stay in bed." As always, he left the hall light on and their door open at least half way. Garett knew that Conner would crawl out of bed and sneak downstairs with some half-baked excuse of needing something to drink. Conner's favorite excuse was to announce that he had forgotten to ask them a question. Upon being asked what it was he needed to ask, Conner was always at a loss. His response was always the same. "I forgot."

Garett spent the rest of the evening describing the events of his trip. Lindsay, Jake, and Maggie sat as he talked about The Flathead Saloon And Cathouse and Randolf's house. They had not seen this light in his eyes for almost two years. He lit up the family room as he spoke about Montana and Flathead Lake. He would have to continue to work at Dean Witter for a few more months because none of this would generate any income immediately. He would spend the time positioning his clients for his departure. He was careful not to elaborate on the disposition of these properties. Selling them would give him the financial freedom he has always dreamed about. Keeping them and moving to Montana was the reason they were left to him. There was no stipulation in the wills to assure this. However, this was not the time to debate the issue. With all of their children asleep, Garett and Lindsay made love in front of the fireplace. Randolf had already given them more than he knew.

*　　　*　　　*

CHAPTER FOUR

There was a sales meeting every Friday morning for the bullpen brokers at Dean Witter. Bruce Carson, the branch manager, would relate any new sales ideas and any stock positions the company had taken during the past week. On this morning, the brokers in attendance were told the company had taken a large position in Hospitality Properties Trust, a REIT or Real Estate Investment Trust. Twelve million shares would be offered and Dean Witter, Chicago, had committed to a large portion of this offering. In other words, the bullpen brokers were strongly encouraged to cold call on this security. Garett Baine was physically in the room but that is where his participation ended. Normally, he would not have cold-called on this anyway. He hated calling on products. The "Have I got a stock for you" approach was never his style. Garett listened to this meeting from another place, and knew he would never make another cold call again. Garett experienced a tranquil confidence as he watched the other brokers taking notes and going over the HPT Prospectus. His copy landed on the seat next to him as did the numerous other handouts tracking market trends, mutual fund purchases for the month, and the recommended allocation of stocks, bonds, and cash. The meeting ended with the usual lame role playing. One broker would simulate an appointment with a prospective client. The client would be played by another broker relishing the opportunity to provide an unwilling participant. Bruce Carson would critique the ordeal and suggest more appropriate methods for uncovering assets. The practice became so redundant, some brokers left anonymous notes pleading Bruce not to waste the time on Fridays. Eventually, he held the ordeal once a month.

"Hey Garett, you know Sunshine thinks he bagged the elephant last Friday." Matt Hipple explained as the brokers were filing out of the meeting.

"Really! Is it the old lady he has been calling since Labor Day with the $2500 IRA?"

"The old girl finally came through." Sunshine chimed in, "She promised me that if I drove to her house in Gurnee, which is almost an hour from here, she would not only transfer her $2500 IRA, she would consider purchasing a CD if the rates were right. So I said to myself. Ken, you can drive an hour to transfer an account that will produce no commission. If everything goes well and the CD is purchased, that CD could generate upwards of four dollars in commission. And to think, there was a time I considered this job frustrating."

Garett and the dozen other brokers attending the morning meeting filed out of the conference room and made their way back to the bullpen area. Daily call sheets were laid out on all of the desks along with the memo, called The Bull Sheet. This sheet listed the top producing brokers for the previous day. Topping the sheets, the President's Club brokers were buried in their offices from the time they arrived until the close of the market. The bullpen brokers rarely saw these men. The sheet also tracked the monthly progress of the branch and how many production days remained until the end of the month. At the bottom of the sheet was the thought for the day. Today's thought: "Better to pay a fair price for a good company than a cheap price for a loser." Garett would spend the morning studying his client list. He would be staying at Dean Witter only as long as the probate period. However meager his income had been, he saw no reason to end it now. He would need a certain amount of time to place his clients with the right brokers. He pulled out his lead file and began shuffling through the hundreds of cold-calling cards in his file. The nights spent enduring this tortuous vocation began to creep through his mind.

"Kenny, are you on the phone?" Garett asked.

"Garett, I'm always on the god damn phone. It's become part of me. In fact, I spend so much time on the son of a bitch, it's about the only part of me that has been getting any activity. After talking to people for ten or twelve hours a day, I barely utter a sound when I get home. This has done spectacular things for my love life. Hey, didn't you have to go out of town for a couple of days? How was that? Something about your grandfather passing away. I remember you saying something about that last week."

"Not much to tell you. I had to go out to Montana and clean up some loose ends from my grandfather's affairs. My father and his father never got along too well, so he asked me to go out there to wrap things up."

"What are you calling on this morning? I can't see pitching that HPT REIT. It's hard enough trying to sell a preferred or a short term, high yield corporate. These REIT's are like speaking Arabic. These people don't have the slightest idea what a REIT is. Shit, I'm not sure I do."

"You know what I love? I love getting these answering machines where the people think their machine is the first answering machine ever put in use. The instructions are nothing short of a Truman Capote novel. "I'm sorry, Rory and Melinda are not home at the present time. We appreciate your call and would love to return your call. After this message, you will hear a beep. After the beep, leave your name, the time

31

of your call, any message, and the number and time where we can reach you. Be sure to wait until after the beep before you begin speaking." My normal response is to act confused and lost. Sound agitated and plead with the machine to repeat itself. Oh my god, was it after the beep or before the beep. Christ, most monkeys can use an answering machine by now." Garett was laughing thinking about the nights this provided the only source of entertainment.

"The single most annoying answering machines are those with messages left by children, barely old enough to talk." Ken was cringing while thinking about these adoringly demonic epithets. "I do not have any kids, yet it never ceases to amaze me, how these parents actually believe someone on the other end of this drivel is smiling. I have always wondered about the length of time necessary to teach these children the scripts, mommy and daddy have written. My God, someone has to cane these sniveling yuppies and their babbling offspring."

"Sunshine, the glow from your desk is blinding, as always." Garett was leaning back on his chair with both feet on his desk. The branch manager made rounds during the day. Bruce would take strolls through the bullpen area to check if the brokers were on the phone. He rarely said anything if someone was not on the phone. He made notes to address at the monthly fireside chats. The key was wearing a headset. A broker with a headset always appeared to be on the phone. Later that day, Bruce Carson took another stroll back to the bullpen. He was looking for Garett Baine.

"Garett, can I see you in my office?"

Bruce Carson's office was what the bullpen brokers referred to as purgatory. Most visits to this office were initiated to rectify some type of broker error. Aside from the monthly fireside progress chats mandatory for all first and second year brokers, Carson's office was the equivalent of the SEC referee's office. Garett entered the office wondering which one of his clients had failed to pay for a trade on time. Maybe, one of them simply refused to honor a trade claiming he never gave authorization. Killing the trade would cost the broker any drop in the price of the stock. If the stock went up, the gain could only be used to offset a previous loss. Garett sat down as Bruce closed the door.

"We have a problem with one of your clients." Bruce Carson began. "Edward and Dorothy Cole have filed a written complaint with the NASD. They have been made aware of the Code of Procedure and have requested an arbitration hearing. The complaint states that you put them in certain investments comprising the entire inheritance from Edward's father. These investments, as the complaint reads, were unsuitable and extremely risky for their needs. The result has been a loss of nearly forty percent in the first twelve months. They claim a total lack of knowledge

32

in the area of purchasing stocks and funds. Therefore, they relied heavily on your advice and your assurances of the safety of their investments. The investments have been proven to be anything but safe. Garett, I looked at their portfolio and the make-up is strictly comprised of volatile high tech stocks, high risk foreign mutual funds, and some aggressive small-cap funds. They appear to have some legs with this because most of them would not fit into a novice investment portfolio. They insist their main objective was safety of principal and long term retirement income."

Garett rolled his eyes and knew the exact circumstances Bruce was referring to. He had been monitoring this account very closely since the money was invested. This complaint, while not unexpected, was surprising in terms of the speed with which the complaint was registered.

"Bruce, this is bullshit." Garett Baine was livid. "This was a broker of the day call. I did not solicit these people. They came to me. The couple had inherited some money from the husband's father. They had done some investing before, but experienced little success, so they decided to work with a full service broker. The father had dealt with Dean Witter in the past, so they called our office and the call was put through to me. After speaking to them on the phone a couple of times, I had them fax me a copy of the accounts they inherited. The money was all invested in some open-ended bond funds which is not at all uncommon for a man in his eighties. I am not a fan of any bond funds and this is reflected in my client portfolios. We arranged a meeting here for the purpose of giving them some options based on the information they gave me. This information was centered on a client profile questionnaire detailing their current financial make-up, their goals for the money, their age, and their risk tolerance. The answers spelled out a conservative couple, mid fifties, a ten to fifteen year time frame, and some liquidity concerns because they were considering buying a vacation home at some point down the road. I spent three hours with them at that first meeting giving them my proposal and some basic investment ground rules. You know the drill. Success is achieved through patience and time in the market. Diversification and the ability to ride out corrections were key to long term gains. I gave them blue chip stocks like Coca-Cola, Disney, Motorola, Intel, etc. The mutual funds I proposed consisted of our best performing funds over the past fifteen years, American Value and Dividend Growth. I told them that I did not personally like bond funds because they defeat the purpose of owning bonds. The main reason to buy quality bonds is to insure the safety of your principal. Bond funds lack the security of that return of investment at maturity. I spent hours explaining this to them. Edward was virtually silent during this meeting. The only comments he made were to praise me on the common sense this proposal seemed to make. Dorothy was another story. She questioned the reasoning behind buying blue chip stocks when the market appeared to be high. She had been in an investment club for a short time and was subscribing to the Money Magazine school of investing through the media. Whatever is hot and on the cover is right thing to do. She also, had a big problem with me proposing Dean Witter funds. I explained the loads on these funds consisted of no-load entry and decreasing exit fees, not unlike most mutual funds on the market. I was much more familiar with these funds and we had the ability to change funds at no charge within our family of funds. My commissions were no higher on in house funds than outside funds. I told her investing through ratings magazines was her prerogative, but if this was what they wanted then there was no reason to hire a broker. They wanted to think about the proposal and conduct some of their own research. At our second meeting, Dorothy had a complete list of new stocks she insisted they wanted. They had found outside mutual funds recommended to them from Edward's sister, but they insisted on keeping me as their broker to monitor their investments. I explained how these investments were not what I would recommend and they involved more risk than I thought they should be taking. This did not change their minds, so we proceeded to invest the money where they wanted it. My daily log details every part of these transactions. I did what the client wanted me to do. The trades were all marked unsolicited."

"Obviously, I will want to look at your log and we will need to send a copy to the NASD. If this couple continues to contend that these investments were not their idea or even if they were, and the board finds them unsuitable for the client, then you still bear some responsibility here. If you deemed these trades unsuitable for the clients and they insisted you execute them anyway, then your position dictates that you decline to take the account."

"That's crap, Bruce, and you know it. Brokers don't turn down accounts because the client disagrees with their proposals. We are hammered about gathering assets and explaining risk. I spent a great deal of time educating this couple and they decided to retain Dean Witter and myself as their broker. However, they wanted to put their money into avenues of their choice. It is still their money. They were not buying junk bonds and penny stocks. They simply chose a more volatile road than I would have taken."

"This process is a long term process. It may take a year or two to reach a closure date on this matter. In the meantime, they have closed the account and requested that we liquidate and send the remaining proceeds. I will need to monitor all of your transactions from this point. Until this matter is settled, all of your trades must be approved by myself or the branch Sales Manager, Kevin Macey. I'm sorry, but my hands are tied. The company dictates this action. You have done well up until this point, but these are the circumstances to avoid." Bruce Carson finished with a condescending tone in his voice.

"Let me review this for a moment." Garett responded, "I took in a client. I educated this client and explained all of the risks involved concerning my proposal and their ultimate choices. Now, I can't execute a trade unless my boss approves it. Exactly, how am I to explain to a client that before I can place his order, I have to go see if it is O.K. True, you might lose the price on that stock or you might lose the bonds completely, but I no longer have the authority to manage your account properly. I'm sure that will have only minor consequences with my current clients and my ability to prospect new clients. I will not be reprimanded for doing my job properly." Seething, Garett's eyes narrowed as he bit on the first finger of his closed fist. He glared at his branch manager and the room became stale in a hurry. Bruce Carson did not make a habit of allowing second year brokers to lecture him. However, he never considered interrupting Garett Baine. He wanted no part of that.

"This is an industry based on numbers." Garett stood as he continued, "How many clients do you have? How much money do you manage? How much commission have you generated? What are your trailing dollars? How many calls have you made today, this week, this month? I can't even explain to my wife what this job is like. She desperately wants to help me get through the bad days and she can't help at all. No one can understand the constant rejection and humiliation associated with cold calling until they have done it. The major brokerage firms work by numbers the same way. For every ten brokers they hire, eight won't last. If they throw enough of us against the wall, some are bound to stick. Excuse me for not kissing ass on this one, but I'm hopping off that boat. You once told me that some of the older brokers in the office thought I was cocky. Fuck them. I take enough garbage on the phone every day. Who are they to judge me? Soft, little men, earning a living by guesswork. They felt my attitude represented an arrogant, overly independent demeanor for this business. They were dead wrong. I treat my clients with respect and dignity, an area sadly lacking among most of them. Most brokers feel the need to page their client books at the end of every month looking for trades to generate some income, regardless of whether it is in the client's best interest. This practice makes my stomach turn. I've made mistakes in this business. I have lost money for people and it keeps me up thinking about it. We take a very arrogant position when we contact total strangers and ask them to put their financial resources in our hands and to trust us. I do not position a client's assets to benefit me. If you think that sounds trite, fuck you! I have spent the better part of two years making myself sick about how I make my living. The only redemption I have felt is knowing that I have been honest to my clients. I don't want a fucking medal for doing what I am supposed to do. However, I will not be reprimanded for it. I don't lie to people and I'm about to start lying to myself. Edward and Dorothy Cole knew exactly what they were doing. You can relay this message to them. Thank them for expediting my departure from this firm. I prefer working for a living, not groveling for one. I have put my family through hell during the past two years. They have seen a man try to justify the means by the carrot at the end. I have endured a steady diet of humiliation, tempered by motivational seminars dressed up in five star hotels and white table cloth dinners. I have watched my last telemarketing evangelist parade around a stage. Dials, people, you have to make the dials. They sing the praises of calling every night. Call on weekends. Call until nine o'clock. Call during dinner. What's the difference. These people are home. That is what matters. That is bullshit. It's not that I can't do this anymore. I won't do this anymore. An old man, I barely knew, recently told me to ditch the suit if it didn't fit. Well, it never did. I quit, Bruce."

Garett Baine waited for his wife in the lobby on the main floor. Lindsay was taking the train downtown. She would take a cab over to the Dean Witter offices. From there, they would be going to the Chicago Bulls game that evening. Garett purchased season tickets for the Bulls in 1983 for one of the restaurants he owned. They were to be used mainly for promotional purposes. The Bulls were not a good team in 1983, so the tickets were readily available and the choices were endless. The purchaser could literally choose the location of the seats. Garett chose four front row box seats. In 1984, the team drafted Michael Jordan. Timing is everything. Lindsay looked spectacular as she climbed out of the cab on Monroe Street in the heart of Chicago's Loop. Her blond hair was growing out, falling to the top of her shoulders. She wore a black sportcoat with a white lace top, jeans and boots. Her figure remained slender and firm through four children. Garett walked outside to meet her and they headed to the International Parking Garage, roughly six blocks from the office. Lindsay talked about the kids, their day, and why the sitter was late.

"I quit today." Garett dropped as casually as his sarcasm would allow. Waiting for a reaction, he watched as Lindsay turned her Irish profile towards him, a stiff breeze sweeping her hair straight back. Without any look of anguish or shock, she just smiled. "Bruce Carson called me into his office this afternoon. He informed me that one of my clients was filing a formal complaint against me concerning some investments. The clients claim that I coerced them into purchasing. The complaint would take the NASD route through arbitration. This could take more than a year. In the meantime, any trading I conduct must be approved by Carson, first. The prospecting necessary with this job has been humiliating and as you well know, very difficult for me to come to terms with. I did enjoy the trading and acting as the architect in creating successful portfolios. Although the prospecting consumed over ninety percent of my time, the trading became the reward. Today, they took that away. Prior to closure of this complaint, my trades and securities purchases for clients must be approved before they are executed. This eliminates my ability to function as an effective broker. Not to mention, his audacity to treat me like some schoolboy. Now, I have to explain to my clients and my prospects that I have been a bad boy. By the way, I am under investigation for unsuitable trading and I am unable to execute a trade without my manager's approval. Besides those irrelevant issues, exactly how much money did you want to invest with me today? After years of working for myself , I missed being able to quit. As the owner of those businesses, quitting was never an option. Today, I called in that option and it felt fantastic. God, I want to get drunk." Garett Baine was happy at this moment. He had not felt this way for years. He was light, his steps were quick. Lindsay shuffled to keep pace. He continued. "I know this puts us in a bind , but I know we'll get by the next few months. By that time, I'll have The Flathead Saloon And Cathouse open and kicking ass. I can't wait to get the hell out of here."

Lindsay stopped near the entrance to the garage. Garett was five or six steps ahead of her before he realized she had stopped. "Garett, what do you mean, open The Flathead Saloon And Cathouse and get the hell out of here?"

The drive from the Loop to the stadium took them over to Randolph Street and west through the trendy new restaurant row. The area formerly reserved as the exclusive home of the produce markets was undergoing a tremendous revitalization. Since the new stadium was built in 1994, Chicago's West Side was systematically being leveled and rehabilitated. Old warehouses were being transformed into multi-million dollar eateries and six-figure brownstones were replacing abandoned buildings faster than the traders at the Chicago Board of Options Exchange could buy them up. The roads were being ripped up and resurfaced. New streetlights and planters were taking the place of old winos and the homeless along Madison Street. The new United Center in Chicago stood as a beacon of wealth among what was left of a very poor neighborhood. Some public housing units still remained scattered in the maze of the corporation owned parking lots. Gone were the days of tipping the parking lot attendants to assure a space for the next game. These new lots sold on a season ticket basis only. The private lots run by the old Chicago Stadium crews were pushed back to the small vacant lots three or more blocks from the new stadium. Garett Baine hated the new parking facilities adjacent to the United Center. Passes for every game must be purchased to use those lots. Garett kept in touch with the old attendants and parked on Washington Street, three blocks away. Bernard always saved him a street space and had the car started and warmed up at the end of each game during the frigid Chicago winter. Garett and Lindsay were meeting Jim and Denise Shane at the main entrance on Madison Street. Game time was 7:30, and they were to hook up at 7:00. The Blazer pulled out of the International Parking Garage at 6:45 and the conversation was heated.

"Garett, exactly when were you going to inform us that you had no intention of selling that property in Montana? You simply decided, on your own, that this family was going to pick up everything and move to Montana. I have always been under the impression that these decisions were made as a family. Who the hell wants to move, anyway? The kids have their friends, school, and their whole lives built in Sheridan Shores. I don't know anyone in Montana. Hell, I don't even know if there is anyone in Montana. We live in one of the best school districts in the country. We have our family and friends in Chicago and you decide we are moving. You're nuts. No one is moving anywhere. We need to put that property up for sale. My God, if we only get half the market value of those properties, we could solve all of our financial problems here. We could pay off all of our debts and you could start fresh with another firm or another business. This is the break we have been praying for and you want to move to a state we know nothing about. Shit Garett, I've never been to Montana, I have no desire to go to Montana, much less live there. You have had some asinine ideas before, but this one sets a new standard."

"Well, at least you are open minded about the possibility." Garett responded, fully expecting the heat. "Obviously, this is something we will have to discuss. We need to examine exactly what we would be leaving. First, we would be leaving a school system ranked nationally for it's excellence in sending an overwhelming majority of its students to college. This school system where most parents can afford to send these kids to school by the time they reach the age of two. Their toughest decision is whether to ski at the University of Colorado or get out of the cold by going to Arizona State. This is the same school system that produces the highest suicide rate in the state because these pampered brats can't cope with having everything handed to them. The progressive academic agenda in these schools has destroyed half of the values we try to teach. Birth control pills and condoms are distributed at school. How the hell are parents supposed to teach abstinence? Our kids are part of a school system gone berserk. The grade schools gave up fundamentals years ago. They create more psychological problems than they solve by trying to put first and second graders in therapy every time they fall behind. The analytical babble coming from some of these teachers is mind boggling. Oh, little Tommy has been having problems in his first grade class. We believe this originated early in his childhood, possibly in the womb, causing a critical crossroads for his emotional well being. Shit, just teach him how to read and write and forget whether his parents spoke to him in the womb or the fact he had a long delivery and his entrance into this world was strained."

"What else would we be leaving? The North Shore. The suburban dream of middle America. We live spectator lives. Our enjoyment comes in many forms of watching others. We relax at night by watching television. On weekends, we go to a movie or watch a sporting event. Some nights, we like to have dinner downtown and people watch. On special occasions, we dress formal to attend a play or a concert. Spectators. This is pathetic. Think about the quality of life we are leading. I am afraid to let any one of our children walk around the block without supervision. If we loose sight of one child for a moment at a mall, a restaurant, or anywhere in public, I panic. High school freshman carry guns to school. We protect our homes with security systems, dogs, and sophisticated lighting on special timers. Judges and the courts are releasing child abusers, rapists, and sex offenders because they don't have the room. What is that? People can't run away from these problems, but they can balance the odds. There is not one place on this planet immune from the atrocities one human being is capable of committing against another. Living in this cesspool simply positions the gasoline entirely too close to the fire. I'm not sure that taking a child from this environment and bringing him to a place where life is a bit more basic is such a bad thing. You know I'm not some nature freak bent on isolation. I've seen what we could have in Montana. I want you to see it before we make any permanent decisions. Randolf was trying to tell us something. For once in my life, I want to listen."

The Blazer pulled into the Red Top lot on Washington Street. It was a few minutes past seven. The area around the United Center was a sea of activity. Lindsay was quiet as they left the vehicle. Garett thanked Bernard and slapped a five dollar bill in his palm as they headed for the stadium. They would cross Warren Street and head down a walkway cutting through one of the fenced parking lots directly across from the main gate entrance. Vendors were out selling peanuts on the street. The United Center had banned peanuts in the complex because they were so difficult to clean up. Now, they must be smuggled in. Garett felt there had

39

to be some conspiracy to slowly destroy all of the traditional bastions of viewing a professional sporting event. The parking lots were full of high priced luxury foreign cars and the sidewalks were filled with young black children from the nearby projects looking for spare change. The homeless were out selling copies of Streetwise for one dollar, a publication comprised of articles written by the homeless. A bronze statue of Michael Jordan soared high into the arches of the brick facade on the east end of the stadium. Garett and Lindsay raced across Madison Street to greet Jim and Denise. They were waiting by the string of limousines lined up in front of the main entrance, anxious to drop off their precious cargo. Overweight men dressed in gaudy Googi sweaters lumbered out of these corporate chariots. Sports fans had become fashion statements. A Bull's ticket was the most prized ticket in town and the owners wanted to show their stuff. Women, not knowing a team foul from a back court violation, looked elegant if nothing else. These were the people spending most of the third quarter talking on the concourse and leaving with two minutes remaining in a tie game.

Jim Shane had known Garett Baine for most of his life. They grew up down the street from each other and spent the better part of ten years reigning over the neighborhoods. Jim moved to Atlanta while in high school, but the two kept in touch, visiting often. Jim attended Georgia Tech on a football scholarship. He was a bad ass fullback, known for a punishing style of running. Suddenly, after one semester, Jim left school and enlisted in the Marine Corps. Jim Shane spent twelve weeks at the Marine Corps Recruit Depot or MCRD at Paris Island, South Carolina. Early 1972 had seen an embattled nation pressing to extract itself from the only war it could not or would not win. Jim Shane did not share the viewpoint of his young college campus companions. He despised the anti-American sentiment adopted by his generation. As a senior in high school, Jim assumed he would be drafted. This did not cause the least bit of apprehension. To the contrary, he looked forward to the service because of the war. He believed that military service should culminate in the active defense of your country. Jim's four year stint in the Marines began inauspiciously. He entered the Marines with a chip on his shoulder the size of New Jersey. Growing up, Jim liked to fight, and his talent with his fists became playground lore at a very young age. Jim was big, strong, fast, and unafraid of being hit. The Marine Corps was an organized extension of the violence he excelled in. The first few weeks of basic training in 1972, harnessed what would have been released in the present day Marine Corps. Over the past twenty years, the Marine Corps has changed. Today, the USMC will not spend the time or the effort to break a recruit. Immediate discharges await the recruits determined to undermine any authority they encounter. Expulsion from the Marine Corps is frequent today. The Marine Corps has concluded that they had been spending entirely too much time on bad recruits. The USMC was spending eighty percent of their time on ten percent of the recruits. Twenty years ago, the Marine Corps would break down anyone who dared to challenge their traditions or their programs. The physical hazing knew very few boundaries. Over the years, the legal climate has changed dramatically regarding the treatment of recruits. The quality and quantity of recruits has increased dramatically. These factors have contributed to the present philosophy of the Marine Corps. The belief now is simplified: a shithead recruit will make a shithead soldier. In 1972, the Corps would make a Marine out of a recruit, no matter what the cost, and in 1972, Jim Shane became a Marine the hard way. Following basic training, Jim attended specialty school at Camp Pendelton. Eventually, he landed as a Marine helicopter crewman in Vietnam. Two tours in Southeast Asia culminated at the United States Embassy in Saigon during 1975. Jim Shane was one of the last Americans to leave the Embassy in 1975. He speaks very little of those days. Garett remembered encountering a very somber friend following his Vietnam tours.

Jim Shane returned angry and quiet, and moved to San Antonio, Texas in 1975. He worked with three other men, building houses. He loved the work in the brutal Texas sun. They worked hard and drank hard. Nights were late in the San Antonio bars. Jim Shane had moved in with a beautiful Asian girl after six months in Texas. Her name was Sanya Tu Lee. Everyone called her Sunny. No one knew where they met. Jim left for a few days. When he returned, Sunny was with him. Sunny stood five feet two. There was a classic combination of high Anglo cheekbones and shining almond eyes. Sunny's waist length black hair fell thick along her shoulders. They met on April 29, 1975 at the United States Embassy, Saigon. Jim was working the CH-46 choppers evacuating Americans from the region. The United States had issued orders declaring that within twenty four hours of April 29, 1975, the evacuation of Saigon would cease. Jim Shane was part of a Marine rescue team that would fly almost seven hundred sorties from the grounds of the United States Embassy to the airport or support ships. At 4:00 p.m. on April 29, there were thousands of Vietnamese storming the Embassy. They were jammed against the gates and the walls so deep, many people expired from the force of the crowd. U.S. Marines were trying to keep the gates clear and knocking people off the walls in their attempts to enter the compound. Caucasians were helped over the wall. Vietnamese diplomatic officials are allowed access. Jim's unit of smaller CH-46's worked the roof of the Embassy while the larger CH-53's landed in the courtyard. As his unit pulled away for the final time, Jim noticed a beautiful young girl huddled near the door of the chopper. She looked horribly out of place as did everyone. She was wearing a Vietnamese Diplomatic Attaché Badge over some American fatigues. The Attaché Badge could have come from anywhere. She may have worked for someone at the Embassy. She may have been related to someone in the Thieu regime. She may have pulled the badge from someone's neck in the streets. It didn't matter now. As the helicopter rose over the chaos below, Jim Shane took the badge from around her neck, explaining that it may have helped her enter the compound, but now it was time to lose the connection. Anonymity would be an asset from this point forward. He introduced himself. Her name was Sanya Tu Lee.

On one sweltering summer night in Texas, Jim Shane had just finished one of many Corona's. Jim and his crew were pounding at the Train Station, a rough working class bar just inside the city limits. On this night, there seemed to be an unusual amount of tension in the room. A group of bikers had found a home for the evening on their way through the state. Jim never thought much of anyone, who relied on the safety of numbers to project strength. A confrontation became inevitable when one individual biker mentioned that a certain stench in the room must be caused by the "slant-eyed hole". He was referring to Sunny. Jim Shane was not one to engage in any verbal exchanges when a physical encounter was eminent. There would be no questions, such as "What did you say? Are you talking to me?" He knew the intent of the remark and he would not disappoint the source of the remark. Jim stood up from the table and walked over to the bar. The man making the remark stepped forward, surrounded by a dozen overage nomads looking for trouble. Without breaking his slow stride, Jim approached the group, and in one violent explosion, swung a six inch metal black jack at his target. The instrument tore through the man's lower jaw, shattering teeth and crushing the facial bone structure. Two more strikes were delivered with tremendous velocity. The man crumbled to the floor. The lower portion of his face had been mangled. Blood had splattered everyone around. Jim backed away and invited the rest of the group out. Jim's crew was now behind him poised to back up any fall out from the first attack. There was no further retaliation and nothing was said. Eleven men left. One was carried out. Word had trickled down over the years that a man died that night at the Train Station. It was Texas. There were no investigations.

At 6'2" and 185 pounds, Jim Shane's forty- four year old physique showed no signs of lost definition or middle age movement. He spewed "Rush Limbaugh" analogies like mortar fire. Coming of age can be described as talk radio. When the pulpits of G. Gordon Liddy and Rush

Limbaugh replace the music buttons in the car, sanity has arrived. His disdain for the Democrats was only surpassed by his disgust with the nation's welfare system in general. Jim Shane is a conservative, middle aged veteran, carved in granite, and struggling to raise his children like millions of Americans. Most similarities end with his basement arsenal and food shelter barricaded behind a lead enclosure.

Jim and Denise Shane have three children, Brian 13, Justine 7, and Jasmine 5. Denise works part-time as an accountant and runs a day care center for their neighborhood. She is a striking forty-year old woman, with long auburn hair reaching the middle of her back. Her Scottish heritage radiates from her green eyes and freckled cheeks. The two couples exchange hugs and moved through the turnstiles. Inside, the United Center is a spectacular reflection of marble, stainless steel, and glass. This Friday night game pitted the Bulls against the New York Knicks, normally a bruising affair highlighted by the defensive style of basketball played in the Eastern Conference.

After securing a couple of draft beers and some wine for the girls, the two couples spent a few minutes visiting on the main concourse before making their way to the court side seats behind the basket on the west end. The first half proved to be nothing less than the war these two teams had been accustomed to. Garett often took his seats for granted, but tonight, he was reminded of just how special they had become. Jim and Denise were ecstatic about their proximity to the court. Michael Jordan sat roughly eight feet from them. The constant trash talking from the players and the instructions coming from Phil Jackson were fully audible from their seats. At half-time, the two couples made their way back to the main concourse smoking area where Jim and Garett grabbed some beers and the ladies retreated to the washroom.

"Hey Garett, do you give Michael any advice from those seats?" Spencer Dryden asked as he approached. "Shit, you couldn't get any closer to the game unless you were on the team. Good to see you, Garett. This is my wife, Judy."

"Jim, this is Spencer Dryden and his wife. Hell, I would expect you to be in Reinsdorf's private box. If he's not one of your clients then he is in a select minority. Where are your seats?" Garett asked as the group exchanged handshakes.

"I'm here with one of my clients and his wife. I normally would decline these invitations because the conversations with clients at these games never leaves the subject of Trexon. I really wanted to see this game, but I have barely had a minute of basketball. Hell, with the SEC hanging over my every move, my clients still don't understand that I can offer no information on the status of the FDA approval, any acquisition

43

negotiations, or any upcoming announcements of any kind. They try to analyze everything I say concerning Trexon. The message remains unchanged. Buy it and wait. Simple. The day to day movements in this stock are meaningless. It will rise or fall a couple of points depending on which analyst has a hard on for it or which analyst sees some mutual fund purchases on a large scale and decides it's the stock of the week. Shit, now they have me rambling on about it. Nice meeting you, Jim. I'll see at the office, Garett"

Garett said nothing to Spencer about his afternoon. Spencer Dryden has been very supportive of Garett Baine's career, unlike most of the senior brokers at the downtown office. Spencer Dryden is fifty-six years old. His daily attire consists of blue jeans, a sweater, loafers and no socks, winter or summer. Garett and Spencer simply hit it off. Garett had come into Spencer's office one day during the second or third week of his new tenure at Dean Witter. All of the new brokers told him to stay clear of Spencer Dryden. He was huge and never spoke to the bullpen. This notion made visiting Spencer a priority. Garett wanted to know why he was so successful and these other guys were so miserable. They spent a couple of hours together that first day. Spencer had originally told Garett he could spare no more than five to ten minutes. He made it clear to Garett, that his success was generated from a number of sources, none of which were cold-calling. Bury yourself on the phone and the business will bury you. Spencer emphatically urged his new colleague to spend his time outside of the office, getting in front of people. Be yourself and bring something unique to the table. Phone robots were cloned examples of how to fail and be miserable in the process. Spencer saw something in Garett that first day, something reminiscent of the attitude from a frustrated lawyer some twenty years ago when he joined Dean Witter.

Spencer's client base numbered over one thousand and he managed nearly seven hundred million dollars in client assets. This ranked him number two in the firm. Spencer came from a prestigious law firm in Chicago. When he made the switch to Dean Witter, Spencer brought with him a tremendous network of past and present law clients. Spencer was also able to transfer the assets of nearly half of the firm's partners. Less than one year after Spencer's move to Dean Witter, his former law firm moved their entire profit sharing plan to his management. This was a multi-million dollar move. Spencer Dryden quickly earned President's Club membership and was named an officer at Dean Witter. Ten years ago, Spencer became involved with a small company out of Sampson County in North Carolina. Trexon, Inc. was a very small tobacco processing firm in the town of Clinton, North Carolina that was involved in some speculative research. The president of Trexon, Phillip Martin, was a law school student with Spencer Dryden. They have been close friends ever since. Phillip came to Spencer in 1985 with information concerning a patent on a completely non-addictive and harmless cigarette. The research centered on a nicotine substitute temporarily called K222 and a revolutionary technique of treating tobacco rendering the specific noxae or poison in smoke harmless. During the 1960's, the application of tobacco residue to skin tissues of laboratory rats produced the first evidence of cancerous lesions. Preliminary testing by Trexon, indicated there was no damage to the skin tissues of laboratory rats where the newly treated residue was applied. Also, no depravation syndrome developed following the removal of the K222 chemical from the animals. The removal of nicotine in the same animals presented a tremendous difference in behavior. The company needed to raise twenty-five million dollars for the research and development necessary to bring this product to market or at least to have an opportunity to market this product. The FDA approval process is long and expensive. The testing phase may take years culminating with human testing in the prison system. Prisoners are easier to monitor. Volunteers can be tracked based on monitored diets. Any damage from the experimental substance can be traced with more accuracy when the subjects cannot alter their dietary intake. After surviving four phases of testing, the actual approval process becomes another hurdle altogether. Following Phase IV release, the FDA will spend up to six months reviewing the tests submitted and subsequently issue a ruling. Spencer sold the concept to nearly his entire client base. Many of them purchased large blocks of stock at the initial offering. Everyone was completely aware of the risks involved. The major tobacco companies have squelched their research on any similar products, due to fears about the consequences to their traditional cigarette business. Successful production of a safer cigarette would catastrophically effect the industry's position as to liability issues concerning the public health related to smoking. In either case, completion of this task by a small company would be extremely difficult at best. The sheer power and resources of the tobacco lobby could present a permanent hurdle. The absolute necessity for protecting the processing and manufacturing formulas was imperative to Trexon's future. The investors understood these risks. On April 1, 1991, the company went public, trading on the NASDAQ under the symbol TREX. Spencer Dryden purchased two-hundred and fifty thousand shares for his own account. The stock opened at eleven dollars per share for an investment of two and three-quarters million dollars. Spencer's clients, two insurance companies, and the firm's officers made up a majority of the difference to reach the twenty-five million dollar goal. Five years later, the stock is trading at nineteen.

45

Rumors abound as to the impending complete approval by the FDA. Rumors concerning licensing agreements or potential buy-outs by one of the majors continue to spring up constantly. Dean Witter, it's clients, officers, and brokers have garnered such a large position in the company, this position has prompted the SEC to place the stock on restricted status for all Dean Witter brokers, including Spencer. This designation simply means that no Dean Witter employees may solicit future orders on this stock. They can accept only unsolicited orders. Any major movement in the price of the stock or any acquisitions, agreements, or block movements will be examined closely by the SEC. Any hint of insider trading from this point will trigger a full investigation by the SEC and assets could be frozen. Spencer wouldn't tell his own mother anything from this point forward. His stake could well exceed ten million dollars with a major acquisition. Lindsay and Denise joined their husbands on the concourse. Garett had just finished telling Jim about Spencer Dryden and Trexon, Inc.

"Why don't I own any of that stock?" Jim inquired somewhat mockingly of his friend and broker.

"You could literally sit on that stock forever. It is pure speculation. If the company is bought out, everyone makes big money. If the FDA approval is not granted or another firm reaches the market first, then the stock dies. You'd be lucky to get ten cents on the dollar. I own a few shares, more out of obligation than anything else. Hell, there is a TREX alert at the office every time the stock moves. I got bored listening to it constantly, so I bought some. Let's get back to the game. Forget about Trexon. I think it would have happened by now if it was going to happen at all. Just thank me later for saving you some money."

The close half-time score quickly became a Bull's route midway through the third quarter. Steven Schirer, a Bull's vice-president and public relation's director, came over to greet Garett and Lindsay. They had been extremely active with the Illinois chapter of the Make A Wish Foundation. Lindsay had been a "Wish Granter", and assisted in arranging many visits of terminally ill children to the Bull's locker room. These special visits were the number one choice for the majority of the children sponsored by the Illinois Chapter. The obvious goal, to meet Michael Jordan and spend some time with him, one on one. Michael never refused these requests. Along with spending as much time as he could with these children, he always provided some fabulous gifts to remember the day. Michael would present each child with an autographed jersey and a pair of the latest Air Jordan's. Steven and Lindsay talked at length about the program and her desire to resume her involvement as soon as all of the children were in school. She had to cut back with the addition to their family of Conner and Christopher. The fourth quarter was well under way. The game was a full blown route as evidenced by the empty seats throughout the United Center. Dinner reservations at Gibson's awaited, appearances complete, the corporate season ticket holders shuffled to the exits. Garett did not leave early, and his guests understood this. Through all of the years, he still believed it was a privilege to see these games in person and he had seen too many things happen in the closing minutes to rush out for sake of avoiding a bit of traffic. As the game concluded, the Baines and the Shanes gathered their coats and hustled up aisle 120 heading for the North side exit doors. The stream of people was steady, not overwhelming. Crossing Madison Street through the buses and limousines, Garett and Jim were walking some eight to ten feet ahead of their wives. Young black children approached asking for their ticket stubs, a seemingly harmless request. Garett declined and explained to the group how these kids used the ticket stubs to manufacture bogus tickets. They would then sell the phony tickets at the next home game to fans hoping to avoid the pricey ticket brokers. Every Bulls game has been a sellout for years and the season ticket waiting list numbers in the thousands. People buy these tickets and are escorted from the stadium when they arrive at the seats only to find them occupied by the legitimate ticket holder. The kids are long gone and the crime is virtually impossible to pursue. The police are obligated to take the report, but they know it is a complete waste of paper and ink.

The traffic was solid but moving fast. Approaching Warren Street, they waited for the Chicago Policewoman to stop the traffic and allow the pedestrians to cross. Garett and Jim hustle across, but the ladies are detained for another flow of traffic. As they finally make their way across Warren Street, their husbands have slowed their pace to allow the women to catch up. Another half block and they will head down an alley to their parking lot on Washington Street, just east of Damen. Walcott Avenue is the short cross street between Washington and Warren. The alley leading to their lot begins midway down that short block. The streets are still full of exiting fans from the game doing their best to avoid the stream of vehicles pouring out of every lot surrounding the stadium. Garett turns to proceed down the alley engrossed in a conversation with his friend concerning the miserable failure of the The Chicago Housing Authority. Some public housing remains visible from the stadium grounds and it's decaying condition has launched Jim into an editorial on the ills of public housing. Lindsay and Denise followed discussing the responsibilities of the volunteers that work for the Make A Wish Foundation. Denise had always wanted to get involved in some way.

Without warning, from the corner of Washington and Walcott, the sullen sounds of mumbled conversations and starting cars, were shattered by the screeching tires of a blue sedan spinning onto Walcott heading south from Washington. Careening around the corner, the car sent people scattering. Garett stopped and whirled around to address the commotion. His eyes became fixed on the window of the sedan as he spotted what appeared to be a gun held by a passenger in the rear seat. In that split second, he screamed as the shots sprayed the west side of the street. One after another, explosions crushing the winter night. The rapid blasts ripped through the instant hysteria. The car turned again onto Warren Street, cutting the corner and slamming into two men on the corner. One of them flipped completely over the car landing limp on the pavement. The blue sedan was now weaving in and out of traffic at great speed, reckless and gone. The area was chaotic. People were still diving for safe cover. The startled Policewoman on Warren Street was calling for back up. Her partner rushed to the injured. Garett and Jim, frantically rushed to their wives, somehow lost among the forms littering the sidewalk and the hysterical bedlam of that one block area.

"Lindsay...Lindsay..." Garett screamed again pushing his way out of the alley. His heart stopped and his world left him when he saw his wife lying motionless on the sidewalk. Her blond hair draped over the curb along with her left arm which laid lifeless in the street. "No...", was barely audible as his own body stopped breathing. Lindsay had been shot twice. Blood stained the front of her white blouse and her right hand which seemed to be clutching her stomach. He knelt beside her, praying for signs of life. Her chest was moving and as he gently cupped his hand underneath her neck. A faint pulse touched against his fingers. Garett curled up next to his wife, wanting to protect her from what had already happened. Sirens began blaring in the background as the ambulances made their way from the stadium. Police personnel scrambled to reach their vehicles. The blue sedan was lost in the sea of departing fans. Garett's eyes and attention never left his wife. Four others were shot. Denise Shane had been thrown back against the chain link fence of the parking lot adjacent to Walcott. Her body sat prone supported by the fence. She had been shot once in the chest. Garett could hear Jim screaming for the paramedics. He stumbled in thought. This simply could not be happening. No time had elapsed. He thought of his children and their arms draped around Lindsay every morning. Pain enveloped his own body. Pain from his thoughts, pain from his vision, pain for his friends, and the pain he desperately wished he could assume for Lindsay.

Less than four minutes after the shots were fired, three ambulances had made their way to the accident scene. Teams of paramedics piled gear on top of stretchers as the equipment was yanked from the trucks. The first team reached Lindsay seconds after the trucks arrived. The first paramedic instructed Garett to back off and give them some room.

"What happened?" The question was directed at Garett as the paramedic established vital signs.

"Shots were fired from a car speeding through this intersection. It happened so fast. We heard the car spinning around the corner. I turned and saw a gun firing randomly into the crowd. My wife was a few feet behind me...how is she? Is she going to die?"

"She has been shot twice in the abdomen. She is alive and her vital signs are strong. I do not know the extent of the damage. We will be taking her to Cook County. You can meet us there."

"I'm not leaving her. I'm going with you."

"No you're not, sir." The paramedic didn't explain. He was relaying information to his partner. They placed a manual oxygen pump on her chest, inserting the breathing tube into her mouth. An IV was started as they immobilized her body on a spine board.

"Move her, now!" The order was barked and the team moved in unison. The board was placed on the stretcher. One paramedic was holding the IV bag in one hand and pushing the stretcher with the other. His partner was squeezing the oxygen bag in sequence as he guided Lindsay to the waiting ambulance.

"Ready, on one." The stretcher was slid into the vehicle followed quickly by the attending team.

Jim Shane yelled for his friend. Denise had been placed in another ambulance and Jim was given similar instructions. Jim had not been told that his wife showed no signs of life. Garett grabbed Jim's arm as he searched the chaos. The two men reached Garett's Blazer in seconds and pulled immediately out onto Washington Street. They drove west one block, then left on Damen, heading south. Cook County Hospital was located very close to the United Center, visible from some vantage points. Jim sat stunned in the passenger seat, his wife's blood covering his hands. Garett lay on the horn as he burned his way through the traffic, leaning forward and wiping a combination of tears and fear from his face. He had never driven to Cook County Hospital from the stadium. Tonight, he knew the way.

Damen crosses the Eisenhower Expressway just west of the stadium. Cook County Hospital was in full view as the Blazer fought its way through the traffic. It was 10:25 p.m., Friday January 26, 1996. The eight story hospital was a landmark in disrepair. Located on Chicago's volatile West Side, this was the last bastion of the trauma center program started by the city seven years ago. The intricate white brick structure was etched in dirt as the in-laid craftsmanship of the original construction housed years of neglect. Single broken down window air-conditioners dotted the front face of the building, looking grossly out of place on the facade of this unique treasure to Chicago's architectural past. The night sky hung a soft layer of white clouds rhythmically broken across the city's skyline. The searing wail of sirens seemed to come from all directions as the police and ambulances recovered from the abrupt nature of this random violence. A stadium flooded in white spotlights took on a sporadic red wash from the hundreds of lights spinning brightly atop all of the emergency vehicles. This city was accustomed to the sounds of transporting crime. However, even the residents of this hardened neighborhood pressed the windows of their high rise apartments to witness this carnage.

The trip to the hospital took less than three minutes. Garett had no idea where the emergency room entrances were and he had no intention of looking. He pulled the Blazer up to the front entrance to Cook County Hospital on Harrison Street. Jim Shane was in shock, deathly silent during the brief ride to the hospital. His sense of urgency was non-existent. When they arrived at the main entrance, Garett's demeanor was noticeably shaken, but demonstrative. He was moving quickly. Jim moved with hesitation and confusion. They entered the glass doors of the main entrance, raced through the unmanned metal detectors standing next to the inoperable conveyor scanning devices. The front lobby resembled an airport waiting area. White plastic chairs sealed together and anchored to the floor stood in neat rows. The area was quiet with a half dozen sleeping homeless sprawled across three chairs. They had no business at the hospital except to land a warm place to thaw until security asked them to leave. Security at Cook County Hospital is an oxymoron. Not enough and not in the right place. Garett wanted to ask someone where the trauma unit was located, but every desk and security point was empty. They simply started roaming the halls following the signs posted in systematic order and printed in English and Spanish. The trauma unit at Cook County is located in the rear of the structure on the first floor, recently moved from the fourth floor. The ambulances had pulled in behind the building as Garett and Jim were weaving their way through the hallways toward the trauma unit, where a Chicago Policeman stood at the entrance way. The room looked huge. Garett was accustomed to the normal sized emergency rooms of suburban hospitals. At Cook County, there were sixteen sections for patient care and operating rooms adjacent to the immediate treatment area.

"My wife was brought in with another woman from the shooting at the stadium. Do you know where they are?" Garett blurted, trying to catch his breath.

"They were brought in two minutes ago. You'll have to go to the ER waiting area. Someone can help you there. This is a restricted area. You'll have to leave now."

"I'm not leaving until you can tell me where my wife is and let me talk to someone who has seen her. The fucking paramedics tell me I can't ride with her. Now you tell me I can't see her and I'm in a restricted area. She just got shot outside the stadium. My friend's wife got shot. Somebody has got to tell us how they are."

Jim Shane exploded through the entrance to the trauma center. He knocked the officer back and was well inside before anyone got their bearings. Garett followed right behind Jim. This trauma unit was staffed with three surgeons in house and on call, eight residents, assorted support staff, and changing shifts of paramedics as they transport and deliver their wounded riders. The policeman called for more security before he gave chase. As the staff security arrived, the two men searching for their wives had found them.

"Denise...Denise..." Jim shouted as he saw her surrounded by a team of medical personnel. The security arrived to impede his progress. "Just tell me what is happening..." He was not out of control. His words were strong, now, as his eyes fought his heart in disbelief of the scene unveiling before him. One of the attending surgeons wanted the swell of people removed from the area. He turned to Jim and met his eyes dead on.

"I'm sorry sir. Your wife has been shot once in the chest. Her heart has taken a direct hit. We are doing everything possible. Let these men show you where to wait. Get him out of here now!"

Jim stared at the area where his wife was lying. He watched as frantic hands became still. They had inserted a breathing tube into her throat with a manual bag attached. Someone pulled the bag away as Jim was led out of the room. Denise Shane had died instantly on the street outside on this January night. Paramedics are not allowed to declare death on the scene unless the victim is decapitated. With the hospital so close, within a five to ten minute time frame, the unit will attempt to revive the victim. There were no vital signs at the scene. The nature of the wound left no doubt. Denise was pronounced dead at 10:32. Jim was out of the room. He took a seat in the waiting area. He began to cry. The trauma unit surgeon who spoke to Jim only minutes before, came out to speak to him. There was nothing they could do. He expressed his sympathy and walked away.

Garett Baine had been escorted to the emergency room waiting area. No one on the staff or the security personnel tried to make things harder on the victims families. There were certain procedures necessary to keep order. Unauthorized visitors were not allowed in the Trauma Unit. Invariably, these incidents occur under the duress of the victim's families. The staff and security are trained to understand this. Their goal is to remove the individual from the restricted area and then assist them in obtaining answers pertaining to the condition of their friends or family

51

members. Garett entered the waiting area as the surgeon was leaving. Jim looked up at Garett while trying to wipe his hands on the front of his shirt. The blood on his hands had dried some time ago, but he continued to slowly rub his hands diagonally across his shirt. Garett didn't ask any questions; the tears welling up in the eyes of his friend spoke volumes. Jim's muscular frame began to crumble and shake as Garett reached out to embrace his friend.

"What am I going to do Garett?" his voice cracking as he tried to prevent his own collapse. "I've got three kids at home sleeping. They have this crazy idea that when they wake up, they will still have a mother. Oh God... I don't believe this... Am I crazy Garett? Did we just go the Bull's game and now my wife is dead? What is that? What am I supposed to tell them? I'm sorry kids, but somebody decided to open fire randomly in a crowd and mom caught one. God, Garett...we just went to the ...game...wasn't it just a... basketball...game." he could barely finish the sentence. His body sunk back into the chair, and began to wipe his hands across his shirt.

Garett Baine wasn't well equipped to be an emotional juggernaut at this point. The emergency room had begun to fill up with the fallout from this shooting. Police were arriving to keep the press outside or at least confine them to the lobby. Since the shooting occurred at a Bull's game, the media trucks and equipment were on sight. Word of the shooting sent these sports reporters out on the street. The current casualty count was six people shot, one fatality, two in critical condition and three in serious condition. Thirteen people were injured by the vehicle. One victim was pronounced dead on arrival at Cook County, three were listed in critical condition, two in serious condition and seven arrived with a variety of minor injuries. Garett looked lost as the families of the other victims began to fill up the room. People moved slowly as they tried to grasp some sense of where they were and why. The immediate aftermath of this tragedy was now being televised live on every channel in Chicago. The two televisions located in the emergency room waiting area projected the horror they had encountered just eight blocks away. The pictures conveyed the sights and sounds of the constant sirens moving about the stadium grounds which were joined in harmony with the whirling frenzy of five television news helicopters and two police helicopters searching for the suspect vehicle.

Two policemen came into the room looking for Jim Shane. They tried to comfort him while having the unfortunate task of questioning him about the shooting. Jim and the two detectives approached Garett.

"Garett, I'm going to go with these detectives. We have to make some arrangements for Denise. They said they will accompany me to the morgue and make sure that I get home all right. I'll make some plans to pick up my car in the next few days." Jim moved closer to his friend and put his arms around Garett. His voice was breaking up but his words were soft and sure. "Garett, I hope to God that Lindsay pulls through this. Denise's mother is baby sitting at our house right now. I've got to make a call to tell her that her daughter has died. I'm not sure how I am going to be able to tell her that. I always wondered how people were able to deliver news like this. How does a parent sit down with his children and tell them. God, I hope you don't go through this." Jim's eyes focused on the crowded hallway.

"I'm sorry, Jim. I never imagined...I never thought this could...I have to stay, Jim. I'm sorry I can't go with you. They won't tell me anything about Lindsay. She got hit real bad. I'm sorry Jimmy...I'm so God Damn sorry..." Garett's voice trailed off. He watched as the three men made their way through the crowd in the waiting area.

"Mr. Baine? Is Mr. Baine in here?" A trauma unit surgeon was asking.

"Right here, right here! How is my wife? Where is she? Can I see her?"

"We are preparing your wife for the operating room." The young doctor pulled Garett to some chairs. "Sit down Mr. Baine." The young surgeon's name was Loren Reuben. He was forty years old but looked thirty, having kept his tight physique from a gymnastics background in high school and college. Loren Reuben had thick red hair, longer than most in his profession. He was a graduate of Northwestern Medical School and specialized in General Surgery. This provided him a wide range of surgical challenges. He did not want to become a 'one trick pony', or a surgeon who would perform the same operations every day of their practice. General surgeons had to be prepared to operate on many different organs mainly concentrating on the abdominal and chest regions. "Mr. Baine, your wife has sustained two bullet wounds to the abdomen. She has lost some blood, but the shock of the injuries is most likely the cause of losing consciousness. Her condition is critical at this point. The bullets have pierced the intestines, and this is the area of first concern. We have to go in and shore up any punctures to the small and large intestines. In most cases where the intestines sustain damage of this type, we remove sections of the damaged intestinal walls. The procedure necessary is called an Exploratory Laparotomy. We have to go into the abdomen and search out any wounds to the bowel areas. Infection from the intestinal fluids is the immediate danger. From the X-rays taken, we can see that one of the bullets seems to have shattered a vertebrae. I will have no idea as to the extent of that damage until we eliminate the risk of infection and close the damage done to the intestines. The spinal cord does not appear to be punctured or severed. Again, this is premature until

I can get in there and assess her condition. Right now, we need to stop the internal bleeding and prevent any infection. This procedure could take three or four hours. I will come out as soon as we are finished and tell you how everything went. I have to get in there, now."

"Don't let her die...just don't let her die." Garett wanted to say so much more.

"I don't intend to. Call your family, Mr. Baine. I'll be out as soon as I am finished."

*   *   *

CHAPTER FIVE

The smell of Captain Morgan rum filled the car and burned Casey Griffin's throat. He sat in the back seat of the blue sedan parked in the lots adjacent to the Henry Horner Housing Projects of the West Side. These projects sit just north of the United Center on Washington Street. Casey was nervously fidgeting with the Tech-9 laying on his lap. Zarvell White sat behind the drivers seat chain smoking cigarettes which were beginning to pile up on the ground outside the car. Casey was twenty-two years old and Zarvell was twenty-four. They were members of the West Side gang known as the Breed. They are watching an old brownstone house sitting at the corner of Washington and Walcott. They are two or three of these row houses still standing on this block. Old and run down, these houses had somehow avoided the wrecking ball of the United Center house cleaning. This location had been the center of Breed drug transactions for the past few years. The gang took pride in being able to operate in the middle of the United Center parking areas. The police of the 13th District had decided not to make this a proving ground during events at the United Center. Most activity at this house took place before or after an event, as the gangs knew when the police would be reluctant to engage their members and risk harming any innocent people. The Breed took pride in flaunting this activity in an area crawling with police. The police would regularly film the individuals entering and leaving this house from strategically placed unmarked cars in the surrounding lots. The Breed didn't care.

Recently, Griffin and White had become aware of some disturbing news. They had been informed that members of the Four Corner Hustlers were bringing drugs into the area and transacting business at this location. No taxes were being paid by the Hustlers. Therefore, no permission had been granted to enter their territory and conduct business. In many cases, gang leaders will extract a fee or taxes from a rival gang to permit that gang limited access to a specific area for the purpose of selling drugs. Anything short of this arrangement would be interpreted as a lack of respect towards the residing gang membership and a blatant attempt to

55

humiliate them on their own turf. On this night, Griffin and White would make an example of those Four Corner Hustlers. The impending activity at the Untied Center would have no bearing on this action. As soon as the Four Corner Hustlers were spotted outside of the premises, they would be gunned down from a passing blue sedan. Griffin and White had spotters inside the Henry Horner Projects on the upper floors. These spotters would relay a certain number through a beeper to the blue sedan. At that point, the vehicle would approach the location, never stopping, identify themselves as members of the Breed, and open fire on their targets.

Born into the projects at the Robert Taylor Homes on the Chicago's South Side. Casey's life quickly became an exercise in survival. The walkways at the Taylor Homes resembled prison corridors complete with wire mesh from floor to ceiling. The elevators rarely worked. Doors were kicked in, beaten badly and covered with gang graffiti everywhere. The stairwells could be used safely only in the daytime hours; at night, these stairwells became stages for drug deals, rapes, and retribution chambers for the gangs. When Casey was six years old and his brother Spencer was eight, they were playing on the walkway in front of their ninth floor apartment. They wandered down to one of the vacant apartments that had been nearly destroyed by various gang members over the last year. They used these vacant apartments for meeting places to conduct drug transactions or simply for places to get high. This was a warm summer evening in Chicago and the daylight lingered on well past eight. The boys knew that after dark was not a time to be wandering about. They had been playing in that vacant apartment during the afternoon and had gone back to retrieve some food they had stashed there. The front door to this apartment had been knocked off its hinges and was just leaning against the general area of the doorway as it had been for the past few months. The boys slipped into the apartment and headed back to one of the bedrooms where they had their stash. Before they could reach the middle of the front room, someone grabbed Casey from behind and smacked Spencer with some kind of club. On the floor in front of him, Casey saw a young girl being held down on the debris littered floor. She was naked and gagged. One man held her arms outstretched above her head and two other men held her legs spread apart.

"Well, you boys just stumbled into the wrong fucking place." The man holding Casey spoke.

"We didn't see nothin, man. I swear. We'll go. We didn't see nothin." Spencer was pleading with the man holding his younger brother.

"You know something, I believe this little guy might be on to something." The man released his hold on Casey. "I believe this little guy is not going to say one fucking thing to anyone." The man walked over to

Spencer and put both hands under his shoulders, lifting him off the floor. This large man carried Casey's older brother over to the window and threw him out of the ninth floor apartment. Spencer's screams were short and the impact came quickly. He turned to Casey, who stood frozen in shock. "Get the fuck out of here, little man. You say anything to anyone and you'll find out what it's like to kiss the pavement from the roof."

Casey ran home to his bed. He listened as the sirens came and he waited for the police to knock on all the doors that night. He told his mother that he wasn't with Spencer. He never cried. He would learn to protect his space. He would learn the code.

Casey Griffin moved to the West side shortly after his brother's death. Zarvell White had spent his entire life in this West Side neighborhood. Their childhood years were remarkably similar, almost eerily mirrored as they marked each passing year with new encounters of criminal activity. Neither had spent more than one year in high school, an home was a location for some occasional food. Fathers never existed and mothers concentrated on the younger children of the family until those futures melted into another pregnancy. Casey and Zarvell began their gang activities as taggers on the same crew. They would team up on 'bombing runs', where members of a crew would go out and try to mark as many places as possible with their gang name and symbols. They would cover entire walls with gang graffiti, or 'kill the walls.' These early runs were made for the Vice Lords, one of the original black stronghold gangs of Chicago. Most other current gangs are from factions splitting away from the main group. The Breed and the Four Corner Hustlers were formed from splits with the Vice Lords. Other offshoots include the Travelers and the Black Gangster Stones. In Chicago today, if the gang population could somehow manage to unite, they would outnumber the police four to one.

As Casey and Zarvell got older, their records grew. Stints in jail became frequent for drugs, assault and armed robbery. Their code became the lifeline of their peers; goals were limited to the preservation of oneself. One had to be willing to prove he was able to take care of himself, which always involved violence. This code was never left alone. It had to be constantly enforced on a continuing basis. The police and death became synonymous with apathy. Neither was a deterrent to any activity necessary to preserve your respect and exhibit your courage. They had moved up quickly in the ranks of the Breed. Each gang had its own system of rank and reward. They were brothers and this was their family.

The two men didn't speak much during their wait. The bottle of rum was empty now and Casey was getting restless. They watched as the streets began to fill with exiting fans from the basketball game. The extent of the early departures indicated the closeness of the contest. Zarvell glanced at his watch. The time was almost a quarter past ten. The beeper on Casey's belt began to sound. Zarvell started the car in an instant and pulled out onto Washington Street gaining speed rapidly. Casey slammed the fifty round clip into the Tech-9 and slid over to the window on the passenger side of the rear seat. He rolled the window down and clutched the weapon firmly in both hands. Two black men had walked down the steps of the brownstone on the corner of Washington and Walcott. The blue sedan had the targets in sight. They were identified by the red bandannas hanging from their back pockets, a trademark of the Four Corner Hustlers. The spotters in the projects would have been looking for these bandannas through their binoculars. Casey and Zarvell knew what to look for as they reached the corner, but were traveling too fast to make a clean turn.

"Slow down!" Casey yelled as the rum and the pedestrians combined to cloud the intended targets.

"Shit!"

The car hit the curb at the corner and jumped the sidewalk, scattering scores of people. Casey had no idea where his targets were at this point and began firing in the general direction of the house and the alley behind it. Three or four bodies had been sent reeling over the vehicle as White struggled to get control of the car. Casey Griffin wanted to release as many rounds as possible to insure his targets were hit. In the event they were not hit, the message would be sent very emphatically to stay out of this territory. Any innocent people killed in this exchange would only serve to remind any ambitious Four Corner Hustlers considering future forays into Breed neighborhoods. White never let up on the gas. The vehicle's rear tires were desperately searching for a hold on the concrete. The intrusion of some mythical borders had become an urban battlefield spilling the blood of men and women blind to the cause and so far removed from the conflict. The muffled blasts from the Tech-9 ceased. Griffin pulled his weapon back into the car as they turned the corner on Warren, weaving through the traffic.

"Did you drop 'em?" White yelled to his accomplice, "I didn't hear Breed."

"Just get the fuck out of here, man. I don't know what the fuck I hit." Casey had turned to view the chaos from the back window. "Try keeping the fucking car on the road long enough to get us out of here." The traffic worked to their advantage. Zarvell White had made his way back to Lake Street and followed the 'L' tracks behind the projects to a garage just past Ogden Ave. There are nearly twenty-five uniformed Chicago police personnel assigned to posts outside the United Center for any given event. Many more plain clothes detectives work inside. The 12th and 13th Districts are separated by Madison Street, as officers working the stadium itself are from the 12th, while those working the surrounding streets north are from the 13th. Descriptions of the vehicle were radioed into the 13th District seconds after the shooting. From there, the Chicago Police dispatch headquarters had a city-wide alert to every patrol car in the area and outside of the area within minutes. The mass of police vehicles converging on the United Center and the surrounding West Side neighborhoods was deafening. Casey Griffin and Zarvell White had disappeared.

*   *   *

CHAPTER SIX

It had been two hours since Dr. Loren Reuben had told Garett Baine that his wife would be undergoing emergency surgery due to the damage caused by two bullet wounds to the abdomen. Since leaving the United Center three hours earlier and for every moment yet to come, Garett Baine had his life irrevocably altered. The short time since attending the game was a view of someone else's life. Garett would continue in his attempts to shake the reality of this night from his mind. Garett had called his next door neighbor, whose daughter was staying with the kids. Jack and Kate Doleman have lived next to the Baines for ten years. Their fourteen year old daughter, Mary Ann, was the sitter of choice for the past few years. The trick was booking her far enough in advance. Their Sheridan Shores neighborhood was starved for teen-age sitters. The window of age was thin. Twelve seemed to be the minimum age, but then only if the child was a neighbor. At fifteen, the hormonal high school distractions immediately remove most of the girls from the available ranks. Kate had answered the phone when Garett called. She had been glued to the television since news of the shooting had taken over the airwaves. Kate was always aware of where the Baines were, when Mary Ann was watching their kids. The Doleman's had expected a call to assure them that the shooting did not involve their neighbors. The names of the victims were being withheld until families could be notified. Kate took the call and held her breath as Garett's voice came with hesitation and anguish searching for the right way to handle this situation.

"Kate, this is Garett. You have to listen to me carefully. I don't think I'm going to be able to carry this conversation very long. Have you been aware of what has been going on outside the stadium, tonight?"

"Yes, we have been watching the news since this story came on around 10:30. Garett, are you and Lindsay alright...I mean....you guys weren't in this...were you?"

"Listen to me, Kate. We were right in the center of this shooting. Lindsay is in surgery as we speak. She was shot twice. She is in critical condition. She was not awake when the ambulance brought her in. I might know more in an hour or so. Denise Shane was killed. We were walking to our car after the game. Out of nowhere, came a car screeching around the corner near our parking lot. It happened so fast...Somebody started shooting from the car. The car was gone and people were lying everywhere. Denise took a bullet directly to the heart. They brought her in, but there was nothing they could do. Jim left with some detectives. I don't know what he's going to do. I couldn't help him...I wanted to...I wanted to help so bad. Kate, take care of our kids tonight. Go over to my house and send Mary Ann home. If any of my kids are up or wake up, don't tell them anything. Make sure they are in bed and then stay there until I can call you or until I get there. I'm at Cook County in the emergency room. I'll call you as soon as I know anything. Please, just make sure the kids are all right. I have to be the one who talks to them about what has happened. Make sure of that, please. I have to go Kate. I don't...I don't know what I'll do if Lindsay doesn't make it. Kate, did they catch these guys?"

"Garett, Jack and I will take of everything. Just stay with Lindsay. We'll pray for her, Garett. You have to put your faith in God. He won't take her from you. Don't worry about the kids; I'll do everything you ask. Go Garett, our prayers are with you."

"Thanks, Kate...thanks for everything. Kate, did they catch these guys?"

"No, Garett. At this time, they have no trace of the car. The helicopters arrived too late, and the car got lost in the traffic after the game."

When suddenly thrust into the teeth of a tragic sequence of events that will change lives forever, Garett Baine is asked to put his faith in God. Pray to him for support. Would he pray and revere God at Denise's funeral? Garett Baine wanted to know where he was tonight. Garett's struggles with religion bordered on condescending sarcasm. Lindsay was lying in surgery and Denise was gone. There was the devastating image of Jim Shane wiping his hands across his chest, trying to erase the nightmare. Garett gained little comfort from the notion of prayer. Retribution filled his soul; not forgiveness at the image of the blue sedan disappearing into the belly of the West Side. Garett was lost, desperately searching, pleading with God to help his wife. He wanted help from the source he blamed. Denise believed in the goodness of God. Lindsay lived by the devout trust in Jesus Christ. Garett searched for something absent in his life. Faith had always been an elusive butterfly. Garett Baine felt alone and helpless.

Dr. Reuben entered the emergency room waiting area exactly three hours after his initial visit. He looked drawn and tired. He found Garett staring at the doors leading to surgery. Garett's eyes opened with fear as the doctor reached out to grab his elbow and lead him back to his seat.

"Sit down, Mr. Baine. Your wife is stable following the surgery. Her condition is not life threatening at this point. She will, however, remain on the critical list and her condition will be constantly monitored in the Intensive Care Unit.. Lindsay is heavily sedated, but should come out of it in a few hours. We have repaired the damage done to the intestines. One section was removed and we were able to close some smaller punctures. It is important to locate all of these punctures. They normally occur in even numbers because of the bullet piercing both sides of the intestinal walls on impact. Her wounds appeared clean and I am sure we found all of them. The risk of infection remains from the bowel fluids released inside the abdominal cavity. No other organs were damaged. Your wife has sustained what is called a comminuted fracture or burst fracture of the vertebral body. The irregular shape of the spine and the vertebra allows for the greater likelihood of fractures in this area. Lindsay's lower spine has taken the impact from one of the bullets. The fracture has sent the bone fragments into the spinal cord. The cord is not severed, it is bruised and some swelling has occurred in the area. From the tests we were able to perform, prior to surgery, it appears that Lindsay has suffered some paralysis below the point of the injury. We were able to administer some sensory tests showing the motor reactions to pain. She responded positively to all tests performed above the point of injury. There was no response from the tests performed below the injury. This paralysis may be temporary; there is no way of knowing at this time. In seven to ten days, we will go in and fuse the bones back together. We must wait to insure the absence of infection to the region. Hardware will be placed to support the spine during the healing process. Lindsay will have to remain in traction until the fracture has sufficiently healed. More than likely, this will consist of one to two weeks in complete traction in the ICU. Lindsay will be placed on a kinetic treatment table or a Stryker bed. These are specifically made for the spinal cord-injured patient. She will be immobilized in this bed. The apparatus can be very intimidating to you and your wife. It is extremely important that you reassure your wife that the immobilization is to prevent any further damage during recovery and is not a permanent situation. The sudden onset of paralysis leaves no time for the patient to adjust, whether it is temporary or not. We need to be candid about the injury when she wakes up and the prognosis regarding recovery. Your touch will mean more than any words at this point. The demeanor reflected by your eyes, your voice, and your body language will give away your own fears if you allow that, and she will have enough fear to deal with. The strength you provide is her strength, remember that.

Once the swelling goes down around the spinal cord and the healing process begins, we will be able to determine the extent of the damage to the spinal cord. Your wife does not appear to have any sensation in her legs. This is not uncommon for an injury of this magnitude. Let me reiterate myself with regard to your wife's current condition. Lindsay is not in a life threatening situation, now. The paralysis may be temporary. Time will provide the answers. You have been very quiet during this consultation, Mr. Baine. Go and see your wife. It will be awhile before she comes around. You haven't lost her, Mr. Baine, but she will be scared as hell when she wakes up. We can talk later."

Garett stared intently as the doctor spoke in a calculating and compassionate manner. He had been given the news that Lindsay was going to make it, but she may never walk again. The unusual silence was not brought on by Garett's anguish. Garett's heart told him what his pen had written for many years. He loved his wife. The threat of losing her had finally erased any doubts that time may have replaced love with complacency and habit. He was quiet because the news that Lindsay was not leaving him became more important than anything else. Garett expected the worst and received much more. They could deal with anything together and that opportunity remained. Garett thanked the doctor. He agreed to stop in every hour or so until Lindsay woke up. They stood to shake hands. This surgeon had others to see. Garett brought his arms up to embrace Loren Reuben, and, to Loren's own surprise, he returned the embrace. Garett Baine headed for the ICU. Loren Reuben thought about his profession. Through all of the imperfections and misconceptions of medicine, he couldn't think of another place he'd rather be.

Immobilization of the spinal cord is imperative to the victim from the scene of the accident through the healing process. When Lindsay was transported to Cook County, the paramedics had taped her head to the backboard and placed sandbags on each side of her head to assure the stability. Any movement to the spine could cause additional damage. After surgery to repair the immediate damage done by the shooting, Lindsay was brought to Recovery Room 3D in the ICU. Garett Baine's breath shortened and his heart fell to his knees as he walked into that room. His beautiful wife was lying in a maze of chrome rings supporting her prone body. There were IV tubes and electronic monitors beeping. Lindsay's head was immobilized in the forward frame of the bed. This bed was a wedge turning frame consisting of an anterior and posterior frame so that the patient can be turned from a prone position to a supine position. The bed allows easy access for skin care and toilet necessities. Fear was the overriding emotion as Garett sat next to his wife. Lindsay had always handled hospitals well. Through four pregnancies and one miscarriage, she had skipped the seemingly mandatory birthing classes. She wanted to have the babies, get some rest, and if needed, use an epidural. If the eighties and nineties dictated natural childbirth, breast feeding, and spousal participation through every phase of the pregnancy, Lindsay Baine was not to be swayed. She felt Garett would be better off in the waiting room even though she didn't mind him next to her in delivery. Through four children, Garett never looked at the delivery itself; he had always wanted to remember certain areas from a sensual standpoint. This was fine with Lindsay, who spent the bulk of the delivery looking at the ceiling. Three of the four children came so fast, that a spinal pain injection was bypassed. Lindsay had the babies on formula from day one. Her family was raised that way and her kids would be raised that way. Garett never had a problem with any of this, and admired the way she ran her own show in the hospital. There was no intimidation. She enjoyed the hospital stay and took advantage of it. He prayed she could retain her composure through the current circumstances.

Garett had called Lindsay's sister during the wait for the surgery to be completed. It was almost three o'clock in the morning. Maureen Nolan lived very close to her sister. Tonight, it would take her an hour to get down to Cook County Hospital from Wilmette. Garett called Kate Doleman again. He explained Lindsay's condition and made her promise not to say anything to the kids, instructing her to stay with them until he got there. If he wasn't home when they woke up, Kate was to tell them that mommy and daddy had to stay down town last night, but they will be home soon. It was Saturday morning, so the little ones would be watching cartoons. Now that Lindsay's immediate danger had waned, he would coming home. Garett would wait until his wife was awake and they had a chance to spend some time together. He wanted to be honest with his kids, but it had to be face to face. The news had to come from him.

Maureen had arrived at 3:45 a.m. This was nearly two hours after Lindsay had been taken out of surgery. Garett asked her to wait in the lobby until Lindsay woke up. He wanted the privacy for her to react naturally. Dr. Reuben was on call all night and had just left approximately ten minutes ago. It was now 4:10 a.m., and Garett sat next to his wife, holding her hand. Recurring images of the shooting haunted each and every thought.

"Garett?" Lindsay's soft voice searched for her husband as her eyes opened slowly. The first sensation consumed her entire body. She was literally unable to move. The feeling in her legs was gone. Her head was in a restraint preventing any movement whatsoever and her arms and midsection were strapped gently but firmly to the Stryker frame. "Garett...are you here? I can't move Garett. I can't move..."

"Lindsay, I'm right here." Garett stood up and looked into her eyes for the first time in what seemed like days. He held her hand and felt her fingers tighten as they made contact. "Listen to me. You are at Cook County Hospital, about eight blocks away from the United Center. Do you remember anything about leaving the game?"

"I remember walking behind you and Jim. Denise and I heard some car coming too fast...I'm not sure...We heard shooting... I'm not sure, I don't remember much more than that..." She was crying and frightened. "What has happened to me Garett? What..."

"Lindsay, listen to me. I love you very much and you are going to be fine, but somebody shot you last night next to the parking lot we use. This was a random shooting. Six other people were shot. Thirteen others were hurt from the car jumping up on the sidewalk. You were shot twice in the abdomen. The bullets did some damage to your intestines. You were unconscious when the ambulance brought you in here. They had to do some surgery immediately to repair the damage to your intestines and to prevent any infection from setting in. You were in surgery for a couple hours and the damage was repaired. One of the bullets broke one of the vertebrae in your spine. This has caused a great deal of shock and swelling around the spinal cord and is the reason you can't move your legs. The spinal cord is not severed. The doctors say there is an excellent chance to regain all of the feeling in your legs. They will have to operate on you in a week or so, in order to repair the damage done to the vertebrae that sustained the impact of the bullet. Once this is accomplished and the swelling goes down, the doctors will be able to give us more answers. Because of the damage to your spine, they have to keep you perfectly still. I know this bed looks ominous, but it is only for a short time. Lindsay, I thought I was going to lose you and I don't think I've ever been more afraid of anything. I say that because I never felt that kind of fear before. I know you're scared, but you will be fine. Kate is at our house with the kids. I told her not to say anything until I can get there. Maureen is in the lobby here, and she will be able to stay with you when I go home and talk to the kids. The scary part is over. You're not leaving us. The rest, whatever it is, we can get through. I wish I could crawl up on that bed and hold you right now, but I don't think you would be terribly thrilled with me if I tried that."

"What about Jim and Denise? Are they all right? Are they here, Garett?" Her voice was barely audible, fighting her own emotions and the lingering anaesthesia.

"Denise was shot once in the chest. You must have been right next to each other and caught the same line of fire. These guys just shot randomly into the crowd. Denise died, Lindsay. They brought her in to revive her,

65

but there was nothing they could do. She never suffered." Garett's voice began to break up. Tears filled his eyes and he continued. "God, I feel so bad for them, Jim is having such a rough time. There was nothing I could do. We never had a chance to warn you. We never had a chance to get you out of the way. We shouldn't have been walking so far in front of you or Denise. I'm sorry Lindsay. I'm sorry it's not me laying there instead of you. If I could change places with you, I would do it gladly."

"Garett, come here." Lindsay tried to look his way. Garett leaned closer, careful not to disrupt any of the tubes or lines draped over the frame.

"Garett, closer..." Lindsay's eyes found her husband's. "Kiss me gently." Their lips touched for only a moment. "Go home Garett. I'm fading. Go home and take care of our kids. I love you. No one knew this could happen...nobody's fault..." Her eyes closed and she drifted. Garett kissed her again and left the room.

Over the course of the next six hours, Lindsay woke up a couple of times, and Garett and Maureen were right there. Lindsay wanted her husband to go home and take care of the kids. She wanted Garett to be honest with them. They would have a hard time with all of this, and Lindsay did not want to make matters worse by lying to them. Dr. Reuben had been in to speak to Lindsay. He spoke to his patients in a very direct manner, conveying respect for the people he treated. His message was not one of ambiguity. He spoke to Lindsay about the complications brought on by the shock of the bullet to her system and her spinal column. Damage of this magnitude was not uncommon and the return to normal movement from this type of injury was not uncommon. He made it clear that this was not a guarantee that the damage done to the spinal column was not permanent. His words were strong, and his candor came as a welcome surprise to most patients. Dr. Reuben detailed the upcoming surgery and the prognosis for recovery time. Everyone felt it might be best to wait until the second surgery was complete to bring the kids down. Completely immobile at this point, Lindsay could not even turn her head. This would add to the children's fear, and it was scary enough for them. The severity of spinal cord injuries is always complicated by the size and complexity of the equipment needed to treat the patients. The immediate aftercare apparatus is tremendously intimidating. The patient coming out of recovery and realizing for the first time the details of the injuries incurred is often complicated by the overwhelming equipment involved. The initial contact and emotional support may be the most important aspect of the patient's recovery. Lindsay had handled her initial shock with her typical composure and style. She had been brought up not to feel sorry for herself, and considering the circumstances, she felt lucky to be alive. She found it easy to thank God for allowing her to see her children and her family again.

Lindsay's head restraints had become unbearable. Initially uncomfortable, the tension had become too great, and Lindsay asked Garett to locate Dr. Reuben. After numerous attempts to find someone to summon Dr. Reuben, Garett approached the ER main desk. The attending nurse behind the counter was a large black woman buried in a sea of charts. Tranella Grant had been a nurse at Cook County for nineteen years, spending eighteen of them in the Emergency Room. She had been there when the late Mayor Harold Washington began the most extensive program of co-operative hospital trauma centers in the United States. None of the trauma centers from the more affluent sections of the city remained.

"Excuse me, do you know where I can find Dr. Reuben?", Garett asked as he approached.

"Who?"

"Dr. Reuben. He was the attending physician when my wife was brought in last night. My wife is Lindsay Baine. She was one of the United Center victims. She needs some help and there seems to be shortage of personnel around here."

"There is always a shortage of personnel around here." The nurse answered tersely.

"Will you locate Dr. Reuben?" Garett grew agitated and abrupt. "Just tell me if that is a possibility. If not, then get someone else to help my wife."

"Lindsay Baine." The nurse looked up and located the chart on Lindsay Baine. She checked the call sheet and paged Dr. Reuben. "I'm sorry for the delay. Dr. Reuben should be down shortly." There was no attempt to mask the sarcasm in her voice.

"You're fucking unbelievable, lady." Garett turned and headed back to Lindsay.

"Is that right Mr. Baine?" Garett stopped. The nurse behind the desk seemed to be working from another agenda.

"What's you're problem, man. My wife was shot last night and I'm terribly sorry to inconvenience you."

"You're a long way from Sheridan Shores, Mr. Baine." The woman replied, gazing at the chart in front of her. " This ain't Lincoln Park and this ain't Bridgeport. The color's a little darker on this side of the tracks. You'all want us to jump whenever you bark, man?"

"Don't you know what happened last night?" Garett was incensed.

"Do you know what we call multiple shootings and multiple fatalities around here?"

"Enlighten me."

"Thursday." Tranella Grant put the chart down and looked directly at Garett for the first time. "This shit happens every night down here. The only time it becomes newsworthy, is when some upper crust from the North Shore gets thrown out of joint down here. You goddamn people slide through this neighborhood and close your eyes. Your idea of a bad day is a drop in the stock market. Daley decides to build the United Center so the North Shore can play fashion police eighty-two times a year. Bull doze the neighborhood because the city needs to accommodate a slew of corporations bent on wasting millions for their skybox drunks. Nobody cared about this neighborhood, these people didn't matter. Walk fast, so the little black boys won't focus their hungry eyes on you. Stop at Marche and valet the car–it's too dangerous to walk a block. I'm sorry your wife was shot, but it ain't no big deal around here. It's a way of life. There ain't no trauma centers left, man. They didn't want no West Side trash dumped in their laps. Cook County is it."

*　　　　*　　　　*

CHAPTER SEVEN

Garett pulled into his driveway shortly before one o'clock. This was a typical winter day on Chicago's North Shore, with the sun breaking through the low cloud cover for a brief appearance. The previous week had been unseasonably warm, so what little snow had accumulated was now gone. The neighborhood was traditional and well established. The large maple and oak trees long since stripped of any leaves cast a skeletal shadow on the homes they framed. Garett Baine prepared himself. Conner, Christopher, Maggie, and Jake were about to find out their mother had been shot. During the entire drive home from the hospital, Garett worded and re-worded what he wanted to say to his children. What he wanted to say was nothing happened. Your mother is fine. No one got hurt and I'm sorry that I'm late. He never had any practice doing this. No one ever does. Lindsay had asked him to be straight forward and honest. Kids are not going to understand half or more of what you tell them. If you confine yourself to the truth, then you never have to remember what you said. Kate Doleman came out to greet him. She had been on the phone with Maureen for the past half hour. Lindsay was sleeping, and the kids were beginning to ask more questions. The older ones suspected something was going on. Garett and Lindsay did not stay downtown because the game ran long. First of all, they would have called home by now. Kate tried to defer the speculation. She put her arms around Garett in the driveway. They stood motionless for a few minutes. Kate was crying. Garett thanked her for everything. He wanted to be alone with the kids now. Kate kissed Garett on the cheek and walked down the driveway. She didn't look back to the house, didn't want the kids to see her crying. Maggie was in the window with Jake. They had never seen Kate Doleman hug their father. Maggie knew she was crying. Maggie looked at Jake and asked.

"Where's mom?"

Conner and Christopher were in the basement watching a tape. They didn't hear their father as he came into the family room from the garage side entrance. Maggie and Jake ran over to embrace Garett. Maggie would repeat the question she was beginning to fear.

"Where's Mom?" Maggie asked. Garett looked down at his only daughter. In her nine year old face, Garett saw his wife. Maggie had the same features as her mother. She had a small face, the high cheekbones, a little turned up Irish nose, and eyes that could charm the stars right out of the sky.

"Mom stayed downtown. Where are the little ones? We have to have a family discussion now. You know, like the ones we had when we all decided that it was time to get the dog. Remember, we all sat down and discussed how everyone had to pitch in to help take care of the dog."

The dog reference threw Maggie off course. She said the little ones were downstairs but wanted to know if the family was getting another dog. Her face lit up as she thought about the prospect.

"Listen Jake or Maggs, go downstairs and get Conner and Christopher. Don't yell. I can do that. Go get them and bring them back here. We need to all sit down for a few minutes. No! We are not getting another dog. Go on. Hurry up, go get your brothers."

Conner and Christopher came rumbling up the stairs from the basement like two midget water buffaloes. Maggie had stood at the top of the stairs by the food pantry and yelled down that daddy was home. Certain that every basement light, bathroom light, TV and VCR was left on, Garett heard the scrambling and jostling to see who would be the first to reach their father.

"Daaaaaaaddy!" was echoing in unison from the two mounds of hair slipping on the oak floors in their stocking feet. Garett grabbed his two sons at the same time and picked them both up in bear hug. His thick forearms cradled each child as their feet dangled from side to side. Garett buried his face in between their squirming little bodies and roared like a big bear. He used his nose to tickle each one of them in the nape of their necks. They never seemed to tire of this routine and for a moment everything felt normal. As always, Garett would put them down and they would both be yelling, "Do it again daddy. Do it again. Just one more time." With children under the age of ten, there is no such thing as 'one more time.' The favorite past time of the Baine household had become a spirited game of tickle-tackle football. This game could be played inside or outside, with outside being the preference of Lindsay Baine. Inside the group would move to the living room and clear out the furniture from the middle of the room. After retrieving a Nerf football, the one holding the ball was to be tackled. Once firmly on the floor, ground or carpet, the participants would then tickle the ball carrier until he or she relinquished the ball. Next! Garett set the two boys down and Conner immediately began jumping up and down in anticipation of the impending game. His long blond hair was full of soft curls. When he got excited and scooted across the family room floor, he looked like a fluffy pillow with hair in motion. Garett gathered everyone around the L-shaped sofa in their family room. There would be no games tonight. Jake was quiet. Maggie had forgotten about the dog. Something was wrong. The kids settled around the wooden coffee table. Garett had to ask the little ones to sit down two or three times before he got their attention. He had to make this short because the attention span of the two small boys would be short. The older ones already looked worried and could sense something was wrong. The family meeting was about to begin without Mom. Something was wrong.

Garett sat on the brick ledge in front of the fireplace. The room boasted a fourteen foot cathedral ceiling with a fireplace centered against the back wall. There was a huge wooden oak beam suspended across the length of the room. The French patio doors sitting behind the couch were framed in oak. There were oak base boards, oak flooring and the main door to the garage was oak. The walls were painted forest green with a white ceiling. There were two octagon windows, one on each side of the fireplace, also trimmed in oak. This room was the room Lindsay had always wanted. Family pictures covered the front wall in no particular order. As the family grew and the kids got older, the collage of pictures grew. The sense of order in the room fit neatly with the disorder of the pictures. All of the frames were different and they ran from the floor to the top of the French doors. Garett felt the butterflies in his stomach. He wanted to do everything right. He wanted his words to be the right ones. He wanted his voice to be confident and reassuring. He wanted most of all, not to cry.

"I'm sorry that Mom and I couldn't come home last night. Something happened that is very hard to explain. Mom and I had gone to the basketball game last night at the United Center. When we were walking to the parking lot, something happened. We were walking on the sidewalk across from the stadium when a car came screeching around the corner and ran everyone off the sidewalk. The car was driven by some very bad people. One of them had a gun and began shooting at the people on the sidewalk. Everyone tried to jump out of the way, but everything happened so fast. The car kept going and no one had a chance to catch the people who did this. Mommy is going to be all right, but she was shot during this drive-by shooting. An ambulance took her to the hospital and they had to take the bullets out. She loves you very much, but she won't be able to see you for a few days. The doctors want her to rest." Garett needed to stop for a moment. He didn't want to break up and he could see the fear in Maggie's eyes. They knew this was not a game. Even the small boys sat in silence. Conner watched Maggie to see what he should do. Christopher walked over to his father and put his five year old arms around his dad.

71

"Daddy, I know Grandma is in heaven and if Mommy is with her, then I want to go, too."

"Listen to me," Garett continued while pulling Christopher onto his lap. "Mommy is not in heaven. She is not going to die. I promise you that. Mommy is hurt very bad and she needs a little time to get better. I don't know why this happened. There are some very bad people in the world and all they want to do is hurt others. The only reason you can't see her right now is because the doctors think she needs some time to rest before she has any visitors. Grandpa and Grandma will stay here for the next few days. I'm going to go stay with Mommy. We will call you tonight and all of you can talk to her."

Jake was trying not to cry because he could see his father on the verge of tears. He couldn't last. The tears rolled down his red cheeks. His arms came up to wipe them away but they came too fast. Maggie wanted to see her mother.

"Can't we go with you Dad? I promise, we'll be real quiet. I just want to give her a kiss and a hug. I'll bring her the green blanket. Please." The green blanket was a scrap of a blanket Lindsay kept on her pillow at night. She has had part of this blanket from the time she was a child.

"Listen Maggie, I promise that we'll call you tonight from the hospital. They won't let anyone in for the next few days except me. It's not my decision or else I would bring all of you. It's OK to cry because you miss Mommy, but she didn't go away. She got hurt and she will be with you soon. We have to say special prayers for Mommy every night to get better in a hurry. I know those prayers will help her to get back here as soon as she feels better. We both love you guys very much and I'm so sorry this happened, but we have to be strong for Mom." Garett moved over to the couch where all the kids were sitting. Garett gathered his children close to him. Conner got up and walked around the table. He stood in front of Garett. His blond curly hair was not bouncing now. He was too young to really know what had happened. He looked at his father.

"I'm strong, Daddy." He brought both arms up clenching his fists underneath his chin. "See."

*　　　　*　　　　*

CHAPTER EIGHT

During the next two days, Garett Baine spent the majority of his time in the ICU at Cook County Hospital. His parents and many of his neighbors took turns watching the kids, taking them to the movies, providing meals, and making sure they had as little time as possible to worry. Lindsay spoke to them two or three times during each day. Her spinal surgery had been scheduled for Thursday. Her condition was improving and the restraints on her arms and mid-section were removed when the bed was in the prone position. This allowed her to hold the telephone and speak to the kids. She deferred all other calls to Garett. By Sunday morning, the news of this shooting was dominating the Chicago airwaves. Television crews were camped at the hospital trying to interview family members and doctors as to the condition of the injured. The owners of the Chicago Bulls franchise and the Untied Center expressed their shock and sympathy for the victims and their families. They put up a $100,000 reward for information leading to the arrest and conviction of those involved in the shooting. Public service announcements were shot by members of the Chicago Bulls team asking for any information about this crime to be passed on to the Chicago Police Department. Numerous television stations shot reports from in front of the Baine house in Sheridan Shores. Garett instructed his parents and the neighbors not to allow the kids to be filmed. These requests were made of the media outside the home. The media consistently ignored those wishes. The incredible insensitivity and irresponsibility present in the news media is rampant. What is accomplished by publishing the address of the victims before any arrests are made? Under the premise of informing the public, television news coverage placed the children of the victims at risk. The victims and their families in these stories became victims all over again. The object of the game becomes the camera. Which station can produce the exclusive. There are rewards for the most intrusive and unauthorized photos. Garett recalled his outrage when a local television station staged a two week promotion based on Richard Speck's homosexual and drug

73

related encounters during his stay at an Illinois Correctional Facility. The lead trailers for these reports showed Speck in bikini underwear snorting cocaine with his boyfriends in jail. Fellow inmates video-taped these prison parties. Richard Speck was the man convicted of killing eight student nurses in the early sixties. Speck was quoted as saying he had much more fun in prison over the past thirty years, than he would have enjoyed on the outside. Retribution and closure would never be achieved for the victim's families. Eight cold blooded murders resulted in years of satisfaction. Speck was shown laughing about the crimes and explaining the best way to choke the life out of a young girl. This was all done to accomplish higher ratings during sweeps week. Garett left strict instructions that no interviews whatsoever would be granted to any member of the media. Garett had called the Sheridan Shores Police Department and requested some additional patrols around his home. The Chief of Police in Sheridan Shores was Anthony Cordell. He responded by assuring Garett and his family that he would have an officer assigned to the house until further notice. Anthony lived around the corner from the Baines. He informed Garett that he would be pulling some of this duty himself. There were no more problems from the media, from that point on.

The flowers and arrangements sent to the hospital were staggering. Lindsay talked to her husband about how blessed they were. By Monday afternoon, the entire ICU wing was littered with these arrangements. Garett and Lindsay marveled at how fast these flowers arrived. The cards were so special. Whatever faith had been lost because of the shooting had been regained many times over by the compassion and concern of everyone they knew.

Bruce Carson made a special trip to Cook County Hospital. On Monday afternoon, he stopped in after calling to see that Garett was there. He personally delivered a beautiful arrangement of flowers from everyone at the Dean Witter downtown office. He also came with a message for Garett. The two met in the emergency room waiting area. Bruce did not want to disturb Lindsay and had no intention of trying to see her. He wanted to deliver the flowers and speak to Garett.

"Thank you for coming here, Bruce. I know Mondays are pretty busy downtown and both of us appreciate the time you have taken to come down here. I'm still in a semi-state of shock. It seems like another lifetime, but we were just walking out of a basketball game. Listen, I was pretty upset on Friday. There was nothing personal there. I simply felt I couldn't continue under those circumstances. I thought the company would back me."

"Garett, forget about Friday. I don't accept your resignation. Your job is waiting for you and your status will be intact. I think I over reacted to the hearing notice without listening to you. I have put everything on hold until you can return. I believe I would have come to the same conclusions regardless of the current circumstances. I have contacted the Coles about this matter. They have agreed to withdraw the complaint. Dean Witter will liquidate their holdings and reimburse their losses. The account will remain in cash until you can return. They want you to remain as their broker. Seems they now remember some of your suggestions and concerns. Remember Garett, these developments are not a result of what happened to you and Lindsay last Friday night. They may have enhanced the time line, but these actions would have occurred regardless. I'll let you get back to your wife. Give her our prayers and tell her everyone downtown is pulling hard for both of you. Let us help in any way we can. That office just wouldn't be the same without at least one rebel broker."

"Bruce, I don't know what I'm doing these days. Like I said, I was pretty upset the other day and I didn't want you to take things personally, but my feelings haven't changed. I need some time to see how Lindsay comes out of this. Thank everyone downtown for me. I'll stop in as soon as I can."

"Take your time. I'll notify your accounts of what has happened. All of the guys have offered to handle them for you until you get back. If anyone wants to change a position, it has to go through me. Don't worry, I won't let Grady stick any of your clients into that micro-brewery stock he has been pushing. I'll have enough problems when the bottom falls out of that dog."

"In addition to the micro-brewery stock that peaked the day it came out, tell Sunshine not to lay that pathetic drivel about Tye IV, Inc. on any of my clients. Tell him, I'd rather have him advise my clients to take their retirement funds and go to Vegas."

"With pleasure. My skin crawls every time I see a buy ticket come across my desk on that stock. His brother sold Grady on that company. Seems as though he works in the industry and had some reliable information concerning Tye IV, Inc. Grady ignored his brother's advice on a similar situation six months ago and the stock tripled in three weeks. This time he was determined not duplicate the mistake. He built a fairly strong position in Tye IV after the offering. Opened at twenty-six, jumped to thirty-four by the close. That was six weeks ago. Yesterday the stock closed at nine."

"Thank the guys for me. Tell them I'll call soon."

"Done."

*　　　*　　　*

CHAPTER NINE

The Bianco Funeral Home In Northbrook, Illinois brought out a pungent memory for Garett Baine. He had pulled into this lot too many times. This evening was for Denise. Bianco's was set back from the main four lane highway running through the heart of the Chicago suburb. The funeral home had been a beacon of tradition in the ever changing landscape surrounding it. Its red brick facade remained unchanged for decades. The fields and small farms visible when the home was first constructed were now replaced with Comp USA, Best Buy, a movie theater complex, and a string of franchise restaurants. Garett remembered his only visits to this funeral home were to pay respects to friends or classmates who were killed accidentally or died well before their time. There was Jason Goodyear in 1969. He was killed in a motorcycle accident. They had played baseball together for years dating back to little league. Gail Evans and David Hinton had been an item for two years in high school. They never made it home from a party on a Saturday night in 1970. A head on collision claimed both of their lives. Russell Joseph and Garett played football together during their freshman and sophomore years at Glenbrook North High School. One morning during Christmas break in 1970, Russell's mother discovered his body in his bedroom. He had stuck a shotgun in his mouth and used his toe to pull the trigger. He was sixteen years old. Two other friends during the eighties were brought to Bianco's. Alvin Keith died from cancer at the age of thirty-one. Brian Martin died from kidney failure at the age of thirty-eight. The wake for Denise Shane was on Monday and Tuesday evening. The funeral would be at Saint Norberts Church in Northbrook on Wednesday. The parking lot at Bianco's was full as cars were lined up on both sides of Waukegan Road, spilling onto the gravel shoulder of the road, extending nearly one-half mile in either direction. Garett decided he would attend the Tuesday wake which was open from 4:00 p.m. to 9:00 p.m. He pulled into a 'no parking' section behind the funeral home directly in front of a rear exit. There were media trucks parked near the front entrance. He would not allow these people near him. A rear private entrance pulled open on the second attempt. It was 8:30 p.m. when he entered Bianco's. The place was packed.

Garett chose to come alone. As he walked into the wake, his eyes tried to focus on finding Jim. The air and motion in the room seemed to suddenly freeze. Garett remembered sitting at a luncheon in the Midland Hotel in Chicago many years ago. He was there to attend the Quarterback's Club luncheon featuring Walter Payton. When Walter Payton entered the room, the air and motion in that room hung still. Every eye followed Payton until he sat down. Garett Baine felt the eyes upon him as he walked towards the front of the room where he could see Jim standing. Two of Jim's children were standing next to him. Jasmine was playing with her Grandfather in another room. This was the second night of the wake. Jim Shane's strength had helped his family through the past few days. His face looked drawn and his eyes looked spent. There would be many more tears to come but not tonight. The friends and family seemed endless and the blessings they brought were heartfelt, but they weren't connecting that night. Jim was imagining what everyone could be thinking. How could this happen? Was there anything he could have done to prevent this. How come the women were shot and the men were unharmed? She was your wife and the mother of your children! She depended on you. Where were you? These thoughts were in his own head, so how could they not be on the minds of everyone else? Jim saw Garett moving through the room. He stood still and waited. Jim Shane closed his eyes for a moment and was glad to see his friend.

Garett approached Jim and the two embraced. Linked forever by the events of January 26, these two men hugged in silence for the better part of one or two minutes. Garett backed away and approached the open casket. Denise Shane didn't deserve this. Her life was taken from her by some deviant bent on avenging his own miserable existence. Garett looked at this young lady and thought about that sidewalk and the car. He questioned the concept of the wake. Why was this ritual of showcasing someone in a heavily lacquered mahogany casket over stuffed with lace and satin considered respect? This religious tradition had been explained to him countless times during his forty-two years on this earth and he had yet to grasp one plausible rationale for exposing family members to the additional grief associated with this public forum. He wanted to apologize to Denise. Garett didn't kneel at the casket. He spoke for Lindsay and himself.

"We miss you, Denise." His words were soft. Jim knew what he was saying. "Lindsay sends her love. She wanted to be here for Jim and the kids, but she won't be going anywhere for a while. I know you can hear me somehow. I'm sorry we weren't there for you. There's nothing I can do about that now. I'll be here for your kids and your husband. If they ever need anything, so help me God, I'll be there. So help me, God? He wasn't there to help you and Lindsay much the other night. He might have been too busy making sure these assholes escaped through a maze of traffic. Thirty Chicago Police personnel conducting the city's largest manhunt has turned up nothing. I'm having a difficult time with the concept of worship these days." He dropped to one knee in front of the casket and was speaking directly to her silent eyes. "Good-bye, Denise. I'm so sorry about this. It was just a basketball game. I was worried about where we would go for dinner and whether we would have enough time to get the sitters home."

Garett rose and turned back to the friend he had known for more than thirty years. "Let's get out of here for a minute. You need to. Have your parents watch the kids for five minutes. These people will wait. I'll meet you in back. Go through the director's office. There is a private entrance to the back. Meet me there."

Garett waited out back while Jim arranged for someone to watch the kids for a few minutes. The idea of getting away from the wake for a brief time was a welcome respite. Garett lit one of the Nat Sherman cigarettes he normally reserved for later in the evening. Jim came walking out of the rear exit pulling out a Marlboro.

"Garett, you remember how many times we walked around outside this building to have a smoke? Seems like all of us have to meet here every few years. Shit, I remember Jason's wake here back in high school. Russell blew himself away six months after Jason was killed. I know there were more, that couple killed in a car accident. You can probably remember their names. I remember how everyone felt at those wakes. But we got to leave and an hour later we were back to our lives." Jim pulled hard on the last draw from the Marlboro in his fingers and then flicked it with his middle finger across the parking lot. He continued, "Yesterday morning I got a call from the people at the Chrysler assembly plant just outside of Rockford. Chrysler has three of my machines in their Rockford plant and four more in their Detroit plants. GM and Ford have purchased eleven different systems from me. The commission on these machines is nice, but the money is made by selling them the plastic compounds used with this equipment. Each machine will use eleven hundred pounds an hour of this compound. My take on this is five cents a pound. When you figure how much compound each machine uses by operating three shifts, twenty-four hours a day and then multiply that by eighteen machines, the numbers are substantial. Well, the general manager at the Chrysler/Illinois plant informed me that they would be switching compounds and wouldn't be purchasing our material anymore. Someone had been able to duplicate the product at a substantially lower cost. Over the next month, more than seventy percent of my income will be eliminated. I can't compete with this new product. It's that simple. I've still got three kids to raise, Denise is gone, and I get this phone call. If Denise was here, I would have gone berserk. I spent years cultivating these sales. I built relationships with these companies to the point they trusted my judgment enough to order multi-million dollar systems from me. Then they turn around and cut the income source the machines were set up to provide. The commissions on the machinery were simply reimbursement for the years of sucking up to get the business. Garett, I was getting dressed to attend my wife's wake when these pricks called. I said nothing. I'm fucking numb, Garett. The only thing barely keeping me together are my kids. If I didn't have them, I'd have checked out by now."

Garett wasn't sure he wanted to go there. "Forget about business, Jim. Nothing ever goes smoothly in any business, so you'll deal with it at a later date. My wife is laying in a hospital and can't move her legs. She is hooked up to a bed that looks like a carnival ride and is about to have surgery to fuse her spine back together. She may never walk again. I haven't spent one waking moment without thinking about what I could have done to take those few seconds back in front of the stadium. But I can't. Neither can you. I've got Lindsay and we'll get through whatever we have to. You still have the kids and I know Denise feels better knowing that they are with you. Just take care of them now. Don't even think about business. Get them through this. That is your new career. Anything else you need, your friends will take care of."

"Garett, I have no words to tell you how I feel. You are the only person I can look at and not feel like I am being judged. I needed to see you today. You and I will talk soon. Tell Lindsay that I'm thinking about her. Take off, man. I'll understand if you decide not to come tomorrow. "

"I'll be there."

Garett followed Jim back into the funeral home. The director's office led them into the main lobby where more than a majority of the people attending had gathered after paying their respects. There were people there that neither one of them had seen for years. They had come to say good bye to Denise and show support for Jim and his children. They did not expect to see Garett Baine. Most were friends from the area, friends from childhood, or relatives. Garett spent more time than he planned talking to the guests. As much as he wanted to get to the hospital, this time with friends helped. They were all asking about Lindsay and offering to take the kids or help in any way they could. He knew they all wanted to know exactly what happened but were too polite to ask. He didn't mind talking about it. After all, he was thinking about it so much. Garett spent forty-five minutes in the lobby of Bianco's. Unconsciously, this became Garett's first step in coping with his own guilt from that night. In explaining the events of that evening, he began to understand the difference between believing you should have been able to prevent this and wishing you could have been in a different position on that night. Nearly two weeks had passed since the shooting and there were four children in Sheridan Shores, who have never entertained any thoughts or questions about blame. Lindsay never spent one minute wondering why Garett was walking ahead of her. Lindsay and Denise chose to walk behind their husbands. Staying close to avoid being shot was not part of the option evaluation for the evening. Lindsay was brought up to understand that certain things were out of her control. She told Garett on the day after her first surgery, that guilt was a characteristic of weakness. Assigning the blame can never alter the outcome. Blame is an after thought for those who should have done much more prior to the incident in question. She told her husband not to seek forgiveness for the actions beyond his control. Answering these questions from friends gave Garett a chance to listen to himself for the first time. Garett simply recalled the events of the evening. His family never sought a further explanation. What else mattered?

After Garett excused himself and began pulling out of the parking lot, he thought about what Jim had said. Jim was right. During all of the other visits to Bianco's, they were merely guests. Their own lives were touched, but not altered by the day. This day was not the same. Garett Baine remembered pulling out of this lot in a red 1968 Mustang convertible with Jim Shane in 1970. They were leaving the wake for David Hinton. They were sixteen years old. David Hinton's body was the first dead body Garett ever saw in person. The other two wakes he attended were closed caskets. A motorcycle accident and a suicide left massive wounds which prevented viewing. Garett was born and raised in a reform Jewish family, and the funerals he attended as a child did not involve wakes. Garett remembered how they were in a hurry to get out of the clothes they wore. Garett's own mortality appeared that day in 1970 and he wanted no part of that confrontation. Twenty-six years later, he couldn't change his clothes. His car pulled out on Waukegan Road. The drive downtown would take him forty minutes without much traffic. He decided to stop in Sheridan Shores first and see the kids again before he headed downtown.

*　　　　　*　　　　　*

It had been a week since Denise's funeral. Lindsay had her surgery on Saturday, February 3. It was February 7. Lindsay had been moved from the critical care unit to the intermediate care unit. The focus of the care at

80

this stage, is to foster independence and to help the patient begin to adjust to the injury. Many patients find this a difficult transition. Many find solace in a state of total dependency. Dr. Reuben had accomplished everything he sought during the surgery. No infection had developed in the abdominal cavity. The repair to the damaged vertebra was completed with the necessary hardware to secure the fracture. Swelling had receded in the spinal column and the surgery would accelerate the healing. Permanent damage could only be detected after the spinal column had returned to it's normal state. The doctor had explained to Lindsay that range of motion exercises would begin immediately to minimize any atrophy and muscle weakness. He pointed out that once the muscle tone begins to return and there is an increased activity of muscle spasms, this would indicate that spinal shock was over. At this point, an inability to generate movement in the lower extremities would reflect a loss of cerebral control over muscle activity. Dr. Reuben emphasized that time was the unknown factor at this point. An inability to generate movement in the affected areas was normal following any surgery of this type. The body's own healing process and timetables vary for everyone. Lindsay was especially excited this morning; her road out of the hospital and back on her feet began now. She would also see her children for the first time since the accident. Garett would be bringing them down after school.

Garett had been spending a tremendous amount of time at the hospital. He had not been back to work yet. Actually, he had not decided if he was going back to work, but that decision was the least of his concerns. He had been in contact with Michael Ramirez in Lakeside, Montana. Garett related the events of the past couple of weeks and indicated that any decisions regarding his family would be delayed. These decisions would be addressed after the condition of his wife was determined. Michael assured Garett that he would maintain the property until such time as they were able to decide which direction the family would be taking. There was enough money in Randolf's account to fund any expense incurred with the maintenance of the properties. The estate was still in probate and as anticipated, there were no claims filed against the estate.

Many patients experience a period of denial and resentment following the realization that the life threatening crisis is past. A common characteristic of this phase is anger. Why did this happen to me? They strike out against those treating them usually with verbal abuse. This often extends to the patients family as they experience fear, humiliation, and helplessness. Lindsay had two things going for her that prevented these symptoms from developing. First, she did not have a hopeless diagnosis. Many spinal cord injuries can be determined to be permanent from the injury date. These patients often cling to false hopes or blatant denial. Dr. Reuben began his treatment by being frank and honest. Her doctor could not give her any assurance that she would regain movement below her waist, but he did allow for that distinct possibility. Secondly, she had decided during the hours of laying immobile that whatever hand she was dealt, her situation was lucky because she made it. Positive mental attitude is not an industry. It is not a storefront that can be conveniently put up and taken down. Lindsay could sincerely find the good in most situations or people. Garett found a hard time locating the good in most situations or individuals when the door smacked him in the face. His instincts led him to pinpoint the areas of mistrust or determining the worst case scenario.

Jake, Maggie, Christopher, and Conner arrived at Cook County Hospital with their father somewhere around five o'clock on the afternoon of Wednesday, February 7. The kids had been in constant contact with their mother over the telephone. They had been consistently reassured that everything would be fine, but their inability to visit Lindsay was beginning to scare all of them. The older ones had been grilled at school because the incident became public knowledge right away. The television trucks in the neighborhood were magnets to the gossip starved grapevine of the North Shore. Children at school were merely repeating the questions of their parents without the inhibitions of discretion. Jake and Maggie were well aware of Denise Shane's fate. Garett had begun to open up concerning Lindsay's condition. He had told them that their mother was not able to walk. The injuries she suffered caused some damage to her back and this was preventing her from walking. The doctors were hopeful that they could correct this, but that was not a guarantee. On the night they had this discussion, Garett waited until Christopher and Conner were asleep. Jake was his mother's son. He loved sports, participating in basketball, golf and baseball. His favorite outing was an afternoon at the golf course with his father. This was the year he was able to play the regulation eighteen hole course. Jake watched ESPN constantly, switching from cartoons to Sportscenter at the age of five. But his nature was Lindsay. He was sweet and non-aggressive. Garett found him upset one day in his room because he couldn't discipline the dog. Garett insisted that dogs understood two things, pleasure and pain, but Jake couldn't hit the puppy, no matter what the mess was. Jake and Lindsay enjoyed a bond that was very special. Garett cherished and envied their bond. Garett's oldest son loved his father deeply, but his heart belonged to Mom.

Maggie was the only girl in the house with Lindsay. Besides being her only daughter, Maggie and Lindsay had become clones. Maggie had her mother's profile and independence. At a very early age, it became strikingly obvious that Maggie would be skipping the tom-boy stage of life and heading directly from toddler to female. Maggie always sat on the bed while Lindsay got ready to go out for an evening. She always gave opinions on outfits and whether it was a good or bad hair day. The boys would be watching sports and the girls couldn't care less. There was a special gold lamé dress that Lindsay wore on a couple of formal occasions that captivated Maggie. This form fitting Christian Dior creation was the most expensive dress Lindsay owned. Maggie and Lindsay often looked to duplicate the look for Maggie at children's shops or costume stores. On each birthday and every Christmas, Maggie searched to find a gold dress of her own among the packages.

This had been an excruciatingly long wait to see their mother. Cook County Hospital was not located in an area these children were familiar with. They wondered why Mom was not at Lake Forest Hospital, a plush North Suburban hospital resembling the clubhouse to a country club. Lake Forest Hospital was where they had gone to see her when she had Christopher and Conner. The entrance at Cook County on this day did have security present. The metal detectors were in working order and the security staff, a bit overzealous, was creating a late afternoon delay by their methodical searches of hand held bags and purses. Garett wondered where this concern for safety was on a late Friday night a couple of weeks prior. Lindsay would be transferred from this hospital on Thursday. She would be able to recuperate at the Rehabilitation Institute of Chicago. The RIC was a major health care facility equipped with a special Spinal Cord Injury Treatment Center. The instability of the fractured vertebra prior to the second surgery was the reason transferring Lindsay to the RIC had to wait until the surgery was complete. Dr. Reuben did not want to take the slightest chance of damage occurring during the move. If the patient had been diagnosed with permanent spinal cord damage then the move would have been made sooner.

Lindsay had been moved to the fourth floor at Cook County Hospital, and she had a private room. Following the second surgery, Dr. Reuben confident that the damage had been stabilized, assigned Lindsay to the private room without the Stryker bed frame. She had not shown any outward signs of instability. Her mid section would remain securely anchored to the bed with the help of side boards running from each shoulder down along the length of her body. Additional boards would run up between her legs impeding any movement from the lower extremities. Straps across the abdomen and legs insured her position during sleep. This was a very intimidating sight for the first time, but tremendously less restrictive than the Stryker frame which allowed no movement from the patient. Here, Lindsay could turn and lift her head without restriction. She had the full use of her arms for the first time since the shooting. Therapy would begin very soon. The stark technology of the room was tempered considerably by the beauty of the flowers. Their warmth took some of the edge away from the electronic monitors, IV tubes, and the long overdue refurbishing of the rooms in general. Brightly colored cards adorned every inch of wall space and table space. Highlighted across the wall opposite Lindsay's bed was a mural poster made by her children. It was simple with the words, "MOM...WE LOVE YOU AND MISS YOU!" etched in colorful magic marker, written by the kids themselves. The six foot mural was covered with pictures drawn by the kids. Each separate artistic creation reflected something from home that was supposed to remind her of happy thoughts. Of course, there were self-portraits of each child and their name bold and prominent below each drawing. Raising children involves contest management. Most endeavors when undertaken as a group evolve into a series of contests. Who is first. Who has the most. Who did the best. Positioning and equality become very important to small individuals, short on years but long on the concept of self. Pictures of the dog, Juneau a two year old husky, were splashed on the mural from different stages of his mischievous puppy days. Garett agreed to get the dog for the kids and Lindsay. He knew this would be an inevitable junction in life that would be discussed each year. The kids were getting too old to continue to use the infant-baby-toddler reasoning of being too small to handle the responsibility of a dog. He decided that putting off the inevitable would only make things worse. The dog arrived with the assurances of Dad never having to worry about taking care of the family's new addition. The kids and Lindsay would handle everything. He loved their sincerity and their convictions, but knew it was false bravado. When Garett awoke at 5:30 a.m., everyone else was at least an hour or more from arising. There were few alternatives to a black and white crying puppy pressing his nose through the small bars of his cage. It was still dark and Garett needed to shovel the snow from the back door and let the dog run. Juneau would start scratching and barking to come back in after a few minutes, eager to be fed. It was barely 5:45 a. m. Garett would recall the family meeting they had before the dog arrived. It was decided that Dad would never have to worry about taking care of the dog. The assurances were ironclad, and would prove themselves this time. Lindsay had been staring at the mural anticipating the onslaught of children. She began smiling at the thought of the dog and her husband grumbling around in the snow before the sun came up. She knew he hated having a dog, but he just couldn't bring himself to hate the dog. As much as he tried to ignore Juneau or simply discipline him, the dog idolized Garett. Lindsay and the kids would marvel at why the dog would constantly seek attention from the one giving none. She wondered if

84

they could sneak Juneau into the hospital. That thought quickly vanished when she remembered Juneau's propensity for vomiting in any motor vehicle. Garett often referred to their beloved puppy as the vomit fleabag.

Lindsay was getting nervous. All of the questions and concerns discussed over the previous two weeks were fostering now. Would they be afraid of all the equipment? How would they handle the paralysis? How did she look?   She definitely wanted to look good for them. God, she missed those faces. She missed chasing Conner back to bed a dozen times before he finally would fall asleep. She missed Christopher clinging to her every movement. He would follow her around the house during the day. He would sit in front of the bathroom door while she was taking a shower. With a towel wrapped around her head and one wrapped around her body, she would open the door and Christopher would be looking up at her from his cross legged position on the floor. "I was just waiting for you." She missed her time with Maggie, the special time when the two of them could have lunch together without the boys. She missed the raspberries. Maggie's tender appearance and angelic face were coupled with the disposition of a crocodile. As a two year old, strangers would approach Lindsay when the two of them were out. The most common comment made was in reference to how adorable this little girl looked. Strangers often commented on how alike Lindsay and Maggie looked. Maggie's typical response was to put her tongue between her lips and blow raspberries at the source of the compliments. Lindsay always apologized for the little display from her daughter and repeatedly told Maggie to be polite. Inside, Lindsay loved the spit and fire in her daughter and hoped she never lost it.   A popular country song captured her connection to everyone and no one.. Garett and Lindsay smiled every time they heard the Faith Hill song seemingly written for Maggie:

> She's a wild one with an angel's face,
> A woman child in a state of grace.

She missed Jake most of all, even though she wasn't supposed to think of things that way. He was her first born and he seemed to need her more than the others. The little ones would grow out of their need to shadow mom, but Jake didn't. There were no connotations towards pushing Jake to grow out of it. He simply had an easier time opening up for his mother. As a small child, Jake was very close to Lindsay's mother, and their bond shattered when she unexpectedly died. Jake used to sleep on the floor next to her bed when she was stayed at their house. He insisted on this again after her first stroke. After her passing, Lindsay and Jake became even closer. Never in the family had this been considered anything but terrific. Garett often joked about the family being three against three because Jake always took Lindsay's side during debates. He was his mother's son with no inhibitions to show it. At a very early age, he displayed remarkable confidence. He found it neither necessary or impressive to imitate others. She missed his Nike baseball cap pulled too tight and rounded perfectly on the edges of the bill. Her strength during this injury had not been calculated. It came naturally. So too, did the butterflies in her stomach anticipating her family's arrival.

Lindsay had a hand held mirror that she was using to make some last minute adjustments on her hair. She couldn't believe how nervous she was. Slamming the mirror down to the bed disgusted with herself for acting like a teenager getting ready for a date, she noticed the door to her room was sliding open slowly. From the bottom of her bed, she could see some curly blond hair just above the edge of the bed.

"Mommy?" a little boy spoke, frightened and looking for his mother.

"Conner, I'm up here honey. Don't worry about all this stuff sweetheart. Come over here. Where is everyone else?"

"Daddy told me to go in by myself. He said that would be best. This looks like it hurts a lot. Do you have to get shots?"

"Sometimes, honey, but they don't hurt. Come up here. I missed you so much. Be careful. You can sit on this chair right next to me." Her eyes couldn't hold anything back. She was crying at the sight of her little 'bean'. They called him that from birth for no apparent reason other than he looked like a bean. Garett had decided to let the kids go in one at a time. That way, they could each have some time alone with Lindsay and react to her without the others around to heighten the fears or confuse them. Conner climbed onto the chair next to his mother. Standing on the chair, his eye level was roughly six inches higher than hers. He stood there with his arms to his sides looking at his mom and all of the medical equipment surrounding her. She reached her hand out to pull him closer.

"Can I have a kiss, Bean?" Conner bent down slowly and kissed her on the lips. He placed his head on her shoulder and his arm across her chest. His left hand was gently patting her back..

"I love you so much and it feels so good to hold you." Lindsay felt the tears fall down against her cheek and into the pillow she was resting on. Conner was very busy most of the time. He rarely sat still for longer than thirty seconds. He was placid and content on Lindsay's shoulder. It had been too long without his mom. At three, his reaction spoke volumes. His head finally rose off the shoulder he had found and his face stood inches from Lindsay's.

"Can you come home now Mommy? I don't like this place." His blue eyes had lashes that seemed to curl up over his forehead. Women marveled at the length and thickness of his eye lashes. He raised his eye brows and looked out from the top of his eyes. He waited for an answer.

"No, honey I can't come home tonight, but it won't be very much longer."

"Tomorrow?"

"No honey, not tomorrow. I'm not sure when, but the doctor will tell us real soon. He just wants to make sure that everything is O. K."

The door opened again and Christopher came walking in. He looked at Lindsay and the mechanical menace surrounding her, turned around and ran out of the room. Lindsay tried to call him back, but he was back out of the door before it closed from his entrance. Conner stood his ground. He looked back to his mother as if to tell her that he would look out for her. Garett opened the door carrying his five year old son and was followed by Maggie and Jake. Garett whispered something into Christopher's ear and put him down. He ran over to Lindsay and climbed up on the chair with Conner.

"Don't be scared Christopher. It's me and I missed you so much. You don't know how happy I am to see all of you. I loved your poster. Look, it's over there across the room. Every time I look at that poster I think of all you guys. And it makes me smile. Can I have a kiss Christopher?" Christopher leaned over the rail and gave Lindsay a kiss. She placed her arm around his back and gave him as much of a hug as she could provide. She whispered in his ear, "I love you sweetheart and I think about you all the time. I'll be fine Christopher, I promise."

"I thought they might like to come in one at a time, but that didn't work out too well." Garett was standing at the end of the bed. Maggie and Jake were stunned by the extent of the equipment. Lindsay looked past Christopher and started crying again as she imagined how this must look to her family.

"I'm so sorry this happened." she said through her tears. "I didn't mean for any of this to happen. I know you guys have been so good and have been helping Daddy with everything at home." She trailed off there and needed to wipe her eyes and gain some composure. Jake and Maggie came over to the other side of the bed. They didn't lose control, but for the first time they were able to give something back. They had thought about this day for a long time . They had practiced all of their lines and wanted to say the things that Daddy had them practice. He wanted everything to go so well. None of it mattered now.

"Mom, we're here now. It's not your fault, and we all know that." Jake spoke first. "Christopher got upset when he saw you in this bed because he wants to have you back the way things were. So do I, and we will have that some day. But, today is for you. We have been so worried about you and have been bugging Dad to bring us here ever since this thing happened. The only thing that is important to us today, is that we didn't lose you. Nothing else matters. We need to spend some time with you. We

87

need to hear your voice and see you smile. No matter how long it takes for you to get back to normal, promise me one thing."

"What's that?" Lindsay asked through a combination of happiness and tears brought on by listening to her ten year old son speak so eloquently and touch so deep.

"Promise that you'll never apologize again for what happened to you. You didn't do anything wrong. God knows it, we know it, and whoever did this to you should be the ones to answer for it."

"I promise, Jake. I don't know where I've been to miss how fast you've grown, but I am so proud of you, all of you. Thank you for being here. I know it might take some time, but I'll be fine. I can't miss with this kind of help. Hey, how's Dad getting along with Juneau. Are they best buddies lately?"

Maggie was holding one of Lindsay's hands while she rolled her eyes thinking about Juneau and Dad. "Mom, Dad is so mean to Juneau. He's always yelling at him, but that dog just sits at his feet and looks up at him. During the day, Juneau sniffs around all over the house. I know he's looking for you. He misses you, too. Not as much as we do, but Dad never gives him any treats like you do."

Jake and Maggie planted huge kisses on Lindsay. Garett pulled up a chair and the conversation began to get back to the normal trials of the kids. Conner and Christopher began wrestling for position on the chair. Maggie and Lindsay talked about how the boys gang up on her. They laughed about how the boys watch basketball every night. She brought her collection of Beanie Babies and laid them out across the bed. Maggie had twenty-two of these little stuffed bean bag animals. She detailed who and where each new one was from. The turnstile of friends, helping to watch the kids while Garett had been at the hospital, contributed to this collection on each visit. The time went quickly as 8:00 p.m. came too soon. The kids didn't want to leave, but they were happy because Lindsay would be transferred to the Rehabilitation Institute of Chicago, located on the grounds of Northwestern Memorial Hospital near Chicago's Magnificent Mile. This commute was substantially shorter for Garett and the kids. Garett promised them they could see her in two days at the RIC. After saying good-bye, Garett asked Jake to take the kids down to the elevators and wait for him there. He wanted to say good night alone. They heard the clan racing down the hall and Garett pulled the chair away from the bed. He stood next Lindsay and held her hand. He leaned down and kissed her. She was quiet. He knew that seeing the kids could be the best medicine in the world, but watching them leave would break her heart.

"I was thinking about some arguments we used to have. I'm sure you remember the delightful conversations about having children we had before we got married. I really didn't want to have kids. You wanted six or more. After we got married and had two, we decided to stop. Actually, you decided to wait a couple years before bringing the subject up again. You talked me into having a third and then Conner was the real surprise, a fourth. I don't remember if I ever told you this before, but we make great babies. Get some sleep tonight. This is your last night at Cook County. I love you."

She heard him yelling from down the hall. Garett was trying to get the kids in the elevator. God, what a sweet sound.

* * *

CHAPTER TEN

On his way downtown, Garett was thinking about the afternoon move from Cook County Hospital to the Rehabilitation Institute of Chicago. They were scheduled to move Lindsay sometime in the afternoon. Dr. Reuben was to arrive no later than two o'clock. The time was nine thirty on Thursday morning, and Garett was going to Dean Witter for the first time since the shooting. It had almost been two weeks. He had decided that he would not be taking Bruce Carson up on his offer. The charade surrounding the Cole's account wouldn't have changed at all, had it not been for the incidents of January 26. Garett knew it, Bruce knew it and the generosity of the offer to come back did not change the way Garett felt about his former profession. The rehabilitation period for Lindsay had also contributed to his decision not to return. He was planning to stay at Dean Witter only long enough to convince Lindsay that moving to Montana would be the best thing for the family and for their lives. Now, moving anywhere would have to be pushed back indefinitely. If and when Lindsay had made a full recovery, Garett could consider addressing the subject again. The Montana properties were mortgage free. They could easily borrow against one of them for living expenses during Lindsay's rehabilitation. Garett had discussed briefly with Michael Ramirez what the rental possibilities would be for the residence in Lakeside. Selling the property was Garett's last choice, but at this juncture, a distinct possibility. Whatever transpired with Lindsay and the Montana property, Garett would be at home helping with the kids and not cold-calling housewives and senior citizens, chasing useless leads, or doing what brokers call The Grovel Slide. This consists of making so many phone calls over a particular period of time that your brain just begins to lie. The brokers make a conscious effort to be straight forward with the prospects but the continual rejection begins to build its own resistance. The body and mind seem to build an alliance to combat this onslaught of insanity. The brain begins to say anything to produce more favorable results. The Grovel Slide is akin to hitting the wall in marathon running.

Getting off the elevator, Garett noticed a new receptionist. Dean Witter took the entire seventh floor, and the woman working the switchboard was engrossed in a conversation obviously not associated with her new employer. The familiar ring as the elevator opened its doors failed to raise her attention. Garett walked right by her as her back was turned towards the atrium. Garett followed a long walkway past many of the private broker offices. Most of these were small and in need of some serious renovations. Yet, they were private and the first step up the ladder as the broker pulled his way out of the bullpen. Office sizes were determined by the amount of production generated by the individual broker. There were specific formulas designed to calculate the square footage of an office based on the commissions billed out for the previous year. As the size of your book increased, the size of the perks increased. Minimum requirements for a broker to move from the bullpen to a private office were $200,000 in gross production for the previous year. This translated to an approximate income of $60,000. Often brokers would reach this plateau and have to go on a waiting list for office space. The walkway continued around the larger producers and their offices. These men were usually in the office early and left after the market closed. There were a minimal number of acknowledgments in the hallways, but the office seemed unusually quiet. Garett entered the bullpen area located at the rear of the space. The area was just under four thousand square feet housing twenty desks for brokers and trainees. A dozen more desks were assigned to the sales assistants. Most of these desks were empty because the advent of computerized trading had reduced the need for an SA. Fifteen years ago, the ratio of brokers to sales assistants was three to one. Today at Dean Witter, many sales assistants working with new brokers handle as many as eight or ten. Stocks, bonds, and mutual funds can all be purchased through the order entry program on every computer. Checks can be issued through the computer for clients. Mass mailings to all of a broker's clients and prospects can be accomplished through the consumer literature program on the work stations. Individual company research, firm recommended lists, and index history can all be accessed through the work station.

Garett made his way to his desk, puzzled by the silence, and when he reached his work station, he got his answer. His desk and cubicle were covered with cards, banners, and flowers. The banners welcomed him back and wished Lindsay a speedy recovery. Ken, Jake, Matt, and many others jumped up to greet him as he reached his desk. They didn't know when he would be returning, but they had choreographed this event for the precise moment. The non- attentive receptionist was in on the plan, alerting the bullpen when Garett arrived.

After wondering where everyone was, it seemed like the entire staff at the Dean Witter downtown office was taking turns coming by to visit

91

Garett. When the procession ended, the bullpen mates brought lunch in and they all took turns getting Garett up to speed on the sales disasters brought in by all of the product people. Brokerage firms are mills churning out clichés. The mutual fund wing of the firm will send their representatives around the country to each Dean Witter office touting the newest fund offering of the company. The brokers will be told to jump on the growing wagon of small cap stocks. Small caps will drive the market for the next year. Two months later, the same reps will reappear to tout the newest dividend and income fund. Techs will take a beating and the Dow will be driven by blue chips and dividend producing stocks.

"Garett, I think our fund managers were all products of the Ralph Cramden school of forecasting. Every fucking thing they bring out is going to the moon." Grady offered with his usual sense of impeccable optimism. "I hate mutual funds now anyway. You have to build positions in a limited number of companies for all of your clients in individual stocks. When they hit a fifteen percent gain, sell the fucker. They do fine and you make money. Fuck these mutual funds. It ties the money up forever. If I'm going to survive in this business, I've got to generate some business."

"Hey Ken, how's Tye IV doing?" Jake asked, knowing the response.

"Hey, I'm a trained professional, armed with the wisdom to search out the true values in the market."

"How's Tye IV doing?" Jake persisted.

"Closed at 6% yesterday. I bought most of it at 28. God, I'm good."

Garett finished filling everyone in on the medical updates and eventually everyone made their way back to work. Brokers have a tendency to look for things to occupy their time. It's called call reluctance. Garett's appearance in the office gave new meaning to the term call reluctance. As the bullpen began to buzz with the usual drivel of cold calling, Garett resumed reading the cards and notes left on his desk. Some of the bigger producers in the office had sent lovely notes expressing their heart felt concern for Lindsay and their hope for her complete recovery. Most of these brokers had never met Lindsay, but today was not a day to dissect anyone's motivation or sincerity. Through the dozens of cards and notes, Garett picked an envelope with his name on the front and Spencer Dryden's return address in the corner. He pulled out the note and began to read:

Dear Garett,

I would like to pass on to you, my sincere wishes regarding the most complete recovery for Lindsay. I am very sorry for your friend, Denise Shane and her family. I remember meeting them at half-time and they seemed very nice. My wife and I were delayed almost an hour by the emergency vehicles and police activity of that evening. We were only able to listen to the radio trying to figure out what had happened. When we got home and the watched the events unfolding on television, we were devastated to hear that you, Lindsay and your friends were victims. I am not going to pontificate on the subject. I'm sure you are up to your eyes in well intentioned insincerity. I am here for you and your family. I think the world of you, Garett Baine. I want you to read this note and understand every word of it. All of my resources are available for you. If I can be of any assistance with your clients, let me know. I know about your situation with Bruce Carson, and his change of heart did not come to him in a vision during the night.

Do what is best for you and your family. Understand what control is, and the difference between action and assistance. Always know who is dictating the decisions around you. Move past the fluff, and visit with me when you can. A week, two, maybe three. Whenever you feel the time is right. Give my best to Lindsay. I'm trying to figure a way out of a commitment I made to one of my clients. I am to be his guest at the Bull's game on Monday, February 19. His seats are in Section 222, aisle K. Those seats are so high, you feel like they're going through the roof. I have no desire to attend any of these games at this time. I know this is something that I do not have to tell you. I've tried to tell this guy gracefully that I can not attend, but he refuses to accept that answer. Hell, it's like I have been waiting for some Fucking Dumb Ass approval to grant me permission to pull out. He dropped the tickets off at my office last week. I think I'll shake him up by waiting until 3:00 on that Monday. Then I'll call and tell him that I sold them all. That will be the last time he ever asks me to a game.

Remember what I said. If you need anything.
Sincerely,

Spencer Dryden

Garett folded the note and placed it back in the envelope.

*   *   *

CHAPTER ELEVEN

The traffic was light during the early afternoon as Garett drove from the Dean Witter offices in the Loop to Cook County Hospital. They would be transporting Lindsay in a specially equipped medical emergency vehicle to the RIC facility. Garett would not be allowed to ride with her, but would be with her at Cook County and then meet her at the RIC, no more than a fifteen minute ride in midday traffic. The Rehabilitation Institute of Chicago was the Midwest's first federally designated center for the treatment of spinal cord injuries. The center is a comprehensive treatment approach designed to put the patient in control of their lives. The goal of this facility is to provide the training necessary to live as independently as each spinal cord injury will allow. Spinal cord injuries are measured by where they occur in the spine. A C1 or C2 injury occurs near the top of the neck and produces the most damaging results. C1 and C2 patients normally are quadriplegic with no movement in any of their extremities. They are on mechanical ventilation for the majority of every day. Life is almost exclusively sustained through advanced mechanical life support systems. As the injury lowers as in C4, C5, C6, and C7, the amount of upper body control increases. These numbers refer to the vertebrae in the spinal column. When the injury occurs in the Lumbar section of the spinal column, as in Lindsay's injury, loss of movement in the lower extremities or paraplegia is often the result. The patient has full use of their upper body and chances for an independent life are much higher. The RIC has twenty-four full time physicians and over eighty attending physicians on staff. The facility is considered one of the finest spinal cord rehabilitation centers in the world. The insurance Garett carried at Dean Witter would provide full coverage for this facility.

Lindsay could sit up during the ride to the RIC. This was her first time outdoors since the shooting and the air felt wonderful. Garett had been with her as they wheeled her down to the vehicle parked at the front of Cook County Hospital. He gave her a kiss and retreated to his car as the attendants assisted her in getting from her wheel chair to the chair in the vehicle.

Lindsay had made substantial gains during the first two weeks. The movement and strength from her upper body was almost normal. This eliminated the need for remaining in a prone position for any length of time. The ride was short. They headed for the Kennedy Expressway and Hubbards Cave exiting at Ohio and heading east through the River North District of Chicago. Lindsay gazed at the enormity of the Planet Hollywood sign. She had driven past these locations hundreds of times and never noticed them like today. The guitar shaped sign at the Hard Rock Café was four stories tall. The Rock and Roll McDonald's took up an entire city block. Left on Michigan Avenue or Chicago's Magnificent Mile, the traffic grabbed them and the movement was slow. Lindsay remembered walking this street many times with Garett. They would spend a night or two downtown every six months or so, just to re-group. Lately, they had to cut back on this because of the money situation. She watched the people flow into Niketown as the van inched along approaching Water Tower Place. She remembered their favorite stay was at the Ritz Carlton in Water Tower Place. Jim and Denise were with them almost five years ago. The four of them sat up until six o'clock in the morning drinking the little bottles from the mini-bars in the rooms. They all ordered cheeseburgers at 5:30 a.m. Jim and Garett were sitting on the floor in the bathroom with little bottles of Jack Daniel's as room service arrived. Right on Superior Street and three blocks to the Northwestern Memorial Hospital facility. Lindsay stared at the vertical sign for the Rehabilitation Institute of Chicago. This would be her home for an indefinite period of time. The door to the van opened and Garett was waiting. He looked at his wife sitting up in the van as the medical staff scurried about releasing all of the safety equipment and preparing for the transfer. Her eyes were red and tears washed her cheeks. Garett climbed into the van, ignoring a request to remain where he was, and put his arms around his wife.

"Garett don't let me stay here very long. I want to go home. I just want to go home."

The van had a mechanical lift to accommodate the wheelchairs. Lindsay's chair was wheeled into place on the lift as the attendant lowered the platform. At the same time the platform came to a rest on the ground, Lindsay's chair shifted on the light impact and slid off it's locking apparatus. Before Garett or anyone else saw this Lindsay's right leg had slipped out of the stirrup and had become wedged next to the stainless steel footrest of the wheelchair. She screamed as the chair pinched her ankle. The medical staff had the chair back in place in seconds. Garett reached for his wife and realized the damage was minimal, but Lindsay felt helpless and scared.

The RIC does a terrific job of easing new patients into their program. There are no forms or paperwork to deal with on arrival, and any

95

remaining or unfinished forms are held until later. Lindsay was brought directly to the floor she would be staying on. The focus and success of this facility is the relationship between the patients and the treatment team. Nurse therapists, occupational therapists, and physical therapists work together with physicians and psychologists to gain the patient's trust and confidence. Lindsay was introduced to the team that would be working with her. Garett felt comfortable with the two women assigned to work with Lindsay. Garett could sense that she began to feel more at ease as they spoke about the initial fear of arriving at the center. Patient denial often resurfaced following the departure from the hospital. In the hospital, everything is done for you. At the RIC, Lindsay will be taught to live with her paralysis and function as if she will not regain use of her legs. This presents another set of fears for the new arrival. The realization that this injury could be permanent is confronted on a daily basis. Patients are not allowed to sit around and wait for some miraculous return of their motor functions. In many cases, this determination has already been made at the time of the accident. Many spinal cord injuries are permanent at impact. The patient has no faint hope of recovery. Lindsay's case would be unpredictable. Walking may or may not be possible. Rehabilitation must begin from the state of the patient at arrival. Therefore, skills and independence will only be gained by dealing with the reality of the condition, not the hope for change in the condition. Lindsay and Garett listen as they are reminded about the importance of patience. As the initial meeting concluded, Garett gathered his coat.

"Why don't you try to get some rest for a couple of hours. I'm going to bring the kids back to say hello. I know they won't let me keep them here that long on your first day, but they want the whole family involved here. They might change their thinking on that issue after a couple of visits from our crew. I love you and I'll be back soon." Garett kissed his wife and headed for the elevators. Less than a minute after he had left the room, Lindsay's door burst open.

"Hey, I have to ask you something." Garett's eyes were lit up and he almost seemed out of breath. "When we got here this afternoon and the wheelchair jumped the latch downstairs, didn't your foot or ankle get caught for a second or two?"

"Yes, my right ankle got caught for a second or two."

"You screamed at that instant. Was that from fright or pain?"

"I'm not sure. I think I got scared, but I seem to remember a sharp pain shooting up my leg at that instant."

"If it's pain Lindsay, then you have feeling!" Garett couldn't locate the therapists fast enough. The attending physician was called in. Dr. Myron Cohen was fifty-one years old, looked forty, maybe. At six foot one, he surprised most. Garett imagined what a Myron Cohen would look like upon hearing his name. He actually had trouble believing parents would name their baby, Myron. This seemed like a name reserved for someone old. People must change their name at a certain age, because there are no children named Myron. Dr. Cohen arrived in Lindsey's room moments after being paged. His thick black hair was not laced with gray. Confident and friendly, with an athletic frame remained remarkably defined for his years. The incident at the entrance was described, along with the pain sensation in Lindsey's leg or ankle.

"We are going to run some tests. These are most likely the same tests that have been run for feeling sensation during the past two weeks. It is not unusual for your mind to create the sensation of pain in circumstances that would have produced pain in the past. Then again, it could have hurt like hell. What do I know? Let's find out." Dr. Cohen began his series of sensation tests. The right leg was tested first. Lindsay had no reaction during the tests. The left leg produced similar results. Myron Cohen had traveled this road many times. "Lindsay, this is your first day at the Institute. You may or may not have experienced some pain in the ankle. Just because these tests haven't worked out, doesn't mean there was no pain. Time will tell us the answer. You are the only one who can ultimately answer the question. Your sensation this afternoon could come back at any time. My mother told me something a long time ago. God rarely shuts the door, without opening the window a little bit. We've got some work to do, but remember what happened today was a positive sign. I'll be around later."

Dr. Cohen left the room. Garett watched as his angular frame sauntered down the hall. Garett turned to his wife. "That was not a Myron. It's impossible. Are you O.K. with this? I'll stay for a while if you want me to?"

"Garett, I'm fine. I believe this man when he tells me that what happened today was a positive sign. I know what I felt this afternoon. If it doesn't come back right away, I know it will. You ask me if I'm alright. The answer is yes. I can't think of a better way to continue this day than to see the kids. Do you mind driving all the way to Sheridan Shores to get them?"

"I'm gone! I'll see you in an hour and a half. I love you."

"I love you." Lindsay was smiling. She thought about the day they would leave together.

*   *   *

97

CHAPTER TWELVE

The ride back to Sheridan Shores took Garett down Lake Shore Drive. No matter how long he had lived in the Chicago area and driven this route, the stature of it remained as grand as ever. Heading north, the high rise condominiums on the west side of the street grew like pillars of wealth stacked in one after another. Ornate entrance drives and pristine doorman dotted the miles of Chicago's Gold Coast. On the east side of the drive, the rolling pathways were dotted with joggers even on this cold February afternoon. The empty harbors and crashing waves of the lake carved the shoreline as the drive lead Garett into Rodgers Park and turned into Sheridan Road. Garett Baine picked up his car phone and dialed Jim Shane.

"Jim, this is Garett. I am on my way back to my house to pick up the kids. Lindsay is at the Rehabilitation Institute of Chicago. We moved her today from Cook County. This is the place on the grounds of Northwestern Memorial Hospital. She seems to be making some progress, but time is the only way we are going to know the extent of her injuries. I thought I'd bring the kids back to see her for a few minutes this evening. This is her first day there and that will definitely cheer her up. I have to ask you a question and I know this is not the time to discuss business."

"What's up? You know what I'm going through. Business is the last thing on my mind at this point. The kids are having a horrible time. They want to know where their mother is. Being honest with kids is not always enough. When they don't understand something, they keep asking for her. Anyway, what's up? It's good to hear from you. I'm glad Lindsay got out of Cook County."

"Jim, do you trust me?"

"Of course I do. What are you talking about?"

"When I got into Dean Witter, you turned over all of your investments to me. You have almost one-hundred thousand dollars in your IRA account. In your personal account, you have nearly seventy-five thousand dollars. We set these accounts up for the long term, buying mutual funds and blue chip stocks, along with some flyers that you knew something

THE FLATHEAD SALOON AND CATHOUSE

about in your industry. Your portfolio is solid. If you leave it alone, your returns should be strong over the next five to ten years. This was the objective when the money was placed. Plan for the long haul and be patient. This is still the prudent course of action."

"I know you didn't call me to review my portfolio. I liked what you did when we set this thing up and I haven't changed regarding any of that. I trust you Garett. What is up?"

"I want you to liquidate your portfolio at Dean Witter. Sell everything to cash. That includes your IRA and your personal account, the Active Assets Account. We will take the cash, which will be approximately one-hundred and seventy-five thousand dollars, and open an account at Charles Schwab in Sheridan Shores. I can handle all of the selling transactions from Dean Witter, but I need your approval. There are certain forms that must be signed concerning access or liquidation of an IRA account. There will be some penalties from this transaction. I know this sounds ridiculous, but I am doing this with our accounts. Nothing will be done with any of your money that isn't done exactly the same way with my money. I am going to liquidate everything I have at Dean Witter and open the same type of account at Schwab. I can't tell you anything else. This move requires your complete trust in me. Think about it and let me know. I am leaving Dean Witter and these will be my last transactions at the firm. Do you trust me? You have to answer that question with more than blind friendship trust. We are talking about your retirement money and your investment money. All I can tell you is that I will not lose your money. Don't worry about saying no, I won't take it personally. Think about it and let me know in a day or two, no more. I know this is not something you need at this point. You know how I feel about you and your family. I need an answer soon."

"Garett, I don't have the slightest idea of what you are planning to do, but I trusted you before Denise died and I will trust you now."

"Understand that you are trusting me to pull all of your investments immediately. You will suffer some early withdrawal penalties and a five percent charge to liquidate all of the mutual funds because you haven't been in them very long. Once we have the accounts set up at Schwab, I will detail the investment instructions before we make the move. At that point, you will still have the option to say no. I am liquidating my accounts tomorrow morning. This will be the last time I will be at Dean Witter. After I make the necessary account changes, I am resigning effective immediately. Can you meet me at my house at noon on Wednesday? I will place all of the sell orders this Friday morning. My instructions will be to issue you a check. That will take three business days. You will be able to pick up a check at the Riverwoods office by your house. It will be waiting for you on Wednesday morning. Bring it directly to my house. You and I will go to the Charles Schwab office in Sheridan Shores at noon. I will have the check from my accounts, also. We will open accounts there and place the instructions for the funds."

"I'll be there at noon. Plan on explaining a bit more of this plan. Trust aside, this family is not in a position to handle any more bad news. I know you and I know you wouldn't roll the dice with my future or the college funding designated for my kids."

"Jim, I don't understand why some things happen the way they do. There are reasons I can't explain anymore at this point. You will appreciate my position in a few days. You cannot tell anyone about these transactions and tell no one about my conversations with you. If anyone at Dean Witter inquires about this liquidation, then you must inform them that all of these transactions were unsolicited. At Schwab, our accounts will be opened individually. The movement in those accounts will not be questioned by anyone at Schwab. The manager of the Sheridan Shores office is a neighbor of mine, Scott James. I have already talked to him about this transaction. We spoke in hypothetical terms and I was very comfortable with his answers. Listen, my phone is starting to break up. I will see you at my house on Wednesday at noon. I'm sorry I have to be so vague. I know Denise is shaking her head right now wondering what is going on. I promise, I won't let her down and I won't let you down. If you change your mind, let me know by tonight, because the accounts will be liquidated in the morning. Take care, buddy. I'll see you on Wednesday."

"I trust you, Garett. Do it."

*   *   *

Garett checked the messages when he got home. There was a call from Loren Rueben, the surgeon at Cook County. He wanted to know how the move to the RIC had gone and how Lindsey was doing. Garett thought that was a class act. Michael Ramirez called from Montana. He had to pay the annual liquor and food license fees for The Flathead Saloon. Total cost involved was nearly two thousand dollars. The money came from the restaurant account left by Kenton Gabel. There were no claims against either estate, and that process would be complete soon. No need to sell or rent any of the property at this point. Two more messages were from friends of Lindsay's calling to see how she was. Garett wrote the names down and would call them back later. The kids were next door at the Doleman's. They would notice his car in the driveway and be streaming through the door momentarily.

The door to the garage burst open. Conner and Christopher thundered through the family room desperately trying to be the first one to greet

Garett. The hardwood floors and high ceiling of the family room amplified these rumbling little feet to a level beyond deafening. Garett grabbed his two young sons as they reached him simultaneously. Maggie and Jake had followed and waited for the attack to subside.

"I won." shouted Conner as he was pulled up in the cradle of Garett's arm.

"No you didn't. I won. Didn't I win, Daddy? Didn't I?" Christopher pleaded as he was raised in the cradle of the other arm. This competition between Conner and Christopher was obsessive. They argued about who ate the first bite, who went to bed first, who got out of bed without permission first, who got dressed first, who petted the dog first, who was faster, who was a better ninja, who had more candy, the list was endless. Lindsay and Garett always talked about spending time with the little ones separately. They were angels alone. Garett ignored the request for a ruling.

"Hey you guys, do you remember what we're doing right now?"

"I do," blurted Jake. "We're going to see Mom. Did she get moved to the new hospital today?"

"Yes. She is at The Rehabilitation Institute of Chicago. We need to get going. Since this is her first day, they want her to get some rest. I had to talk her doctor into letting me bring you guys down there to see her. He gave us permission to see her tonight, but we can't stay long. Who wants to go see mom, now?"

They were in the car and headed back downtown almost as soon as the question was asked. Conner and Christopher took the middle seat of the mini-van and began to argue about whose gloves were better. This led to a confrontation on the merits of their head gear. Conner had a knit hat, red, white and yellow. The hat had knobs pointing up from the middle and following a straight line like a Mohawk down his head. This was a dinosaur hat. Christopher's knit hat sprouted court jester like protrusions with bells on them. Garett followed the same route back to the city. Sheridan Road south into Evanston, eventually leading to Lake Shore Drive with the final exit at Michigan Avenue. Garett glanced in the mirror at the melee brewing between the two runt passengers. The jester was jingling during his tirade. The miniature T-Rex argued his case with the exaggerated animation of those egotistical car dealers who insist on starring in their own television commercials. These men find it impossible to speak without waving their arms in some contorted fashion. Jake had his headphones on. Maggie sat next to Garett in the front. Her profile was her mother's. Garett stared at his daughter. The city, the skyline, and the Drake Hotel silhouette drew closer as the daylight disappeared.

*   *   *

101

CHAPTER THIRTEEN

The streets around the United Center on Chicago's volatile West side had somehow weathered the intense scrutiny brought on by the drive-by shootings in front of the stadium. The 12th and 13th Police Districts experienced an expanded police presence from the night of the shootings. Television stations sent their investigative reporters to the neighborhood to examine the roots of this behavior, and the gangs toyed with these reporters. Abrasive criminal reporters questioned the lack of success by the police in finding the killers. The media fed the well, sustaining the growing fear of attending events at the United Center. The mayor announced the placement of an additional sixteen squad cars at strategic corners surrounding the stadium. The police deployment on foot at the stadium and on the grounds adjacent to the stadium would be doubled. The Blackhawk and Bull's games came and went without incident. A Disney children's show on ice, Beauty and the Beast, ran without incident. Nearly three weeks after the shootings, the television crews were gone. The psycho-analytical pontificating from the media about our society and it's inability to manage the inner city had run the course. A new field awaited the columnists and self-appointed media saviors. Closure and journalism have nothing in common. How much interest could there be in the welfare of the victims from that night? Will the difficulties of three children who have lost their mother produce ratings? How have the injured fared?   Three weeks after the shooting, the police were no closer to finding the shooter or the driver. The information they received on the night of the shooting remained the only information they had. There was one driver and one shooter in the back seat. Both men were black. They had the color and the make of the car. Three weeks later, they had nothing else.

Zarvell White and Casey Griffin were unaccustomed to the position they found themselves in immediately after the shootings. Statements are the core of gang life. The statement being made on the night of January 26 was that of territory. Most crimes are not committed on the orders of

102

a gang leader or at the bequest of the gang itself. Individual members, sometimes in the company of homeboys or non-gang members are responsible for the vast majority of gang associated crimes. The individual gang organizations normally do not share in the proceeds from these crimes as in the case of gang members selling drugs. Our judicial system has intensified the penalties for gang-related crimes. In it's haste to quench the public thirst for vindication, our system has stumbled. Families getting lost and taking wrong turns end up shot to death. Gang membership spreading into the lily white suburbs. Our political follies erect a bridge of balsa wood. Prosecutors, mayors, state's attorneys, and a variety of legislators mount a tough talking campaign designed to scare the offenders. Tougher penalties and more prisons are inevitably the standard fare. Abolishing parole for callous crime is another constant. They make good copy, and they accomplish nothing. More prisons for individuals that don't mind being there. Tougher penalties for individuals with no fear of the police. Capture and incarceration are simply a part of life. Individual gang members need to find platforms for their actions or an identity within the gang. Their actions need to be noticed, and the violence feeds on itself. The younger gang members are consistently trying to surpass their predecessors as their violence becomes more brutal, more frequent, and random. Reputation and the ability to produce cash or material possessions can dictate the position one assumes within the gang. White and Griffin's dilemma began with the intangible luck stumbled into on the night of January 26. The exact placement of the police on foot and the placement of the police vehicles at the stadium enabled them to slip through clean at the moment of the shooting. The Four Corner Hustlers came out of the brownstone on Walcott and Washington at precisely the same time traffic began to clog. There is a window of movement in the flow of traffic from the United Center after a full house. This window is short, maybe five to ten minutes following the end of an event. The first fans reaching each parking lot manage to race out of the area without much congestion. White and Griffin made their attack during this short window of movement. Timing or planning had nothing to do with it and the result was no pursuit, no leads, and no arrests. They had committed one of the most publicized crimes in the history of the city. The police would not find them. Their only enemy would be the tool of advancement and respect. Reputation. There was no apparent monetary gain from this crime. The gain would come from the recognition of their ability to take risks and perform. Admiration and respect can only come from the knowledge of who the participants were. Fear did not take the form of avoiding capture or prison. Prison stints and life on the streets were synonymous. A prison stay would simply be a change of venue with no change in priorities. Illegal activities dominate life within the penal system and they dominate life on the streets. Progress in either venue is measured by deeds. Griffin and White never entertained the notion of not taking credit for the stadium shooting. Their objective in sending a message to the Four Corner Hustlers was always secondary to the act itself and its implementation. Notoriety and respect for the act within the Breed would come. The price for this notoriety seemed to be the natural order of their system. They would not be concerned about the police getting this information. The police never got this information.

The twelfth district police station sits at 100 South Racine. From the outside, the building stands four stories of white brick that has yellowed over the years. The small Chicago Police decal in the window of the main doors was very hard to see. The City of Chicago flag and the American flag were the indicators of the building. Joe Cortez walked past the unorganized front desk.

"Joe, who's up in Tac now?"

"How the fuck am I supposed to know? I just walked in. Wallin, if you ever checked something on your own before asking about it, my heart would freeze up on the spot."

"Fuck you, Joe. I don't know everyone's goddamn schedule."

"Isn't that your job? Isn't your responsibility as the desk officer to know the officers on duty?" Officer Wallin chose not to continue this. Joe Cortez was a Tac Unit officer in the 12th district. He was in his nineteenth year on the Chicago Police Department. He had passed the sergeant's exam years ago, and chose to return to the Tactical Unit. He loathed the clerical responsibilities of higher rank. His goal of a gold shield would not be helped by his decision to return to Tac, but it really didn't matter. He was not that far from retirement, and wanted to spend his remaining years doing what he liked. Joe Cortez was born to an African American mother and a Mexican American father. Both worked hard and stayed together. His mother died five years ago from cancer. His father moved back to his hometown of Zacatacus, Mexico. Joe was forty-six years old. He grew up in Evanston, Illinois. Evanston borders the northern city limits of Chicago and is home to Northwestern University. He went to Northern Illinois University on a football scholarship as a nose tackle. At six feet one and two hundred sixty pounds, Joe was the immovable object. After earning a bachelor's degree in physical education, Joe was convinced he could land on a pro football roster. He took a teaching job in January each year with the understanding he could spend July and August at someone's football camp until he latched onto an NFL team. After five years of trying, he took the police exam and found a home.

Two messages were taped to the telephone on his desk. The third floor TacUnit offices were stark. Seven desks, two separate offices, and stacks of filing cabinets filled the room. Joe threw away the first message, but sat down as he read the second.

Joe Cortez,

Considering the efforts combined to apprehend the scum of this community and the disappointing results culminating from these efforts, a gift awaits. We believe your intentions were admirable. In the future, remember that you cannot penetrate the walls that don't exist. Malcolm holds the answer to that elusive butterfly you have been chasing. This charity will not reoccur. I owed you this. Discipline stays home from now on.

T.C.

T.C. stood for T.C. There was no name. Joe Cortez had arrested this man at least fifty times over the years. He had spent time in Joliet on four occasions. Their paths have cris-crossed the west side of Chicago for more than a decade. T.C. owned the Four Corner Hustlers, and they were his gang, whether he was inside or out. Cortez grabbed his coat and marched into the Unit commander's office.

"I'm taking Taxman and Bondo with me. The Hustlers dropped something on me, but I'm not sure what it is. T.C. must remember last year when I let his nephew walk. He wacked little Frankie Fell under the Lake Street 'L' last year. Did us a favor, but he happened to do it in front of a squad. They pulled him in here, and he asked for me. He claimed it was self-defense. I talked to the arresting boys and they didn't have a problem with me cutting him on the stipulation that he told T.C. who made this disappear. The note said Malcolm knows. We'll start at Malcolm X. I don't believe it's going to be too hard to find. I know T.C. and this is something he wants us to find. He wants me to owe him. Send some back-up around the perimeter of the school."

Taxman and Bondo were part of the 12th TacUnit. Taxman got his name from his constant obsession to obtain a receipt for everything he bought. Candy bars or soft drinks were not excluded. He would never buy anything from a machine because there were no receipts. His neurotic orations on why cops shouldn't have to pay any taxes never changed over the years. Bondo was always getting hurt. He had been shot three times in the last ten years. Most cops never get close to a bullet. He broke his leg at a softball game and tore knee ligaments falling down the stairs at the 12th. They arrived in the parking lot at Malcolm X College on Tuesday afternoon, February 13. The college is situated one block south

105

of the United Center. Cortez pulled his Ford slowly through the lot. The car came to an abrupt halt. Joe got out of the car slowly. His eyes were fixed on the blue sedan. There was an arm hanging out of the trunk. He motioned for his companions to move slowly around opposite sides of the car. They had been to this dance many times before. Joe approached the trunk which was not completely closed. He gave the hanging trunk lid a tap with his foot and it rose slowly. Inside the trunk were two black male bodies. They had been shot numerous times in the head and face. Laying on top of them was a partial calendar. It was the month of January. One date was circled, Friday the 26th. Joe Cortez called for the coroner and homicide. The United Center shooters were just hand delivered.

*   *   *

CHAPTER FOURTEEN

The Rehabilitation Institute of Chicago has seen an alarming change in the demographics of their patients. Since the inception of the Institute, the highest percentage of spinal cord injuries had always been caused by automobile accidents. During the past five years, the overwhelming majority of spinal cord injuries have occurred from gunshot wounds. Many police studies are presenting the possibility that gang members are targeting victims with the intention of inflicting these wounds. Permanent damage serves as a constant reminder. Garett had just finished putting the kids to bed. They had spent over an hour with Lindsey. It had been particularly hard for them to say good bye. Lindsay's composure and faith had begun to wilt. The combination of her new surroundings and watching the kids leave again became too much. She began crying before they could leave and Garett finally asked the nurse for something to help settle her down.

Garett flicked the remote and the 35" Mitsubishi television rose to life as he sat down on the leather couch encircling their fireplace. The couch was nine years old and showed the wear of four children and a myriad of pets. A flick of the answering machine button before heading to the couch released a flurry of messages. Reporters from three television stations had messages on the machine. A Chicago police officer named Joe Cortez left a number. Quickly, the number was scribbled on the edge of the Tribune, and that call would be made in a minute. Garett was shoveling through the mound of mail that he had been ignoring. He began reading a letter marked urgent from the school district in Sheridan Shores. The letter began by describing three separate incidents involving similar circumstances. A brown sedan, possibly a Chevrolet Impala, beat up and rusting was spotted in connection with these reports. One male occupant of the car attempted to coerce three children to get into his car. This was reported by three children, each incident was approximately three days apart. No one had been abducted and no one had been arrested or questioned. The police had been unable to locate this vehicle since the reports surfaced. The letter went on to explain that these children had run away from the man on each occasion. Garett thought about the amount of time he had spent talking to his kids concerning the same subject. He wondered if they would remember what they had been taught. Don't talk to strangers and don't trust anyone. People will come up to kids with a puppy or a story about losing their puppy. They will ask for the child's help in locating a puppy. The puppy will be used as a lure. Garett had tried to drill this message into his kids. He never liked teaching his children to lose the innocence that will never come again. Unfortunately, it could cost them their lives. The letter concluded by warning parents to take extra precautions when schooling their children on what to do if they see anyone like this. Garett stared aimlessly at the television. His wife was gunned down going to a basketball game. His children couldn't walk the four blocks to school without the fear of abduction. At forty-two, Garett didn't want to test the envelope with his family. How can men focus on producing an income sufficient to sustain their lifestyle when they cannot protect the very ones they seek to provide for. He shook his head and ran his hands through his hair searching for some sanity in this abstract version of the American dream. Every day, he felt his children were target practice for anyone believing that the world had sold them short.

He continued through the mail. Magazine subscriptions recently renewed, were now sending notices to take advantage of some special offer to sign-up now. "Only Six Months Until Your Last Issue-Sign-Up Now For A Special Rate" Garbage. Every club and organization on the North Shore was soliciting for donations to their silent auction or their casino night. These groups were mostly well-intentioned, but one had to wonder how much of this money collected actually got to the target. Garett leafed through the 'everyone needs a cause stack'. There was a letter from the insurance company that held his health insurance through Dean Witter. Garett opened the envelope. There was a cover letter attached to a stack of bills from Cook County Hospital. The letter read:

Dear Mr. Baine,
    This letter will refer to covered expenses and deductible amounts. For the purpose of this letter, a covered expense is one that is allowable under the terms of the HMO plan you selected through your employer. More information will be needed to process the attached claims. There is some question as the existence of a pre-existing condition. Please complete the forms enclosed and they will be evaluated with the forms sent back from the physicians involved.
    In the event that a claim has been denied, in whole or part, you can request a review of your claim. This request should not be sent more than

sixty days after you receive notice of denial. All information will be evaluated and you will be informed of the decision in a timely matter. "

"What the fuck are you talking about?" Garett was yelling at no one in particular. "There is some god damn question about a pre-existing condition. My wife was shot. Do they fucking think that her paralysis was a pre-existing condition only aggravated by having a bullet slam into her spine." He threw the papers across the table sending them spewing. Garett's experience with the insurance industry does not come riddled with accolades. From his days in the restaurant business, Garett has seen claim after claim denied for some insane technicality. In 1985, one of Garett's employees, a cook named Henrique and his wife had their first child. Henrique was covered under the medical plan Garett had for the restaurant. The child developed a heart condition two weeks after he was born which required open heart surgery. The surgery was successful and Henrique's son was fine. The hospital bill was over $12,000, and the insurance company denied the entire claim because the notification of birth was not signed. Henrique forgot to sign the form adding his son to the medical coverage. After many formal protests, the company stood by their original position. Henrique was able to have his medical bills taken care of by a Mexican/American agency in Chicago specializing in cases such as these. Garett wasn't surprised by the latest contact with the insurance industry. This, however, represented a bit of a stretch. Denial based on the fact that a gunshot wound was a pre-existing condition seemed unlikely. The phone rang. Garett let it ring a couple of times before he closed his eyes and picked up the receiver.

"Hello."

"Garett, have you been watching the news?"

"Jim?"

"Turn on the fucking news."

"It's on, but I haven't really been paying any attention to it."

"They got 'em. They're dead. The mother fuckers that shot Denise and Lindsay are dead. Zarvell White and Casey Griffin had their fucking heads blown off by some of their brothers. The reports just say that the police were tipped as to the location of the bodies. They were in the trunk of the car they used on the night of the shooting."

"That's why I had all those messages. Some Tac Unit cop from the 12th called me along with all of the television stations. Are they sure about these guys?"

"Garett, they got the gun."

"I'll call you back. Are you home?"

"Yes."

109

"I'll call you right back."

Garett grabbed the remote and started switching channels looking for anything on the news concerning this report. Channel 7 flicked past the screen with an image of the United Center above the newscaster's shoulder. Garett stopped and turned the sound up. Channel 7 news anchor Dianne Burns was just beginning her report:

"...unexpectedly, the Chicago Police reported a break in the case of the United Center drive-by shooting of January 26. Late today, the 12th District Police station reported the discovery of two male bodies in the trunk of a car at Malcolm X College located across from the United Center. The two black men, identified as Zarvell White 24, and Casey Griffin 22, were found in the trunk of a blue sedan. This car was similar to the vehicle described by eye-witnesses on the night of the shooting. Two automatic weapons were uncovered and one was positively identified as the weapon used in the shooting. Test results on the blood taken from the front fenders were still pending, but a police spokesman left little doubt as to the outcome. Both men had extensive criminal records and were reported to be members of a predominately black gang called The Breed. Police would not elaborate on how they were led to the bodies other than to say they had been tipped. Speculation centers on the gang battles on-going in the area. Channel 7 had received information the day after the shooting that the drive-by was targeting members of another West Side gang called the Four Corner Hustlers. Sources inside the police department unofficially confirmed that the two men were executed by the Four Corner Hustlers and dropped in the laps of the Chicago Police Department. Repeating, police have confirmed the discovery of two bodies in the trunk of a blue sedan on the West Side. The car is believed to be the vehicle used in the United Center drive-by shooting of January 26. Ballistic reports on the weapons found in the vehicle matched those from the shooting at the United Center that left six people shot and more than a dozen hit by the vehicle. The two black men were identified as Zarvell White 24, and Casey Griffin 22. Stay tuned to Channel 7. We will update this story as soon as more details become available."

Garett fell back into the couch and stared at the ceiling. He had spent hours and hours since the shooting wondering about the ones responsible for this. He had often wondered how his own values would stand up under these circumstances. He was glad they were dead. Garett did not want to go through a trial. He did not want to look at the men who shot his wife on a daily basis. He did not want to hear about their abuse as children or that society had turned it's back on them. Garett found himself wandering politically over the past few years. During his years as a business owner, he felt compelled to back the Republican party, although he personally

110

never experienced any tangible benefits from a Republican President. He believed in a woman's right to choose but didn't see why men were so involved in this issue to begin with. He believed the nation's largest problems were being completely ignored. Overpopulation and hand gun violence. The gun problem could be greatly reduced if the manufacturing of these weapons were illegal. The government would continue to pass law after law limiting the purchase and possession of hand guns. Yet they condone and encourage the industry by allowing unchecked production and token restrictions on imports. The number of people in this country and on this planet would be it's ultimate closure. Garett was not consumed by some demonic fear of being overpopulated, but he felt the cities were being stretched to their limits. Too many people, frustrated and lacking opportunities, turned to lashing out at those perceived to have more than their share. The persistence of people in this environment to bring more children into the same struggling existence with seemingly no regard for their future confirmed Garett's own racism, but the questions still stood. Where did White and Griffin fit into this puzzle? Death by statistics will trivialize life. Full circle in this web leaves nothing. Were there any safe venues left in this country? Children had become targets in this society. Inner cities, affluent suburbs, schools playgrounds, malls were all potentially poisonous to our worst fears. Were there any communities where a family did not have to be afraid for their children? Shipping your children off to the service used to represent fear in our society. Two men were killed for their sins. Would anything change? Garett spoke volumes over the years on the merits of capital punishment. He knew it was not a deterrent. It was revenge, a concept that did not offend him. Some flaws in our system of justice were troubling. Sending an innocent man to death bothered him. Our system continues to render unfair jury decisions on both sides of the fence. When these decisions concern executions, where is the boundary for mistakes? Griffin and White deserved what they got. Their sentence was not a product of some warped judicial parade on Court TV. Their sentence was produced by the society they entered unwillingly, yet helped to sustain. Vigilante justice appealed to Garett because it couldn't hide behind any system. It produced swift results. It's consequences would not be debated or considered on this evening; the results were acceptable to Garett Baine.

Garett returned the Tac Unit call from the 12th. The desk officer would try to locate Officer Cortez.. The phone at his own home had begun to ring with the airing of these reports. Garett waited for the machine to screen these calls.

"This is Officer Joe Cortez, Tac Unit."

"This is Garett Baine. I am returning your call." The answering machine was shut off as Garett pulled the receiver up to his ear.

111

"Mr. Baine, I am assuming that you have heard about the bodies discovered today at Malcolm X College in the trunk of a blue sedan."

"Yes, I have heard about this. Are the reports accurate? Are these men responsible for the shooting last month at the United Center."

"They are accurate. I wanted to call you personally to cut through all of the bullshit you might hear in the next few days. I'm sure you and your family have been through enough without enduring the endless speculation from the media. I'll give you everything we know. Relay this information to Mr. Shane and leave it there. This is an unauthorized call which I will deny making if asked. Is that alright with you?"

"Fine, continue."

"The shooting at the United Center on January 26 was a result of some territorial dispute between two West Side street gangs. Members of the Four Corner Hustlers had been selling drugs out of the brownstone located on the corner of Washington and Walcott. This location is outside of the area controlled by the Four Corner Hustlers. It falls into an area controlled by the Breed, another West Side gang. On the night of the shooting, two members of the Breed decided it was time to teach the Four Corner Hustlers to stay out of their territory without permission. On this particular evening, there were two members of the Four Corner Hustlers conducting some business at the brownstone. Two members of the Breed waited by the Henry Horner homes for them to complete their business and exit the house. The blue sedan would drive by and the occupants would conduct an execution of those gentlemen. The intended result would remind the Four Corner Hustlers how hazardous conducting this type of business had become. The program seemed to loose control when the men left the house at the same time the Bull's game was ending. The men in the blue sedan approached the target too fast and the car jumped the curb. Shots were fired randomly and the car disappeared into the traffic before anyone could get a handle on what happened. Our department conducted as complete an investigation as I've ever seen. I would tell you if they didn't. One problem, however. We never got a thing. We were no closer to this case today than we were three weeks ago."

"That's comforting."

"It was not from lack of effort. Sometimes, by dumb luck, the worst planned crimes get by. Trouble here was, these guys couldn't keep their mouths shut about the incident. It meant nothing if they didn't take credit for it, so they took credit for it. Word got around and someone from the Four Corner Hustlers owed me a favor. I won't get into that one. They would have killed these guys anyway; the favor was dropping the shooters in our laps. Trust me, they are the ones. Zarvell White and Casey Griffin were responsible for the injuries to your wife and the death of your friend,

Denise Shane. Would there be enough evidence to convict them in a publicized trial? We'll never know. The police will issue statements that will be vague and focus on meaningless aspects of this case. They will remind the media how much attention had been put into this case. They will extract as much credit for this closure as possible. It wasn't us. I don't condone how this case was concluded but it's not my place to judge. I called you for one reason. This case will stop now. There will be a homicide investigation as to who killed White and Griffin, but that will never be solved because no one on this end cares who did it. The guns are already dismantled and floating somewhere at the bottom of the Chicago River. They would be untraceable if they were found. Unless an eyewitness comes forward with glittering details of the murder scene, Zarvell White and Casey Griffin's demise will remain unsolved as nearly eighty percent of all internal gang homicides do not end in convictions. The men responsible for the shooting on January 26 have been found. They are dead. I am not asking you to agree with it, like it, or even understand it. Just accept it. Your family and your friend deserve to know that."

"I have been listening to you for a few minutes and I am confused. You have explained why you called, but why me? Have I ever met you?"

"Yes. We met briefly at Cook County Hospital. You pushed me aside in the emergency room at Cook County on the night of the shootings. Personnel had been called in to restrain Mr. Shane. You told me to put my own wife in the same position and back off. I let you go and I do not normally do that. For that moment, however, I pulled half the staff back. Mr. Shane was out of line, but I let you handle it. My call came from that night. Respect is a scarce commodity on this job, but I admired the way you held your ground. I saw the media converge on your home and your family. I have an ex-wife and two young daughters. It's in the eyes. It was in your eyes that night Mr. Baine. It's always in the eyes."

"Thank you for the call. Will I get the chance to see you again?"

"Unlikely. Good luck to you and your family. You have my number."

"One more question before you hang up. Did these men act on their own or does the responsibility for this crime extend up into this gang?"

"These men acted on their own. There are ways to prove yourself in these gangs and there are ways to increase your stature within the gang. Planning an attack on an intruder and implementing that plan through violence is catamount to a promotion. They acted on their own. Responsibility for this crime is another subject. Good night Mr. Baine."

Garett called his wife at the RIC. He asked for the floor supervisor first. He wanted to be absolutely sure that no one from the media was going to bother her. After being reassured that no calls would be put through to his wife, he asked to speak to Lindsay.

"Hi. I hope I didn't wake you."

"No, I was up watching the news. I'm sure that's why you are calling. Garett, do you think these are the men that did this? At this point, I don't even know if I care."

"They are the men responsible. I got a call from a police officer from the district involved. His name is Joe Cortez. I met him briefly on the night of the shooting. He called to clear up some details for us. Officer Cortez assured me that this case would end here. These men were the two involved in the shooting and they were killed by the men they originally targeted. Cortez wanted us to know certain details that would be withheld by the police. He was sincere and I believe he was trying to give us an understanding of the circumstances. His call was off the record. He said the police would explain things in a manner that would leave them in a favorable light. They would take the credit for solving the case, attributing the results to the massive effort that was portrayed through the press. He explained that they did conduct as thorough an investigation as he had seen, but the results were non-productive. These men were killed because of the gang warfare that instigated the incident in the first place. Cortez was tipped to the whereabouts of the bodies and who they were. They did it, Lindsay. They got what they deserved. How are you? I can come down there if you want? I'll call next door and tell Jack or Kate to come over. I'm sure they won't mind staying with the kids."

"Garett, get some sleep. I'm fine. Retribution has a way of finding it's recipients. This wasn't done to me. I was a result of something else happening. I have thought about this for more hours than I would like to admit, but this helps to close something that would remain unknown. As a Catholic, I know I shouldn't be happy about two men losing their lives regardless of what they did. I'll need some time to understand this. My concern is us and when I am going home. What happened tonight doesn't change anything that I choose to focus on. They made certain choices and our family has been impacted. That hasn't changed. I know you and I know this is some consolation for you. Leave it there. I had a good day at rehab today. Are you coming down tomorrow?"

"I'll be there in the morning after the kids go to school. Kate is going to take Conner and Christopher after they get out at 11:15. I spoke to the floor supervisor and asked them to screen any calls from the press regarding this. I'm sure they'll be trying to get your reaction."

"Thanks. I love you. What are you doing now?"

"I'm going to call Jim. He was the one that called me and told me to watch the news. I want to tell him about the call I got from Cortez. I'll see you in the morning. I love you."

"I love you, too."

Garett hung up the phone and walked over to the refrigerator. He pulled a Genuine Draft from the box and dialed Jim Shane. He knew his wife would have a better handle on this than he did. Her faith was not fashionable nor was it born from circumstance.

"Jim, it's me. I just got off the phone with one of the Tac Unit officers at the hospital on the night of the shooting. He called me off the record. He wanted us to know what went down with these guys and to tell us that they were definitely the ones that did it. It was some gang bullshit. Somebody was invading somebody else's territory. White and Griffin planned some hit that would go down at Walcott and Washington on the night we were at the game, but they fucked up and just started shooting. That's when Denise and Lindsay got hit. They couldn't keep their mouths shut about it and got whacked because they bragged. The cop that called me was cool. These were the guys. The case is over, Jim. I'll give you this guy's number if you want to talk to him. His name is Joe Cortez. He is a Tac Unit officer with the 12th district. He was at Cook County on the night of the shooting. He remembered both of us. Do you want to call him?"

"Fuck it, Garett. There is nothing this guy can tell me that will make this thing go away. My life seems to be a series of people taking things away from me. I have been sitting here watching the news and drinking some of my finest scotch. My tolerance to Glenlivet has heightened this evening. You know, when I left Chicago and moved to Georgia, I thought my life would end. My parents took my friends away from me because my dad wanted to take another job. I was a freshman in high school and he decides to pull us all out of school and move. Shit, I told him I wasn't going. The South, as it turned out, was good for me. I started at fullback for three years in Fulton County. I got a full ride to Georgia Tech. I blew my knee out and football became a memory. Everything in my life up until that point had been centered on football. Coaches were telling us that we had a legitimate chance at the national championship. Pro scouts would be watching everything we did. The injury changed my entire focus. I had a horrible time with school after that happened. I ran to the Marines. Where did that get me? A four year correspondence course to lose whatever shred of faith I had left. After the Marines, I just wanted to work, not think. In less than a year, we were building houses from Texas to Utah. I had a son in Texas the year after I got back. I didn't find out until years later. I was barely twenty-two years old. Shit, they took him away from me and I didn't even know it. He is twenty years old today and I have never seen him. They took my son away from me, and would have gotten a court order to prevent me from having any contact with him. I finally went back to Tech and graduated with an engineering degree. I came to see you in '85, and was going to stay a couple of weeks. After meeting Denise, things changed. We went through the days of rage. You know, staying out until the 4:00 a. m. bars closed. A couple of lines, some misplaced sentimental bullshit and we all had fun. Denise made us a family. She gave me the sense of what I was never able to find alone. They took her away, Garett. Every fucking thing that was ever good for me was taken from me. I'm scared to death looking at my kids, like they're going to be next. I thought about those guys, whoever they were. You know I carry a 357 Magnum in my glove compartment. I have a gun cabinet in my office. There are fourteen rifles, eleven hand guns, and two automatic weapons in there. I collect them as a hobby, right? Bullshit. I collect these guns because this fucking society is spilling out of the cities. There is no more security in Libertyville or Sheridan Shores. I always thought that no one could walk into my life and take my family or my property without paying dearly for the attempt. And they did just that." The scotch was beginning to dominate the words from Jim Shane. Garett heard his friend swallow and release a long sigh. "Garett, I wanted to kill them myself. I wanted to look them in their eyes before they died. I wanted to tell them that they can't have my kids. They're not going to get the kids now. Right, Garett? They can't get the kids, now?"

"They can't get the kids, Jim. No one will get your kids, Jim." Pursuing this conversation on a rational level would be useless. Garett had known Jim for so many years that he also knew his tolerance and his patterns. Alcohol brought out the ultra-conservative, semi-militia mentality that Jim possessed. Too many nights wallowed into the Rush Limbaugh remedies for what is decaying this country. More importantly, the alcohol made him emotional. He missed his wife and it all came back with the reports on television this evening. "Jim, put the fucking scotch away and go get some sleep. Your kids will need you in the morning and you're going to feel like shit. They are not going to care about what happened to the assholes that shot Denise or the fact that you stayed up until three in the morning drinking your brains out. I'll call you tomorrow morning and maybe I'll swing by for some coffee. Is that all right with you?"

"What'd you say, Garett?"

"Get some sleep, Jimbo. I'll come by in the morning." Garett hung up and wished he could take a ride out to Libertyville at that very moment.

The snow fell in Sheridan Shores during an early morning storm. When Jake came downstairs to turn on ESPN at 6:30, the Blazer at the end of the driveway was buried with nearly eight inches of new snow. This kind of storm will slow things considerably in the Chicago area but certainly would not shut anything down. Jake had made an enigmatic transformation at the age of six. He shunned cartoons, to the dismay of his mother, for the constantly repeated program know as ESPN Sportscenter. This show is replayed throughout the morning and consists of almost every imaginable highlight from the previous day in sports. Lindsay would often congratulate her husband on cloning himself in the body of a six year old. Maggie came down at 7:00 a.m., immaculately dressed for the fourth grade. The sound coming from the television never received a glance from her. She stood in the French doors and watched the bevy of activity outside and down the street. The village was a symphony of whirling snow as residents with driveways no longer than two car lengths employed snow removal services. Maggie watched as they cris-crossed paths with the village plows. As soon as the main plows cleared the streets, the smaller plows of the private firms seared their paths across the newly cleared roadways. Conner and Christopher rumbled downstairs at various times. Christopher would get himself dressed and even attempt to make his bed. At five, his ensembles were better assembled than Garett normally provided. Conner would bounce downstairs in his boxers clutching two tattered blankets. His long blond curls framed an angelic face hiding a friendly menace with long eye lashes and bright blue eyes. Conner paid little attention to his blankets after he awoke. But come bed time, there would be no sleep without those beleaguered bedfellows. Garett and Lindsay would often look at each other in horror when Lindsay had accidentally left the blankets at someone's house or forgot they were in the wash. Jake and Maggie left for school at 8:00 a.m. Conner was in Junior Kindergarten and Christopher was in Senior Kindergarten. Garett knew these were simply the modern version of getting the kids out of the house at an earlier age. All the progressive fortyish new mothers could elaborate on the virtues of early inter-action among toddlers when all they truly wanted was some daytime hours to speak to an adult. The neighbors were providing transportation for the little ones to and from pre-school. Most days, Kate would watch the two little ones until Garett could get home from the hospital or the RIC. All of their neighbors and friends showed up to help when the shooting occurred and they hadn't disappeared yet. Breakfast was an interesting phenomenon with the Garett in charge. Bagels and Sprite were the menu for the day.

Garett had been to see Lindsay all day on Tuesday. She didn't seem obsessed with anything having to do with White and Griffin. They went to physical therapy together working with two of the therapists assigned to Lindsay. Ninety minutes were spent on leg massage and movement. Muscle tissue had to be maintained to some degree. One hour was spent on handling the wheel chair. Lindsay's strength in her hands had returned to normal. The movement she retained above the waist was virtually restriction free. This indicated the location of the wound, but could be misleading as to the return of leg movement. The degree of movement and strength associated with the body above the wound did not necessarily indicate the probability of full recovery. Lindsay wanted to get home. Walking would come at someone else's pace. Home was her goal. Lindsay had one hour for weight training associated with the upper body. After the physical therapy concluded, there was a meeting with the physician in charge and a discussion of the time table to go home. If progress continued at the present pace, Lindsay would be home in ten days. Her eyes sparkled with this news. Since the shooting, her fist day home would come some five weeks later. They discussed their first day at home together and Garett promised not make it into a big production. He was lying.

It was Wednesday, February 14, Valentines Day. Garett sent the two little ones next door at 8:15. They would leave for pre-school at 8:20. Jim Shane was due at the house before noon. Today was the day to open the accounts at Schwab. Garett had not told Jim anything more than they discussed one week prior. Garett had liquidated his accounts at Dean Witter. He did the same to his wife's accounts. The money was left in Money Market in their Active Assets Account. This was a checking account that paid interest. Their cash totaled $110,000. Garett had sold all of the mutual funds they owned, including the ones in his IRA. The penalty would be minimal considering the potential gain from this move. These transactions would turn out to be his last trades at Dean Witter. He had not discussed any of this with Lindsay. He didn't have the luxury of waiting and now was not the time to discuss this with Lindsay. He not only had committed one felony by unauthorized trading in his wife's account, he liquidated the custodial college funding accounts. This was strike number two.

Jim Shane wheeled into the sprawling Riverwoods Dean Witter/Discover complex just outside of Deerfield, Illinois. This facility housed one large branch of their brokerage business, the headquarters of their Discover card division and the nationwide distribution center for all of their literature. The sole purpose of this visit was to pick up a check from the liquidation of his accounts. Clients may pick up checks at any Dean Witter branch office. He felt better this morning. The previous day had been tortuously long. Hangovers could be categorized: beer and wine binges were the most tolerable, while Scotch residuals were brutal. Gone were the days of hibernating for twenty four hours with nothing more than brief appearances to obtain sizable portions of junk food. After forty, his body doesn't seem to rebound as quickly from the inebriated state he entered only hours before. He seemed to be going through the motions of this transaction. Jim picked up his check at the cashier's window of the Riverwoods branch. He began observing his own actions, watching himself jump from one irrational act to another. He kept asking himself if any rational human being would be doing this without having the slightest idea of what was coming. Hadn't these accounts been doing fine? Dividend Growth was up nearly twenty-five percent over the past eighteen months. His aggressive growth portfolio fund group was up more than that. His individual stock portfolio was up seventeen percent over the past eighteen months. Was he jeopardizing the one thing he did have some degree of control over? Of course he was, yet he continued to proceed. The liquidation had already occurred. Every fiber in his body was screaming at him to abort this transaction before finding out exactly what Garett was leading him into. Every thread of common sense told him to cancel the liquidation before he gave up his time on the five year back end package. Why would anyone with a shred of intelligence close out an IRA account at a sizable penalty when the money wasn't needed. Jim Shane stuffed the envelope into his coat pocket. The drive to Sheridan Shores would take twenty minutes. His curiosity was now reaching a crest. The loss of his wife pre-empted the more conventional approach to Garett's invitation. Denise never would have allowed a move of this kind. Jim would never have broached the subject in this format. Answers to all of the questions would come first or there would be no movement of any funds. Rebellion and anger precipitated his decision to proceed. His justification became Garett. Lindsay must know if they are liquidating everything they own. Her compliance gave him some confidence. After all, he thought, the money was not committed yet. Garett would explain the deal before he turned over anything.

Jim Shane arrived at Garett's house nearly an hour before their appointment at the Schwab office in Sheridan Shores. Jim parked his four year old Mitsubishi Montero along the snow bank in front of the house. Sheridan Shores in the winter resembled a small New England village with massive oak trees forging wooded archways over the streets. The community was established well before the turn of the century and the architecture reflected an era dominated by large Victorian homes and brick laden streets. Jim reached over and checked the glove compartment to make sure it was locked. He walked along the black iron fence surrounding Garett's house until he reached the garage. He didn't knock, knowing Garett was alone in the house. Garett was sitting at an oval shaped pine table drinking coffee and glancing at the Wall Street Journal.

"Want some coffee?"

"Sure."

"I take it you made it to the Dean Witter Riverwoods office with no problems. They had a check cut for you?"

"The check is in my wallet. There were no problems whatsoever. I have to tell you Garett, that I'm not feeling all that comfortable with what I have just done. Why don't you explain to me what this transaction is all about. At this moment, I am having serious reservations about why I pulled myself out of a decent portfolio for some kind of scheme. In fact, I am having serious reservations about my sanity regarding this deal. My life is fucked up enough. At least I had some continuity with my money and some security. My saving grace at this moment is that I still have the money . What are we doing, Garett?"

"You're right Jim. You still have your money. I am not going to talk you into anything. I have been given, what I believe is an opportunity to take advantage of some information that is not available to anyone else. I want you to read this note." Garett handed Jim a card.

Dear Garett,

I would like to pass on to you, my sincere wishes regarding the most complete recovery for Lindsay. I am very sorry for your friend Denise Shane and her family. I remember meeting them at half-time and they seemed very nice. My wife and I were delayed almost an hour by the emergency vehicles and the police activity of that evening. we were only able to listen to the radio trying to figure out what had happened. When we got home and watched the events unfolding on television, we were devastated to hear that you, Lindsay, and your friends were victims. I am not going to pontificate on the subject. I am sure you are up to your eyes in well intentioned insincerity. I am here for you and your family. I think the world of you, Garett Baine. I want you to read this note and understand every word of it. All of my resources are available for you. If I can be of any assistance with your clients, let me know. I know about your situation with Bruce Carson, and his change of heart did not come to him in a vision during the night.

Do what is best for you and your family. Understand what control is and the difference between action and assistance. Always know who is dictating the decisions around you. Move past the fluff, and visit with me when you can. A week, two, maybe three. Whenever you feel the time is right. Give my best to Lindsay. I'm trying to figure a way out of a commitment I made to one of my clients. I am to be his guest at the Bull's game on Monday, February 19. His seats are in Section 222, aisle K. Those seats are so high, you feel like they're going through the roof. I have no desire to attend any of these games at this time. I know this is something that I do not have to tell you. I've tried to tell this guy gracefully that I cannot attend, but he refuses to accept that answer. Hell, it's like I have been waiting for some Fucking Dumb Ass approval to grant me permission to pull out. He dropped the tickets off at my office last week. I think I'll shake him up by waiting until 3:00 on that Monday. Then I'll call and tell him that I sold them all. That will be the last time he ever asks me to a game.

Remember what I said. If you need anything.
Sincerely,

Spencer Dryden

Jim handed the note back to Garett.

"This is a nice thought, Garett. Exactly what does this have to with the money we are about to invest?"

"Do you remember meeting Spencer Dryden at the game?"

"Yeah."

"Do you remember the conversation we had about Spencer Dryden and his involvement with Trexon?"

"Vaguely. Trexon is a company working on some sort of nicotine substitute. If I remember correctly, this was something you were not very excited about."

"You remember well, Jim. The company has been working on this nicotine substitute for years and it seemed like the stock would forever float in the ten to twenty dollar range. Spencer's note was a risky foray into the land of insider information. His motivation to choose me is not as clear as the message he has sent."

"You're losing me, Garett."

"Here, look at the note again and follow me as I go through it." Garett handed the note back to Jim. "Sit down and follow me. The first part of the note is fairly clear. They had a difficult time leaving the game due to all of the chaos created by the shooting. Skip to the line, ' I want you to read this note and understand every word of it.' He continues...'understand the difference between action and assistance...move past the fluff..' Then all of a sudden he begins to tell me about going to a Bull's game. This seemed very strange considering that it has nothing to do with a sympathy card or a get well card. It didn't take me long to read into this note. Skip down a couple of lines and stay with me. He talks of being asked to attend the Bull's game on Monday February 19. There is no game on Monday February 19. His seats are to be Section 222, row K. There is no row K in Section 222. The rows in that section go by numbers. I checked with the United Center. K222 is the name given to Trexon's nicotine substitute. He talks about the seats making you feel like you're going through the roof. A bullet stock on the market goes through the roof. He speaks of waiting for some Fucking Dumb Ass approval not to attend the game. His message now becomes brilliantly clear. Trexon has received FDA approval. The announcement will come on Monday morning. The stock will go through the roof during the day, but peak before the close. He talks about selling these Bull's tickets by 3:00 p.m. on Monday. Spencer Dryden is telling me that he will sell all of his Trexon stock by the close of

121

the market on Monday. The stock is at seventeen. We buy it today at seventeen. Thursday and Friday are a wash. The news leaks before the bell on Monday morning. This could alter some of the nation's largest corporations and create a day on Wall Street never seen before. This would be the day to sell short on Phillip Morris. I could shake up the options desk with one phone call, but that would draw the SEC in a heartbeat. TREX will fly at the opening bell. Where it goes is anybody's guess. I'll put a sell order in at four times the buy price. If it hits, we're out. If it doesn't hit, then I'll judge when to sell based on the peak. The peak will surface when the stock begins to fall. I won't wait. The first drop in the price of the stock will trigger my sell. If it opens flat, then UPI has no information. I'll wait until the stock drops. If it drops at all then we're out. Worse case scenario is that we lose a point or two. Best case scenario is that we quadruple our money in less than three days. There are no guarantees Jim. If we buy this stock today and the FDA approval falls through or they deny the product categorically, then this could be devastating. I know Spencer was giving me this information to act on it. I can't call him on this and I can't ask him any questions regarding this. He put it in my lap and told me to make sure about who was making the decisions in my life. I've made this decision. My grandfather left me some property out West. If we lose any money in this deal, I'll cover all of your losses. The property is worth about a million dollars. You cannot talk to anyone about this transaction. I want you in with me. I have not talked to Lindsay about any of this. This is not the time, but the circumstances won't wait. Neither will I."

"If we do this, are we putting ourselves in Harm's way? Isn't the SEC going to come down on anyone making a major move on this stock?"

"Spencer is going to get investigated whenever this stock makes a move or whenever he decides to liquidate his position. We are not employees of the company. We have no relatives in the company. We have no direct link to Trexon. We were not employed by Dean Witter at the time of the stock purchase. Will it look like we had some knowledge of this? Yes. Will the SEC pursue an investigation past the mandatory inquiry of an unusual purchase? Not likely. What's their case? I used to work for Dean Witter. I knew Spencer Dryden from a distance. He owned a significant percentage of the stock. He sold his stock on the same day as many other people. That much movement in any stock will trigger a tremendous flurry of activity. Why did we buy so much at the time we did? I followed the stock when I was with Dean Witter and I felt the timing was right. The downside was minimal because the most recent financial statement from the company showed plenty of cash to continue research toward FDA approval."

"Why do you think he gave you this information? Is this some consolation prize for getting our wives shot and losing one?"

"Maybe."

"I don't know this guy at all."

"He didn't give you the information."

"Why you? I don't get it."

"I've met very few people in my life that don't crave some degree of notoriety for their generosity. Few that didn't need to be recognized for everything they accomplished. Spencer told me once that everything in this life must be earned or it has no value. Success will never be the measure of quantity. It is simply the constitution of the path. The effort can produce the unexpected. He gave me some information and baited me to ask questions. There would have been no answers. Technically, he told me nothing. I would imagine that my circumstances prompted this note, but we'll never know that. There will be no questions."

"I'm in Garett. I'm in on my own. I don't want you to underwrite me for any losses."

"Let's go. We've got some stock to purchase."

"Exactly when the fuck were you planning on telling me about this property, anyway?"

*   *   *

CHAPTER FIFTEEN

Scott James greeted Garett and Jim as they entered the Charles Schwab office. He had been looking forward to this meeting because Garett had been somewhat mysterious about the details. He was unaware of Garett's departure from Dean Witter. Brokers from any of the big three firms, Dean Witter, Merrill Lynch, or Smith Barney making appointments at Charles Schwab would attract a margin of concern and a larger degree of curiosity. The three men walked through a series of corridors spotted with cubicle offices, many of them empty. The advent of Internet trading from a central location is making the local broker obsolete. This is not portfolio management. It is discount trading for the active investor or the large block trader.

"This is it gentlemen. Have a seat. Garett, everyone in town is still in shock over the shooting. How is Lindsay doing?"

"Lindsay is doing much better. She is scheduled to come home very soon. She still has no movement in her legs, but we're hopeful this is a temporary condition. This is Jim Shane. He has been a close friend since we were kids and I don't want to tell you how long that has been."

"Nice to meet you, Jim. I am sorry about your loss."

"Thank you."

"What can I do for you, Garett? I see the Dean Witter stock has been rising steadily. In fact, some of the brokers here have been purchasing sizable chunks for their clients. Where do you guys see it going?"

"It's going to crack one-hundred without a doubt. Don't sell it until it passes the century number. Jim and I are here to open two accounts. I left Dean Witter. Together, we would like to purchase nearly sixteen thousand shares of TREX. I know the commission structure of your firm, but I figured you could discount the standard deals for us on a purchase of this size."

"TREX. Let's pull it up here. Trading at 17 1/4 on the buy side."

"Lock it in now. I'll be depositing one-hundred and ten thousand dollars. Jim will be depositing one-hundred and sixty thousand dollars. We will each be purchasing TREX with the entire account. I am figuring the fees to be under a grand combined. Let's open the accounts and book the trade now."

Scott knew he was expected to accommodate this client without asking any questions. The forms were filled out and the accounts were opened. Checks were deposited, the trade was booked, and fees totaled $790.00. Dean Witter fees would have been triple this figure. The three men engaged in some small talk after all of the paperwork was completed. There was relatively nothing more said about this transaction. Garett made sure that Scott would be in on Monday. There would be an equally important transaction done on Monday, but the time would be tentative. Scott agreed to meet Garett for coffee at 8:15 on Monday morning. The market opened at 8:30 Central time. Moments after Garett Baine and Jim Shane left the Charles Schwab office in Sheridan Shores, Scott James sat at his own computer and placed a trade for his own account. Checking the sell price of TREX, which had jumped a quarter, he purchased eight hundred and fifty seven shares of TREX for his personal account. It is important that the price not be lower than the price your client just paid for the stock.

"How many shares did you buy, Scott?" Garett startled Scott as he popped his head back into the office. " Never mind. Don't tell me. I don't care. If I find out you called anybody else and divulged any information about these transactions, I'll make sure the SEC becomes an integral part of your life. Monday at 8:15 for coffee. Have a good week-end Scott."

*   *   *

CHAPTER SIXTEEN

Garett Baine never imagined four days could drag on so long. He was convinced that in between his visits to see Lindsay someone had managed to squeeze another ten to twelve hours into the day. There was a constant need to be accessible to a television or a computer. News about the FDA approval could come at any time and through any media source. CNBC, America Online, Reuters, Dow Jones News would all be dominated by this announcement. Ideally, sources within the FDA or Trexon would release the news upon confirmation to one of these news wires. Through Sunday night, no information had been released. He kept his television on all night, taking sporadic naps, waking to another CNBC wrap-up show. Still no news. At 4:45 a.m., the news hit. CNBC announced a special report:

"Our sources have confirmed the approval of a nicotine substitute by the FDA. This is the first substance approved for use in commercially made cigarettes that would make the product virtually risk-free and completely non-addictive. The FDA approval was issued for Trexon, Incorporated, trading under the symbol TREX. It's formula K222 has been in development for years. It has been widely speculated that the major tobacco companies had the resources to produce a safe nicotine substitute, but this product would seriously damage the current billion dollar plus conventional cigarette market worldwide. Repeating...The Food and Drug Administration has announced formal approval to Trexon's K222 as a nicotine substitute. This news will drop like a bombshell on the tobacco industry. Trexon, Inc. trades on the NASDAQ under the symbol TREX. Shares closed on Friday at 17. Activity on the overseas markets has already begun and TREX has been the entire focus. More details will follow as we get them. Based on what this news means to the small North Carolina company and the potential impact to the tobacco industry, this promises to be an active day on Wall Street..."

Kate Doleman knocked on the garage door at 6:30 a.m. Garett had asked her to come early on Monday morning. He told her that he had a business appointment to attend before 8:00 a.m. and he needed some help with the kids.

"You look like shit, Garett."

"Good morning to you, too."

"How's Lindsay? I talked to her last night. She seemed up. I think the closer she gets to going home, the better she feels."

"You amaze me, Kate. At this early hour, you're still as sharp as a tack."

"Of course, you'll still be here. That could be incentive enough to prolong any stay."

"That's why I love you, Kate. You're just like me and I'm a sarcastic prick."

"Two of a kind."

"Thanks for coming over. The kids will be up shortly. I'm going to jump in the shower. I've got an appointment at 8:15, but I want to prepare some things in the office downstairs before I leave. I don't know what we would have done if you and Jack hadn't been there for us while Lindsay has been gone."

"That shower idea sounded like a good one. Beat it."

Garett had called Jim Shane a few minutes after the CNBC report on Trexon aired. The message conveyed was simple. The FDA approval was announced. Movement on TREX would be a certainty. Garett would call him from the Schwab office as soon as the market opened. The shower felt great. Conner and Christopher wanted to know how many more days before Mommy comes home. Kate had poured two bowls of Waffle Crisp for the little ones, while urging Jake to turn off ESPN and let the kids watch cartoons. Garett finally made his way to the basement and his private little office. Garett had set up this office after he sold the restaurants. This became the only room in the house that the kids would not be allowed in. As with most edicts or absolute rules in the Baine household, this one crumbled quickly. This happened to be the only room in the house with a computer. The older kids had to use the computer for some homework assignments. This morning, the office became the information highway. News of the FDA approval was all over the Internet. Garett turned the small television in the office to CNN then CNBC. On the Today show, the financial news was the lead. Trading had been reported at record levels on the Third World Markets. Details were scarce. Certainly, these transactions would affect the opening price. Garett had nothing to prepare. He simply wanted to watch as many different outlooks as he could find before the opening. It was nearly eight o'clock. He faxed some paperwork to Michael Ramirez concerning the estate in Montana and the end of probate. There were no challenges to the Gabel or Baine estates. Garett seemed amazed that the probate period did not produce some distant relative contesting everything from page one. He left the office before the fax finished and arrived at the Charles Schwab office at seven minutes past the hour.

*   *   *

CHAPTER SEVENTEEN

Scott James had a fresh pot of coffee ready and a few questions that were burning a hole in the back of his brain. They would not be answered on this morning because they would not be asked. Garett entered the office not knowing if he would be there for an hour or seven hours. Investments have the technical lure of gambling, yet the respectability of protocol. Garett certainly knew the difference between buying shares of blue chip giants for the purpose of long term holds versus liquidating your entire portfolio to throw it on one small company stock based on some information you may or may not have perceived correctly. Garett listened to some mindless rhetoric with Scott James without hearing a word. He was thinking about what Spencer had said concerning the importance of working for your accomplishments. Had he misread Spencer's leads? Could they have possibly been a test to determine greed or shortcuts. If this was a test, Garett thought, then what was his motivation? Spencer would have nothing to gain or lose. He shook his head in an effort to snap out of his paranoid daze. The FDA approval had been announced. Garett knew he read the note correctly. The dryness of the air inside was typical of a frigid February morning. The dryness in his throat had nothing to do with the air.

"Call it up, Scott." Garett instructed as they took seats in Scott James' office.

"Don't worry, we've still got three minutes until the opening. Here, I put TREX at the top of my main screen. Still not open. Shit, your boy was all over the media this morning. Isn't there a major position at Dean Witter in this company?"

"Don't go there, Scott. I came to you with this trade. I knew you would pick up on it for yourself. The market's open. I can't read your screen. Where did it open?"

"It's halted."

"Shit." Garett got up and walked across the office.

"See if you can get some information on Dow Jones News. I'm sure there was a shit load of activity on this stock overseas." Garett watched the screen as Scott switched over to the news services pages. Dow Jones read as follows:

6:07 a.m. Monday 2/19/96...trading frenzy on NASDAQ's Trexon, Inc., TREX, followed an early morning announcement granting FDA approval for the nicotine substitute K222. Third World markets have reported jumps from an opening of 17% to 31 or 32. This jump is unprecedented on these markets. Speculation will continue while the opening is anticipated to be halted pending the appropriate level to set the bid and ask. Orders placed at the opening bell are expected to be high. Merrill Lynch sources confirmed the company will direct all Merrill brokers to caution clients attempting to purchase TREX. The fills will not be guaranteed at any price and the gap could be staggering...

7:08 a. m. Monday 2/19/96...massive activity continues on TREX. Overseas prices have been reported to be 40 or higher. The price has been fluctuating rapidly. Veteran Wall Street analyst Arnold Rapport warns against purchasing TREX at the opening. Rapport sees the possibility of a backlash to the approval announcement. He cautions speculators to wait until the expected announcements from American tobacco giants Philip Morris, R. J. Reynolds, and Brown and Williamson. Dow Jones News has learned that there will be statements forthcoming. Rapport spoke to CNN reporters and expressed concerns that the buying frenzy overseas may become a selling frenzy once the stock opens...

8:21 a.m. Monday 2/19/96...Dean Witter, Merrill, Smith-Barney, and other major brokerage firms are expecting TREX to be halted at the opening. Caution is the word as investors speculate the impact of a non-addictive nicotine substitute. Barron's spokesman Miles Tanner questions the comparisons to the Netscape IPO or Boston Chicken and reminds investors that this is not an IPO. Speculation rarely lives up to reality when it comes to timing the short term buys...

"What do you think Garett? Halted trading doesn't guarantee anything. The Street seems to be advising investors to proceed with extreme caution."

"What else are they going to say. Proceed with caution could mean buy like hell. Shit, Rapport has so much tobacco money in his pocket, of course he's going to down play this. Where's your phone? I've got to call a friend of mine." Garett dialed Jim Shane's number as Scott handed him the telephone.

"Jim, it's Garett. The exchange opened a few minutes ago with TREX halted. What this means is that there is so much activity on the stock, they

130

need time to determine the proper opening bid and ask price. Overseas trading during the night showed huge gains from 17 to near 40. The Dow Jones News service and other Wall Street analysts have issued statements about proceeding with caution regarding any purchase of TREX. They have to say that Jim, to cover their ass."

"How long before you get an opening price?"

"I don't know, Jimbo. With all of the technology today, halted stocks stay closed for a minimal amount of time. Exactly how long is anyone's guess. I'll call you as soon as we get a reading on this. Do you have CNBC on? What are they saying?"

"Yeah, I've got it on. They are running all kinds of shit on past flyers like Netscape and Iomega. They are showing how the vast majority of these companies come crashing down before most investors will see a nickel. The officers in these companies often accumulate vast fortunes, but the investors rarely see the same results. This has not been comforting to watch. They are also talking about the statements from the tobacco companies. What is that all about?"

"Jim, the tobacco companies are going to issue statements repudiating the claims of Trexon, Inc. They are going to attempt to discredit this company. Some may announce lawsuits claiming that they have already produced this product. My guess is that they will claim the product is not risk free or non-addictive. The statements may all be bullshit, but they will have some impact on the movement of the stock. The key question for us is...Can they release these statements before the stock opens? Christ, we don't care what the stock does tomorrow or next week. We care what it does today, especially the opening. I'll give you the number of Scott's office if you want to call. Otherwise, I'll keep you posted as soon as we do anything. Don't worry Jim. All that has happened up until now has been positive for us. The press creates tremendous movement on certain stocks by panhandling theories and quoting redundant analysts who are far removed from the firms they speak of. They are adding to the interest in Trexon. Count on it."

At 8:51, the stock opened at 51. Garett pulled his chair right next to Scott as they watched the screen blinking faster than either had ever seen it. At 8:58, the stock had reached 57. The phone rang. It was Jim Shane.

"Garett, CNBC said the stock has almost quadrupled. What is it at?"

"58% and climbing. "

"Should we sell it now! "

"Not yet. I told you, the instant it starts to fall. I've never seen anything like this, Jim. I'm a fucking nervous wreck, but the note was on the money. It's at 60. Stay on the line. I'm going to put a sell order in at 68. If it continues to rise after that, then we can bitch about it later. Four times our money would be more than I ever dreamed possible. I talked about it, but I never thought it would jump like this." Garett held the phone. "Stay on the line, I'll keep you posted. 61% at 9:04." Garett's hands were beginning to sweat. He was watching the volume on TREX and the numbers were staggering. "I'm putting you on the speaker."

Time exploded into an excruciating exercise of guessing right. The walls of the office began creeping ever so slightly toward the middle of the room. Garett asked Scott to temporarily eliminate the clock from the computer screen crowded with quotes of individual stocks and index levels. Prices were leveling off. No jumps for what seemed like an hour. Garett Baine stood up and began pacing the office. He would not lose voice contact with Jim Shane. Ten minutes would go by in silence. Neither man anxious to reveal how they felt. Both trembling to get out now with a substantial gain, yet not willing to bear years of second guessing if the stock continued to rise. Worse yet, would be a sudden jump moments after they sold. If they had just held out for a bit more time. Eventually, Garett knew the decision would be his. Scott James was continuing his commentary and updates on TREX, neither of which were requested or desired. Garett never wanted to have the responsibility of Jim's financial future in his hands. Ironic, coming from an ex-broker who presumably was handling just that for his clients. This client list included Jim Shane and his family. The note from Spencer was a gift and for whatever reason, Garett did feel the circumstances at the United Center ultimately produced the note. Garett knew Denise Shane paid the ultimate price from that evening. Anything from that evening had to be shared with Jim and his family. The pacing continued.

"What time is it?"

"Should I put the clock back on the screen?"

"Just tell me what the fucking time is. I don't want to stare at it. I just want to know what it is at this moment." Garett always wore a watch. Today, he did not.

"It's 9:45. You're pretty tense for a man with nearly a four hundred percent gain going."

"Jim, you still there?"

"What do you think, Garett?"

"Jimbo, I've got a feeling this is going to peak. No signs, yet. The stock is at 63. I know I told you that I wanted to wait until the stock dropped before we sold it. I've changed my mind."

"Do what your gut tells you, Garett. Don't second guess yourself."

"Let's sell it now!"

"Do it."

Scott James placed the order to sell now and abort the sell order at 68. The order for Garett's account was accepted at 65. Jim Shane's sell order was accepted at 65 _. The stock was still rising.

"We're out, Jim. Your shares sold at 65%. Your account total is $539,392.50 less fees. My account total is $420,550.00. We nearly quadrupled the investment Jim. Capital gains will take a chunk, but that is one check I'll enjoy writing. We fucking did it, pal. I might have jumped the gun a bit, but you won't find me complaining. The stock is at 67... and.. wait. It's at 66%. It dropped for the first time today."

"It's done? We're out? I don't believe this."

"Believe it, man." Garett was watching the screen. Scott James had placed his sell order. It got filled at 62. The stock was dropping. "Jim, the stock is falling. I think we got out at the peak or near it. The high was 67. Scott got filled at 62 and it continues to fall. Wherever it levels off is anyone's guess at this point. I'm going to hang out here for awhile just to see what happens. Relax today. Nobody took anything from us today. I'm going to go downtown to see Lindsay after the kids get home from school. I know she'd love to see you."

"Tell me what time you're going and I'll meet you at your house."

"Be at my house at 4:30. I want to get the kids situated at my next door neighbor's before I leave. I'll have Scott James put our funds in Money Market for the time being. This is not something that we should be yapping about to anyone. We'll tell Lindsay when we get down there, but be careful about who you talk to regarding this transaction. The less said about it the better."

"I'll see you at 4:30. Garett, I don't know what to say to you."

"You just did. I'm hanging up. See you at 4:30." Garett punched the speaker button and ran his hands up through his hair. "Scott, put these accounts in Money Market for now. Where is Schwab at?"

"4 3/4."

"Fine. Thanks for your help. I'm sorry if I was a bit tense. That's why I didn't make a good broker."

Garett had walked up to the Schwab office on this particular Monday morning. Scott James placed the funds in the Money Market accounts. He knew this would be a very temporary home, but insisted on print out sheets of both accounts and confirms of the trades. After thanking Scott for a second time and wondering who should be thanking who, Garett walked out of the Schwab office and adjusted his coat as the wind swept into his chest. Garett rarely wore a hat and at forty-two, still preferred his hair long. The rush of air was exhilarating. His hair blew straight back. His beard was speckled with gray now, an aspect of age he didn't mind. The attire of blue jeans and boots wrapped by a long black overcoat gave him the appearance of a mountain man. His stroll was slow and without any time restraints. He made more money in the last two hours than he did in the previous five years combined. The will in Montana and the subsequent acquisition of the property had been a shock. Their value hadn't touched him in any tangible manner because they were not yet in his possession. Lindsay's desire to sell the two properties would have to be addressed. None of that concerned him now. For the first time in his life, he could afford to think about the aspects of his life that mattered. His mind raced through the past few weeks. He passed through the general business district of Sheridan Shores. Recent renovation to a major portion of this business district had left the original character of this community intact. The ornate brick work on the village hall greeted visitors as they entered the village. The five story structure majestically overlooked the main intersection of Sheridan Shores. The Victorian hall was immaculately maintained. The brick facade was scrubbed every spring, The wrought iron railings framing the two stone staircases leading up to the main entrance were painted every summer. Cobblestone streets, one-hundred year old Oak trees, and small independent businesses where the owners knew the customers were cherished here. Garett walked past the snow covered gazebo in the park shadowed by a World War I Memorial. This park rolled along behind the post office. Two ball fields bordered the North end of the park. Garett always wondered why they were situated so close to the street. The backstops butted up against the sidewalk. The middle of the park held a spectacular configuration of slides and climbing apparatus. The equipment grew from the sand surrounded by jumbo railroad ties. Along the border of the railroad ties were toddler tractors and mini-trucks immobile in their space. Six large swings propelled little bodies into the limbs of the rumbling Oak trees guarding the park like centurions of tradition. All children should grow up in a town just like this one. Garett trudged around the bases on the baseball diamonds blanketed by winter. Norman Rockwell might have created this scene on a canvas in a different time or a different place.

The park brought him back to his unexpected ride of the past few weeks. He had spent the better part of the past ten years struggling to meet the monthly expenses. These expenses were growing steadily with the additions to his family. There was not a day nor an evening that he did not think about his income. The past two years had been the worst. His financial position was beginning to consume his entire life. The time spent with his family was becoming much too infrequent. He loathed his new vocation from the beginning. Garett despised getting up in the morning. Lindsay Baine watched her husband slide into this descending ride of frustration. The roller coaster crept back up the hill with the unexpected news from Montana. This roughshod ride took them to the United Center late in January. He looked at an empty park and saw images of Conner and Christopher digging on that simulated tractor in the sand. What would be the cost for this financial gain? The sun was disappearing from above. A rolling sheet of gray winter clouds slipped into their rightful place overhead. Norman Rockwell still couldn't slip out of town. Garett brushed the snow from the brass plaque.

           *   *   *

CHAPTER EIGHTEEN

Garett spent part of the afternoon taking Conner and Christopher to McDonald's. There was nearly a ten year span in Garett's life of absenteeism from the Golden Arches. The onslaught of children brought the reunion back together. Adolescent fascination with Big Macs and the ever expanding jumbo sized order of french fries generally evolves into a post teenage boycott of Ronald and company. After marriage the boycott usually continues. It is the children that will resurrect the cycle. The first born will always receive the vow of a healthy diet. Garett and Lindsay vowed to feed their children only the purest form of nutrition. They would have no soft drinks, no deep-fried food of any kind, and candy or cookies would be only a rare form of reward. This well meaning proclamation began to crumble about the time their first child was old enough to hold solid food. By that time, the daily parental goals change, tending to conform closer to threads of reality. French fries often become as dear to parents as the second floor nursery. The McDonald's near the Baine household contained a children's play area. Twentieth century technology filled this play area with a gargantuan white pipe and net configuration containing thousands of plastic balls situated to sustain little bodies hurling themselves off small platforms. After an hour of plastic ball jumping and some less than nutritional deep fried little brown things, Garett brought his two young sons to the same park in town he had walked through earlier. He parked the Chrysler Voyager mini-van amidst the empty spaces on this cold mid winter afternoon. Since Lindsay had been in the hospital and the RIC, his forays with the mini-van had become much more frequent. Garett Baine did not like driving this vehicle. The practical functions accomplished with the van had no bearing; it was a vehicle that he had no desire to be seen in. There were certain holdovers from his adolescent years and young adulthood that remained intact despite years of becoming his father. Garett's abhorrence with the station wagon of the sixties and its connotations evolved into a station wagon reincarnation called the mini-van. During the frustrations of the past few years, one thought has remained ironclad. This thought surfaced during the Randolf Baine tapes as they were played in Montana. This flash thought reoccurred as the TREX stock soared. Success could be defined as not losing sight of goals set years before. It could be defined as having your family together and healthy. It could also be defined as unloading the family mini-van to the first legible offer. Garett Baine spent over an hour chasing two boys in the snow. Cradling Conner and Christopher in his arms, snow began creeping into the gaps between their gloves and coat. Rosy cheeks were tucked under crooked hats. Garett cherished this day.

Jake had a basketball practice and Maggie came home with Kate's daughter on the bus. Garett told Kate that Jake would be getting a ride back to her house after practice with Jack Costner's mother. He kissed the little ones good-bye and headed back to his house to meet Jim Shane. It was nearly 4:30. They would be going to see Lindsay. The Montero was parked in front of the house.

"Do you know where TREX closed?"

"Actually, no. I decided to take the boys out. When the market closed, I was tossing Conner and Christopher down an ice covered slide at the park up town. By the way, it's nice to see you, too."

"The son of a bitch closed at 32%. How long did you watch after we sold?"

"I didn't. I tried, but something told me not to press the issue. We were out. What difference would it make it to us where the stock closed. At that moment, I had no desire to stay. Until you just asked me, I had not thought about it all day."

"What happened?"

"It reacted like an IPO. There was tremendous speculation on the announcement that Trexon would be approved to market an FDA sanctioned nicotine substitute. Owners of the stock before the announcement were the ones to potentially make the windfall. The scramble to purchase the stock after the announcement was already too late. An investor that relies on news service information to pick his flyers won't be in the market for long. Thousands of investors placed orders on the stock this morning. They knew it closed at 17 on Friday, but they had no idea of where they would get filled this morning. Many bought the stock in the sixties and watched it fall to, where did it close?"

"32%."

"Thank you. Watched it fall to 32%. Son of a bitch, we got out at the right time. Listen, did you talk to anyone about this deal?"

"No. Denise's mother is still staying with the kids. I haven't mentioned a thing about this to her or anyone else. Christ, they would have thought I was an idiot if I talked to them prior to this morning."

"Come on in. I've got to make a call and then we'll head downtown."

*   *   *

Rush hour traffic in Chicago has experienced a complete transformation over the past ten years. Years ago, the traffic entering the city in the morning would snarl shortly after sunrise. Those lucky enough to be driving out of the city would encounter no serious delays. In the afternoon, the order would be reversed. Traffic flowing out of the city would move at a crawl, while in-going traffic would flow freely. Today, rush hour in the morning or afternoon backed up in both directions. Garett and Jim left Sheridan Shores at 4:45 p.m. They would take Sheridan Road and Lake Shore Drive. It would take them one hour to reach the Rehabilitation Institute.

The elevator doors opened to reveal a sedate hallway devoid of the frantic activity associated with hospitals and nurses stations. The tile floors glistened with care. Two physical therapists were conversing at the main desk across from the elevators. One young lady looked up to greet the two guests approaching.

"Hello Garett. How are the troops? I told you, the next time you come down here, you better bring the kids. They're my little assistants."

"Hi, Gina. The kids were scattered about this afternoon so I'll be sure to bring them down later in the week. Hopefully, they won't have many more visits if Lindsay's progress stays on track. Is next week still looking good?"

"Everything is looking great. Your wife is remarkable. We might even bump that release date up a bit. She works so hard in therapy. I'll let Lindsay fill you in."

"Is she in her room?"

"Yes, we finished about an hour ago."

"Thanks Gina. This is Jim Shane."

"Nice to meet you. Lindsay has talked about you and your family quite a bit. I'm terribly sorry about your wife. She sounded like a terrific lady."

"She was. Thank you for saying that." The two men walked up the east wing of the floor. Lindsay's room was on the end. Garett pushed the door open slowly as he entered the room. Jim stood back in the hallway, waiting. After a couple of weeks, the room was cluttered with plants, flowers, posters from the kids, and numerous baskets of various arrangements. The blinds were semi-closed and Lindsay was sound asleep on her side. Garett stood motionless for a moment. Her hair was brushed back along the white pillow case. Both hands were cupped together under the pillow and the look on her face was serene. He had not seen that picture for much too long. She was as beautiful at this moment as he had ever seen her. He closed the door slowly and turned to Jim Shane.

"She's sound asleep. If you're not in a hurry, why don't we go down to the solarium on this floor and wait until she wakes up. The therapy probably knocked her out. Let's let her take a nap. I'll wake her up in an hour."

They walked back up the east wing stopping at the main desk. Garett explained to Gina that Lindsay was sleeping and they would be in the solarium if she woke up in the next hour. Each floor at the RIC had a special solarium built for the patients. The abundance of sunlight and the accessibility of the space provided every patient a place outside of their room for visiting with friends and family. Upon entering this room, one of the striking characteristics that stood out was the seemingly sparse furniture within the room. The unusually wide spaces between each separate cluster of chairs and couches was to accommodate the variety of wheelchairs and bed frames that are moved in and out of this room on any given day. Garett walked over to the windows overlooking Lake Michigan and Navy Pier. The nation's largest Ferris wheel was dormant. Even from this vantage point, Garett could see the snow covered seats frozen in the wind. The dinner cruise ships and sight seeing vessels were missing from the docks. Lake Point Towers stood as a misplaced beacon of timeless architecture. Looking south along the Drive, Grant Park appeared as a manicured garden in the snow. With his eyes fixed on this magnificent view, Garett spoke to his friend.

"Is it possible to miss a place you have grown to despise? I remember coming down here as a kid. My dad would take us to Soldier Field. I remember going to the history museum or the Shedd Aquarium when I was in grade school. The city used to scare me. It was so big and I was so afraid of getting lost. I thought of it as a great big animal. It was exciting to view in it's movements and lines. But if it got of hold of you, this animal would eat you alive. I'm forty-two and the city scares me again. Leaving this area might have been hard a couple of years ago. Today, this decision has almost been made for us. It has taken enough from me. It's time to leave."

"Montana?"

"Definitely. My grandfather left me property that literally is an extension of the Canadian Rockies. I'll own a tavern and restaurant overlooking a lake the size of Rhode Island. The house he left us could sit on any postcard promoting the Pacific Northwest. It's small town all the way. Lakeside, Montana has one flashing yellow light to mark the town. It sits twenty miles south of Kalispell, the largest city in the county. The population of the entire county is less than Evanston. My kids can grow up without having the Black Gangster Disciples or the Latin Disciples creep into their high schools."

"What about Lindsay?"

"Lindsay doesn't want to move. She wanted to sell the property when I told her. This was before the shooting and before the transaction with Trexon. Our financial position was potentially disastrous. Her outlook may change after she learns how much money we made on the TREX deal. She might want to strangle me for risking the money, but the results will ease the pain. None of this matters at the moment. I want her home and well. I will not broach the subject of moving until our first priority is accomplished. The money is there. The property is there. They will wait. We just want Lindsay home. I wish it was different for you and the kids."

"Jasmine asked me last night if Mommy was mad at her. I said, God, no. Why would you ask that? She wanted to know if that is why she went away. Justin cries for hours and Brian barely speaks anymore. It isn't getting any easier. They miss her more than I could have possibly imagined. I am there for them. Trouble is, I am not her. I can't spend enough time with them at night because I have to leave the room so often. I don't want them to see me cry."

"I'm so sorry Jimmy. I'm dumping my problems on you about whether or not we should move to Montana. My kids are lucky. Their time with Lindsay has only been interrupted and changed physically. I hate what this place has done to your family. Hell, I hate what it's done to mine."

"I'm sorry, Garett. Maybe coming down here was a mistake. We should be happier today. Shit, we almost made a million dollars between us. This is a time for you and Lindsay. You know what I thought about after I found out the Trexon stock quadrupled in value? I thought about how mad Denise would have been if she knew that I took that risk. I didn't care that I made over four hundred thousand dollars in one day. I didn't want Denise mad at me. I should go, man. Talk to Lindsay. I'm sure she'll warm up to the idea of moving."

"You're not going anywhere right now, Jim Shane!" A voice came from a silhouette seated in the hallway. Both men turned abruptly and watched Lindsay wheel herself into the room. She stopped ten feet into the room.

"How long have you been sitting there?" Garett asked unable to shake the whiter shade of pale from his face.

"Long enough." Lindsay retorted as she slowly moved her wheelchair toward the window while eyeballing her husband. He was dumbfounded and fumbling now for a way to retreat from the conversation regarding Montana..

"Lindsay, I don't care about Montana. I don't know how much you heard, but you are the only thing important to me right now. Our goal is to get you home. All of us need you there. We don't have to move. I was just rambling." Garett was stuttering. Jim sat quietly. He rose and reached for his coat. When he spoke, his voice was slow, his eyes jumped around the room looking for a way out.

"I'll leave you two alone. I know there are some things to be discussed that don't concern me. Garett, I'll grab a cab to the train station. The Northwestern will drop me near your house, right? From there, I'll pick up my car." Jim was putting on his coat.

"You're wrong, Jim," Lindsay spoke up before Garett had a chance. "Sit down, please." Her eyes pierced his. "Please."

Jim Shane sat down. He followed Lindsay as she wheeled herself next to Garett. She turned the chair around as it was positioned next to her husband. She was now seated beside him. Lindsay reached up and took Garett's hand. Jim Shane hadn't seen Lindsay since the shooting. He fumbled for words. They were both nervous.

"I missed you Lindsay." Jim stopped. Looking at Lindsay brought back Denise. Lindsay's grip tightened on Garett's hand. It seemed unusually tight. Lindsay's other hand bore into the handle on the left side of her wheelchair. Both men stumbled for their words. The brief silence was uncomfortable. Garett stepped in to break the tension.

"Lindsay..." His words were abruptly cut off.

"Shhhhhh..." Lindsay looked up and softly instructed her husband to wait. Her right hand began to pull for support. In an instant, the bottom plates were kicked out from the wheelchair and Lindsay stood up while pushing the chair back out of her reach. Her left hand released from the chair and grabbed onto Garett's arm. She was standing tall on her own. Her eyes stood bright and proud. Garett, again, fumbled for words.

"Lindsay, when..." He was cut off once more.

"I said, shhhh..." Lindsay put her finger to her lips requesting quiet. A smile crept around the edge of her mouth while a deep breath drained what was left of the air in the room. She turned her head to look at Jim. Her voice was barely audible.

"I couldn't hear you Lindsay. What did you say?" Jim asked, leaning to catch the words.

"I asked you to come closer." Lindsay's voice was becoming stronger. Jim took a few steps towards Lindsay.

"Closer." She turned and touched her lips again knowing Garett was about to burst. Jim Shane was standing inches from Lindsay. She looked into his eyes and took the first steps her husband had witnessed since the shooting. She released one hand from Garett's arm and reached out to

141

grasp Jim's hand. There would be no mistaking these words. "Come with us."

"Come with you?"

"You heard me. You and the kids come with us to Montana." Lindsay replied and waited for a response. Garett couldn't speak. Jim Shane looked at Garett but didn't hesitate.

"Love to." It was done.

Lindsay took her arms and threw them around Garett. She whispered in his ear. She wanted him to hold her. The questions would be answered in a moment. For now, they would freeze this frame. Lindsay buried her head in the shoulder she claimed fourteen years ago. They were both crying. Garett couldn't wait.

"When?...How?...Why didn't you call me? How long have you been able to stand? What happened?"

"Garett, this just happened today. I knew something was different last night. I wasn't sure what, but there were definite sensations in my legs. It was late and I finally fell asleep. You were gone in the morning, so I called Dr. Reuben. Both of my therapists were at a conference for the weekend and hadn't returned yet. Dr. Reuben was kind enough to come by. Well, I think I'll let him describe this."

Dr. Loren Reuben walked through the doorway, taking Garett back to the emergency room of last January. The athletic look was still there but a broad smile had replaced the grim tasks of that previous meeting.

"Garett, It's good to see you. This is one of the more pleasant trips to the RIC I have had to make in quite some time." The two men shook hands.

"Doctor, do you remember Jim Shane?"

"Of course, I do. I don't remember if I had a chance to tell you how sorry I was for your loss. That was a very sad night for us in the emergency room."

"Thank you doctor. I know you did everything you could."

"Let me start with some background. I know you are both bursting with questions. Garett, do you remember the sequence of events on the night of the shooting? Specifically, I am talking about the steps taken after Lindsay was brought to the emergency room."

"I remember most of what occurred but I couldn't walk you through the medical steps taken, if that is what you're referring to." Garett's arm was wrapped firmly around the shoulder of his wife. "Lindsay, do you want to sit down?"

"Garett, that is the last thing I want to do." Lindsay turned her attention back to Dr. Reuben. He continued.

"Garett, when Lindsay called me this morning, she had already been able to move her legs. It seems as though the feeling in her legs began to

142

return last night and almost completed the journey overnight. If you remember the night of the shooting and the next day, I talked to you about the trauma done to Lindsay's spine. We had determined that the spine had not been severed. This determination made it possible for us to allow for some hope. Lindsay's injuries had rendered her a paraplegic. The location of the wound had not impaired her upper body movement. When Lindsay was brought into the emergency room, we immediately injected her with massive doses of Methylprednisolone. This is a steroid given intravenously to minimize the swelling around the spinal cord. This steroid was administered for a couple of days. The side effects would be harmful if the drug was continued at those levels for any extended period of time. The purpose of using this drug was to impede swelling of the spinal column. Lindsay's injuries were the equivalent of a concussion to the spine. In other words, the nerves were bruised. The nerve cells are located in the spine. The nerve axons carry the orders to the muscles from the nerve cells. These axons were not damaged. The axon sheaths carry messages from the spinal nerve center to all parts of the body. If these are not damaged and the cord is not severed, full recovery is a possibility. This case presented two possibilities in my opinion. First, since the damage done to the nerves did not result in any severing of the spinal column, there was the possibility of a quick recovery. In most of these cases where movement returns, the results are evident in a matter of days. If the nerve is damaged extensively, they will grow back or repair themselves over an extended period of time. This brings us to the second scenario possible. If Lindsay would regain the movement in her legs, the time frame could be very long. The damage to the nerves can be superficial and sensation can return in a matter of days. If the nerves are damaged more severely, the recovery time is usually very long. The phone call I received was a surprise. We felt the steroids had kept the swelling down initially. The surgery done to repair the damage to the spine itself was successful. All of the pieces were in place to see the return of movement in a short period of time. When this did not happen, the possibility of regaining movement still remained but the time frame would be greatly increased. Nerves damaged beyond an initial shock normally repair themselves very slowly. In other words, we have seen spinal cord injuries act as superficial damage and recover in a matter of hours or days. We have seen spinal cords patients regain movement over an extended period of time. This could be many months or years. We have not seen a patient recover in five or six weeks. At least we had not seen that time frame until today. There is one constant in medicine. Things never stay the same. Your wife will be fine. We completed an extensive examination before you arrived. I've got to get back to Cook County.

143

Lindsay can go home tomorrow. We'll get together with the therapists before you leave." Dr. Reuben leaned over and kissed Lindsay on the cheek. "You're a lucky lady."

Dr. Loren Reuben walked out of the solarium. The triangle of emotion bantering about the room was exhilarating in its scope. Garett and Jim had come downtown to visit Lindsay with news of an extremely profitable day in the market. Lindsay's remarkable recovery had tabled everything else. Garett was continuing to stumble with the excitement. Nothing he had done since the shooting had any fulfilling meaning because of Lindsay's condition. Everything in his life had taken the back stage to the act of recovery. The windfall with Trexon was not complete. The recovery of their financial freedom was not complete. Until now. Garett had to sit down.

"Talk about having a good day!" Garett ran his hands through his hair with a smile that was creeping into his eyes and his cheeks. "We came down to tell you about a transaction on the market that proved rather profitable. The minute you stood up, I forgot what I was doing here. The kids are going to go berserk. When did you change your mind about moving to Montana?"

"Just now. The girls at the desk told me that you and Jim had come down. I was up most of the night because I knew something was happening to me. When the feeling came back to my legs, I kept standing in my room. I was determined to practice until you got here today. This was going to be the best surprise of your life."

"It was."

"Well, I didn't envision myself falling asleep. When I woke up, I went to look for Gina at the floor therapist's station. That's when they told me where you guys were. I was about to come in. Something stopped me. I sat outside this room and listened for some time. I agree with you, Garett. I had been so afraid to leave what we had become accustomed to. I didn't realize that what we had become accustomed to was a comfortable notion of complacency. I constantly associated the aversion to any change with our own security. We have been living where I felt, we were supposed to live. This was the American Dream. Well, my American Dream has changed. I thought about Denise and your family, Jim. We are not privy to the split seconds that will change our lives. They go off like the flash from a camera. Afterwards, we have to look at where we are standing in that picture. This is not where I want to be. I thought about the tapes you heard from your Grandfather, Garett. He told you that there was one regret he had in his life, and that was not taking your Grandmother to live in Montana. This was from a man that regretted nothing. Why should we make the same mistake? Our kids are being taught to cement their rear end to a chair while watching a computer for their education, their social interaction and their recreation. They are told not to go outside alone. We hold training sessions to show them what to do when they are approached or attacked walking to school. I don't know what the right answer is, but this isn't it. I listened from the hallway and realized that this city was scaring me, too. It isn't simply an isolated incident anymore, it's a way of life. It's here and it will not be changing soon. When I first heard about the property in Montana and your ideas of moving there, I was dead set against it. My God, there are no Nordstroms in Montana. The schools must be backward and what the hell would I do in Montana, for God's sake? This shooting has changed all of us forever. I want to leave. I don't care if I ever see a Nordstroms or a Crate & Barrell again. I hope the schools are backward and teach old-fashioned reading with fundamentals. The North Shore can keep their whole language crap. I hope we can kiss our kids good-bye in the morning and not worry about never seeing them again. Jimmy, I'm sorry I couldn't go to Denise's funeral. I can't take her place, but I'd love to help with the kids. She wouldn't mind. I'm sure of that."

"I know she wouldn't mind a bit." Jim answered, happy to be talking about Denise. He wanted the four of them to make this decision. "It seems as though this is the week for acting on impulse. We are not working well as a family. Every room in our house screams of Denise. She is there. We all feel it but nobody talks about it. I don't know what I'm going to do in Montana. Hell, I'll work as a carpenter if I have to. Those were the happiest days of my working life. I built houses in Texas, New Mexico, Arizona, and Colorado. Before Denise died, I was questioning the business I had created. My turnaround time on any sale was over a year. I worked on many projects for a year or more that fell through. I know exactly what Garett was going through in sales. Our personalities are similar. Kissing up is not an occupation I aspired to. When the dollars are good, you lose perspective on the things in your life that count. When the dollars aren't there, you look for any reason imaginable to justify the losses. The economy is down, therefore my business is suffering. The President's economic policies have made industries reluctant to purchase any capital equipment It's crap. I lost two deals this year that have taken two years to cultivate and thousands of dollars to romance. I accept your invitation to Montana. Garett, I'll tend bar for you if you want. That prospect sounds like heaven. Because of you, we have the funds to make this all work. Lindsay, the sight of you walking brought the first smile to my face in a very long time. Your invitation brought the second."

"Tend bar, my ass." Garett chimed in. "You and I will be partners in this place. Shit, it's too big for me to run alone."

145

"Wait a minute, boys. Aren't we forgetting something?" Lindsay announced, a mischievous smile wrapped in those high cheekbones. "There's the small matter of some money made that I am somewhat curious about. Garett, would you like to tell me what is going on?"

"Hell, I forgot about that! It would be my pleasure to tell you about a small transaction Jim and I completed this morning. Do you remember when I bought that stock from Trexon, Inc. I believe it was over a year ago. This was the stock from the company that Spencer Dryden had acquired such a large stake. The company was run by one of Spencer's college roommates. Trexon is a small tobacco company that had been working on a nicotine substitute. Spencer became one of the majority stock holders when the firm went public. His client base purchased large blocks of the stock based on Spencer's advice. This company would develop a nicotine substitute and receive FDA approval to market the product. This had not been accomplished by any firm. The stock has done very little since going public. Spencer's position never changed. As the stock wallowed in mediocrity, Spencer continued to strengthen his position. Many of the original investors sold after a year or two. We bought one hundred shares. The office kept talking about it every day so I finally bought some. It never really moved from the purchase price. It was not a stock the I had been advising clients to purchase. That alone, should have been a clue to buy it. Anyway, I bought the one hundred shares and left them alone."

"Lindsay, do you remember seeing Spencer and his wife at half-time on the night of the shooting?"

"Vaguely."

"The first day back to the office after the shooting, I was going through some get well cards when I read a card sent to me from Spencer. It was a strange note from start to finish. He talked about controlling your own life and seemed to ramble on about knowing the difference between actions and reactions. The last part of his note talked about his desire to tell one of his client's that he couldn't attend a Bull's game. This was a game he had already committed to attending with this client. I thought, why would he want to talk to me, of all people, about going to a Bull's game? I'll show you the note when you get home. I kept thinking about the note. Something was wrong. Spencer Dryden would not waste his time telling me about this. He would not be so insensitive and insulting as to discuss attending a Bull's game after what had happened to us. After reading the note again and again, I realized what he was doing. Without breaking the law by releasing inside information, he was trying to tell me that Trexon had received or was about to receive FDA approval. He gave me indirect dates and instructions as when to buy and when to sell the

146

stock. Jim and I followed the instructions. Last week we bought a substantial amount of Trexon at seventeen dollars per share. This morning we sold all shares. The shares sold for nearly sixty-five dollars per. We quadrupled our money."

"How much did we make?" Lindsay finally sat down.

"Over three hundred thousand dollars." Garett's response hung in the air.

"Three hundred thousand dollars?" Lindsay was struck. "How much did we buy to start with?"

"I cashed in all of our accounts at Dean Witter and put the whole thing in Trexon. I knew this could have upset you, so I waited until the transaction was complete before telling you. We now have nearly a half million dollars in money market!" Garett braced for something to come hurtling through the air.

"Garett, darling. What if this deal had fallen through?" Lindsay asked, knowing the answer would be good for a few laughs.

"It didn't!" Garett smiled, leaned over and kissed his wife. "The money is safe. Let's talk about your coming home. I can't wait to get home and tell the kids. They'll flip."

"Don't tell them about me walking. Let's make it a surprise. Tell them I'm coming home and that we both have a surprise for them."

They all sat in the solarium for a couple of hours, talking about Montana and watching Lindsay pace the room. She was wobbly and visibly tired from using muscles that have been inactive for so many weeks. But she was happy. There would be some closure from this experience. She could take control of her family again. So many nights were spent envisioning the burden her presence would create. Love and obligation would have kept them silent. Lindsay had learned that the majority of spinal cord injured patients experience a tremendous level of guilt following the trauma of the injury itself. Not only have their lives been altered dramatically, the lives of their loved ones have been equally disrupted. The burden of their disability on family members can be as devastating as the injury. Sometimes, much more devastating. The staff began to remind the trio of the time. The visitors would have to leave soon, but the reminders fell on deaf ears. It was almost nine o'clock. The hallways were quiet. Lindsay sat on Garett's lap, one hand kept fiddling with the hair resting on Garett's shoulders. Her other hand rested on her right thigh. The sensation of feeling her own leg was exquisite. The city generated a symphony of lights darting from the lakefront boundaries of Lake Shore Drive and flickering through the glass structure surrounding them. The stars grabbed the activity of Michigan Avenue and sent meteors of light across the room. The high sky over the lake stretched into a sea of tiny mirrors and splattered the night like an elegant dance floor.

"Remember when we were kids?" Garett got up and walked to the edge of the room. His back was facing Lindsay and Jim. His body cut a silhouette against the night sky. His hands tucked into the front pockets of his jeans. He turned back slowly to face the others. "I remember when I was a kid. I always wanted to change places with the man in the Marlboro commercials. Funny, it had nothing to do with cigarettes. You saw that guy everywhere. Magazines, television, billboards. I begged my dad to buy me that suede vest. Actually, I think it was lambskin. He kept telling me that I was old enough to get over the cowboy thing. One day, that vest was lying on my bed. I think I was eight or nine. It didn't fit after a year or two. I still wouldn't mind being a cowboy when I grow up."

Another reminder about the time, as the floor supervisor suggested that the time to go had arrived. They all agreed.

*　　　　　*　　　　　*

CHAPTER NINETEEN

Preparations for a welcome home party would have to be abbreviated. Garett made it home just after ten. Kate had brought the little ones back to the house and put them to bed. Jake and Maggie waited up for Garett with Kate. Garett pulled the Blazer into the driveway. The light from the television illuminated the family room. The children rushed to greet their father as he entered the room. Garett grabbed his daughter as she jumped into his arms. Maggie buried her head into his shoulder and wrapped her legs around him. Jake quietly put his arms around Garett. Maggie's greetings had always been extremely demonstrative. Often, she would choreograph her steps well in advance. If the desired effect was not garnered, the steps were repeated. Jake would wait until the scene had played its course. Maggie worked at grabbing attention in a world of brothers and males. This had become even more pronounced since Lindsay was absent.

"Kate, thanks for all your help tonight. Are the little ones asleep?" Garett asked.

"Sound asleep, Garett. How's Lindsay?"

"Yeah, Dad. Did you find out when Mom is coming home?" Maggie chimed in.

"As a matter of fact, I've got some good news. Mom is coming home tomorrow."

"Yes!" Jake closed his eyes and made a fist. Garett watched his son and couldn't have put it any better.

"I've got to pick her up at noon. The doctors seem to feel she is doing great and the time has come to send her home. Of course, we'll have to prepare the sun room as our bedroom. She won't be going up and down the stairs for awhile. I'll move the dining room furniture over to one side of the room. That way, she'll have a clear space to move the wheelchair throughout the first floor."

"Garett, don't worry about the sun room. I'll set the whole thing up. By the time you get home from the hospital, the room will be done. She'll be grateful that you didn't try to arrange the sheets and the bed." Kate got up and wandered into the living room to survey the room that would have become Lindsay's home for the next few months. Garett and the kids followed. The sun room off the living room was the coldest room in the house because the floor was not insulated. Garett had insulated the floor one year, but the combination of squirrels and raccoons had found their way underneath the room and ripped up every shred of insulation. Still, it was the one room that Lindsay loved to sit in. The room was bathed in windows, wrapping the small area with the shade of the giant Oak trees hovering high above the roofline. A black baker's rack held a white desk phone and albums of family photos. Hanging plants grew in happiness soaking in an abundance of sunlight. Against the east wall sat a white sofa bed that somehow had survived the onslaught of four children. One of the first things taught in the Baine household was that the sun room was off limits to children. Garett wondered about Lindsay's sudden desire to move. How would that change when she returned to this home? This was the only home their children knew.

"Garett, I'll have Jack come over when Lindsay gets home and he can help you bring down any dressers that have to be moved."

"Thanks, Kate. We'll wait until Lindsay gets home. I'm sure she'll have her own ideas of what needs to come down."

"Dad, are you guys going to stay down here?" Jake asked.

"Yes." Garett lied.

"Can I stay on the floor here for a couple of nights when Mom gets home?" Jake continued.

"Me too?" Maggie added.

"Honestly, guys. I don't think your mother would let you sleep anywhere else." Garett sat back in the sofa bed joined by the kids. "Kate, I can't thank you enough for everything you've done."

"See you guys tomorrow. I'll get Christopher and Conner from pre-school. We'll be waiting for you when you get home."

Garett walked upstairs with Maggie and Jake. They spent some time on the floor of Jake's room. Bedtime meant prayers. This night brought some excitement and cautious anticipation regarding the homecoming of the next day. Lindsay had always helped them with their prayers before bed. Tonight, Jake asked Garett to fill that role. Garett knelt next to his oldest son as he climbed into the bottom level of his bunk bed. He fumbled for some words but discovered his son knew the way.

"God bless Mom, who finally is coming home." Jake started. "God bless the doctors who helped her get better. God bless Maggie, Conner and Christopher. God bless you, Dad. Mom would have been proud. I know this hasn't been easy for you. I'm just glad you're my Dad. Amen."

Garett kissed his son goodnight. He knew the next day would bring a special surprise for this young man. He closed the door to his room and his eyes watered. This young man was eleven years old and continued to teach him the humility and innocence that he never possessed. His selfish image of an aggressive athlete dominating the children around him had melted into a sensitive young person proving to his father that character had everything to do with pride and accomplishments. He watched his son curl up in the blankets on his bed and drift into a peaceful state of anticipation. The next day would bring his mother back. Garett thought about how proud she would be of this boy. He could never love anyone more.

Maggie had fallen asleep in the short period of time Garett spent with Jake. Garett pulled the covers up around her shoulders and kissed her cheek. He missed the little joys of parenthood like kissing his children when they were asleep. Garett could sit for hours and watch them sleep, divorced from the pressures clouding his days. He sat next to Maggie on the floor leaning up against the white rattan dresser. The immaculately dressed Molly dolls perched in school desks watched with him. As usual, Maggie's outfit for the next day was precisely placed on the floor next to her bed. The corduroy pants were laid flat with the red turtleneck strategically placed above the pants. The black tie shoes rested at the end of the cords. Maggie wanted to look good for Lindsay. Special care was taken for this outfit. Garett kissed his daughter again before he closed the door and made his way downstairs.

Garett hit the message button on the answering machine. There were two messages. The first message was from Matt Hipple at Dean Witter. He wanted to know if Garett had heard about Trexon. The time was 4:10. The second message was from Joe Cortez at the 12th District Tac Unit. The time was 4:22 p.m. Garett would call Matt when he could. He dialed the number Joe left him. It was a pager number. Garett entered his home number.

*   *   *

CHAPTER TWENTY

Tuesday, February 20 logged in just shy of four weeks from the shooting. The kaleidoscope of activity at the Baine household was a stoic tribute to Kate Doleman. Garett had left in the morning to pick up Lindsay from the RIC. The short notice on her return home made any plans for an elaborate celebration virtually impossible. However, this presented a challenge for Kate. Her best friend and next door neighbor was coming home from almost four weeks of confinement in a hospital or rehabilitation center. She was given a few hours notice. At dawn, Kate began calling neighbors, waking them and explaining the circumstances. Requests were made to forgo work or previous commitments to help welcome Lindsay home. Kate did not expect many to accommodate this request based solely on the lack of notice.

By eleven o'clock in the morning, there were sixty people at the Baine household to welcome Lindsay home. This was the first time since the shooting that the kids felt any type of celebration. Jake and Maggie were busy putting the finishing touches on the banner that had been in production for some time. Completion had to be pushed up. Conner and Christopher were bouncing off the walls. They went from one center of attention to another. The kitchen boasted a myriad of luncheon dishes brought from everyone in the neighborhood. The sun room had been transformed into a first floor bedroom suite. Jane Sheehan, a neighbor who lived four houses south on Birch was the linen buyer for a prominent Midwest department store chain, Lord and Taylor. She brought over treatments for the bed and windows that would take Lindsay's breath away. Jack Doleman led a group of men moving the upstairs dressers down to the sun room. Conner and Christopher continued their playful meandering, all the while keeping a watchful eye from the family room for the Blazer.

The drive from downtown went very quickly. There was very little traffic at noontime on the expressways. The RIC made things very easy for the patients to check-out. Dr. Reuben had made a special trip to wish Lindsay and Garett well. Lindsay felt even stronger after a remarkable nights sleep. She was deathly afraid that she would not be able to fall asleep at all. On the contrary, after Garett and Jim left, Lindsay fell sound asleep for nearly nine hours. Garett turned onto the Willow Road exit ramp and headed into Sheridan Shores. They were less than a mile from home.

"I see them!" Christopher shouted as he raced for the garage door. Kate went to slow him down, but gave that up in a hurry. Conner followed, as did the others. By the time Garett pulled up to the front of his house, it seemed like the whole neighborhood had amassed. Lindsay put both hands up to her cheeks. She was thrilled. All of their friends stayed a respectful distance back behind the black iron fence surrounding the house. Jack and Kate Doleman stood by the front gate and waited. There were four jumping children wrestling together to open the handle where Lindsay sat. She looked at Garett a moment before the door would open. She said nothing. Her eyes sparkled and one eyebrow popped up.

"It was Kate, I swear."

The door to the passenger side flew open and Lindsay was mobbed by her children. Conner and Christopher had hopped into her lap with Jake and Maggie adding to the reunion in the front seat. Garett jumped out of the driver's seat. As he ran around to the other side of the vehicle he held up one index finger to his neighbors poised behind the fence. They all assumed he wanted a moment for the family together.

"O.K. Guys, give Mom some air." Garett spoke with little conviction, preferring to observe. He eventually had to start peeling the children away from his wife. Jack Doleman came over and asked if Garett needed any help with the wheelchair.

"No, Jack. Thanks anyway. We can manage." Garett responded, patting Jack on the shoulder and motioning the kids to wait by the sidewalk. "Come on sweetheart, Let's give the crowd what they all paid to see."

Lindsay pushed the Blazer door as wide open as it could go. Garett backed up slowly giving everyone a clear view of the car. The kids didn't know what to think. For a brief moment, everyone looked confused. Those thoughts ended abruptly. Lindsay swung both legs around while dropping one foot to the ground. Her right arm grabbed the door as she stood up and left the vehicle. Garett held his left hand out . Lindsay put her hand in his and they walked toward the fence. Kate couldn't hold anything back. She burst into tears of joy as she ran to embrace her friend. The kids froze dumbfounded for a second.

"Mom's walking!" Jake announced. "Mom, you're walking!"

The kids just realized what had happened. All of the guests spilled out of the yard and formed a spontaneous receiving line next to the Baine family. Conner and Christopher slithered back into the house and began

153

raiding the desserts spread out on the kitchen counter. Maggie stood riveted next to her mother with both arms wrapped around her waist. Jake occupied the other side while Lindsay held court with the neighborhood. Garett backed away for the moment. Jack and Garett leaned against the Blazer.

"Congratulations, Garett. You guys know how to shock the hell out of everyone."

"This just happened yesterday. We wanted to surprise the kids. I had no idea that Kate would mobilize half the town, although I should have guessed."

"Are you and Lindsay moving?" Jack asked, catching Garett off guard with the direct nature of the question.

"We've discussed it." Garett replied. "Up until yesterday, that had not been the priority."

"And now?"

"Jack, after this homecoming, any talk of moving might be tabled."

"Have you talked to the kids?"

"About moving?"

"Yes."

"No, we haven't. Look at Lindsay, Jack. Does that look like a woman that will be moving anywhere?" Garett responded, somewhat annoyed at the persistence of the inquiry. The chill in the air had not diminished the excitement in the crowd at the Birch Street residence. Kate finally convinced everyone to move inside and start working on the buffet. Once inside, the guest filled their plates and searched for a seat in the family room. Lindsay had been led to the fireplace by Jake and Maggie. There, the three of them curled into a maze of pillows surrounded by some very special people. A detailed recounting of the last couple of days began. Everyone in the room expected to watch nervously as Lindsay arrived home. They knew she would have to be helped into a wheelchair upon her arrival. Now, everyone had questions. Lindsay Baine answered every question and savored each query. Hours passed.

The afternoon melted into the evening. Most of their neighbors left just before six o'clock. Jack and Kate ordered some pizzas for the kids. They continued to talk until eight o'clock. After the Doleman's left, Garett began to straighten up the family room. Lindsay smiled and told him that it was her turn to put the kids to bed.

"I thought you'd never ask?" Garett answered, knowing this night had been a long time coming.

Lindsay took the kids upstairs at ten after eight. Garett finished cleaning up and did the dishes. He grabbed a Genuine and planted himself on the couch. Just before he could grab the remote, the phone rang.

"Hello."

"Garett Baine?"

"Speaking."

"Garett, this Joe Cortez. We seem to have been playing telephone tag the last day or two. I'm glad I caught you in."

"Joe, I'm sorry I missed you. This was the day I brought my wife home from the Rehabilitation Center."

"That's great Garett. How's she doing?"

"She's walking. Two days ago, she regained the feeling in her legs. The doctors don't really have an explanation for it. They told us all along that this may or may not occur. To tell you the truth, I don't care whether anyone can explain it. She's home, she's walking again, and the prognosis is back to normal. The doctors seem to confirm that the injury was like a blunt trauma to the spine or a severe bruise. There was no severing at the spinal cord. The bruise apparently healed. What's going on? I assume this is not a social call?"

"The last time I spoke to you, I explained how this investigation would most likely proceed. The conclusion of the case would leave Griffin and White's murders unsolved, but the Department would wash it's hands of the Stadium shooting. The shooters had been discovered and turned up dead. The gang conflicts causing the deaths were insignificant to the closure of the Stadium shooting. None of this has changed. I simply wanted to call you and confirm exactly what I suspected would happen. They have shut this down as an active case. Everyone working on this case has been re-assigned including myself. This has not been a full time assignment since the week after the shooting. Now, it is closed. The one thing I can pass on to you is a long shot. You and Mr. Shane may want to call my Captain. His name is Kevin Kontel. While investigating the two deceased individuals, we discovered the garage they used on Lake Street. It seems as though this location had been used as a residence for them as well. My partner and I found twenty-two thousand dollars in cash buried inside the drywall in one of the non-bearing walls. We always look for cuts in the walls that are too clean. Under a new program for victim's rights, you and your friend can put a claim in for all or part of this money. I'm not well versed in all of the details, but Captain Kontel can give them to you. You can reach him at the main number on my card. I know it's a long process, but it could be worth something."

"Thanks, Joe. I'll talk to Jim. Was this drug money?"

"Honestly, this is a bit unusual. These guys normally wouldn't have this much money anywhere near them. It could be that they were unaware of the money. Someone else could have been using the location without their knowledge. This would be the more likely scenario. Griffin and

155

White were four and five time losers looking to exist from day to day. Doesn't matter now. The money got filed under this case. Put your claim in. Good luck, Garett. Let me know if I can help you in any way."

"Thanks again, Joe. You have been a tremendous help already. Good-bye."

"Good-bye, Garett."

Lindsay made her way back downstairs after nine. Garett knew there would be some special prayers with the kids. She stayed with Conner and Christopher and watched them fall asleep. Considering the day they had, this took no more than ten minutes. They were so happy to have Lindsay home, but they couldn't keep their eyes open. Lindsay then spent time with Jake and Maggie in the master bedroom. They collected some blankets and pillows from their respective rooms. They were camped at the foot of Garett and Lindsay's bed. It would be almost a week before they wanted to sleep in their own rooms.

"We have some company in our room tonight." Lindsay remarked as she entered the family room.

"No surprise there. They wanted to sleep next to you. I told them you wouldn't have it any other way." Garett replied while he got up and helped Lindsay maneuver between the magazine rack, the assorted toys, and the coffee table. Successfully encamped on the couch, Lindsay threw her head back against the cushions and closed her eyes briefly.

"What are you thinking about?" asked Garett while staring at his wife.

"I'm thinking about how this day couldn't have been more perfect if I had written a script for it." Lindsay answered, her eyes open wide now.

"I was watching you today with all of our friends and neighbors. I know how important this community has been to you. I imagine you are going to be having second thoughts about moving. I don't blame you. It's hard to spend fifteen years in one place without developing some very strong roots."

"That's what I love about men. They have no idea of what women think. While you were developing this post Rehab center diagnosis of my mindset, I was talking to Wendy Tass. You remember Wendy, don't you? She and her family live around the corner on Cherry. She has been with Century 21 for fifteen years. I told her to call me tomorrow. I needed to meet with her. I didn't get into the details with her, but my mind has not changed at all. Our friends are terrific and I will miss each and every one of them. But they are not my family. I never want to be separated from any of you again. We are moving."

"I just thought..."

"Stop thinking. I love you more than I ever imagined. My God, I thank you for holding this family together during the last four weeks. If it wasn't for you, I don't know where the kids would have been or where I would have been. You are the reason I am walking today. Make no mistake about anything. You are the explanation."

"I don't have many words to tell you how I feel. I knew you were the strongest one in this family and God was going to find out one way or another. Thank you for coming home. I love you very much." Garett whispered and leaned over to kiss Lindsay.

"I didn't have a chance to tell you about my last conversation with Dr. Reuben." Lindsay announced right before Garett kissed her.

"Is this something we need to discuss right now." Garett continued kissing her.

"I asked him how long I would have to wait before we made love." She spoke through the kiss. Garett stopped and pulled back a bit.

"How long did he say we would have to wait?" Garett asked.

"He suggested that we wait until we got home." Lindsay whispered back in his ear. She then sat back on the couch and unbuttoned the four buttons on her vest. The vest slid from her shoulders. She continued to unbutton a silk white Tommy Hilfinger top, leaving it open. They were nervous. Lindsay slid ever so slightly down into the cushions. Her breathing was pronounced as her chest rose with his touch. Garett slowly placed both hands inside her shirt while running them gently over her small firm breasts. She closed her eyes as his touch slid lower. They made love slowly. Her arms were stretched around him, pulling him further inside. The small fire bathed their perfect fit, as her perfume brought him back to a place he never wanted to leave again.

*   *   *

CHAPTER TWENTY-ONE

Six months later...

Garett pulled into the back spaces at the Flathead Saloon and Cathouse. It was almost nine o'clock in the morning. He wanted to survey any damage done during the night by the local wildlife. Fresh tracks from the mountain lions decorate the loading dock and refuse area in the morning. The curious cats carry their wet, muddy paws down from the adjacent mountains during the early morning hours. The deer and elk roamed freely throughout the night but rarely disturbed the trash. Black bear would occasionally venture onto the grounds, while the grizzly stayed in the mountains. The cats would cause the most damage. They liked to tear up the area. It seemed to Garett that they enjoyed the act.

It was the start of the Labor Day week-end. Traditionally, this has been one of the biggest week-ends of the year for area businesses. The northwest regions of Montana have an abbreviated tourist season. The session can only be described in terms of June, July, August, and September. Historically, June is the weakest of the four month summer resort season. The region is what Colorado was prior to the sixties. Winter brings skiers to the Big Mountain ski resort in Whitefish, but too few to clog the roads or fill the bed and breakfast stops. October through December encompasses the hunting seasons including deer, elk, boar, etc. There is no legal hunting season for grizzly. The Flathead Saloon and Cathouse rests thirty feet from Highway 93 at the foot of Flathead Lake just outside of Somers, Montana. Kenton Gabel had transformed three and one half acres of an old lakefront tavern into a spectacular roadside eatery. Garett Baine and Jim Shane had arrived in early April from Chicago. Lindsay and the kids waited until the school year was complete. They arrived in mid June. Garett and Jim were leaving similar situations in the Chicago area. The Baines had purchased their Sheridan Shores home in 1982. The real estate boom of the eighties had pushed the value of their home to nearly $500,000 from a purchase price of $139,000. Jim

Shane had purchased his home in the mid eighties and experienced similar property appreciation. They resided further north in Libertyville. Lindsay and Garett met with Wendy Tass about the move to Montana and the options available for placing their house on the market. Wendy suggested that they consider renting their home. They could lease on a one or two year term. Many corporations move executives in and out of the Chicago area. These people prefer to lease on a short term basis and the Sheridan Shores/North Shore area is the area of choice. Wendy explained to them that rent could go as high as $3,000 per month on their home. The mortgage was less than $1500 per month. Renting would accomplish their move without relinquishing property that continued to appreciate. If they did not like Montana for any reason, they could return to the home they left. Proceeds from the homes were not needed to purchase property in Montana, so Garett and Jim decided this would be the way to handle the move. After all, everyone had some concerns and fears about such a drastic change in lifestyle. People talk about a simpler life amid a safer environment but responsibilities and financial restraints generally put an end to those thoughts. Wishful thinking reflects a general resignation that life is past the point of meaningful change. Change comes with risks that few are willing to endure. Losing a comfort zone, however uncomfortable it may be, becomes a way of life. Jim Shane's comfort zone had exploded. He discussed the impending move with his children. Jim spoke of spending the summer in the mountains out west. There, they would make a decision on any permanent move. Denise's mother, Barbara, would watch the kids for six weeks while Jim left for Montana with Garett. Barbara had been a widow since 1989, and would stay at the house during the summer. Certain of their return, she remained silent. Jim never asked her to move in after Denise was killed, but he knew she was where she belonged. If there was a permanent move to Montana, as Jim anticipated, Barbara would be there. The Baines signed with Tass. Leasing their home took less than two weeks.

The state of Montana covers nearly 150,000 square miles with a population of less than 900,000. Flathead County sits in the northwest corner of the state near Glacier National Park and the Canadian border at British Columbia. The Swan and Mission ranges of the Canadian Rocky Mountains slice down the middle of the county. The cities of Missoula, Butte, Great Falls, Billings, and Helena are situated hundreds of miles apart. From The Little Bighorn Battlefield in the state's southeast corner to Glacier National Park in the northwest corner, Montana remains an enigma of independence in a country overrun with the need to legislate every facet of daily life. Montana yearns to be left alone. In recent years the property value in the state has soared. The absence of any major industry outside of the tourist and service industries has placed the tax burden squarely on the property owners. The influx of newcomers and the scarcity of any true open country in the states has driven prices skyward. The locals tend to blame the outsiders for the problems created with the higher property values. Many long time residents of Montana cannot afford to pay the taxes on their property anymore. They have owned land for years or have acquired the property from their families. Many farms cannot produce enough revenue to cover the taxes on the land. Relief is being bantered about the Montana legislature with no tangible results to date. Some local residents point the finger to the locals who are selling the land, therefore driving up the price. There would be no outsiders moving to Montana if the original residents would not sell their property.

Flathead County occupies 5300 square miles of raw territory in the northwest corner of the state. Kalispell anchors the center of the county and is the largest city at a population approaching 14,000. Total population in the county is somewhere just under 70,000. The county is comprised of the Canadian Rocky Mountains, the Flathead Valley and Flathead Lake. Glacier National Park would occupy county land if not for the Federal Park designation. Flathead County reaches the Canadian border to the north including Whitefish, Columbia Falls, and the Big Mountain Ski Resort. Traveling south along the Flathead River sits Glacier International Airport eleven miles north of Kalispell. Kalispell brings back the twentieth century and all the retail nightmares associated with franchise capitalism. Four Corners, Somers, and Lakeside fill out the southern boundaries of the county meandering mid-way down the western border of Flathead Lake. The eastern border wraps the county line just past the town of Big Fork. The 5300 square miles of territory in Flathead County are patrolled by the Sheriff's Department, headquartered in Kalispell. The total force numbers forty-two with five officers patrolling the county on any given shift. They also can be summoned to Glacier National Park on emergencies such as avalanches, search and rescue calls, and all coroner calls. The new residents are somewhat disturbed when their calls to the county for non-emergency assistance are answered in a matter of days.

The are roughly two dozen African-Americans in Flathead County and a slightly higher number of Native Americans. These groups would comprise less than one percent of the county population. There are few opportunities for employment in the county. The tourist industry is a service related industry consisting of numerous low paying positions. Garett Baine had little trouble finding staffers for the Flathead Saloon and Cathouse. Many young people waiting to leave the county are constantly looking for work, as are many young people returning to Flathead County after spending some years away. This territory permeates a tradition of finding that the grass is seldom greener on the other side. There are no illegal aliens to speak of in this county. All restaurant positions are filled by white locals, ranging in age from twenty-one to forty-one. Northwest Montana barks up a male mentality that neither embarrasses the populace nor begs for change. The number of home schooled children steadily rises as the debate over sex education in school resurfaces each year. Federal laws prohibiting religious worship in school, fall on deaf ears. Aspen is Los Angeles East with breathable air and better scenery. Flathead County is a two-lane road winding out of the Rockies littered with fresh debris from an undetected nighttime rock slide. A logging truck barreling down from Canada, traverses the asphalt like a mogul skier on a slalom course. The truck disappears at the horizon line sometime before the ten o'clock sunset. No Lexus would follow.

Garett Baine and Jim Shane arrived in Montana as the snow was melting in the April sun. They drove in separate vehicles packed with everything that would fit into the Blazer and the Montero. Interstate 94 brought them from North Dakota into Montana near Glendive. They chose to take the longer route along the interstate through Billings, Bozeman, and Butte. Heading north on 90 carried them through Missoula to Highway 93. After finishing breakfast in Polson, at the southern tip of Flathead Lake, they made the final short push into Lakeside. The early morning of Thursday, April 4 saw the brilliant wash of the sun brushing a purple haze from the lake onto the base of the mountains framing Flathead Lake. Highway 93 carved a statuesque pathway through nearly thirty miles of the Flathead Indian Reservation and the remaining coastline drive into Lakeside. On cloudy days, the mountains rest hidden in the distance, a mere background of strength peering through a steady mist hugging the lake. On this day, the sunshine and shadows dared to expose every stationary movement of these massive peaks, scrawling a razor's edge against the blue sky. It was well before noon, when the two vehicles from Illinois pulled into the mini-mart at Lakeside, Montana. Garett walked over to the Montero gesturing to the direction of the home they would occupy. The highway ran directly through the center of town, whose traffic lights consisted of a single yellow flashing light. A couple of roadside motels combined with two restaurants, both closed for the season, a mini-mart, and a gas station comprised the business district of Lakeside. The two car caravan crossed 93 at the yellow light and headed down a small road past two lakefront motels and the office/bank building housing Michael Ramirez. Lakeside Boulevard emerged where the piers began. Lakefront homes graced the west side of the street and their adjacent piers slung into the water on the east side of the street. Garett and Jim followed Lakeside Boulevard as the street narrowed and pulled away from the lake. The pavement shot up a steep hill where the front of the Blazer became the only sight visible from the windshield. With the engines straining to creep up the hill at such slow speeds, the hood dropped from view when the road flattened out. Lakeside Boulevard became a segue of gates and security fences hiding estates buried into the hillsides and coastline of Flathead Lake. Blistering out of place amidst the callous wealth of these Hollywood retreats were the remnants of the original residents. Small, immaculate log structures and wood frame bungalows dotted the roadside. Dust trailed the two vehicles as the road lost it's asphalt base. The post held mail boxes scattered in between the iron gates disappeared in the dust disturbed by the passing vehicles. Garett slowed to a crawl searching for the drive at 9 Lakeside Boulevard. His brake lights locked on. The Blazer stopped. Jim Shane pulled to a halt behind the Blazer. Garett got out of the vehicle and waited for Jim to do the same. They had arrived at 9 Lakeside Boulevard. They were home.

The gates to Randolf Baine's home were shut. There were two large black iron gates slightly rusted and anchored by twin stone towers standing nearly eight feet tall. The stone walls extending from each tower wrapped the property from the gates to the water. The walls stood roughly four and a half feet tall. Years ago, when these walls were built, they were meant for the designation of property lines and not intended as protection. Garett walked over to the gates and began to test the keys sent to him by Michael Ramirez. Jim Shane hopped up on the wall and threw his legs over towards the lake. He stretched his long muscular arms in the speckled sunlight filtering through the trees. He gazed at the property in front of him.

"Garett, did I just waste the first half of my adult life?"

"I guess I never really described this property accurately. I knew you had to see it for yourself. I was not going to oversell this site. The decision had to be yours without any pressure from me."

"I spent the better part of two years building homes in Colorado and Texas. I used to talk to Denise about where I would like to end up. We fantasized about opening a hardware store in Idaho or Utah. Colorado had become overrun with wealth from the east and west coasts. Shit, the condominiums have fucking ruined half the landscape. I never wanted to leave the city for a dressed up version of the same thing. I told Denise that we would build a home someday that would neither offend nor insult the land we bought. I pictured the work on a daily basis. I drew full blueprints of different designs. We would spend hours in front of a fire arguing about the size of the kitchen or the location of the guest house. I am looking at what I dreamed of building. Randolf Baine never cut himself off from the rest of the world. He found it right here, and they never came to him."

162

Garett had located the key to the gates and pulled them open. He walked down the terraced driveway to what appeared to be a tool shed and carport resting fifty feet down from the gates. Jim followed Garett down the drive leaving the vehicles up on Lakeside Boulevard. The lot covered over two-hundred and fifty feet of lakefront. The property stretched one hundred and seventy feet up the hill and away from the lake. There were four structures on the property. Each was built of full cut timbers. Randolf had torn down the original home on this property in the seventies. The only original structures still intact were the walls and the gates. The drive was re-constructed along with the residences. The tool house and carport were located closest to the road. One wall in the carport held an array of axes, saws, shovels, and tree trimming paraphernalia. There were two large tree stumps sitting adjacent to the carport used exclusively for cutting wood. The drive widened around the carport leaving room for three vehicles but only one could be under roof. The guest house sat twenty feet further down the drive. The house was constructed using the hillside as the anchor. The main floor was built straight out from the hillside resting on an extensive cris-crossed support beam network reaching eighteen feet from the ground up to the deck. The three bedroom house featured an expansive kitchen feeding a large deck overlooking the lake. The shoreline began one hundred feet below through a maze of two hundred year old pine trees. Expansive windows hugged the guest house from end to end. A wrought iron six burner stove, rough pine cabinets with glass window fronts, oak floors throughout, blended with modern touches such as the Sub-Zero refrigerator, twin wall unit oven and micro-wave, an indoor grill with intake fans and triple stainless steel sinks to create a magnificent rustic kitchen. The island eating area spewed out to a warm family room. The large stone fireplace looked almost new. Randolf had few opportunities to use the guest house. The cathedral ceiling and skylights draped the room with broken sunlight, at all times guarded by a Canadian moose mounted above the fireplace. Three small bedrooms hugged a small hallway and one bathroom. The guest house was immaculate, aside from the dust.

The drive ended at the guest house. A narrow stone pathway lined by larger rocks led to the main house. The trees thinned in front of the main house. Randolf had removed some of the pine trees when he rebuilt the main house. The back of the main house was close to the ground. The windows of the four back bedrooms reached almost to ground level and the roof line was at six feet. The rising landscape provided an abstract perspective of the home from the rear. Sitting between the main house and the carport was an outhouse. Although Randolf had to rebuild this particular structure, he made sure to preserve the character of the years past. The outhouse was constructed from the old timber of the main house. There were no windows. Near the top of the front doorway to the outhouse was a slot for air. The years had ravaged the obsolete outhouse. Area rumors had Randolf using the outhouse on a regular basis.

Jim and Garett wandered almost spellbound on the property. Their steps were careful and light as they reached the front deck of the main house. The sun had burned off the mist from Flathead Lake. The surrounding mountains provided a natural windbreak. The water lay perfectly still reflecting the snow capped peaks as if a mirror lined the shore. The pathway followed the south wall from the main deck down to the water. Twin piers extended on opposite sides of the property. The south pier came from a two story boat house constructed out of the same rough cut logs as the four other structures. In between the piers, in the shallow water reaching twenty-five feet from the shore, sat a miniature lighthouse amidst a sporadic formation of rocks. An exact replica of an original lighthouse from an imaginary coastline off the North Atlantic, the nine foot white tower whirled a beacon at night that became a fixture through the years on the west edge of Flathead Lake. The main house focused entirely on the lakefront view. The kitchen, family room, and master bedroom fronted the lake with sliding glass doors extending the entire length of the house. The kitchen and family room ran together on the first floor. The master bedroom sat above the kitchen and family room giving the appearance of a loft. The glass rose to the top of the A frame front design. Any morning could bring a turquoise haze glistening back to the house, pulling the mountains out of an endless sky. The still pine trees played a symphony of silence framing the view of a lifetime. The four other bedrooms and a small den were located on the first floor at the rear of the house. There were fireplaces in the kitchen, family room and the master bedroom. No curtains, blinds or shades were hung on the deckside. The privacy was the lake. Garett and Jim were standing on the deck after examining the main house. The deck stretched the length of the family room and kitchen. Jim was leaning on the railing shaking his head at the mountains in the distance. He turned his back to the water gazing up at the profile of this magnificent log structure.

"It'll do." Jim lit a cigarette and smiled at Garett.

*   *   *

164

CHAPTER TWENTY-TWO

During the first two weeks Jim and Garett arrived in Montana, they decided to separate their focus initially. Garett concentrated on The Flathead Saloon and Cathouse. The task of preparing the restaurant for re-inspection and opening had grown immensely due to the down time of the operation. Jim Shane would focus entirely on the property at 9 Lakeside Boulevard. His engineering, home-building, and construction background incorporated everything necessary to restore the homes on Flathead Lake. Work began at each venue almost immediately after they arrived.

The Lakeside Boulevard residences had fallen into some disrepair due in part to Randolf Baine's age and the lack of any regular use or maintenance on any part of the property. Randolf slept and ate on the grounds. The guest house was seldom used. The piers and boat house were not used. Over the years, some neighbors had inquired about leasing the slips on Randolf's property. The answer was always no. He was getting along fine without the intrusion. Since rebuilding twenty years ago, these structures begged for the maintenance Randolf ignored. Jim's first task was to build a tool center on the grounds. Garett agreed that for the time being they would convert the tool shed into a fully enclosed garage housing a complete workshop. They would address the need for an enclosed garage during the summer. Jim could construct a garage from the ground up in less than two weeks. The workshop contained newly purchased hand tools of every kind, numerous work benches, electronic tools including belt sanders, jigsaws, table saws, drill presses, two lathes, welding equipment, and a drafting table. Their financial independence was never more evident than the purchase of Jim's new vehicle. This was God's own truck. Purchased in downtown Kalispell and possessing the energetic embodiment of the Montana Male mentality, Shane lectured the sales staff at Ponderosa Dodge/Plymouth/Chrysler on the innovative design of his new Dodge Ram T-Rex 6 x 6. This was a prototype vehicle sold regionally on a limited basis scheduled for national release during the next year. This vehicle engaged three axles with six wheel drive, capable of pulling 26,000 pounds or the equivalent of eight cars. The club cab would seat six behind a power plant housing an eight liter V-10. With off-road lights below, a light bar over the cab, power windows, seats, locks, leather, a CD player, cruise, and a dual gun rack, the vehicle rang in at $51,000. Jim built a temporary enclosure for the truck attached to the guest house at the end of the drive. The truck represented much more than transportation. Since Denise died, Jim's life had begun to evolve from the abstract image of Rush Limbaugh to the realities of financial freedom. Jim had desired for years to bring his children up away from the city. Suburban life was not his idea of leaving the city. Financial considerations had kept him close to Chicago, but Jim knew that was an excuse to play out a conventional lifestyle. The children had to go to the "right school." His own mask had been so abruptly removed. Those fireside chats about hardware stores and Idaho were products of too many Garth Brooks' ballads mixed with an abundant supply of Merlot, or any '84 Cabernet. The morning calls to 3M or Kimberly-Clark came crashing through a 7:00 a.m. headache. Jim Shane did not choose these circumstances. They chose him. His responsibility to continue the hypocrisy of his vocation ceased on the day his wife died. Jim had not changed dramatically from his rebellious youth. Responsibilities, marriage, and parenthood had failed to produce a puppet. Jim believed that God never intended men to be supported by the starch in their shirts. That is why he gave them backbones. Jim welcomed the affection and respect of his family, but sought neither to please a neon society or participate in a mindless value system predicated on image and devoid of substance. Lost innocence of the child is a right of passage. It returns only when traumatic circumstances deal a crushing dose of reality. There are no guaranteed paydays for living within the boundaries. Jim Shane paid the ultimate price to discover what he already knew. He spoke to his children nightly. Ultimately, Jim would return to Chicago in early June to bring his family to Montana.

Garett's task of opening the Flathead Saloon brought him back home. Seventeen years in the restaurant business came back, quickly. The progression of opening became a welcome strategic process. Over the years, Garett had learned that the purpose of those municipal bodies granting the appropriate licenses, walked a very fine line between public interest and a diluted power syndrome. Experience had shown that many of these governing bodies were staffed by frustrated neophytes determined to thwart the entrepreneurial spirit they so glaringly lacked. There were expected objections to the license applications for the Flathead Saloon and Cathouse. First, there were no specific documents leaving the business to Garett Baine. The business and property were left

166

to Randolf Baine. His death put the Flathead Saloon in Garett's possession. The paper trail and unusual nature of this transaction provided ample ammunition for the Flathead County Commission to recommend that the existing license not be transferred. There would have to be an application for a new license, a process that could take up to eight months to complete. It is much simpler to transfer the existing licenses while merely changing the officers of the entity involved. A new license application involves changing the county charter to accommodate one more liquor license. Hearings are held for the residents to voice any objections on the proposal or to revisit any objections from the original license granted at that location. Secondly, the property had been closed for months. Inspections would be needed from all county departments including building, electrical, plumbing, fire, and health. No licenses could be issued without those agencies signing off. These agencies, however, could not inspect the premises until the issues regarding the new license were resolved. Michael Ramirez was hired to handle the county licenses. Local representation and the overall desire to see the business operating combined to successfully avoid the prolonged process of a new license. The old license did finally transfer and the inspections eventually were conducted with routine favorable results.

Once the legalities were concluded, an account was set up to fund the opening and operating expenses of the business. Rule of thumb in the restaurant business is to place one year of operating expenses in the business account, expecting to support the business for twelve months. Of course this occurs in dreams and large corporate restaurant operations. Garett Baine and Jim Shane formed a partnership and placed $100,000.00 in the new Flathead Saloon and Cathouse account. There was no mortgage on the property. The taxes based on 1995 figures were $6500.00 per year. All perishable products had been disposed of during the probate period. A full cleaning service from Kalispell was hired to scrub the building inside and out. Ads were placed in the papers for staff positions. Signs were posted outside for staff positions. Garett determined he would need sixty five employees to operate the restaurant. This would include bartenders, wait staff, bus staff, dishwashers, and a hostess for evenings. The total number of people hired would exceed eighty people. During the first two weeks of a new restaurant venture, a tremendous turnover occurs. Thirty percent of the initial staff may be gone during this time. With each venture, Garett was amazed by the number of employees hired that simply never showed up for their first shift. Training has been completed. Uniforms, shirts, and aprons have been distributed to the staff. Schedules are made, posted, and finalized. Nine people fail to report for their first day of employment. One called. This was common.

Menus were collected from thirty-six restaurants in the area, some as far as Missoula. Garett noticed an extraordinarily high percentage of fine dining restaurants in a predominately rustic, mountain region of the country. Garett developed the menu for his Flathead Saloon as a saloon menu. A great BBQ selection, large sandwiches, nine ounce burgers and other tavern items would dominate the menu. Garett did not want to re-invent anything. He believed in quality food, large portions, and simple selections. Food presentation has always been equally important to taste. If the meal looks great, chances are it will taste great. Garett instituted a dessert cart. This table on wheels was brought to the customers on request. The subsequent display centered on the final presentation of a flaming Gran Marnier Ice Cream Sundae. Thick, twenty ounce, schooner glasses were brushed with Gran Marnier and sugar creating the illusion of a frosted glass. The special sundae ingredients were added including a rich French Vanilla ice cream, hot fudge, and fresh strawberries. A float of 151 rum was poured over the edges and ignited. The plate was served in flames which lasted approximately ninety seconds. Extraordinary presentation and simplicity with this dessert provided a spectacle of taste attracting the attention of the room.

The restaurant was scheduled to open in early June. There would be announcements placed in all of the local papers featuring a sample menu. There would be no grand opening party. Garett planned to avoid this needless ritual of giving away the house. Lindsay and the kids were driving to Montana with Jim Shane and his children. They shipped everything before packing seven children into the Tahoe. Garett and Lindsay had finally relegated their mini-van to a suburban Chevy dealership in trade for the Tahoe. Garett could not get away due to the opening of the Flathead. Jim's schedule allowed him tremendous flexibility. His position at the Flathead Saloon would wait until he brought everyone back from Chicago. Jim's mother-in-law was not convinced of the permanent nature regarding the move. Jim estimated she would be ready to move by the end of the summer or the end of her first visit, whichever came first.

Two days before the opening of the Flathead Saloon and Cathouse, Garett Baine drove to Missoula, Montana. A two hour drive from Lakeside was extended by the back end of a spontaneous truck caravan numbering more than a dozen rigs. They were crawling through the passes on Interstate 90, stretching the miles through the Flathead Indian Reservation and into Missoula. The Blazer curled off on South Avenue West in Missoula. Three hours later, with the afternoon gone, Garett was heading home. The drive back to Lakeside crept like the last Waltz at Fort Nightly. The sun was sinking behind the tribal pine forest. A muted orange Montana sky saddled the Mission Range mountains with a warm promise for tomorrow. The temperature was seventy-six degrees. A dry breeze skirted through the truck slapping Garett's long hair, pulled back under a Nike cap. Garett couldn't take his eyes away from the rear view mirror. Locked in the frame of his mirror and resting on the bed of a Kendon single bike trailer, was a twenty-one year mirage. Garett had just purchased a brand new black XLH Harley-Davidson 1200 Sportster. There was a little circus to chase and it would begin soon with a flip of his right wrist.

*   *   *

CHAPTER TWENTY-THREE

Early June in Chicago is unquestionably the most pleasant weather on a consistent basis the city experiences. Consistency and weather define a plurality rarely used in the same sentence with reference to the Chicago forecast. Jim Shane arrived at O'Hare Field at noon on a Monday, the first week of June, 1996. The rented Ford Taurus took him to Interstate 294 heading north towards Milwaukee. Winding his way through Chicago's Northwest suburban sprawl, Libertyville sat forty minutes north of the airport, barely fifteen minutes from the Wisconsin state line. Jim and Denise had originally moved to this village because of the rare small town characteristics exhibited in the ever-growing Chicagoland area. A one hour ride on the Metra trains to the loop, commuting time continued to expand. Young couples were moving further away from the city to find affordable housing with enough room to sneeze. Ten years ago, Libertyville offered affordable housing, quarter to half acre lots, and horse farms bordering a downtown district built in the twenties. Now, ten years later, the high schools are over crowded, drugs permeate the grade schools and junior high schools, and the gangs have found the tollways. A gaudy amusement park called Great America has replaced thousands of acres of farmland. Located five minutes north of Libertyville, the theme park has a partner. Across from Great America along Interstate 294 sits the Gurnee Mills Shopping complex. Billed as a shopping center featuring factory outlet stores, this three hundred store dumping ground has destroyed Gurnee and all of the surrounding communities. The commercial magnet had drawn many multi-million dollar franchise contracts, including the Rain Forest Café. Construction permits for the center had drawn many unnecessary state exemptions concerning ground coverage, drainage and sewage regulations, and numerous tax exemptions. These projects were literally raping the area of its history and appeal. As Jim drove past the White Fence Farms, he remembered driving with Denise past these same acres. They would stop and watch the horses run without distraction. The equestrian clubs would put their rides through a series of choreographed exercises resembling the precision of a Marine drill team. Today, the fences were considerably shorter. The owners had sold most of the land to corporations of urban masturbation. Where young colts had learned how to run, now stood a repulsive series of car dealerships, fast-food franchises, oil change garages, and one strip mall after another. In less than ten years, this community had become the grotesque home of factory outlet nausea. Quiet Sunday bike rides had been replaced by overweight mall walkers afraid of the outdoors.

Jim received a warm embrace from his mother-in-law as he walked through the front door. The kids were down the street, not sure about the time of his flight. He walked down two driveways and stood watching Justine and Jasmine running through an elaborate sprinkler system, showering the neighborhood kids on a bright June afternoon. When they noticed the tall figure at the end of the drive, they ran to his arms. In a dripping embrace, Jim closed his eyes, planning to never let them go again.

Brian's last day of school had been yesterday. A quiet recluse since his mother died, he resented the way Jim left for Montana. Brian resented the way his mother was taken from him. Though he never admitted as much, Brian would always have some questions as to what happened that night at the stadium. Through some poignant letters from his father discussing his own guilt, that tension had eased a bit. Jim and Brian hadn't been to the playground in a long time. Brian walked off the playground on January 26; it wasn't that easy to find his way back. At 13, he was caught between a child, a big brother, and his father's son. Jim sat with the kids for hours when he got home. After dinner, Jasmine and Justin settled in to watch a tape before bed. Tomorrow, they would begin packing. Jim and Brian would take a ride together. They would go visit Denise.

It was a twenty minute drive to the cemetery in Woodstock. Jim couldn't stop talking about Montana. He told Brian about the truck he bought. Brian did the math. He would be sixteen in two years and two months. Strangely, Brian looked forward to moving. When his mother died, Brian pulled away from many of his friends and the activities that they had enjoyed. His friends were uncomfortable around him and unaccustomed to his grief. At 13, they moved on. Brian didn't follow. He had inherited his father's independence and moving did not scare him. Woodstock had remained a small island in a sea of concrete. Large farms dotted the roadside. Woodstock, Illinois had a small chance to retain it's small town facade. The community was predominately owned by very wealthy individuals whose purpose in attaining the land was for personal use as opposed to commercial use. Many of the ordinances prohibit development of the land within the village. Jim and Denise did not spend any time discussing their final resting place. Denise would rest with her father. Resurrection Memorial Park was a Catholic burial park.

Jim guided the rental car through the maze of drives and headstones. Denise was buried towards the back of the park. The car slowed to a stop. The trees had taken the late May bloom and washed well against the June sunset. The leaves held firm in the stiff breezes that so commonly sweep the flat lands of northern Illinois. Jim and Brian closed the doors to the Taurus. The winds seemed to pick up at that moment. Something was wrong. Jim looked down at the tracks carved into the manicured grass of the west lawn. These were not the marks left by the tractors used to dig the graves. Jim followed the tracks up a small hill and stopped. He was looking over the land that held his wife and father-in-law. There were hundreds of headstones mixed in between a variety of large and small burial crypts. The tracks leading from the drive had destroyed the grounds. Brian ran up to his father and froze when he realized what had happened. Someone had taken at least two, four-wheel drive vehicles and carved chaos in the cemetery. Again, Jim would be unable to shield his son from another senseless act. Jim, quickly wrapped his arms around Brian.

"God damn it." Jim voice was barely audible. "Damn it."

Jim pictured a carload of gang-bangers, full of heroin and bravado, carving a name for themselves in some adolescent hierarchy. This fuel knocked over more than one hundred headstones, destroying many of them. Graffiti had been spray painted on the crypt walls, and the grass had been mangled with the spinning tires of gunning engines. They walked the one-hundred yards to Denise's grave. Her plot had been violated. Tire marks creased the lines of where she lay. The engraved headstone lay broken and covered in mud.

"Who did this?" Brian asked, looking up at his father.

"I don't know, son." Jim pulled his oldest son closer. "I don't know. Someone that will eventually pay for this."

"Why would someone do this?" Brian continued. "Can't they just leave her alone?"

"There are no reasons for this. Some people feel this is some sort of fun. The older I get, Brian, the more I learn about what cannot be explained. Some people continue to cross the boundaries of decency. There is no explanation for what they do. They have to pay for it at some point." Jim's patience was gone, but he held together for his son. He looked at the Taurus on the drive. He thought of the T-Rex in Montana with a 357 Magnum in the dash and two shotguns in the rear window. They invaded his wife, again. This society had gone over the edge.

Jim and Brian cleaned the headstone and placed it back in it's proper position. They pressed some roses to the polished finish. Jim spoke to Denise about Montana and how they would be happy to get away from all of this. Brian said good-bye to his mother, again. They would be moving, but he asked her to stay with him forever. Brian and his father cried together. They had not done that before. In that moment, when a father and his son broke down, the toppled headstones wept in silence. The disrespect for a sacred place set with the sun. Brian held that callused hand. A boy had tried to understand too fast.

"I missed you too, Dad." They walked back to the car.

Jim stopped at the chapel near the entrance to Resurrection Memorial Park. He told his son to wait in the car. There were some answers he needed to find. Jim walked through the open doors to the chapel.

"Is anyone here?" he shouted. There was no answer. Jim walked through the chapel to the residence.

"Is anyone here?" He repeated.

"The chapel is closed. There is nobody here." came a voice from the kitchen off the back residence. The caretaker did not welcome this intrusion.

"What the fuck happened to the graves out there?" Jim asked, unconcerned with the man's annoyance, "When did this happen?"

"A couple of days ago," the caretaker replied.

"Who did it?"

"I don't know? We discovered the damage in the morning. Must have been done sometime in the middle of the night."

"You live here?"

"Who are you?"

"My name is Jim Shane. My wife is buried in one of the graves damaged. Do you live here?"

"Yes."

"So, you slept though this?"

"Go ask the cops. I called them as soon as I saw the damage. I just handle the daily maintenance."

"Did you see anything that night?"

"Take off, man. I already told the cops that I didn't see squat. I guess I was sleeping."

Jim walked towards the man. He was fat, jumpy and smoking a cigarette. His dirty long hair hung on a white T-shirt stained from a day's work. He never made eye contact with Jim and his distillery breath easily cut through the smoke. In one swift combination of movements, Jim knocked the cigarette out of his mouth, grabbed the back of his hair, and slammed his head into the kitchen table. Jim repeated this action before abruptly pulling him back up. Blood flowed from his nose. Jim released the caretaker.

"Sit down, asshole." Jim's voice invited no resistance. "I have a thirteen year old boy in the car, who doesn't have a mother anymore. All

I ask is that we can visit her grave in peace. Nobody could sleep through what happened out there. I don't have time to go to the police, because they won't tell me shit. I'd like to know who is responsible for trashing my wife's grave, and I suggest you tell me something now. I don't have much time and I have no patience left. Make something up, I don't give a fuck, but I better hear something soon."

"There's some Latino gang crap going on out here. They painted that shit on the crypts. I don't know any names. They .like to mess up cemeteries. There was a bunch of them. I don't know how many. They were gone in a few minutes. That's all I know. Now, leave me alone."

Jim drove back to the house. Asking the police for any information would simply result in a lecture on how they would handle the situation, while keeping him informed. Justine and Jasmine were ready for bed when Jim and Brian got home. They had been packing with their Grandma. Tea sets had to be in order. Molly dolls were searching for traveling clothes.

"Daddy, can we take Sweetie Pie with us? Justine said we couldn't."

"Of course, Sweetie Pie can come with us. She's part of the family." Jim lied with conviction about the dwarf rabbit in the basement. He would ship the rabbit. He refused to ride in the same vehicle with an animal that had a bowl movement every twelve seconds. With his two youngest children in tow, Jim paraded upstairs. At the foot of Justine's bed, Jim held the girls on his lap.

"You guys ready for a special prayer tonight?" He asked.

"Sure, Daddy. Is it about Mommy?" Both girls raised their eyebrows, excited to talk about Denise. They wanted so hard to believe that someday, they would see her again.

"God bless the father, the son, and the holy spirit, amen." Jasmine began.

"God bless Daddy, Brian, Grandma and Grandpa in heaven. God bless Grandma and Grandpa in Georgia. And God bless Mommy in heaven. Is that right, Daddy?" Justine asked.

"That's perfect, sweetheart. But, I want to add a special message to Mommy. I want to ask her to find a special place for us to live in Montana. A beautiful place with lots of friends and animals to play with. While we are packing tomorrow, maybe Mommy can make sure we find that special place. Remember the humming birds from Scottsdale. Jasmine. Do you remember when you tried to talk to them? You didn't think they could hear you. After a while, they knew exactly what you were saying. They were afraid of everyone else, but they came right up to you. The reason they liked you so much was a wish. Some people might say that Mommy can't hear us. I say no way. If we wish real hard, I'm sure she can hear us.

We love you Mommy and we miss you so much. Don't worry. We'll meet you in Montana. We promise Amen. Now, can you guys wish real hard?"

"Can we wish for Mommy to come back?" Jasmine wondered out loud. Jim sat still for a brief time staring with his eyes closed. Jasmine's eyes searched his face for an answer.

"Get some sleep, now. We all have a big day tomorrow. I love you guys." Jim leaned over and kissed Jasmine on the forehead, whispering, "I'm sorry, sweetheart. I'm so sorry."

Brian and his father would stay up late. The incident at the cemetery had, surprisingly, closed the gap between them. When Jim had stopped the car at the chapel, he had instructed his son to wait in the car. Brian did not. He followed his father into the chapel and stayed as close as he could when Jim ventured back to the residence. It was difficult to see everything going on, but he had no trouble hearing every word. Brian rushed back to the car before he was seen. When Jim got back to the car, Brian knew he was tense. The veins were about to burst in his hands as the grip on the steering wheel grew tighter. Brian sensed his father's heart rate pounding along with his own. Jim Shane had no idea that he had just erased whatever doubt had lingered from that January night. Brian stared straight ahead and spoke briefly.

"Can you find these guys, Dad?" Brian asked. His father looked at him and he knew.

"No, son. I can't. But, I'll make sure that never happens to your mother's grave, again."

After the girls were asleep, they finished up talking about Montana and all the things they would do together. Brian finally fell asleep on the couch after 1:00 a.m. They would be leaving in a couple of days. The pictures of Denise surrounded them in the family room. Jim wanted that to continue. Montana was not a place to lose memories. She was going with them. That, they would never forget.

*   *   *

Sheriff Jack Hagan drove the sixteen miles to the Flathead Saloon and Cathouse. The start of the Labor Day weekend would normally provide better things to do than waste a couple of hours at a local restaurant. Jack Hagan had first met Garett Baine at the hearings discussing liquor license approval for the Flathead Saloon. Hagan was required to be there, as the county sheriff had to sign any liquor license for the county. Garett had called Hagan on a couple of occasions concerning the damage being done to his grounds by the animals. Garett wanted to know if he could shoot any of the offending animals if they were seen disturbing the property.

Hagan didn't want to waste any of his officer's time by examining some garbage dumped on the grounds. He didn't have a problem with eliminating some isolated offenders. The sheriff explained to Garett that he would have a problem with this action if it became chronic or excessive. Hagan also told Garett to lock the dumpsters if the locals were invading. This suggestion was encouraged before Garett Baine embarked on critter warfare. Hagan had little patience with city people. Strange, considering he came from Los Angeles.

Jack Hagan learned to fly in the Air Force. A double tour of duty in Vietnam as a fighter pilot, left the airlines competing for his services. Jack chose to fly for United Air Lines based in Los Angeles. Jack was married, with three children living in the exclusive Malibu section of the city. His one passion during the years had been the solo fishing expeditions to northwest Montana. Jack had purchased some land outside of Big Fork in the early seventies. He would fly up to Montana, at least five or six times a year, to fish or simply escape Los Angeles. In 1980, on a flight back to Southern California, Jack decided to cancel his dinner reservations and cancel his lifestyle. Arriving home that evening, he informed his wife that he wanted to sell their house and move to Montana. Just like that. There had been no discussion. His wife told him that she wanted no part of that plan. He packed and was gone the next day. He quit the airlines and spent the next year fishing and hunting in the Northwest territories of Montana, Washington, Idaho, and Wyoming. He built a home on his property near Big Fork, Montana. In 1985, Jack Hagan was elected Sheriff of Flathead County. He was completing his sixth term and would be unopposed in the November election for a seventh term.

His honest demeanor and a no-nonsense approach to the county appealed to the electorate. He believed in leaving people alone until they gave him a reason to come calling. The residents of Flathead County did not need the Federal Government running their lives. Jack Hagan kept the politics out of his county. His constituents cradled their independence, cherished their guns, knew how to use them, and disdained the Brady Bill. His philosophy represented the center of his appeal. Do not come to Montana to change Montana. It has done just fine without you. Come to Montana and live as we live. If that creates a problem, don't come. Since his divorce fourteen years ago, he has remained single. Garett had not yet arrived at the Flathead Saloon.

It was a warm, early September morning. The fishermen were the center of activity across the street from the Flathead Saloon. A steady stream of four wheel drive vehicles, pick-ups, and RV's with boats perched atop their trailers, would wait for access to the lake. The sunrise calm over Flathead Lake welcomed the visitors from Somer's Boat Docks. The time crept up on

9:00 a.m. A small group of tourists had congregated near the road. They were looking up at one of the telephone poles anchored adjacent to Highway 93. A bald eagle was perched atop the pole eating a catfish, recently pulled from Flathead Lake. Two stray cats had claimed the position directly under the pole. This location provided generous scraps of fish falling from the eagle's meal. Jack Hagan leaned against his county police vehicle parked in the front lot of the Flathead Saloon, overlooking the dock area and the southern expanse of Flathead Lake.

The smooth deep rumble could be heard approaching. Gliding north on 93 from Lakeside, Garett guided the Harley around the steep highway banks hugging the lake. A more distinctive sound could not be found on any roadway. The sun flashed from the chrome pipes sweeping along the right side of the motorcycle. Approaching the Flathead Saloon, the engine throttled down as Garett's foot tapped through the gears. The lake was racing by in the black enamel of his gastank. Garett pulled the bike next to the police Ford Explorer parked in his lot.

"Been waiting long, Sheriff?" Garett asked while removing his helmet. Montana had repealed a helmet law for motorcycles the year before. Garett hated wearing them, but promised his wife and children that he would.

"No." he shrugged, peering through dark glasses with his arms crossed. The success of the Flathead Saloon only contributed to his contempt with Garett Baine and his group from Chicago. Jack Hagan felt that Mr. Baine had fallen into some fabulous property. The home and the business were laid in his lap. "Just got here. Do you want to tell me why it was so important for me to meet you here?"

"Can I ask you a personal question?" Garett pulled his sunglasses down to wait for an answer.

"No." The sheriff looked bored.

"Good. Are you a Mormon or a member of some religious organization that is diametrically opposed to the use of alcohol? Is there an underlying philosophy behind the reason you have treated us like shit since we moved out here?" Garett was pressing the issue. He caught Hagan's act from day one. Didn't care for it much, but gave him the benefit of simply not being friendly. Every encounter since has produced the same patronizing attitude. He continued. "Or is it, you simply don't like outsiders moving into Montana?"

"Mr. Baine, you called my office and specifically asked me to come out here. I have no personal ax to grind with you or your family. I wish I had a chance to talk to Kenton before he died. I can't do anything about that now. You were given a small fortune in property by a man you never knew. Another estranged relative left you a spectacular lakefront estate.

177

In Flathead County, you appear to be a very blessed individual. Most of the people in this county are having a tough time getting by. My apologies if I have behaved inappropriately." Jack Hagan finished. The two men stood staring at each other. One peering over his sun glasses, the other looking through his.

"Sheriff, I am not going to apologize to you or anyone else in this county for the circumstances that brought my family and me to Montana. Kenton Gabel's relationship with my Grandfather was between them. Apparently, they did not feel the need to enlist your advice on any number of personal matters. As a man elected to deal with the facts, I find it offensive that you can characterize my relationship with my Grandfather as estranged. Gossip seems to be an odd source of evidence for a man in your position. My wife knew very little about my relationship with Randof Baine. How you are qualified to judge this relationship is, quite honestly, beyond me. Most people in this county have given us a warm welcome. My business has reflected none of the resentment you imply. I understand the economic struggles people are having these days. As you will see, this is relevant to why I called you here. Mr. Gabel and my grandfather did not sell their property to the highest bidder as many have done. You once told me that the high property taxes in the county are partly due to the original residents putting their land up for bid. The inflated prices have contributed to the inflated tax base. This, in turn, hurts those on a limited income that prefer to keep their land. This was your assessment. However, when Kenton Gabel and Randolf Baine choose not to sell their land, their wishes failed to meet your approval. Tell me, what would you have preferred they did with their property?"

"Mr. Baine, I did not drive out here to get into a debate with you. I have 5300 square miles of land to patrol. Again, is there a specific reason you called me out here? Because if there is not, I will be on my way. The next time you want to talk to me, please make an appointment. I'll be happy to see you in Kalispell."

"Let's take a walk around back, Sheriff." Garett had made his point.

"More damage by the animals?" The sheriff followed Garett through the main parking lot. The gravel lot rose with the property as the drive curled around the back of the restaurant. The building was constructed with the main entrance in the rear. The roadside view of the Flathead Saloon and Cathouse consisted of a two story structure with the cathedral beams extending well above the second story. Two decks lined the entire lakeside frontage. The top deck was occupied by the dining room patrons. Dinners and lunches were served from this deck with a seating capacity of seventy. The lower deck was adjacent to the bar area. Appetizers and a limited bar menu could be obtained from this level. Kenton Gabel's intentions for this level included a casino. The design incorporated the space necessary for operating a three thousand square foot gaming room. The parking lot was located on the east side of the property. The lot wound around the main structure to a log staircase leading to the rear entrance. This entrance rested at the same level as the second story. Upon entering the Flathead, patrons were at the dining room level. The lower level housed the bar area. There were two small houses behind the restaurant, also part of Kenton's rebuilding project. They were built to house some of the kitchen and bus staff. Years ago, help did not come as readily. When it did come, it was very hard to depend on. Alcoholism among the restaurant industry has always been rampant. Somers, Montana was not immune. Kenton figured that if he could house the help, they would show up. Garett was not using the houses for employees at the present time. The final structure on the property housed the dumpsters. In this county, the structure surrounding the dump site had to be exceptionally sturdy. Kenton built his from the same rough cut timber as the main building. A wire mesh cover prevented the wildlife from entering. Garett and Jack Hagan reached the top of the drive near the rear of the restaurant. Garett was standing still. Jack Hagan was slowly turning, surprised by what he saw.

The two staff houses in the back had every window shattered. An ax had been used to collapse the front porch on each house. The lattice fence was destroyed. The structure surrounding the dumpsters had been pulled down. Shredded blocks of stockade fence used to house the refuse containers were piled among the open bags of garbage from the night before. The landscaping leading up to the rear entrance was torn apart.

"It doesn't appear that everyone is completely enamored by your presence." Hagan's sarcasm was not without a ring of truth. "When did this happen?"

"It had to happen between the time we closed last night and sunrise, this morning. The bread truck driver delivers the bread before 6:00 a.m. He called his company to contact me. I was notified at 6:15. Immediately, I drove up here. That is when I contacted your office."

"Well, we can eliminate the wildlife theory."

"Come here." Garett led the Sheriff over to the main entrance door. These were double doors towering twelve feet tall. Many women and men had trouble opening them. "Somebody left their calling card."

Carved in the doors were numerous Native American symbols. Below these markings, the doors were signed as follows:

CS & KT
Blackfoot/Southern Piegan

Sheriff Jack Hagan stood before the vandalized doors. Eventually, he knelt close to the signatures, examining the carefully carved letters. He stood, running his fingers over each of the drawings. Jack Hagan was a well educated man.

"What do you think?" Garett was the first to ask. "Do you have any ideas as to why the Indian or Native American people would want to do this? Have you had other problems that were similar to this? Christ, is there one place in this country where a family can live without the fear of becoming targets from some frustrated minority. I didn't move across the country to go through this shit again. Enlighten me, Sheriff. Tell me something about the Indians. Are the young people still pissed off at the way the United States stole their land? Jobs are scarce. There is little opportunity for these people, so they lash out at new targets. Is there a single message here or should I expect this to continue?"

"Mr. Baine, I was not born in this county. I was not raised in this county. When I moved here nearly sixteen years ago, it became my home. When I was elected Sheriff, I began a very unique relationship with the Native Americans in this region. With their help, I became familiar with the history of the Northwest territories and the individual Indian tribes." Jack Hagan had lost his sarcasm. "You are absolutely right. They are still pissed off about losing their homelands, and they have every reason on earth to remain pissed off until that land is returned. Assuming that possibility is remote, they will stay pissed off. Do I think this is some kind of message? Maybe. Have I had trouble with Indians before? No more than anyone else. To answer your question about frustrated minorities, I have no answer. The Native American population of this county and the surrounding counties have many problems concerning employment and economic frustration. These are problems experienced by the entire county. This frustration does not discriminate. In the future, you may or may not find frustrated minorities lashing out against you. I cannot take you to a place that is immune from this. It does not exist. I can tell you, however, that the Native Americans in this territory did not touch your property." Jack Hagan viewed the damage. He was not happy about crime in his county.

"What do you mean, Native Americans did not touch my property?" Garett was growing impatient with Hagan's 'read between the lines' rhetoric.

"CS & KT are the initials for The Confederated Salish and Kootenai Tribes of the Flathead Reservation. This tribe is one of the more financially successful tribes in the nation. They are involved in land, mining, oil, oil refineries, hotels and resorts, and numerous other corporate ventures. They employ fifteen staff attorneys on the reservation, alone. The Kootenai Tribe did not go to war against the white men.

Because of this, they were able to negotiate treaties with the government, where they retained all water, hunting, and mineral rights to their land. These century old treaties have stood up in court from day one. They stand ironclad today. The Kootenai does not travel the county knocking over garbage dumps." Hagan had Garett's attention. He continued, "The other signature is Blackfoot/Piegan. The Blackfoot Confederacy consists of five bands. Four are located in Canada. One is located in the United States at Browning, Montana. They are called the Southern Piegan Band of Blackfeet. Their reservation occupies over 1.5 million acres east of Glacier National Park. They have not had the financial success of the Kootenai, yet their birthright instilled the pride from generations past. The Blackfoot Confederacy fought for their land and their way of life. They do not hide in the night and strike as cowards. The Southern Piegan Band of Blackfeet do not address themselves as Blackfoot. The Blackfoot are in Canada. This distinction is not misrepresented among Native Americans. They would prefer that we not make the same mistake. Mr. Baine, somebody wants us to think that this damage was done by Native Americans. Trouble is, they didn't do their homework."

       *   *   *

CHAPTER TWENTY-FOUR

In nearly three months, the Flathead Saloon was exceeding the expectations of the new owner. Garett had projected a break even figure and was meeting that figure on a consistent basis. This was the first project he had ever been associated with that had some financial breathing room. The weekly gross normally becomes the Holy Grail to an independent business owner. Garett was able to operate without the pressure meeting the bills on a weekly basis. If the Flathead Saloon's receipts did not cover the weekly expenses, there were ample reserves to weather the down times. Jim Shane had become a welcome addition to the Flathead Saloon. His projects at home were complete or near completion. Jim took two weeks and three days returning to Chicago for the purpose of bringing Lindsay and the children back to Montana. Shortly after their arrival in Lakeside, Jim would begin his stint at the Flathead. Garett taught Jim to tend bar at first, and he trained him personally. After so many years in the business, Garett rarely took it upon himself to train anyone. Jim Shane had very little trouble grasping what occurs behind the bar. The first lesson that Garett ever learned behind a bar, was that drink recipes were the easiest part of the job. A valuable bartender has mastered the task of consolidating movements. Order, flow, and preparation produce an efficient bar. In a matter of three weeks, Jim had assumed responsibility for the bar, including scheduling and ordering.

Lindsay appeared to be fully recovered from the paralysis. The last examination prior to leaving Chicago, gave her the green light to resume all normal activities, including jogging. There were no remaining injuries. The timing of the move could not have been better. Lakeside and the county were teaming with activity by the middle of June. During the first two weeks following the arrival of their children, Garett and Lindsay took them horseback riding, sailing, hiking, and fishing. Of course, they took turns on the Harley. Garett and Jake would ride up into Kalispell or over to Big Fork. Maggie always loved the ride into Big Fork. They would visit a small antique doll shop, where Maggie found her heart wrapped in the expressions of the hand made toys. Garett took Conner and Christopher on shorter rides, staying close to the lake. He did not take the two younger boys on the main roads. Everything was new. It was summertime. There was no school. No one missed Chicago.

Lindsay wasted little time in decorating the Lakeside homes. Jim and Garett had done nothing to address these needs. Jake, who had just turned 11 and Brian, 13, became friends from the start of the trip to Montana. Brian had no hang ups about relating to someone younger. Jake, of course, was thrilled to hang with an older boy. They made things very easy with the little ones. During the trip, Jim and Lindsay did not have to beg the older boys to watch Conner, Christopher, Justine, and Jasmine. When they arrived, Brian and Jake seemed to aspire to taking some of the responsibility for watching the younger ones. Lindsay was able to shop for the homes without bringing everyone along on each trip to town. The shopping venues were quite limited in comparison to Chicago. Lindsay had always loved Native American art, but could never feel comfortable with that style in Chicago. Reflecting that motif in their Montana home was pure joy. Lindsay became immersed in the history of each addition to their home and its rightful place had to make sense. As the weeks rolled by, their property began to paragon an attachment to the Northwest territory. All of the furniture purchased for the homes bore the natural foundation that the structures permeated. There were over-sized sofas made from discarded timber. Lindsay had found a special hand made furniture outlet that specialized in turning the scraps from the lumber yards into beautiful sculptures and wonderful, imaginative pieces of furniture. From kitchen tables, chairs, hutches, sofas, and bedroom furniture, the statements were clear. Nine Lakeside Boulevard became as natural inside as the unique construction outside. The decor echoed the surrounding land. The large glass exposures framed the rustic comfort exuding from each room.

Each room was given an identity with the artwork displayed. The bedrooms were named based on their art history. Native American paintings, sculptures, woven art, and turquoise adorned each room. Justine and Jasmine's room was called Sun Rising. Brian's room was called Fierce Plains. Conner and Christophers' room was called the Cowboy Room. Maggie's room was called Hypnotize the Moon. Jake's room donned the moniker, Eagle's Cross. Lindsay allowed the children to assist in each selection for their rooms and they all had a final say on the name. Lindsay cherished the change in lifestyle. What would have felt terribly out of place in Chicago, became the surroundings of home. She took each day as a gift. There was no added burden by taking care of Jim's children. Justine and Jasmine stayed in the main house, as did Conner, Christopher, and Maggie. Brian and Jake were allowed to have a room in the guest house with Jim during the summer. As soon as school started, Jake would move back to the main house.

On many nights after putting the girls to bed, Lindsay would walk out onto the deck overlooking the lake and the mountains. At 9:00 p.m., the remaining sunlight was often skimming the summer snow capped peaks while casting a warm red glow on the water. Lindsay stood on the deck and spoke to Denise. Her arms folded in contentment. Her long deep breaths somehow reinforced the reality of her new roots.

"God, I miss you. We all miss you." Lindsay's voice was soft. "Justine and Jasmine love the bunk beds that came last week. Sun Rising is pretty much complete. I know you hear their prayers at night. I never helped them with any of that. Those girls are you, Denise. Last week, Jim bought Brian and Jake some kind of ATV. I think that stands for all terrain vehicle. Whatever, this thing will go anywhere. They are not allowed off the property with it unless Jim or Garett is with them. That works out just fine, because they spend the whole day giving rides to all of our kids. Justine and Jasmine adore Maggie. They spend hours matching beanie babies on the deck. I miss you, girl. I love you." Lindsay smiled, tears washing her high cheekbones. The tall pine trees moved slightly in the wind. The warm summer breeze kicked up and washed the deck. Lindsay walked inside and whispered good-night.

Jim pulled into the parking lot at the Flathead Saloon at 10:00 a.m. The day shift at the Flathead was quite busy during this season. The business opened at 11:00 a.m. Lunchtime at most restaurants consists of a small window of business between the hours of approximately 11:30 and 1:30. In a resort setting, those hours are considerably extended. The Flathead has averaged over two hundred lunches per day for the past two months. The average tab at lunch has been just under ten dollars per person. Dinners have been averaging 150 to 175 covers per night. At nearly fifteen dollars per person, daily totals have been averaging over four thousand dollars per day. After bar totals are calculated, the summer numbers exceed thirty thousand dollars per week. Garett had five servers at lunch, one bartender, two busboys, two dishwashers, and four cooks. Jim handled the bar when he was working lunch. Garett handled the main floor, the kitchen, the staff and all of the seating. Jim hopped up the steps inside the main doors. He was looking for Garett. After a quick check of the dining room, Jim hurried through the kitchen toward the back stairs. They led to the bar level and the offices.

"Hey, Cosmo. Have you seen Garett?" Jim asked the lead lunch cook, bearing a striking resemblance to Kramer from the Seinfeld television series.

"Yeah, boss. He's downstairs in the office. The Miller rep was just looking for him. Hey, Jimbo. What's with the Halloween welcome out back?"

"I don't know, Wolfgang." Jim replied in reference to Cosmo's idol. "My guess would be, another one of your fans showing his appreciation for the excellent cuisine you prepared."

Cosmo flipped him the bird while Jim winked and made his way downstairs to the office. Garett was sitting behind his desk going over the beer orders for the week.

"Give me fifty cases of Genuine Draft, fifty cases of Lite, and tell your boss that I've been waiting four weeks for the patio umbrellas he promised. The Bud guys will have them here in two days if he doesn't produce. I'm sure he'll be happy to see the entire patio lined with Bud and Bud Lite umbrellas. If this is the last week for the long-neck deal, double the order. But if he can't deliver the umbrellas, tell him to kiss us good-bye." Garett finished with the Miller rep after being assured the umbrellas would be in place by the end of the day. Jim sat down and waited for the office to clear.

"What the fuck happened out back?" Jim lit a cigarette and reached for the coffee pot. "Looks like some Indians got drunk at one of the casinos after a bad night at the machines. Shit, we haven't had any trouble from them."

"It wasn't the Native Americans." Garett pulled a long sip from a large cup of coffee. "Jack Hagan met me here this morning. He seems to think all of the carvings are bogus. Somebody just wants us to think that the Indians are responsible for this. I have to agree with him. What he told me makes sense. Some of the markings are wrong. You haven't tossed anybody lately that might have a grudge against you or us?"

"No. We haven't had anybody tossed lately. I think I cut off a couple of guys the other night, but they were harmless. No hassles. They just left."

"Well, I guess we have now experienced the ever expanding national crime epidemic. We are not immune in Montana. Listen, don't mention this to Lindsay. There's no need for her to hear about this. I'm sure this is the result of some over-served punks venting their displeasure with the policies of the Flathead Saloon." Garett grimaced at the cold coffee he just swallowed. "Listen, Jim, you had a call from the cemetery where Denise is buried. The director was very coy. He wouldn't leave a message."

"Shit, I know what this is about. I am trying to have Denise and her father moved to Montana. I never told you about my last visit to her grave. Brian and I went to the cemetery the day I got back in June. The place had been trashed by some fucking Latino gang punks. They tore up the grass with a couple of four wheelers, knocking over a couple hundred headstones. They spray painted their logos over a dozen crypts along with various other

185

messages. We were able to salvage Denise's headstone. It had been knocked over, but was not damaged. I promised Brian that I would never let that happen again. Before all of us left for Montana, I had made arrangements with the cemetery to have the bodies moved. A permit must be issued by Cook County in Illinois to have the bodies removed. As long as the next of kin authorizes the transfer, the whole procedure may take a month to complete. Denise's mother did not want to have her husband moved until she felt the move to Montana would be permanent. She also felt that I had not properly invited her to make the move with us. Obviously, she was not happy about having her grandchildren taken cross country. She has prevented any movement at the cemetery, and the director has advised the county to delay the move. Our recent change of address must be considered permanent for the county to permit the transfer. My mother-in-law and the Sunset Memorial Director have been able to block the move temporarily. They have sought a twelve month delay to establish permanent residency. I'll call him back later."

"Have they arrested anyone for the damage?" Garett inquired.

"No."

"Has anything happened since?"

"So far, no more repeat performances. Supposedly, they have instituted strict access hours to the cemetery.

*   *   *

CHAPTER TWENTY-FIVE

The years of football had taken their toll on Joe's knees. At 8:45 a.m., he lumbered slowly up the concrete stairs leading to the 12th District station of the Chicago Police Department. The 1949 structure, located at the corner of Racine and Monroe, had seen better days. Joe dropped some coins into one of the two vending machines across from the main desk. He grabbed the Milky Way bar and dropped it into his jacket pocket. Joe always nodded to the list of slain officers commemorated on a plaque next to the front desk. Each year, one or two more names would be added to the list.

The Tactical Unit at the12th consisted of three teams. The eight man teams worked in shifts. The day shift worked 9:00 a.m. until 5:30 p.m. The night shift covered the hours between 5:00 p.m. and 1:30 a.m. The third team worked the off days from the first two teams as well as the special duty assignments from downtown. Tac officers are plain clothes officers usually chosen from the patrol roster at any given district. All special events in the city required additional police. These events could include any major demonstrations, protest marches at city hall or other venues, and visits from political dignitaries such as the President of the United States. Destructive celebrations from winning the NBA title or a Super Bowl victory would turn out the Tac officers. For this duty, they would be back in uniform. Third team Tac officers from each district would pull a variety of duties. These duties could also include additional patrols in volatile neighborhoods. A young black man killed in the predominately white neighborhood of Bridgeport would draw additional police patrols Qualifications for Tac duty must include an active arrest record. Tactical officers work on their own much of the time. Tac Unit officers are expected to make arrests. Their assignments include the crimes of the district. Who has been responsible for the gang deaths. Who is moving the narcotics in and out of the neighborhood. New faces in the district are checked. The tactical officer is restricted to his or her district. This is where they differ from the gold shield Area detectives. The Area detectives have a wealth of resources to assist them including the most up to date criminal technology at each Area headquarters. They enjoy total freedom of movement within the city limits. Tactical Unit officers work more from the streets and their own network of information. The Chicago Police Department is split into twenty-five districts and five Area headquarters. The Area gold shields will be assigned cases covering five districts. Joe Cortez worked the 12th.

Roll call came at 9:00 a.m. The watch Commander reviewed the past twenty-four hours in the district. What were the significant developments or crimes that had occurred within the district during the past twenty-four hours? Joe and his partner took notes during the review. They were looking for any familiar names from the previous days reports. These names would garner their immediate attention during the shift.

"The Travelers and the Stones seem to be mixing it up real good, lately." Jackson Bartles barked. He was in his fifth year as watch commander at the 12th. "In the past seven days, we have had two homicides and way too much noise." He was referring to the random gunfire at night. Car keys were handed out at the end of every roll call.

Cortez and Taxman pulled out of the lot onto Monroe. They drove four blocks and parked in front of a coffee shop. The owner of the coffee shop never charged police officers. The twenty four hour coffee shop insured a wealth of protection for this practice. The Monroe Diner had not been robbed in nine years. It was located in one of the highest crime districts in the city. Joe and his partner chose to eat immediately after roll call. This gave them an opportunity to plan the day. Once busy, they rarely stopped to eat during the remainder of their shift. At ten minutes before ten o'clock, Joe Cortez and his partner were looking for Maslind Denard. Maslind was a four time resident at Joliet for a variety of gang related activity. Cortez had sent him up on three occasions. Since his last release, Maslind Denard and Joe Cortez reached an understanding. There would be no more trips to Joliet for Maslind as long as there was a steady stream of street information. In his eleventh year as a Tac officer, Joe knew dozens of Maslind Denards. The car rolled to a stop at a church, one block north of the Eisenhower Expressway and Damen Avenue. Generally, the morning hours after sunrise produced the fewest number of gang members out and about. Maslind sat in front of the First Church of the Latter Day Order of Hope. Maslind was alone.

"Good morning. How was mass?" Joe asked.

"Fuck you, Cortez. I gave you everything, last Friday."

"That was last Friday. Since then, the bandeleros have been busy. Two dead on Saturday night. A drive-by near X on Sunday, and way too many new faces in the district. Who's moving in?"

"A lot of Stones are way out of their area. I think they are working Greek Town. The Breed and the Four C's are not happy. They want the trade on Halsted to stay local."

"Any names?"

"Shit, why don't you just give me your badge and I'll do your whole fucking job for you. No. I don't have any names. Check out Plaka's on Halsted. Late afternoon is happy hour."

"That's it? Tell me something I don't fucking know, Mas. Late afternoon? Plaka's? What the fuck is that?" Joe Cortez grew up around Halsted Street. He spent his early teen years drinking Roditis wine at Diana's on Halsted. They served anyone with a buck. No one ever busted them. Every night was a Greek New Year. Joe and his friends would watch the suburban kids come into the city and get drunk on cheap Greek wine. Petros would break plates with them and dance. Eventually, most of them could be seen heaving in the parking lots while searching for their cars. As a cop, Halsted Street had not changed much. Over the years, the window dressing may have improved, but the routine remained unchanged. Cheap wine had been replaced with heroin. Tossing plates at midnight had given way to bodies in the dumpsters. "Liberate me, Mas. I've been checking out Halsted Street for almost twenty years. It's getting old." Joe held up two twenties. Maslind walked over to the car and reached for the money.

"A black Ford Bronco."

"Thank you, Mas. Get some food my friend, you look emaciated."

The majority of the day was spent on two in-progress calls. Tac Unit officers will respond to in-progress calls in their district. Joe Cortez and Taxman got hung up for two and a half hours at a domestic dispute that escalated into a homicide, involving three small children. A woman had called police because her boyfriend had become violent with her children. When police arrived, the boyfriend pulled a gun and shot the woman in front of her kids. He was barricaded in the apartment with the kids for three hours. The stand-off ended when the man shot himself.

Joe Cortez kept a gang card file on everyone he knew in the district. There were too many to remember. When they encountered strange faces in the neighborhood, the procedure was the same for everyone. Name, current address, and gang affiliation. Simple. They would be on their way. Halsted Street had been going through a recent renovation due to the 1996 Democratic National Convention at the United Center. The stretch on Halsted called Greek Town consisted of five or six blocks of restaurants and clubs. Days were generally quiet in Greek Town. Joe had watched the upscale night life return over the last couple of years. With it, came the yuppie drug mongers and their wallets. Typically traders, attorneys, or professional types, they migrated from the Gold Coast or Lincoln Park to satisfy an ever-growing taste for heroin. At least half of the row restaurants served much more than Loukaniko. It was after 3:00 p.m. Joe and his partner had been trolling the neighborhood for nearly an hour. A few of the female regulars on the strip were rolling out of bed to begin their day.

"Hey, Joe. When are you back on nights? We miss you."

"Shit, you guys caused my divorce. They pulled me off nights for my own good." Joe recognized one of the hookers from his patrol days. They were making loops around the district. Taxman and Joe knew what they were looking for and how to look for it. Their path took them on a cris-cross pattern throughout the strip. Up and down Monroe, Adams, Jackson, and Van Buren, while crossing Greer, Peoria, Sagamon, Thorpe, Racine, and reaching as far west as Ogden. On their fourth run through the district, they were heading east on Van Buren approaching the light at Halsted. Plaka's Restaurant was located on the Northwest corner. Both cops noticed the parking lot behind the restaurant. Joe nodded at Taxman. Taxman pulled the car around the block and entered the rear lot behind Plaka's. Taxman stopped the car, blocking any movement from a black Ford Bronco with three occupants. Joe called in.

"Squad, Boy 1224, we need to run an Illinois Plate # RS 44533. We have three occupants." Joe Cortez and Taxman got out of the car. The three black men in the vehicle did the same. Joe approached the driver. Cortez carried a 357 revolver with four speed clips on his right side. Most of the younger guys on the force carried 9mm automatics. The sixteen shot clips seemed to even the playing field. Joe liked the traditional revolvers. The automatics carried the possibility of jamming in a crucial moment. Joe also carried a Smith and Wesson '38 on the same side of his belt. Two guns closely latched onto his belt. Many officers choose to carry an additional weapon on their ankle or under their arm. In a close struggle, suspects often go for an officer's weapon. Joe knew both weapons could be protected with one arm, while keeping the other arm free to strike the suspect.

"Afternoon, gentlemen." Joe greeted his targets with his badge and weapons clearly visible on his belt. A white cotton shirt wrapped tight around his muscular arms. Deep lines creased the forehead and cheeks. His demeanor spoke of streetwise experience. "Haven't seen you around here before. I like to know who is doing any business in my district."

"Who said we were doing any business here?"

"What are you doing, here?"

"Visiting."

"Who?"

190

"None of your fucking business."

"Wrong answer. What's your name, asshole. I suggest you answer the question or this could be a very long afternoon." Joe did not like the way this started. Most guys knew the drill. A couple of questions and they could go. This guy was definitely dirty.

"I think our Latino policeman doesn't want any niggers on his streets. At least, not in the daylight when everyone can see us." The two men near the front of the vehicle were silent. Taxman was standing near the passenger door .

"Boy 1224." The call came back on the portable radio. "Do you have the occupants."

"Yes."

"Detain occupants." Some dispatchers are careful not alarm the suspects. Joe knew this vehicle was stolen or there were warrants on the owner. As soon as the garbled message of detain the occupants was heard, the three black men took off. Three men running in three different directions. Joe yelled to Taxman.

"The driver."

Both officers gave chase to the driver only. In this circumstance, if the vehicle is stolen, they can only charge the driver with PS&V, possession of a stolen vehicle. The other occupants would be charged with criminal trespass of a stolen vehicle. Possession is a felony. Criminal trespass is a misdemeanor. The driver cannot be charged with stealing the vehicle if there is no evidence to that fact.

"Boy 1224 in pursuit of one black male, heading west on Van Buren. Six feet tall, two hundred pounds and fast." Joe called the chase in at full speed. Taxman was falling behind. No guns were pulled during the chase. Police officers were prohibited from using a firearm to stop a fleeing suspect. The current public mood regarding the police and their use of deadly force has severely limited any such use. If the life of the officer or the lives of others are in imminent danger, only then can the use of deadly force be an option.

"Boy 1224 still in pursuit of suspect now heading north on Sagamon. This son of a bitch is fast. He's doubled the distance between us in less than three blocks." Joe wasn't slow, but forty-six years old could only travel so fast. "He's west on Jackson, now. No, he's in an alley off Jackson, west of Sagamon. Where's the squads?" Joe ran into the alley splitting two warehouses. The suspect had not been in the alley more than a few seconds. The end of the alley was at least, one hundred yards to Adams. A world class sprinter would need at least ten seconds to reach the end of the alley. This guy was fast, but not that fast. He was gone, however. Joe stopped quickly to listen for someone out of breath. His own pounding chest was the only thing he heard. Two squads closed off each end of the alley. Joe headed for the car at the Adams Street end. The suspect couldn't have made it that far.

"Did you see anyone on Adams?" Joe yelled to the patrolman exiting his vehicle.

"No."

"He's still in the alley." Joe motioned for the patrolmen to cover opposite sides of the buildings. Two more squads had now converged on each end of the alley. Taxman entered the alley from Jackson. Cortez was almost at the other end. Six police officers walked slowly along each side of the alley, knowing any doorway or dumpster may prove deadly. Weapons were drawn. The alley grew silent except for the methodical crunching of slow calculated footsteps hitting the gravel and glass of the pavement. A rat, the size of a Cocker Spaniel, darted across the pavement drawing an errant shot from one of the younger patrolman. The bullet spanked the bricks four feet behind Joe Cortez. The police continued to check the doorways and docks. No open doors. No broken windows. They would have heard that. They had lost the suspect. He was not in the alley. Joe Cortez had been to this dance before. Suspects sometimes disappear.

"Get somebody in the front of both these buildings. Somehow, he had to get inside one of these buildings." Joe knew he was gone. They would not find him.

Back at Plaka's, the Ford Bronco became the focus of the afternoon. It was stolen one week ago from a parking lot in Wrigleyville. The vehicle was registered to an Alan Hyman from Highland Park. He reported the vehicle stolen one week prior. Joe shook his head while Taxman briefed him on the dispatch information concerning the vehicle.

"There's no help there. South or West side gangs do not travel to Wrigleyville to steal cars. If these guys wanted to move any kind of drugs, why would they travel in a hot truck? This guy disappeared in broad daylight. He's not stupid." They searched the vehicle, careful not to disturb any possible prints. No weapons. No drugs. Joe reached under the seats. Nothing. In the pocket on the driver's door, Joe pulled out a number of business sized manila envelopes. Three were empty. The fourth contained two round trip airline tickets from Milwaukee's Mitchell Field. The destination was Kalispell, Montana.

*   *   *

CHAPTER TWENTY-SIX

School had started in Flathead County the day after Labor Day. All of the kids were anxious about leaving the security of their own compound. The move from Chicago seemed to enact the extended vacation or the notion of what a vacation was all about. They drove a long distance to a place very different from their home. There were mountains everywhere. There were campers, hunters, hikers, fishermen and families at every corner. The onset of classes burst the bubble. Most children loose their enthusiasm for school when the difference between summer and the school year becomes pronounced. The summer is still there, yet it has been pulled from them. Swimming trunks and baseball hats are replaced with baths at night and pressed clothing. Children learn very young to fear the first. The first day away from Mom. Why would she leave me here with all of these strangers? The first trip to the bus stop. The rumbling in the stomach at the thought of boarding a strange bus that will arrive at a strange school filled with strange people. The first day of school beckons the beginning of a year that will never end. Summer may never come again.

Conner was one year away from the Montana version of kindergarten. Christopher and Maggie would be attending the Lakeside Elementary School. Lakeside Elementary houses the grades kindergarten through fifth. The school is located only two blocks from Highway 93 at the flashing yellow light representing downtown Lakeside. The Baines and the Shanes lived exactly one mile from the school. Justine and Jasmine Shane would also attend the Lakeside Elementary School. Christopher and Jasmine would begin in Senior K. Justine would begin the second grade. Maggie entered the fourth grade. Lindsay did not want the little ones taking the bus. She would drive them and pick them up each day. Christopher and Jasmine began at 8:30 a.m. and were out at 11:15 a.m. Justine and Maggie would take the bus home once they became accustomed to the school. The drive to the Lakeside Elementary School began on Lakeside Boulevard heading north along the lake. The road turned away from the lake after a quarter mile. The climb took a steep turn next to the array of new homes being built above the lakefront lots. All of the new construction was approved to be built within the landscape. Montana is a way of life. The state and county governments do not intrude on the residents. They do, however, protect the state from architectural butchers buying land in blocks. The Blazer rolled off Lakeside Boulevard onto Highway 93 for the short ride into town. A quick left turn bounced the kids onto the dirt road leading to the school. Flathead Lake filled the rearview mirror. The front end of the vehicle rose above the road as Lindsay climbed toward the school. A small line of classrooms appeared through the dust. Behind the small structure in disrepair rose a framework of studded two by fours surrounding the concrete pillars and iron beams of the new school. The new school would be complete for the fall of 1997. Lindsay spent the first week of school staying with the kids in class. By the fourth day, she slipped out after an hour. On the fifth day, she left after twenty minutes. They were fine after that. Conner became her shadow during the morning. This shadow came with a big curly head of hair and eyelashes, large enough to provide shade for small animals. Lindsay and Conner drove to the Flathead Saloon every morning after dropping off Justine, Jasmine, Maggie, and Christopher. They would bring Garett and Jim some blueberry muffins or gingerbread cookies from the mini-mart in Lakeside. Conner and Lindsay would sit on the deck overlooking the lake. If Jim was setting up the main bar, Conner could be found sitting on the stools waiting to steal cherries from the bar caddies. Sometimes, Jim would run Conner down to the docks and they would watch the boats sliding from their trailers into the waters of Flathead Lake.

Jake and Brian had been taking the bus since the first day of school. They were attending Somers School, seven miles north of Lakeside. Highway 93 rolled north to Kalispell while School Addition Road split off towards the Flathead Valley and Big Fork. Somers School was a middle school housing grades six, seven, and eight. Students from the valley graduating the eighth grade at Somers would next attend Kalispell High School. Jake and Brian would walk the quarter mile to the bus stop at the intersection of 93 and Lakeside Boulevard. They followed the same route on foot as Lindsay drove with the younger ones. Lakeside Boulevard winds around the lakeside lots rising fifteen to twenty feet above the tree bed line. The ground rose from the lake creating a steep incline moving away from the water. All of the lakefront roads were built to cris-cross the hillside due to the incline. The thin reflective guard rails on Lakeside Boulevard barely provided a buffer to a misdirected vehicle. The final one hundred and fifty yards of Lakeside Boulevard approaching

Highway 93 boasted a severe decline through a thick ravine. The ravine bore the jagged rock edges left by the road cutting crews. Lakeside Boulevard never went through to Highway 93 until five years ago. It took one year to extend the road an additional one hundred and fifty yards. Vertical rock walls and their spectacular descents lined the falling roadside to the main highway. Brian and Jake traversed the morning climb clad in full Montana hiking apparel. Each wore Nike hiking shoes rising above the ankle. Khaki shorts were teamed with denim shirts and backpacks for school. Brian enjoyed the relationship with Jake more than he expected. He finally had someone that would listen to his advice and actually care about what he said. Jasmine and Justine did not divert any speakable time to the pastimes deemed acceptable by their older brother. Brian had become fascinated with hunting since his move to Montana. This fascination was not discouraged by his father. Brian would spend hours with Jake passing the knowledge from his father. Jim insisted on his son becoming comfortable with many types of firearms. This tutorial included hunting rifles to handguns. Garett did not permit Jake to handle any firearm at this age. They practiced with the hunting bows. Garett allowed Jake to participate only if Jim was supervising. Jim held the same rules for Brian.

The boys were almost to the intersection of Lakeside Boulevard and Highway 93. The last forty to fifty yards slid down the incline while veering almost ninety degrees to the left. The highway was not in view until the intersection itself. It was 7:45 a.m. The sun had already cracked the tree line.

"Move up closer to the road." Brian barked as Jake tested the gravel near the guard rail.

"Look Brian," Jake ventured even closer to the drop off beyond the rail. "I see six or seven deer at the foot of the ravine. The lead rack is huge."

"Cool." Brian joined him at the guard rail. The group was barely visible through the rising montage of pine trees and underbrush. Brian braced himself against the railing to focus on an imagined prey. He aimed an imaginary Remington at the majestic silhouette shadowed by the brush. "Bam!" The pack dispersed as if they had a set play in mind, each darting in a specific direction without hesitation or indecision. "Got him."

"In your dreams."

"Uh-oh. I think I hear the bus." Brian turned to hurry up the hill to the road. Highway 93 was still blocked by the steep bend in the road, although the traffic could be heard approaching. The gravel rolled beneath their feet as they raced up the incline. When they reached the roadside, they were surprised to find their way blocked by a pick-up truck hauling a camper. The passenger door opened quickly. The man appeared to spring from the truck. He was wearing a ski mask. Another man darted from around the back of the camper. It took less than two minutes. The pick-up was gone.

         *   *   *

CHAPTER TWENTY-SEVEN

The phone rang at 9 Lakeside Boulevard.

"Hello."

"Mrs. Baine?"

"Yes."

"Do you have a son, Jake Baine?"

"Yes, who is this?" Lindsay demanded. Anger and fear raced through her veins like dominos on a vertical slide.

"This is the Flathead County Sheriff's Department calling. Your son Jake, and another boy, Brian Shane, are at the Kalispell Regional Hospital. They have been taken to the emergency room."

"No, God, Please. What happened to them? Are they all right?" Lindsay's knees were buckling. She leaned over the counter to brace herself. The words couldn't connect with this scene that every parent imagined and prayed would never happen to them.

"Please, Ma'am. We believe you should come to the hospital right away. The boys were in an accident. The doctors are with them, now. Do you have transportation to the hospital? If not, we will send a car for you."

"I have a car. What kind of accident? How bad are they hurt? Were they hit by a car? What?" Why wouldn't they tell her what happened?

"Do you know where Kalispell Regional Hospital is located?"

"What has happened to my son?" She was demanding an answer. She would not receive one.

"Mrs. Baine, your son's condition is not information that is available at this time. He is in the hospital. Do you know how to get here?"

"Yes, I've been there a couple of times." He was dead, she thought. Why else wouldn't they tell her anything. "Is he dead? For God's sake, tell me that."

"He is not dead, Mrs. Baine. He is in the emergency room."

Lindsay slammed the phone down, grabbed her keys, and yelled for her youngest son. She scooped him up in a frantic race to the car. Spinning gravel and dust followed the vehicle as she sped to the road.

197

There were too many things to do. Conner had not been buckled in. She did not overlook Conner's seat belt. She did, however, fumble with the buckle in her haste to leave. Lindsay was on the phone to the Flathead Saloon. Conner had pulled the belt out of the clip. Her driving was erratic and reckless. She had to stop. The belt was reconnected. Conner didn't understand why his mother was crying. The receiver had fallen while she strapped Conner in. The Blazer skidded back onto the road. She heard someone. Oh God, she thought, Garett. Her right hand searched the floor for the receiver. Her right foot had buried the gas pedal.

"Garett?"

"Lindsay, what's wrong?"

"It's Jake. The police called and they have Jake and Brian at the hospital in Kalispell. They wouldn't tell me anything except that they were in the emergency room. They said there was an accident."

"What kind of accident?"

"I don't know, Garett. they wouldn't tell me." Her voice was breaking. Tears rolled from her cheeks as she struggled to control the Blazer.

"Where are you, Lindsay?"

"I'm on 93, not far from you."

"Just pull in the lot, here. I'll be waiting outside with Jim. How far away are you?"

"Three or four minutes, that's all. Conner's with me. He's scared, too. He has no idea what's going on."

The time was 9:00 a.m. Garett and Jim had just arrived at the Flathead Saloon. They drove together in the Ram. Garett was not comfortable bringing the Harley since they discovered the mess out back. He wanted to identify those responsible for the damage before he brought the bike back. Tuesday morning was payroll time. Garett was calculating the hours and tips for his staff in anticipation of the payroll service phone call. The bi-weekly pay periods were called in on Tuesdays. Payroll checks were delivered on Wednesday for the pay day on Thursday. Garett left his desk as soon as he hung up with Lindsay. The office was on the lower level with the main bar. Jim Shane was in the liquor room behind the bar.

"Jim, where are you?" Garett's voice was strained..

"What's up, Garett? You sound upset." Jim answered, peering out from the liquor room door.

"Lindsay just called. She is on her way here right now. The Sheriff's Department called the house a few minutes ago. Brian and Jake are in the hospital. They were involved in some kind of accident, but the police would not tell us anything else. They are in the emergency room in Kalispell."

They were upstairs and outside as Lindsay was pulling into the parking lot. She unbuckled Conner and moved to the back seat. Garett and Jim climbed into the front seat. Garett threw the vehicle into reverse and spun the tires on the gravel parking lot. The dust rose like white smoke. The abrupt movements and the short silence in the car scared Conner. He started to cry. The Blazer was slammed back into gear and the eight cylinder engine roared out of the Flathead parking lot onto Highway 93, north towards Kalispell. Conner struggled to catch his breath.

"What did they tell you, Lindsay? What kind of an accident could the boys get in walking to the bus stop? Were they hit by a car? What? They had to tell you something." Jim was frustrated.

"They wouldn't tell me anything, Jim. My God, don't you think I tried to find out what happened?"

"I'm sorry, Lindsay. I know you tried. I'll try from the car." Jim leaned over to the console phone and picked it up.

"Give me the number for the Kalispell Regional Hospital, and please hurry." The operator put the call through. The automated phone system at the hospital explained the options. Jim pressed the number for the emergency room.

"Emergency Room, can I help you?"

"Yes, my name is Jim Shane. My son, Brian and his friend Jake Baine, were brought in this morning. Jake's parent's and I are on the way to the hospital, now. Can we find out how the boys are? What is their status? Somebody has got to tell us something."

"Hold, please."

"No, I don't want to..." The line was put on hold. Jim looked at Garett, who was staring straight ahead. His hands were tight around the wheel. The veins were blue and pronounced as the speedometer hovered near eighty miles an hour. The two lane road flew behind them. Lindsay said nothing about the speed. She was scared to death, but wished he could go faster.

"Jim Shane. This is Sheriff Jack Hagan. Where are you?"

"We are about six miles south of Kalispell. What's going on Sheriff? Why won't anyone tell us what's going on?"

"I'll explain everything when you get here. The boys are pretty banged up, but there are no life threatening injuries. I'll see you in a few minutes."

"Sheriff, what happened for Christ's sake?" Jim heard the phone cut off on the other end. "God damnit!"

The red brick structure, north of the main downtown district was in view. Garett pulled the Blazer right up to the emergency room entrance. They jumped out of the car. Lindsay had already unbuckled Conner as

Garett helped her out of the back. Jim was inside. A hospital security guard approached.

"I'm sorry sir. You cannot leave this vehicle here."

"Fine." Garett tossed the keys his way. "You move it." They entered the hospital.

Jim Shane was talking to Jack Hagan as Garett and Lindsay approached. The hospital was barren. The emergency room at Kalispell Regional was not a hub of constant activity. The quiet and sterility of the halls had the new arrivals agitated even more. Jack Hagan led them to a waiting area. He insisted that they sit down. Lindsay sat with Conner. Garett and Jim stood erect with no intention of having a seat. Jim Shane spoke first.

"Where are the boys? This is bullshit. What happened and where are they? Enough of the God damn games. You are talking about my oldest son. I just went through this with his mother." His voice with anger. "If you don't tell me what's going on right now, I will find someone in this hospital that will." By now, Jim was face to face with Jack Hagan.

"Jake and Brian were attacked this morning by two men, maybe more. The boys were beaten up pretty bad. They look worse than they actually are. Their bus driver called the para-medics. He found them near the bus stop. Apparently, the boys were attacked less than one hundred feet from the stop. I will take you to see them. Please leave the little one with one of my officers. There is some significant swelling and discoloration. It is not pretty."

"Oh, God." Lindsay's words were soft. Garett and Jim were following the Sheriff.

"What do you mean, Sheriff." Garett did not like this matter of fact explanation. Their pace was quick down the hall. Garett was side by side with Hagan. "You have got to do a little better than that, Sheriff. The boys were beaten up? What is that? By whom? Why? Did these men do anything else to our sons? Give us a little more fucking information than, hey folks, two men beat up your kids."

Jack Hagan had walked down a short hallway lined with medical equipment and empty beds. He knew Garett was upset about his son. He, also, knew that Garett Baine was right. His explanation was incomplete and vague. They had very little to go on. The bus driver saw nothing. No other witnesses had been found as yet. The sheriff had not talked to the doctors about the boys condition since they were brought in. He had no idea if these boys were sexually molested. At the end of the hall, the activity began.

The emergency treatment area consisted of two ER stations. Adjacent to the ER stations were the ICU stations. The ER stations were two complete mobile operating rooms. The array of medical equipment was overwhelming. All of the equipment was moveable from one room to another.

"They are not here!" Lindsay turned to Jack Hagan. She turned back to the scene through the glass. Nurses were pulling the padding off the mobile bed. It was covered in blood. Lindsay searched the room and then held her breath. "Garett, it's Jake's clothes." On the floor was a blood stained denim shirt and the remains of some shorts that had been cut off the patient. Khaki shorts, spotted with dark stains.

"Are these the parents of the boys brought in this morning?" The question came from the head of the trauma unit at Kalispell Regional. Dr. Trevor Miller had been chairing a resident meeting when the call came in from the para-medics. Dr. Miller was forty-four years old. A graduate of the University of Southern California Medical School, he had spent the past eleven years practicing in Los Angeles before moving to Montana. Kalispell had been given a gift. Trevor Miller was a talented physician looking for a better way of life.

"Yes." Garett wheeled around at the question. "Where are they?"

"The boys are in the ICU." Dr. Miller spoke with authority. "I will take you there as soon as I explain what has happened. Brian and Jake have been beaten up pretty bad. Their condition is stable; there are no life threatening injuries. Your boys will recover. Brian's injuries include three broken ribs and a ruptured ear drum. The ear drum will heal itself in roughly two weeks. He has sustained numerous cuts and bruises requiring some stitches. Jake has sustained multiple facial fractures around the mid-face area. This is the region between your eyes and mouth. We will have to go in and surgically repair the damage after the swelling goes down. It will take three or four days for the swelling to go down. The surgery will stabilize the bone structure of the face that has been knocked free. I will go into more details later, but figure on his hospital stay to be a couple weeks. Both boys have some damage to their fingers and hands. I'm sure this was in trying to defend themselves. They were attacked with a blunt instrument. The blows seemed to have been delivered with such concentration and force that this would normally rule out a fist as the sole cause of damage. Before we go see the boys, remember that the swelling and discoloration will subside. They do not look good, but they will be fine. Follow me. The ICU is right down here."

The short walk down the hall was agonizing. Dr. Miller pushed open the glass door to the Unit. Two beds were side by side, separated by a long white curtain. Dr. Miller held the door open. Garett and Lindsay moved in slowly.

"They are awake, but sedated heavily. They may wander in and out a bit. Don't try to ask them questions at this time. Just let them know you are here."

Jim walked over to the bed next to his son. He stood there frozen for a brief time. In a split second, he knew what uncontrollable rage felt like. He had been there once before. Brian's face looked like he had some grotesque make-up on for a play or a movie. His eyes were a mixture purple and black extending through his cheeks. His lips were twice their normal size with sutures across the bottom lip. His left ear was wrapped with a white pad and white gauze extended around his head to hold the pad in place. Blood had dried on his neck below the ear that had been ruptured. Jim's body stumbled with the onslaught of helplessness and the deja-vu pictures of Denise in his mind. He stood next to his son and reached for his hand. Brian's eyes were focused on his father's eyes. The hand Jim reached for was taped and braced. Two broken fingers were taped together under a metal brace. He leaned over and spoke to Brian.

"I love you, son. The doctor told me that you guys will be fine. Don't try to say anything, now. I'm so happy I didn't lose you. I don't know what I would do in this world without you, Brian. I love you so much, Brian." Jim leaned over and kissed his battered son. Brian slowly mouthed a message to his father. No words came through, but the message was clear.

"I love you too, son."

Lindsay walked over to the bed with her son. There were some IV bottles partially blocking her view. When she cleared the medical support apparatus, the first clear view of her oldest son paralyzed her. She turned to reach for her husband. Her eyes appeared ready to burst.

"Lindsay, hold on." Garett whispered while his own throat grappled for air. "Don't let him see what you see."

"Look what they did to my beautiful child, Garett." Her eyes and her voice were beyond control. "Didn't we come here to protect them from this?" The question hung from every corner of his mind. It would not go away. Jake was virtually unrecognizable. His face was swollen to twice its normal size, masking any distinguishing features. The facial fractures had closed his eyes with the swelling. The doctor had told them that it may be a few days before he would be able to focus clearly. Jake's blond hair was crusted with dried blood that had been carefully wiped clean from his face. The doctor explained that Jake had a fractured nose and cheekbone. The entire mid-face structure had been knocked loose and there was a slight fracture of the lower jaw. Jake's hands were taped and bandaged. His right hand suffered two broken fingers. A fractured thumb was braced on his left hand. Jake had faded out before his parents arrived. He never saw the reaction from his mother or the tears falling down the cheeks of his father. Lindsay leaned over and kissed Jake on the chest. She searched for an area that held no pain.

"I'm so sorry I wasn't there for you. You are my first born and I love you more than anything in this world. My baby, we came here to protect you and look what we've done." Lindsay turned and walked from the room. Her hands were cupped over her mouth and nose. The door to the ICU closed behind her and Garett heard his wife crying. Jim Shane was standing at the end of the curtain. Garett locked into his stare.

"I'll be out there." Jim Shane was brief. He turned and walked towards the door to the ICU. Garett stood by his son. He stood alone watching and wondering who could do this to his son. This boy came into the world with the sweetest disposition on the planet. Jake had stayed sweet in spite of his peers. As Jake got older, he never ventured into the territory his friends had invaded. Garett never told his son how proud this made him feel. Garett always followed the crowd as a kid. Jake followed no one. It may have left him alone more than he would have preferred, but he refused to walk in mindless adolescent footsteps.

"Jake, I know you can hear me." Garett started very softly. "Please don't let this change you, son. You are so special to me. Let me take the rage from this. It's here and I've already got it. It's all right to be scared and confused, but waste no hatred on these cowards. Never feel shame or fear from cowards. You have shown me what God could not. I cannot explain why, at such a young age, you are asked to endure this. God, simply cannot control everyone. They will not change you because they are weak and you are strong. Be afraid for them, not of them. I will take your rage and I will act upon it. They will never come near you again. I love you so much, Jake. You are my oldest son and believe me, you are everything a father could hope for. Christ, I wish I could be more like you. I love you, little buddy." Garett kissed his son and stared down at his battered face. Garett had never felt such unbridled tension. Every muscle in his body was wound up tighter than an iron fist. "You will be a man some day, Jake. But, not now. That's my job." He was just about to leave when Jake opened his eyes. They couldn't open much, but Garett could see their light. Jake's lips moved slightly. Garett bent over to hear his son. The words were short and they came so slowly.

"I'm sorry, Dad. I promise...I...won't change."

Garett walked out of the ICU space where Jake was lying. Lindsay was standing next to Dr. Miller. Lindsay was listening to the doctor with her right hand cupped over her mouth. Her red eyes bore the pain administered to her son. The tears had stopped flowing. Lindsay stared at Garett. These eyes, he had never seen before. These eyes had been down the road of compassion and forgiveness. They were not there, now. Garett saw Jack Hagan down the hall. He was giving some instructions to one of his men. Garett approached.

"Can I speak to you, Sheriff?"

"Of course, Garett." Jack Hagan finished with his instructions and turned his attention to Garett Baine. Jim Shane was next to Garett. The Sheriff knew the questions about to be raised.

"What exactly happened to these boys, Sheriff?"

"I'm sorry that we don't have much to go on. The boys had never quite made it to the bus stop on 93. It appears as though, they were confronted about two hundred yards from the stop. We know it was two men from the tracks at the scene. There were no witnesses and obviously, no apparent motive. We know the vehicle is an RV or a large truck/van. The rear axle had four tires. The vehicle was pulling some kind of trailer. We have no make, model or color. Why would two men stop and brutally beat two kids? This is not a crime that we have experienced in this county since I've been here. We have Sheriff's deputies from Flathead County combing the area. Any vehicles matching this description will be stopped. Road blocks have been set up by the state police as far south as Missoula and as far north as Whitfish and Columbia Falls. Can you think of any reason, why anyone would want to hurt your boys?"

"What is that supposed to mean?" Garett was incensed. "Don't go there. They did not provoke this type of an attack. When boys provoke a fight, they get punched in the mouth and maybe, lose a tooth. They don't get beaten to within an inch of their lives."

"Excuse me, may I interrupt?" Dr. Trevor Miller was going over some charts as he approached. "We have concluded our tests. There is no evidence of any sexual abuse, whatsoever."

"Thank God for that." Sheriff Hagan replied.

"Thank God, for what?" Jim Shane questioned. "We should be thankful that our boys were almost beaten to death and these mother fuckers decided not to play house with them? I'll thank God, when they look like that." He was pointing to the ICU Unit they just left.

"Doctor, do you have any idea, when we can talk to the boys?" The Sheriff asked.

"Jake will need more time than Brian. If it's agreeable to Mr. Shane, you can ask Brian a couple of questions, now. He's awake, but very groggy."

"Mr. Shane?"

"A couple of questions only. I go in with you."

"Agreed." Jack Hagan and Jim Shane walked back into the ICU. Lindsay was leaning against one wall in the hallway. Garett walked over to her. He put his hand in her hair and kissed her forehead. Her reaction startled him. Lindsay pulled her head away and grabbed Garett's hand.

"Are they going to get these men, Garett?" Lindsay asked.

"Yes, they will catch these men."

"What if they don't?"

"They will, I promise."

"Garett, what if they decide to visit our other children? Maybe they want a couple of five year-olds to bust up. Oh, God! What if they decide to go after the little ones at school. We have to call the school now."

"I've already done that. The Sheriff sent a car over there to get the kids. They're fine. I'll go stay with them."

"This is crazy, Garett. This isn't supposed to happen again." Lindsay's voice was breaking. "I don't have it in me, again. These are our children, Garett."

"I know that!"

"They went after our children." Lindsay's eyes tore into his.

"I promise, you. No one will touch our children, again."

"Garett, I want you to do something for me. I don't know what kind of an animal can do this to a child, but if the police don't find them, what's to stop them from doing this again? You can't promise me they won't touch our children again, if you don't know where they are." Lindsay's cheek was next to his. "If the police don't find them, soon..." Her voice trailed off.

"What, Lindsay?"

"I want Jim to find them!" She backed away. She wanted Jim Shane to kill these men, an inconceivable thought prior to this day. Clear thinking had been left on the roadside next to the blood of her son. Gone, was the confused, forgiving nature that followed the United Center shooting. "I know what I'm saying Garett."

Garett Baine stood silent. A man can only lose so much in one day.

"For God's sake, Garett," Lindsay answered the pain in his eyes. "He's been there before. I've heard the stories for years. I know he killed a man in Texas. He spent two tours in Vietnam. No one talks about that. Denise knew. This is not about you or me, now. Can you understand? This is not about you!"

Garett pulled his wife close, pressing his fingers into her back. She felt the pressure of his arms closing with the strength she needed. Her arms wrapped around his neck. She had her answer. His would come later.

Jack Hagan burst out of the ICU Unit. He ran down the hall and out the emergency room exit. Jim Shane and Dr. Miller followed. They stopped for Garett and Lindsay.

"A red pick-up with a white or beige camper." Jim announced. "Two men. One black, one white."

Jack Hagan was in his car and on the radio in seconds. All police vehicles were alerted. An APB was issued statewide. He estimated that the crime took place less than two hours from the present time of 9:45. His instructions focused on the interstate highways within a radius of no more than one hundred and fifty miles. If they stayed within the county, Hagan knew he would find them. If they fled, his concern was keeping the field of play as small as possible. The expanses of the state would make it extremely difficult to locate this vehicle as time passed. If they headed north to Canada, they could not have reached the border, yet. The roads would not allow them to travel at seventy or eighty miles per hour. Hagan notified all ports of entry into Canada, especially those at Roosville, Flathead, Carway, Piegan, and Del Bonita to detain anyone or any vehicle matching the description given by Brian Shane.

*   *   *

CHAPTER TWENTY-EIGHT

Back at the 12th District station, Joe Cortez was pissed off. It wasn't just losing the suspect, although that did not sit very well with him, Cortez knew something was not right. He couldn't remember why Kalispell, Montana stuck in his mind. He had never been there, yet there was something very familiar with it. The black Bronco had been impounded. There were no new clues from the garage. This vehicle was a stolen vehicle. Other than the airline tickets, the subsequent search turned up nothing. The airline tickets revealed very little. The names on the tickets were Michael Smith and Albert Turner. Both names proved to be phony. Why was the departure from Mitchell Field in Milwaukee? Cortez called the authorities in Wisconsin and was awaiting the results of their check on the names. He expected nothing. Airline tickets have certain information printed on each ticket. The airline is listed on the top. These tickets listed Delta as the airline of choice with routing through Salt Lake City. The travel agency or issuer of the ticket followed below the name of the airline. This was blank. Every ticket agency had a code that had to be used to issue any airline ticket. The code on these tickets were not registered with Delta. Cortez had Taxman checking with the other airlines.

Joe Cortez phoned a girl he had dated during the past year. She ran a Loop travel agency on Michigan Avenue. He explained the information on the tickets they found. He needed to know if there was any way to trace where these tickets had been purchased. They had phony passenger names, no issuing agency, and the agency code proved to be false as well. Cynthia Hayden was not all too happy to hear from Joe Cortez. A torrid two month relationship had been cut-off without much explanation.

"I'm stuck, Cyn. Is there something that I am missing or some way to trace the ticket?"

"Joe, airline tickets are printed by Rand McNally. They are numbered. All issued blank tickets are logged by Rand McNally. The stock control number at the bottom of the ticket will tell you what you need to know. Rand McNally is headquartered in Skokie. Go there."

"Thanks. Can I call you?" Joe didn't mean it, but it came out anyway. "Why not. See you, Joe." Cynthia Hayden hung up.

Driving up to the northern suburbs of Chicago did not involve traveling a great distance. Heading north out of the city along the Edens Expressway, Joe Cortez split the Sauganash/Lincolnwood sections of the city and sliced right into Skokie, Illinois. Skokie is a tremendously diverse community from the heavy Jewish population to the Mexican/American east sections of Skokie that border Evanston. Skokie is a blue collar sliver in the affluent North Shore. The recently renovated Old Orchard shopping center has brought Bloomingdales and Nordstroms to a saturated shopping landscape. Old Orchard sits on the east side of the Edens Expessway at Old Orchard Road. On the west side of the highway, at the same exit, sits the Rand McNally Building. Joe Cortez pulled into the parking lot in front of an impressive array of fountains and marble.

"What a fucking waste of money." He spoke to no one as the revolving door pulled him inside the lobby.

"Can I help you?" A polite voice came from a front desk that swallowed the receptionist.

"Yes, I hope so." Cortez had always possessed some indelible charm, smiling at the gorgeous young woman behind the counter. "My name is Joe Cortez. I am a police officer from Chicago." His badge was displayed in his palm. "I'm not sure this is the right place, but I am trying to locate some suspects from an airline ticket. The information on the tickets was false, so I need to speak to someone about the numerical order of your airline tickets and how I can locate a particular client through those numbers. Does any of that make sense?"

"This is a new one, but I'm sure we can find someone for you to talk to. Would this client be local?"

"I don't know."

"Let me call Sammy Weller. He is the Regional Sales Manager for the Midwest division. I know he's here today."

"Thank you...I don't know your name." Cortez pretended to search for a nameplate.

"Mallory."

"Thank you, Mallory."

Business people always take time to talk to a police officer. Most of them love the intrusion into what is normally a tedious day. Most have nothing to hide and relish the opportunity to actually be involved in something not originating from their television sets. Sammy Weller came down to meet Joe Cortez in a matter of minutes. Joe explained his task. After a brief visit to the seventh floor, Joe Cortez was heading to his car with the name and address of the purchasing travel agency. Pedian Tours,

Inc., located on LaSalle Street near the Chicago River, had purchased the block of tickets last November. He looked at the card in his hand. Scribbled on the back of a Rand McNally business card was *Mallory 847-673-9387.*

Joe called Taxman at the station. He wanted him to check into the travel agency. Cortez wanted to know how long they have been in business, who the owners are, and if they have any kind of criminal record. Meanwhile, Joe Cortez would visit the offices of Pedian Tours, Inc. Summer in Chicago meant the vibrant influx of activity to the Loop and surrounding River North areas. Architectural boat tours and historical boat tours split the Chicago River as the lines of tourists hugged the entrance ramps on either side of the river. While the Wrigley Building and the Tribune Towers split the bridge at Michigan Avenue, the stairways down to the river marked the forum for the start of the ninety minute tours. A short ride past Navy Pier and into the locks, produced an unexpected gorgeous view of the city's lakefront skyline. Pedian Tours, Inc was located two blocks south of the Chicago River at La Salle St. The second floor offices were difficult to find for any street traffic. This agency conducted business exclusively for corporate clients. Therefore, the location was of little concern for visibility. Joe Cortez took the elevator to the second floor. The owner of the agency was available. Michael Pedian seemed to be an affable man despite the mid-life crises screaming from his clothes. As he waited for the information he needed, Joe Cortez wondered what possessed some men to take the normal balding evolution and turn it into an absurd attempt to mask the obvious. Joe Cortez showed the confiscated tickets to the owner. Could they identify the customer from the stock control number on the ticket. In the event, that they could not identify the customer from the ticket, Joe had requested the client lists for the agency. They would reveal the names of each business client and the individuals authorized to receive tickets. Michael Pedian turned over a computer generated list of over one-hundred companies that have done business with the agency in the past twelve months. He was trying too hard. Along with the client list, Michael Pedian identified the ticket in question. It was purchased by Lappin/Sigman Properties at 55 W. Jackson, Suite 1200 in Chicago. Ira Lappin and Harold Sigman, principals.

The 12th District Police Station was teaming with summer high school youth programs. Most of the second floor offices were being used each day for these programs. Some were designed to create jobs cleaning up the neighborhoods. Some were formed to assist the senior citizens. Joe made his way up the stairs past the heavy influx of Latino youths. He entered the TAC offices and placed the lists he had received on his desk.

209

"Hey, Tax." Joe shouted. "We're going back downtown to visit someone. We know who purchased the tickets. Some firm on West Jackson. Lappin/Sigman Properties."

"Lappin/Sigman Properties. That is the largest property management firm in the city. Ira Lappin sits on the board of directors at the Lincoln Park Zoo, Children's Memorial Hospital, The Greater Loop Preservation Commission, and is an advisor to the Mayor. Lappin and his wife also vacation with the Mayor and his family. During my stint on the Mayor's service, I drove behind Ira Lappin and the Mayor to Galena for three days. Myself and Hargrove were assigned to baby-sit these two while they played golf somewhere near fucking Iowa. Harold Sigman is semi-retired. Lappin runs the show."

"My, aren't we a plethora of information today. Call the firm and see if he's in town." Joe sat back at his cluttered desk. Their other cases would wait for a day or two. He rearranged some files on his desk and vowed to organize the entire mess when he had time. He couldn't find the file for his court appearance in the evening. Chicago courts had become so crowded, they scheduled night court to help move the cases along. As he searched the desk, Joe noticed a letter he had received some time ago.

"Kalispell, Montana. What the..." He mumbled to himself.

Nothing unusual about the letter, except the return address was from Kalispell, Montana. The letter was from Garett Baine. Garett Baine had written to Joe Cortez to thank him again for all of his help during the months following of the shooting. Garett, also, described their move to the Northwest and the Flathead Saloon and Cathouse. There was an open invitation to visit anytime. Joe groped his desk for the file they were working on. He pulled two photocopies from the manila folder. There were the two confiscated airline tickets to Kalispell, Montana. Joe leaned back in his chair and ran his hand through his hair.

"Hey, Taxman. Come here. Look at this."

*   *   *

CHAPTER TWENTY-NINE

The trip to Lappin/Sigman was brief. The trappings of wealth hung like a fog in the opulent lobby of Lappin/Sigman. Marble flooring led to an expansive marble reception desk. Mr. Lappin's secretary summoned the two Chicago Police Officers after a short wait. Mr. Lappin was waiting in his office. Ira Lappin greeted the two officers. After some obligatory small talk about the view and Ira Lappin's relationship with the mayor, Joe Cortez explained why they wanted to talk to him. Mr. Lappin acknowledged that they do business with Pedian on a regular basis. Pedian Tours handles their international clients for most of their travel arrangements. Ira Lappin explained that his firm is heavily involved with foreign investment interests which require extensive travel arrangements. Lappin/Sigman is constantly bringing in people from overseas interested in leasing or purchasing property in the city. They manage well over one million square feet of office space in the city for firms all over the world. He explained that it may take some time to trace one or two tickets.

"Mr. Lappin, I appreciate your help in this matter. We believe these tickets have been purchased within the last week or two. Does that help?" Joe Cortez was disgustingly polite. He looked at Ira Lappin and wondered who handed him this wealth.

"Yes, that could speed things up considerably. I'll have a couple of people on this for you. If you gentlemen would like to wait in my office, that would be fine. My secretary, Jennifer, will let you know what we discover. In the meantime, I am late for a meeting. If you'll excuse me." Ira Lappin shook hands and left.

Taxman and Joe Cortez waited in an office the size of Rhode Island. The entire twelfth floor of the 55 West Jackson building was occupied by Lappin/Sigman. Ira Lappin's office epitomized corporate success in Chicago. The deep walnut desk stretched over eight feet and sat in front of the floor to ceiling windows overlooking the heart of Chicago's Loop.

"Kind of like our office at the 12th, hey? We're at the 12th and he's on the twelfth." Taxman was wandering about the room. There were pictures adorning every wall. Each one depicted Mr. Lappin with some famous person. He was pictured with Jimmy Carter, Ronald Reagan, Charlton Heston, Sinatra, etc.

"Excuse me, gentlemen." Jennifer entered the office. "I believe I have the information you need. Those tickets were purchased some time ago. I don't have the exact date, but the client requested these tickets to be left open. This is not an unusual request. Schedules change and our clients need to be able to alter their travel plans on short notice. The client was a joint venture between an investment group from Vietnam called Nagr Industries and a local firm called PDS, Inc., or Plastic Design Stategies, Inc. Nagr Industries is headed by Park Huu Chau. We represented Mr. Chau in an attempt to purchase approximately one acre or one city block on the West Side. Nagr Industries would purchase the land for $1.3 million. They had planned to build a three story office and manufacturing facility for the site and lease it back from the builders. Lappin/Sigman would manage the property and collect a percentage on the land purchase. Nagr Industries had planned to manufacture diapers at the site. PDS, Inc. was to provide the equipment and machinery necessary to manufacture diapers. The deal collapsed sometime before the first of the year. Nagr, Ind. has continued to search for a suitable location. He has sent his representatives to Chicago sporadically since this first deal fell apart. Their trips are always arranged through Pedian."

"Why did the first deal fall apart?" Joe Cortez wanted to know.

"I have no idea. You'll have to speak to Mr. Lappin about that." Jennifer replied.

"Do you have any idea why two airline tickets purchased by Nagr Industries would end up in the hands of a Chicago street gang?" Cortez was thinking out loud rather than expecting an answer.

"I'm afraid not." Jennifer didn't have a clue.

"What else can you tell us about Park Huu Chau?" Taxman inquired.

"Not much. I'm sure Mr. Lappin is the one to speak to about Park Huu Chau. He handled this account personally. The size of this potential deal almost always warrants the involvement of Mr. Lappin. The clients request his involvement."

"Thank you for all of your help." Cortez shook her hand and gave her one of his cards. "Please tell Mr. Lappin that I will be calling him." The two TAC Unit officers left the building.

*   *   *

Lindsay and Conner stayed at the hospital with Jake. Lindsay and Garett had told Conner that Jake had been in an accident, but he would be fine. Conner and Jake had a special relationship. Conner was the youngest of the family. His unplanned arrival caused barely a ripple in the Baine household. Jake and Maggie loved the idea of another baby in the house. There was never any jealousy from any of the children. They preferred more. Garett took some time to warm up to the concept of four children. When Conner learned to walk, he became a pint sized shadow of Jake. Conner learned to watch SportsCenter on ESPN, early in the morning with Jake. Conner had no clue, but Jake explained who they wanted to win and why. Conner usually leans to the teams with horses or animals in their logo. The Lions and Broncos are perennial favorites. Conner showed almost no fear of the wounds on his brother. He just wanted to sit by his side. They told Conner that Jake would be fine, but Jake was scared. Conner could see it in his eyes, even at his young age. Jake was glad to have him there. Lindsay sat in the recliner next to the bed. Conner and his mound of curly hair sat on the bed. His eyes were fixed on the television. His small hand was resting on his big brother's bandaged hand.

It had been nearly three hours since Sheriff Hagan left the hospital with the description of the vehicle involved. Garett and Jim had gone back to the Flathead Saloon. Garett had to arrange some coverage for the restaurant. He did not want to leave his other children alone. The ride from the hospital to the Flathead was slow. Both men silently searching for a red pick-up with a white camper.

"Lindsay asked me something before we left the hospital." Garett spoke up.

"Did she ask you, why the fuck we moved here?" Jim responded tersely.

"She wanted to know if you could find these men."

"Me?"

"You."

"What did you tell her?"

"I didn't answer. Lindsay and I have been married for fifteen years. Now, she wants me to ask you to find these guys."

"Your pride is making you blind, Garett." Jim Shane was not guessing. "What would you do if you found these guys? Would you go after them or would you call the police?"

"I don't know. I know what I'd like to do."

"Garett, you don't know about this. It doesn't make you weak or less concerned." Jim turned to look at Garett. "You and Lindsey have done so much for my family and me."

"Can you find them?" Garett asked rhetorically.

"Who knows, Garett." Jim went back to driving and nothing else was said.

Garett hardly had his mind on the lunch crowd at the Flathead Saloon. Business was unusually brisk on this day. Garett was explaining the circumstances to one of his managers.. Jim had left the restaurant shortly after they returned from the hospital. He told Garett that he would drop a car off at the hospital for Lindsay. First, he wanted to stop at home and pick up a few things for Brian. Garett asked him to bring Jake his Gameboy and his Sports Illustrated for Kids magazines. Jim would come back to the house after a couple hours and watch the kids so Garett could visit Jake. Garett would have to check on the Flathead sometime during the evening. They did not have any time to prepare for a prolonged absence. His first thoughts were to close the restaurant for a few days. Garett did not want the distractions of this business. On a good day, the restaurant business can be a constant series of quelling one small crises after another. On a bad day, the mindless whining of the general public could test anyone's forbearance. His conversation with Lindsay before he left the hospital had not left his mind.

The restaurant business becomes an extension of the owner. The small nuances of his business will be overlooked or ignored on his absence. This general aura of indispensability disintegrates during any onset of common sense or during a personal crises. Garett told his manager that he would be leaving. He explained the circumstances and his instructions were simple. Handle it. I am not available. The Flathead Saloon and Cathouse would survive. No one on the staff would let Garett or Jim down during this period. Business was supposed to fall off the table after Labor Day. It had not. The Flathead had developed a loyal local clientele in a very short period of time. For so many years, this location had been thought of as an institutional landmark and a tavern. The food had been edible, but not much more than that. Kenton Gabel's physical transformation of this location failed to erase the tavern perception, which he did not want to erase. After three months, The Flathead was filled with families on any given lunch or dinner.

Jim Shane had a police scanner in his Ram. The usual quiet static had been replaced this day by a constant stream of broken check-in reports on the search for the red pick-up. Jim was headed to the Kalispell Regional Hospital while he listened to the scanner bursts come up with empty reports. The radio then crackled louder than usual.

"1710 riding east on Thunder Hawk Road and following a red pick-up with a white camper. We are south of Hungry Horse Dam. The number of occupants is unknown, plates unknown, too far away..." The transmission fell off.

The sheriff came back on requesting 1710 stay with the vehicle until others arrived. Jim Shane would be late getting to the hospital.

*   *   *

CHAPTER THIRTY

It was a brief trip to Area 4 Headquarters. The detectives for homicide, violent crimes, narcotics, and burglary assigned to the West Side, including the 12th District, were located at Harrison and Kedzie. Joe Cortez would meet Taxman at the 12th. It had been a couple of days since Cortez had met with Ira Lappin. This case was beginning to annoy him. First of all, this wasn't really a case, yet. Secondly, Cortez had dozens of active files that were being ignored. Something had to make sense, soon. There was nothing here. Pieces of what? They were begging to fit somewhere. The tickets were wired to something. With Sawyer Brown on US99, blaring from the radio, Joe made the short trip to Area 4. Joe could easily listen to country music and still hear the police calls affecting his ride. Detective Jonathan Marchuk and Joe Cortez graduated from the Police Academy together. They have remained good friends ever since. Joe wanted Jonathan to check on Nagr Industries, Inc. and Park Huu Chau. TAC Units and most district stations are not equipped to conduct any investigations involving foreign individuals or foreign companies. Jonathan could provide the information or answers that Joe Cortez was looking for. From losing two suspects in possession of a stolen vehicle, this case had taken some strange turns. As he pulled into the Area 4 lot, Joe waited for Billy Dean to finish, "Only Here For A Little While."

Joe entered the building with rising resentment that this was not his home. Jonathan would never be the cop that Cortez was. Jonathan Marchuk was a homicide detective. He was three years younger than Joe Cortez. Jonathan Marchuk had a better pedigree. A graduate of the University of Illinois with an M.B.A. in business, Jonathan Marchuk was the material that made Gold Shields. The growing displeasure from the general public towards the Police Department left little room for street smart cops to advance past TAC. Street cops tend to resent the political obligations associated with advancement. Downtown was looking for refined fluff over old school leather. Cortez wore leather in his cheeks. Marchuk greeted Joe in the lobby.

"Joe, good to see you." Jonathan Marchuk was sincerely glad to see his friend.

"Chuk, good to see you. Seems like you guys get more spoiled every time I see you. Look at those   threads. Have you been assigned to Michigan Avenue or are you getting married later?"

"This is a suit, Joe. Have you ever owned one that didn't shine?"

"I like the glitter. How's your wife, Chuk?"

"She's great and expecting. Sometime around the end of November."

"Congratulations. Give her my best. And give my best to the father."

"Tell me again, why we're friends?"

"Because I've been your idol since I carried your ass through the academy."

Joe Cortez endured the slow growl of envy churning in his stomach on the way to Jonathan's office, a far cry from the TAC Unit barracks at the 12th. The Area 4 Police Headquarters is situated on the corner of Harrison and Kedzie. The sprawling brown brick structure anchors a devastated neighborhood on the West Side of Chicago. Street corners are filled with young and old men unable or unwilling to find work. Each boarded up gas station is a gathering hole. Two-flat porches and abandoned buildings attract the continuous arm chair traffic amid the late summer squalls. Nowhere in the nation's third largest city is the cycle of poverty harder to break than it is on Chicago's West Side. The predominately African-American residents, epitomize the stereotypical urban nightmare. High unemployment, high crime, and frustration feed the recurring cycle. The West Side progress seems to stop at the United Center. The Area 4 building had become much more of a fortress than a beacon of communication between the community and the police. The sterile lobby is barred off on either side from access. A half dozen disinterested female police officers congregate behind the front desk. It is the only visual access to the space beyond the lobby. A lone male police officer guards the one entrance to the detective quarters. Joe Cortez wondered what solitude this guard sought to desire this position? Perhaps this position had been a punishment? Regardless, the two men walked past the guard and through the barred turnstile leading to a stairwell. Jonathan led the way to homicide. They settled at Jonathan's desk. The detectives had their own bullpen of desks. Large charts reflected the daily case load and the working roster for the month. The large white boards hung like menus among the array of cluttered desks.

"Whose job is it to update the boards?" Joe asked.

"It's not mine, thank God. Shit, don't these things look like the leader board at Augusta?"

"The what?" Joe snarled.

"Never mind." Marchuk dropped his jacket when they reached his desk. He pulled a chair over for Joe. Then, Marchuk reached for an organized folder on his meticulously organized desk. Cortez remembered his anal organization at the academy. This has made him a good cop and a good detective.

"Nagr Industries, Inc. and Mr. Park Huu Chau have been busy, lately. Nagr Industries is an international company with locations in Vietnam, Mexico, India, Turkey, Hong Kong, and Colombia."

"Colombia?" Joe asked. "For diaper plants?"

"Bogota, Columbia. This firm has a major presence in Bogota to manufacture diapers. The firm principals are masked. They turn up to be land trusts and aliases. Park Huu Chau has been investigated for years by the DEA. They have him on money laundering associated with the shipment of drugs into a variety of countries. They have him on drug trafficking. Mr. Huu Chau made a fortune during the Vietnam War as a major player in the heroin traffic in and out of Southeast Asia. The United States Marine Corps had him in custody at the U.S. Embassy in 1975. The end of the war and the evacuation of the compound took precedent over the prosecution of any suspected drug dealers. Following the evacuation of the United States Embassy, he seemed to disappear for about ten years. In the mid-eighties, Nagr Industries surfaced with some intense funding. They began building diaper plants all over the world. There is no doubt that these plants are fronts for the importation of cocaine and heroin. The plants present a formidable mask for moving large quantities of processed and unprocessed cocaine and heroin. I spoke to Monte and Darnell in narcotics. They have each spent considerable time following the main characters in this case. The DEA conducted a special training session for our narcotics division using Nagr Industries as a major example of importation techniques. Seems like Chau has disappeared again. The Feds haven't seen him in years." Jonathan Marchuk was reading from some material gathered from this DEA symposium. Cortez marveled at how this attention to detail had mushroomed from the conscientious and nervous recruit he had known years ago. Marchuk continued, "The raw materials used in making diapers consist of non-woven plastic film for the diaper itself, super absorbents to fill the diaper, Lycra for the elasticity, tape, and hot melt adhesives. The super absorbents used in this process are shipped in 2000 pound bags. They are in the form of white powder. Any major shipment of these super absorbents may consist of hundreds of these bags. Huu Chau and his group intersperse the cocaine or heroin in these shipments. The drugs are buried inside the super absorbents. The plant locations mirror an international drug pipeline. Aside from the protection afforded Huu Chau's group in Columbia, Mexico, Turkey, and Hong Kong, the ability to mask the shipments make detection extraordinarily difficult. With one hundred pounds of cocaine buried in the center of a two thousand pound bag of super absorbents, not even a canine unit can detect the drugs. These plants may go six or seven months without receiving any contraband. The next three weeks will be heavy, then nothing Our narcotics unit has tracked Huu Chau's representatives while in Chicago. We knew they were looking for a location in the states to anchor distribution here. Chicago was centrally located and did not have the sophisticated import tracking that New York, Los Angeles or Miami had implemented. Huu Chau's distribution network will be the gangs. To date, Mr. Huu Chau has been indicted in four states. There seems to be a shortage of co- operating governments. The Republic of Vietnam will not extradite him regardless of the indictments. They claim his whereabouts are unknown. Unless he shows up in the states, we can't touch him. This country has no extradition treaty with Vietnam. Without a treaty, we must rely on comity or the extension of courtesy between two countries. Our relationship with Vietnam has been less than cordial over the years. There is a fragile softening by the State Department. There is still hope to account for the MIA's. The State department is not about to jeopardize those efforts. Consequently, Vietnam would not voluntarily turn over it's citizens for prosecution in this country regardless of the reason. With the current uneasy softening of hostilities between the two countries, there is no way we would go in there and snatch Mr. Huu Chau and bring his ass back here. The DEA Commando Unit would love to oblige, but the State Department will hear none of it. The DEA has not successfully been able to establish any foreign vacation patterns for Mr. Chau. If he does not show up in the states, the only place to grab him is in a co-operating country. One that would look the other way, while our guys packed him away on the first flight out of there. To date, Mr. Chau has been very careful about where he goes."

"Why the West Side? This seems like the last place in the world this guy would want to operate?"

"The West Side is perfect. The gang activity has never been greater there. Some land is still relatively inexpensive and the city is giving huge tax breaks to any employer willing to re-locate to the West Side. Huu Chau's group would have paid no taxes on the property for ten years."

"What happened to kill the deal?"

"We're not sure of that. As far as narcotics could tell, Huu Chau's deal with the equipment supplier went sour. Narcotics tracked a five million dollar letter of credit and then a bank transfer from Nagr to the United States. This money was full payment on the equipment line used in the manufacture of diapers. The DEA named the 3-M Company or Kimberly-Clark as the two suppliers capable of selling used equipment. New equipment would not be necessary for Nagr's purposes and could cost nearly three times as much. 3-M and Kimberly-Clark are continually updating their plants. This makes much of their equipment available after a few years. Nagr's contract called for used equipment to be purchased from a 3-M plant in Wisconsin. 3-M would not begin dismantling the equipment without an irrevocable deposit equaling 50% of the purchase price. Full payment would reduce the price by one million dollars. Nagr Ind. chose to pay full price in advance. The equipment would take longer to disassemble, ship, and re-assemble than the construction of the building. Therefore, the money had to be in place before the land deal was consummated. Once the full amount was wire transferred to Chicago, Nagr began to have problems with city hall. The mayor's office received affidavits dating back as far as 1968 concerning Park Huu Chau. These reports would eventually affect the land deal."

"Affidavits concerning what?" Joe Cortez was intrigued.

"Mostly military reports compiled during the Vietnam War concerning Park Huu Chau's involvement with the drug cartels in Saigon."

"Where did these reports come from?"

"We don't know. They surfaced in the fall of '95. By Christmas, Nagr's deal was killed."

"Did narcotics talk to Ira Lappin or anyone from Lappin/Sigman Properties?"

"Yes, but they claimed they knew nothing about what transpired at city hall. Hell, they stood to loose a tremendous commission base from Nagr, Ind. Lappin said that the Mayor's office had frozen any permits regarding Nagr, Industries pending an investigation into the charges levied in the reports that had surfaced."

"Where does it stand, now?" Joe asked.

"Nagr and Huu Chau have apparently backed off," Marchuk continued. "Lappin claims the company is still looking for another location. Monte and Darnell say that is bullshit. Monte told me that Nagr got hosed on five million to 3-M. They lost the entire five million dollars."

"3-M kept it?"

"A company spokesman claims that there was no contract with Nagr, Industries."

"Is that true?"

"We don't know. Frankly, narcotics doesn't give a shit if Huu Chau loses five million dollars or not. They are relatively certain that he will not continue to pursue a location in this city. The heat and attention generated from those reports are not the type of advance publicity that Nagr is looking for."

"So, where's the five million?"

"Monte and Darnell assume it is stuck in escrow with the agent."

"What agent?"

"Nagr would have to employ an agent, capable of locating the right equipment, negotiating the right price, and overseeing the transaction from start to finish. The agent would be an engineer trained to oversee the dismantling and installation of the equipment."

"Man, you are a fucking expert on making diapers."

"You asked me to check out Nagr, Industries. It got interesting. It's a nice change from looking at decomposed corpses."

"Have they talked to the agent?"

"No, the company shut down. Nagr and Huu Chau did not appear to be coming to Chicago, so the boys at narcotics have not pursued this. We had nothing on his mouthpiece, a guy named Jeong Chan Seo. No one has been able to isolate Huu Chau in more than a decade. The DEA has no desire to chase one of his puppets around the country. The only possible crime involved the five million dollars. Not our concern. Our biggest concern was Nagr establishing a distribution center in Chicago."

"Who was the agent?"

"The company name was PDS, Inc. or Plastic Design Strategies, Inc. The only employee was the owner, an ex-marine named Jim Shane."

*   *   *

CHAPTER THIRTY-ONE

Jim followed the police calls, delaying his trip to the hospital. The first calls for assistance would be in vain. The nearest deputy sheriff's vehicle was nineteen miles away. Sheriff's vehicle 1710, radioed in a plate number. Montana plate number Alpha, Charlie, Susan, 9,9,8. The vehicle had been pulled over. Transmissions from 1710 ceased.

Jim Shane drove the entire length of Flathead Lake searching for the red pick-up with a white camper. Jim stopped in Polson at the very southern end of the lake. Police had converged on the lake, but no one had located the red pick-up or 1710. Twenty seven minutes had elapsed since the last call from 1710. Flathead Lake is thirty seven miles long. Searching the east coast of the lake would take hours. Jim headed south on Highway 93 towards Missoula. The Montana State Police had set up roadblocks within twenty minutes of the last call from 1710. The red pick-up would be relatively easy to apprehend if the vehicle remained on the main roads. If these men planned on eluding the police by staying on the main highways and driving the same hot pick-up, their capture would be certain. Jim Shane stopped heading south after seven or eight minutes. He turned the truck around and headed back to Lakeside. If these guys were going to run, then why were they spotted at the north end of the lake hours after the attack? They weren't trying to run. The likelihood that the attack on the boys was random continued to erode. The main package remained. These men weren't running. They were simply identified. This was the first sign they had that their vehicle was identified. Jim guessed that this would be the time they would change vehicles. Jim took Highway 93 north past Polson, through Big Arm, and pulled up to a service station in Elmo, Montana, halfway up the west side of Flathead Lake and only seventeen miles south of Lakeside. Elmo is a tiny town with one service station situated on the east side of 93. On the other side of the highway is a small diner, grocery store and post office rolled into one. There are scattered houses along the hillside leading up from the lake. The population has never exceeded two digits. Jim pulled the Ram

221

up to the pumps at the Amoco station. The newly remodeled station had been owned by Royce Barweather for twenty-seven years. He fashioned himself as a mechanic as well, but his repertoire was limited to oil changes, tune-ups, muffler, and light brake work. He continued to run the business as a full service station. Royce just liked talking to people. He didn't charge any more for the full service. Royce was fifty-six years old, bald as a billiard ball under his John Deer cap, stocky, and not likely to sport an earring.

"Nice ride." Royce barked as he admired the Ram truck. "Haven't seen one like this before."

"Thanks." Jim replied. "This is the first year for this model. Believe me, a V-10 will not win any mileage awards."

"V-10?"

"Yeah, this son of a bitch could pull the fucking Eiffel Tower up the Alps."

"Fill er up?"

"Thanks. Let me ask you something. Have you seen a red pick-up with a white or beige camper come through here recently? Or simply a red pick-up in the last twenty minutes or so?" Jim assumed that they could have dumped the camper, once they knew the vehicle had been identified.

"Why, are you a cop?"

"Nope."

"Why are you looking for a red pick-up? I'm not much for rattin on folks. Their business ain't none of mine."

"My thirteen year old son and his ten year old friend were beaten within an inch of their lives this morning by two men driving a red pick-up truck with a white camper. They may have ditched the camper and they may have just killed a police officer. Can you help me or not?"

"There is a red pick-up behind the diner across the street. They came in a few minutes ago without a camper. One black guy and one white guy. I filled the truck and they asked about some food. I sent them across the street and noticed that it seemed odd that they would pull around behind the building."

"Thank you."

"What should I do?"

"Nothing." Jim Shane signed the twenty eight dollar receipt.

The Elmo Depot anchored the east side of Elmo, Montana. The two story log structure fit the surroundings like salmon swimming upstream in the frothy white currents of the Missouri River. Seven wooden spooled tables and an eight seat counter comprised the diner. Anna Barnes wore several hats at the Depot. Her regular customers bragged of no finer waitress

222

in the Northwest. Menus were for visitors. Anna was forty-nine years old and a widow. Her husband died nine years ago of cancer. His father had built the Elmo Depot. An antique map of the Northwest draped the back wall of the diner. The map was originally made by the early settlers to the territory. The bright colors tracked the lands of the many Indian Nations native to the territory. The map was priceless. The Sioux and Cheyenne colors meshed into what became the Little Bighorn Battlefield and the demise of General George Custer and his entire U.S. Cavalry division. Anna Barnes was the check out lady for the depot grocery store, the bagger, and the only individual capable of running the Elmo post office. The business was open when she was there and closed when she wasn't. On this particular day, there was a visitor in the depot picking out some groceries. Anna didn't pay much attention to the red pick-up parked in the back of the diner. There was a hose out back and maybe someone wanted to wash down the gravel spray from all the logging trucks. The regulars would constantly wash their vehicles in the back while Anna got their meals. She never noticed the black man sitting nervously in the drivers seat.

Jim Shane parked the Dodge Ram truck in front of the Elmo Depot. One doorway led to the diner. Jim opened the door slowly, but was careful not to appear cautious. He walked up to the counter seats, sat down, and grabbed a menu wedged next to the napkin holder.

"Hello, anybody home?" Jim spoke while reading the menu.

"Be there in a minute," came a voice from the grocery shelves.

"Take your time, no hurry." Jim replied to the voice.

"What can I get for you?" Anna appeared in no time. "Got a customer in the store, but he's still pickin out food. You look hungry, baby. We got fried chicken that'll make a man wonder where I've been all his life."

"Sold, darling. Give me two glasses of milk with that." Jim smiled as he stood up. "Mind if I stretch my legs? They're all cramped up from driving."

"Go ahead, pumpkin. This'll take a few minutes." Jim watched Anna disappear through the kitchen door. He turned his attention to the general store area. Whatever attention he garnered during his entrance had subsided during his stint at the counter. The tall white male in the store had watched the vehicle pull up to the Depot and followed Jim Shane's entrance through the sparsely filled grocery shelves. Relieved the intrusion was not law related, the lone shopper returned to his task. His hand held basket was almost full. He shoved another package of lunch meat into the basket. There was no mustard. The man could not locate the mustard.

"I can't fucking believe this dump doesn't have one god damn jar of mustard." A grown man was mumbling to himself in the aisles.

"Maybe I can help you find something?" Jim Shane was standing in front the tall stranger.

"I don't think so. What are you, the local stock boy?" The man was startled and took a couple of steps backward.

"No, I'm just a father." Jim Shane's body stood calm while his fingers closed like a vice around the metal black jack in his right hand.

"Congratulations, pal. Honestly, I don't give a shit how many kids you have. I'm just hungry. Nothing personal, pal." The man walked past Jim Shane. Jim looked to the ground and seemingly cowered out of the way.

"Wrong." Jim Shane spoke softly without picking his head up.

"Excuse me, asshole?" The stranger turned back around, fully annoyed by this backroads hick.

"It is very personal." The metal club tore through the air slamming into the cheekbone of the stranger in aisle 3. Jim Shane watched as his target was thrust against the scattered boxes of the depot aisles. The hand basket filled with groceries tumbled to the wooden floor. The black jack came crashing back the other way, caving in the other side of this stranger's face. The blows landed with incredible speed and accuracy. A third blow to the temple severed the light from the day. Jim pulled his prey closer, refusing to let him fall. Jim buried the metal weapon into the stranger's groin, pulling it back quickly and repeating the process. The stranger went limp. Jim let him fall to the floor. The man dropped like a wet sand bag hanging over a highway pylon. Blood flowed freely from a disfigured face. One hand twitched in convulsion. Less than a minute had passed. Jim stepped back and heard Anna yelling about what was going on. Jim swung his right foot back and slammed the toe of his Nocona boot into the bleeding remnants of someone's face.

"It is very personal, pal." Jim Shane repeated himself. His short burst of rage drained his breath, but his attention and focus turned to the partner out back.

"Oh, my God!" Anna Barnes was lost. She froze as Jim Shane marched past her without a glance. "I don't have any money here," she pleaded.

"I'm not here to rob you, ma'am. These men are wanted for the savage beating of two young boys in Lakeside this morning. One of those boys is my son. Call Sheriff Jack Hagan in Kalispell, now. Tell him to get out here right away. Tell him the red pick-up has landed." Jim Shane barked this response without breaking stride. He was past the diner and through the kitchen. The back door to the kitchen had been propped open to reveal a tattered screen door. The events inside happened with such rapidity, the black man waiting in the front seat of the pick-up had little time to evaluate the commotion. The screen door to the kitchen was thrown open, dislodging both hinges.

The red pick-up was parked no more than fifteen feet from the building. The black man in the front seat lunged for the pistol under the front seat. He was not anxious to discover who or why someone was charging the truck. Jim Shane expected the weapon. He charged toward the rear of the driver's side, thus cutting the angle and making any attempt to fire on him much more difficult. The black man swung his arm around and out the window of the pick-up. Jim came up from a low position near mid-truck. He grabbed the arm holding a Smith and Wesson 357 Magnum pistol. Lacking any leverage from his seated position, the man's arm became a defenseless tool in a feeble attempt to stop Jim Shane. Jim's left hand locked onto the wrist just below the gun. The arm locked out against the open window on the driver's side. Jim pulled the arm back towards the rear of the truck. In one horrific sequence, Jim Shane thrust his full weight behind his right forearm, slamming it into the back of the locked out arm. The arm snapped grotesquely at the elbow evoking an excruciating scream from the recipient. The bone jettisoned through the skin on the front side of the arm breaking at a ninety degree angle. The gun fell immediately to the ground. Jim Shane pulled open the door with no resistance coming from the man wreathing in pain and falling into shock. Jim prevented the man from falling out of the truck. He reached into the cab and grabbed the black man by the throat. Jim pulled his head forward slightly, then slammed it back into the rear window of the cab. Jim Shane crawled into the front seat in an effort to literally extricate the passenger through the rear window. A sliver of sanity interrupted his reign of revenge. His hands fell to his side. The battered body fell near death across the bench seat of the truck. Jim pulled himself out of the truck. He was washed in exhaustion and exhilaration. Jim stumbled back through the diner coming face to face with Anna Barnes. He stood in front of her and wanted to apologize for subjecting her to this carnage.

"Are they dead?" Anna asked.

"Close. " Jim answered. "Did you call the sheriff?"

"Yes. It'll take them twenty minutes to get here."

"Thank you, ma'am."

"They hurt your boy?" Anna continued. She stared at Jim with his eyes down, his chest heaving, and blood covering his hands and arms.

"They hurt him bad."

"Get out of here, mister. I didn't see a thing. I'll tell them that one of them shoved me in the storeroom. One guy comes in to rob me. The other guy waits out back. Somebody must have stumbled in on a robbery. I stayed in the storeroom. Didn't see who it was."

"You don't have to lie for me."

"I said get out of here. This isn't Flathead County. Just south of it. Hagan doesn't know me. They're probably fifteen minutes out. Head south first."

"I owe you."

"Maybe. I'm not worried. It seems like you're pretty good at payback."

"Thanks, again."

"Hope your boy is O. K. He's got one hell of a father."

Jim Shane drove south for fifteen minutes, turned around and headed back north on Highway 93. There were three sheriff's cars and two state police cars at the Elmo Depot as Jim's truck wheeled back through Elmo, Montana. Three minutes up the highway he passed two ambulances headed in the opposite direction. Jim would make the short drive to Lakeside. He avoided changing at the house because Garett would be there with the rest of the kids. Jim drove to the Flathead Saloon. It was late afternoon. There were a few employees left from the lunch shift. Jim pulled the truck up to the back houses where some of the Mexicans lived. He tossed his shirt under the front seat of the truck. The hose by the dumpster provided the cleansing he needed. Jim entered the restaurant shirtless through the rear delivery dock doorway. He grabbed a shirt in the office. After grabbing a pack of Marlboros, Jim rushed back to the truck and headed north for the hospital. It would only be a matter of time before Royce Barweather described the Ram truck he so much admired, as well as the driver. Even if Anna, in all her goodness, kept quiet, Jim knew that Royce would tell the sheriff about his inquiries concerning a red pick-up. Royce would tell the sheriff that Jim asked him to do nothing when he discovered that the truck he was looking for, happened to be sitting behind the Elmo Depot. Jim Shane didn't care what anyone told Jack Hagan or the state police. It would be impossible to convene a jury in the state of Montana capable of convicting Jim Shane for anything he did during the afternoon hours of that September day. No Flathead County Grand Jury would even pursue an indictment. In Montana, they don't punish justice. They embrace it. There are no mitigating circumstances tarnished with vigilante retribution. An eye for an eye works fine for Flathead County.

This day appeared to be entering it's fortieth hour. Jim arrived at Kalispell Regional Hospital during the late afternoon hours of this terminal September day. He strode past the emergency room where only hours earlier, his son had checked in. The sterile white corridors echoed the sound of boot heels hitting the floor in stride. A young nurse turned back to study the man as they passed in the hall. Jim Shane's eyes were

226

barely visible from under a black Stetson. Montana was Texas, twenty years removed. The hallway led to the block of rooms in the ICU, where the boys would remain for a couple of days. The extreme trauma to the head that both boys endured would precipitate a mandatory stay in the ICU. Jim could see Lindsay sitting next to the bed in Jake's room. The rooms were enclosed by windows, enabling the staff to be in visual contact with the patients as well as electronic contact. Brian's room was visible to the right. His body looked lost in a montage of computer generated monitoring devices. His small silhouette was framed against the white sheets. Jim remembered him as a newborn, cuddled in the arms of his mother moments after his birth. When Denise fell asleep on that day, Jim stood and watched his new son through the glass in the maternity ward. Wrapped and safe, he promised that little boy a family forever. Jim's father taught him many things. Martin Shane was father to four boys. Authority bred nothing without example. Martin Shane's belief became the foundation of his existence. Martin Shane was a poor man driven form the heart of eastern Europe to America. He came here to find a place where dignity was not feared by weak men in the wrong places. Lacking a high school diploma, Martin Shane built a successful electrical supply business in Chicago and later, in Atlanta. His four sons grew past his discipline early, only to return closer. Jim Shane would think about his father often.

"Think about your actions and what you stand for. Answer to God, but don't hide behind the veil of your religion. True faith is not asking for forgiveness. God didn't create man to grovel in his own vanity. You must be able to move on each day without the burden of shame from the day before." His own actions belied these words from his father and he loathed the example he had become. Jim stood staring at his son, again making promises.

Lindsay Baine smiled when her eyes caught the man in the black hat. Jake was asleep. Lindsay was expecting to see her husband as well. She walked out of Jake's room and wrapped her arms around Jim. Lindsay never cared much for most of Garett's friends. Many of them seemed to be stuck in a time warp, refusing to change with age. Wisdom had eluded most of them, while alcohol clouded memories seemed sufficient to fulfill the present. Jim Shane was never viewed in this light. Lindsay met Jim over sixteen years ago. Garett and Lindsay had just gotten married and Garett asked her if a friend could stay with them for a couple of days. Jim Shane was moving back to Chicago from Atlanta, but needed a few days to find a place. A few days became six weeks. Many nights were spent waiting for Garett to close the restaurant. Jim and Lindsay would wander up to the restaurant, shortly before closing. The three of them would stay until three or four in the morning, drinking Gran Marnier and listening to stories reflecting four years in the Marines, including twenty months in Vietnam, a five year stint in college culminating in two engineering degrees from Georgia Tech, and tumultuous construction forays into Colorado and Texas. Lindsay never linked the embellished fables of the barstool junkies to the almost timid recollections of Jim Shane. Jim never sought the adulation of his friends. After his wedding to Denise, Jim's armor began to fall. He became his father. Lindsay relaxed her grip around his neck. She pulled the hair back from her cheeks.

"Brian was up for awhile. I stayed with him until he fell asleep. Is Garett at home?"

"Garett is at the house. Everyone else is fine. The kids are all with Garett. He's anxious to get back here. I can't stay long. Something's come up, so I'll go back to the house and watch the kids. Garett can meet you here and bring you back when the two of you are ready."

"What's going on, Jim. I thought someone was going to bring me a car." Lindsay was talking to a man looking right through her. There was activity at the end of the hall. The emergency room suddenly filled with para-medics, nurses, police, and residents. Jim put his hands on Lindsay's shoulders.

"I found the men that beat up Jake and Brian."

"Where?" Lindsay became rigid.

"In Elmo, a few miles south of Lakeside."

"Did you call the police? Did they catch them?" Lindsay put her hand over her mouth, never connecting the scene at the end of the hall with what Jim was telling her.

"Lindsay, I almost killed them. Two ambulances are bringing them in right now. One or both of them might be dead, for all I know. I assume, the Sheriff is looking for me, as we speak." The words had barely left his mouth when Jack Hagan walked directly through the ER doors. He saw the Ram in the parking lot. "I take that back, Lindsay. The Sheriff has found me. Tell him that I just arrived. I have told you nothing."

Sheriff Jack Hagan walked down the hall with two officers behind him. Jim Shane never moved. He did not attempt to run. Hagan carried his hat in one hand. There were no weapons drawn. Hagan stared at Jim Shane as he approached, garnering nothing in an attempt to judge his demeanor. The two officers behind Hagan looked like official window dressing in a department store two weeks past the holiday.. Hagan brought questions. The Sheriff offered no greeting on his arrival.

"We have the men suspected of beating your sons." The Sheriff spoke to Lindsay. Jim Shane knew, at that moment, that Anna Barnes and Royce Barweather had disclosed nothing. "We got a call from Elmo, a town thirty miles south of Kalispell. Two men driving the vehicle described by Brian Shane were at the Elmo Depot. According to the owner of the Elmo Depot, the men tried to rob the store. They forced her into a store room upon their arrival. Someone interrupted the robbery attempt and nearly beat the men to death. They are being brought in right now. Neither one of them is in good shape. Anna Barnes claims that she saw nothing. When the noise stopped, she came out of the storeroom and found the men. One was in the store. The other was in the truck behind the Depot. She saw no one. She did not see a vehicle leaving the scene. The owner of the gas station across the street claims to have seen nothing. Nothing unusual. Didn't notice any vehicles at the Elmo Depot. Claims he didn't notice any vehicle fleeing the scene in a hurry. It's hard to imagine that someone would not be in a hurry after this beating. On the other hand, if they stopped a robbery, then why didn't they stick around?" Jack Hagan's focus had drifted to Jim Shane.

"I really couldn't tell you, Sheriff." Jim Shane never blinked. If Jack Hagan was searching for a reaction, he would be greatly disappointed.

"An officer from my department was found shot to death shortly after calling in the vehicle. He was thirty years old, married with two small children. His wife used to call me about her fears regarding her husband's job. I always told her that Montana was different. What do I tell her now?"

"I couldn't tell you that, either Sheriff." Jim responded devoid of expression.

"Can you tell me anything about the two men being brought in? One man has a fractured skull among a variety of other facial fractures. The other man is in surgery to salvage his arm. He, also, sustained a skull fracture. This beating was brutal. It had to be rage. Revenge breeds rage. Wouldn't you agree, Mr. Shane?"

"Always."

"I checked the receipts at the Amoco Station across from the Elmo Depot. Mr. Shane, it seems as though you bought some gas at that station today."

"Congratulations, Sheriff. I bought some coffee in Big Fork and some windshield washer fluid in Polson."

"Where were you this afternoon?"

"I was looking for the two men who beat my son."

"Did you find them?"

"No."

"Mr. Shane, we ran a check on the identity of the two men brought in. They are from Chicago. Both of them have extensive criminal records. We are still waiting for a complete sheet on these men. There seems to be circumstances that inexplicably fall under the coincidental category. Wouldn't you agree?"

"Is this going somewhere ?"

"There is a bloody shirt on the floor of your truck. I glanced in the cab on the way in."

"The bloody shirt on the floor of my truck is splattered with ketchup. My late wife used to chastise me for eating in the car."

"May we have the shirt?"

"Get a warrant."

"Should I?"

"I don't care, Sheriff. I have no idea what you are talking about. If you want to charge me with something, go ahead."

"Mr. Shane, what would you do in my shoes? Should I applaud whoever took matters into their own hands? Shit, these maggots deserve everything they got. Right?"

"I don't think I bring an unbiased opinion to this matter."

"What if those men were not the men we were looking for?"

"Were they?"

"That is not the question. What if they were not?"

"That would concern the individuals who did this, Sheriff."

"Do you believe in vigilante retribution, Mr. Shane?"

"Absolutely. The law doesn't work for the victims, Sheriff. Our society has less compassion for the victims of violent crime than it has for the criminals and the unfortunate circumstances leading them to commit the violence they dispense. Our transparent benevolence will cater to the black tie event of the month club. Save the whales or save some lab rats. Protect the victims, Sheriff? Hell, if there isn't someone stalking the playgrounds where your children play then some closet pedophile is conversing with your children on the Internet. Is it vigilante retribution or divine intervention?"

"God's will?"

"Was it God's will that my son was almost beaten to death?"

"There is not a Grand Jury in Flathead County or any county in Montana that would indict a father for this. If these men recover enough to speak, they may identify the person or persons responsible for this beating."

"There's that possibility." Jim Shane did not travel the road drawn for him.

"Under Montana law, Mr Shane, an individual could be facing charges raging from assault, obstruction of justice, to attempted murder. If one or both of these men die, the charge could be murder. Hypothetically speaking, Mr. Shane, does the prospect of standing in a police line-up disturb you?"

"Hypothetically speaking? I suppose the prospect of standing in a police line-up may disturb me to some degree. Being disturbed is a fact of life, Sheriff. How disturbing is it to wait for a system that coddles the guilty and places the victims on trial. The justice system is no longer a forum for justice. Our judicial system is now a perennial magic show for the legal profession. It is deeply disturbing that these men may have been denied their constitutional rights before this incident. Hypothetically speaking, that is."

"Do you ever read the bible, Mr. Shane?"

"I'm vaguely familiar with the work."

"The Old Testament, Deuteronomy 19, Verse 21, Show no pity, life for life, eye for an eye, tooth for tooth, hand for hand, and foot for foot."

"Something like that."

"Divine intervention?"

"Something like that."

"I'd wash that shirt if I were you, Mr. Shane. Ketchup sets in after awhile." Jack Hagan put his hat on, adjusting the brim. "Mrs. Baine, these men will not bother your son, again. I hope it ends here." He turned and walked back down the hall towards the emergency room.

"What does he mean by that, Jim?" Lindsay couldn't fathom anything else making this day worse.

"I don't know. I think he's upset that someone else did his job."

"Hey, Mr. Shane." Jack Hagan had stopped halfway down the hall and turned back facing Jim Shane. "Did you say that you could think of a reason someone would be sent to Montana for the purpose of hurting your family?"

"Sheriff, I don't agree with your premise that someone was sent from Chicago to hurt me. Chicago is a big place. Finding two people from Chicago in another part of the country is not exactly a mind boggling coincidence."

"I guess not." Hagan turned and continued walking.

Lindsay waited inside Jake's room. Jake was asleep and Jim Shane had gone in to see his son. The rooms in the ICU were life saving cubicles dripping with technology. The methodical hiccups measuring Brian's vital signs became the silence. These tortuous tones in daily life became a soft symphony of comfort to a nervous father. Brian had drifted during the day. His young body was unaccustomed to the assortment of drugs suppressing the effects of the morning encounter. Jim pulled a chair up next to his son. Brian's eyes opened on cue. Jim rested his hat on the bed. Brian spoke first. His voice barely audible.

"I love that hat."

"Me, too."

"Fits better in Montana, huh, Dad?"

"Much better, Brian. Kinda blends. Don't ya think?"

231

"Absolutely, Dad."

"Brian, they caught the men who hurt you. They killed a police officer before they were caught. They will not hurt anyone else, ever again."

"Thanks, Dad." Brian's head turned to his father. He knew the man much better than the man knew him.

"Why thank me, Brian? Christ, I wasn't there for you guys this morning. I dragged everyone out to Montana and look what happened."

"It's nobody's fault, Dad." Brian grimaced and closed his eyes. The ruptured ear drum began to cause the room to swirl. He forced himself to continue, afraid he would lose the connection he had sought for so long. "You miss Mom, too. Don't you?"

"I miss her so much, Brian." Jim's eyes rolled to the ceiling in an attempt to mask what his son could easily see. "I have to talk to you, now, Brian. Just listen, son." Jim Shane pulled closer to his son. "I had assumed a role for so many years in order to provide the money to raise this family. I, also assumed, that my role as money maker in this family afforded me some special consideration. Every day became my struggle to achieve the financial success we lacked. This struggle became an obsession to me. It was noble to struggle for your family and it certainly would take precedent over the everyday tasks of raising a family. As you got older, I spent less time with our family. I wanted to prove things to my family through the amount of money I made. When my expectations fell short, I began to panic. You and I began to drift further apart. I wasn't home much. Work became a constant excuse to stay away. Men, actually, accomplish very little by spending an excessive amount of time at work. The illusion is for themselves. When I was at home, everyone was tense. My own family was afraid of me and I created all of it. I vented on you, most of all, Brian. The girls were little. They kissed me goodnight while I barked at your mother about something trivial. I was an ass. I had trouble living up to my own expectations. Most days, I jumped down your throat about nothing. You became nervous to see me. I pushed you closer to your mother and then resented you for going in that direction. We could talk about sports, but our conversations ceased when that subject was exhausted. I wanted you to be more like me as I grew to think less and less of myself. I used to think that the bond between you and your mother would make you weak. Brian, I was so wrong. I never wanted affection through fear, but I created that. My business began to falter and we had to borrow money to live on. I borrowed money from Grandpa. After almost fifteen years of marriage, we were broke. I hated getting up in the morning because I had to spend the day with myself. Your mother never gave up on me, although I tried to give her every reason possible. I made

232

some bad decisions back then, but those mistakes were not unlike many families experience. I needed to make some changes, but I kept clouding the issues with my own sense of morality and self-pity. I became very strict at home, demanding near perfection from my children. I covered my own failures by being an asshole to my children, you especially. I don't know if I'll ever be able to forgive myself for that. Trouble is, I just got worse."

"Dad, we all loved you. Mom told us about the money. She said you'd come back, soon."

"I never did, Brian. My choices were all wrong. Having good intentions is not a blanket excuse for all that goes wrong. I have caused a great deal of pain to those I love the most. I've got to go back to Chicago, Brian. I might be gone a long time."

"How long?" Brian did not want to hear this. His father was letting him inside for the first time and now he was leaving.

"I don't know, Brian. What happened to you and Jake was my fault. I've got to make sure it never happens again. While I'm gone, you guys have to listen to Garett and Lindsay. You'll be out of here in a couple of days. Take care of Jasmine and Justine. Watch out for them. I know you will."

"When are you leaving?" Brian was crying. He tried to sniff back the tears and his injured ear throbbed with each attempt. "Why?"

"I'm leaving now, Brian." Jim was gently rubbing his hand over Brian's forehead. "I can't undo what I've already done. I can't ask anyone to forgive me for what I've done. But, I can stop it, now. I will tell your sisters that you will watch out for them. When this is over, I'll come back. I swear to you Brian, I love you more than you will ever know. I'm so sorry for this. Someday..." Jim's voice trailed off without finishing the sentence. Jim kissed Brian on the forehead as he slid his arms underneath Brian's shoulders and cradled him in his arms. Jim tried repeating himself and fell short again. "Someday...Brian...I...good-bye, son. I love you." Jim stood up and walked toward the door. Lindsay was standing outside the glass. She knew something was wrong.

"Dad." Brian's voice barely carried. Jim had reached the door. "It doesn't matter what you did."

Jim Shane couldn't look at his son. He opened the door and left.

"Jim, what happened with those men? You started to tell me about this before the Sheriff walked up." Lindsay approached as Jim left Brian's room. "Have you talked to Garett, yet?"

"No, I haven't talked to Garett. I'm on my way there, right now." Jim Shane was not making eye contact with Lindsay and that was beginning to create some tension.

"What happened, damnit? Why won't you look at me?" Lindsay's patience was gone.

Jim Shane said nothing. He grabbed Lindsay's arm and led her down the hall to the emergency room. They walked past the attending nurse despite her mechanical objections. The bevy of activity had not subsided since the two men were brought in from The Elmo Depot.

"If you want to know what happened, Lindsay, take a look." Jim let go of her arm as they reached the glass surrounding the ER treatment area. The floor was covered with bloody clothes, recently cut from the two new arrivals. One man had a breathing tube stuck in his throat. His face was a grotesque array of disfigured flesh bursting through a hazy shade of purple and black. His eyes were swollen shut. The other man was completely immobilized. Restraints and straps cris-crossed his forehead, upper body and arms. His left arm seemed to be disjointed. Lindsay covered her mouth as she realized that the left hand and the left forearm appeared to be severed. The arm laid at an inconceivable angle. Both men were unconscious. Suddenly, one man was pushed through the double doors and taken to surgery. Two Sheriff's officers followed the surgical team. Two more officers remained guarding the other man. An attending resident approached Lindsay.

"Can we help you?" The doctor inquired.

"Those men were responsible for beating the two boys brought in this morning. One is my son. What is happening to these men?" Lindsay wasn't sure what to ask.

"They took one man to surgery, just now. His arm has to be reconstructed at the elbow. They may not be able to save it. The other man has tremendous trauma to the face. He will need extensive surgery when the swelling subsides. He sustained some other injuries, as well." The doctor stumbled in his words and shook his head.

"What is it?" Lindsay was not swayed.

"Excuse me, ma'am. His genitals have been crushed. I'll tell you something. I grew up in East L.A. I never saw a beating like this. It's almost like this guy knew how close he could bring these guys before they died. Then he stopped. Someone wanted these men to experience a level of pain, just shy of expiration. Do you know who did this?" The young doctor inquired.

Lindsay turned to Jim Shane. He was gone.

*   *   *

CHAPTER THIRTY-TWO

Kalispell faded in the rear view mirror. A couple of seedy trailer parks hugged Highway 93 on a late September afternoon. The gray clouds tumbled along the peaks in the distance trying to keep the pace. The Dodge Ram motored south without regard for any speed limits. Jim stared long and hard at the Flathead Saloon but didn't stop. The one conversation he had hoped to avoid was about to occur. The spectacular setting swallowed the highway. Lakeside drew closer and Jim Shane could have been driving towards Cedar Rapids or through an Indiana cornfield. Jim was oblivious to his surroundings. Montana never marked time by traffic or movement. Rush hour in Lakeside meant that the sun baked the tips of the pine trees lining the slopes of Flathead Lake. The tall trees appeared illuminated marking the distinction between the tree line and the horizon. The driveway crackled under the large truck tires. The black Harley sat covered in the garage that Jim had finished a few weeks back. Flathead Lake was smooth on this afternoon. Through the trees that guarded the house, the lake sparkled with the mirrored images of the adjacent shores. Jim turned the truck off and the day stopped for that moment. He stood there and wished he could disappear. If there ever was a way to let someone else handle what remained, now would be the time. He knew that his faith had been masked in convenience, a shallow redemption for the paths he chose. Self pity tasted bitter. Jim Shane didn't have time to sip it.

The doors to the house swung open after they heard the truck pull down the drive. Two little girls had been informed that their father was home. Pigtails and pink rushed up the hill to smother the man on one knee. A father scooped his daughters from their sprint and raced back to the house. Jim carried the girls to the deck and fell back on the swinging loveseat with his giggling cargo. He gave bear growl kisses and forgot for a brief time what he was going to do.

"Is Brian coming home?" Justine asked abruptly.

"He'll be home in a couple days. The doctors want to make sure he's O.K. I just saw him and he wanted me to tell you guys that he missed both of you and to stay out of his room."

"Garett said that Brian and Jake were in ... a axdadent...what's that?" Jasmine stumbled in her question and wasn't sure what was going on.

"Listen pumpkin, Brian and Jake got hurt on the way to school. They will be fine, but they have to stay in the hospital for a few days." Jim tried to be brief.

"Did they get runned over?" Jasmine asked proudly as though she figured the whole thing out.

"No Jas, they did not get runned over." Jim knew this wouldn't go away. "It seems like they were playing too close to the guard rail and somehow fell down the side of a really steep hill. I promise, Brian will be fine. He got banged up, but he's tough. Hey, where's Garett?"

"Daddy, I heard Garett on the phone and..." Justine's age soared past her seven years.

"Sweetheart, let's go inside and find some treats. I'll bet I know where they are." Jim cut her off and carried them inside. Jasmine scurried into the kitchen. Justine waited next to her father, looking up at him.

"Some bad people hurt Brian and Jake today, Justine. They have been caught and the police put them in jail. They won't hurt anyone else, ever. I don't want to scare Jasmine." Jim was kneeling and looking his daughter straight in the eyes. He knew that Justine was aware of what had happened. "Can that be our secret?"

"Sure, Daddy." Justine got just what she wanted. She raced into the kitchen. Jim followed her and they waited for him to reach the cookies.

"How are the boys?" Garett's voice came from an arched doorway to the great room. Maggie, Conner, and Christopher joined the cookie demolition. The bag of cookies stood no chance.

"Only take three." Jim's hollow command was wasted on an array of crumbs from an empty bag. Little hands scooped up five or six and were gone. Jim shook his head and looked back at Garett. "Did you ever notice that the words ' parental authority ' must be the origin for the term oxymoron?"

"Lindsay called." Garett's voice rang clear through the fading rumble of five kids. "What happened today, Jim. Shit, Hagan called, my wife called, but I haven't heard shit from you. Lindsay said you ducked out of the hospital without a word. Hagan told me that the men we were looking for were nearly beaten to death this afternoon. Lindsay said you did it." Garett hadn't moved in the doorway.

"Outside, Garett." Jim responded and walked past Garett towards the deck. "Let's go down by the water. The kids don't need to hear any of this."

Jim Shane and Garett Baine walked down to the water. The property included two piers protruding like winding platforms floating effortlessly on the glass-like surface of the lake. The rising shoreline and tree studded cocoon prevented this part of the lake from freezing in the winter. Randolf Baine left the piers in the water for most of the year. Only the coldest winters forced him to pull them from the water. He often sat for hours at the end of the pier, preferring late January to the summer visitors. The shoreline was not a beach. Smooth, large rocks provided many small islands among the shallow water along their property line. The lighthouse sat between the two piers, a scaled down replica of New England lore. Jim reached the water and hopped from stone to stone until he reached the lighthouse. He turned and faced Garett, standing nearly fifteen feet away. Garett sat on the rocks marking the shoreline.

"Talk to me, man." Garett wanted to go back to the hospital as soon as he could.

"I over heard the police calls from up near the damn. They spotted the vehicle we were looking for. One unit decided to stop them. They killed the officer. I tried to follow the general direction of the call, then realized that these men were not running. If they were, then they would have been long gone. I back tracked around the lake and got lucky in Elmo. The two had stopped for some food at the Elmo Depot. I caught up to them, there."

"Did you call the Sheriff?"

"I had the woman at the Depot phone for the Sheriff."

"And you waited for him?"

"No."

"What happened?"

"I showed them that there are consequences for attacking children, especially our children. They're in pretty bad shape at Kalispell Regional. The Sheriff assumes that I did it, but he's not going to pursue it. He tried to exercise his elected duties. A feeble attempt to warn me about my alleged vigilante behavior was less than convincing. He knows that this county would never indict a man for defending his children. Hell, he would have done the same thing. Bottom line, is that these guys won't be bothering anyone. If and when they recover, first degree murder charges for the officer they killed, will be waiting. Garett, this isn't about them. It's about me. I brought them here. They were trying to hurt me."

"What are you talking about, Jim?" Garett turned to check on the kids. The house was still standing. He stood up. The sun had begun to set, casting long shadows across the lake. The wind swirled uncharacteristically through their cove.

"Garett, when I was in Vietnam, each soldier had two families. Your real family was not there. Wives, children, mothers, fathers, sisters, and brothers were back stateside. They wrote you letters that made you cry. Your tour was marked by how many months or days until that reunion date. Your other family was with you. I spent the better part of two years watching members of that family die. The time together was marked by the knowledge that many of us may not survive the week, the month, or the tour. I watched members of my unit get blown to pieces. I watched snipers pick the eyes out my closest friend. Pieces of his skull hit me in the cheek. These were eighteen year old kids. Kids were sent on patrol at night. Sometimes they didn't come back. The NVA or the VC made examples of them. Mandow got sliced up like a Halloween pumpkin, stuck on a pole with his genitals severed and crammed in his mouth. The NVA set him up near the roadside like a speed limit sign. They wanted to scare us. It worked rather well. Most of my unit survived by sending enough heroin up their veins to cloud whatever grasp they retained on the madness around them. In Saigon, I watched as many men destroyed by their own needles as I saw killed in action. A man named Park Huu Chau was one of those responsible for the network providing heroin to our troops. The money and the drugs flowed, virtually, unchecked during the last two years of the war. More people died in the year following the Paris Peace Agreement than in any other year of the war. The body count did not include the breathing stiffs sent back to the states with blank eyes and cold veins." Jim dropped to a squatting position. His eyes looked straight into the water. "I never met that fuck, Huu Chau. That last chopper barely made it off the Embassy. I hung on the doorway watching a helpless mob that knew we were not coming back for them."

"Man, you have lost me." Garett remarked while shaking his head and checking the house for wandering children.

"My return to the states marked the beginning of my days of rage. This stage lasted some ten years including Texas and my on again/off again Tech years. You remember, Garett. Those were the days that included at least a dozen Genuine Drafts, a half bottle of Gran Marnier, and a couple of grams of blow almost every night. I finally came back to Chicago to stay. You guys put me up. Denise and I got married. The kids followed. We had a great house in Libertyville Perfect, right? Then the shooting at the Untied Center. Denise gets killed and Lindsay barely avoids the same fate. We end up in Montana, due to the forgotten wisdom of your Grandfather and the remarkable properties he left. Here were two families connected forever by some random city violence. You and Lindsay took a high road to give the kids a better chance. My children were given the same chance. I could never express how grateful I was. I've always hated the pretentious arrogance associated with big cities. We are told to appreciate the accessibility of the arts. What fucking good is culture if it's defined by tuxedos and limousines? Chicago is like one big fucking race, except there is no start. You just end up in it. Everyone is spinning around the track and we're going nowhere. You've got too many people in a confined space without any money. It doesn't take a fucking

Rhodes Scholar to figure out where this is headed. The minorities are not the fucking minorities, anymore. They are exploding out of the city and blaming everyone that has nothing to do with their particular misfortune. Garett, they would have been knocking on our doors in Libertyville. Montana was perfect." Jim reached up and brushed some dirt from the lighthouse. "I brought the violence to Montana, Garett. I brought it on last January in Chicago. My actions got Denise killed and I nearly got Lindsay killed. There was nothing random about the shooting in Chicago. They were trying to get me." Jim Shane stopped. The words hung like the air on a humid summer night in Chicago. Garett Baine stood in stunned silence. Jim would continue. He would tell this story for the first time. "For the last few years, things hadn't been great at home. My business had been sporadic, almost dictated by the political tides. Big business rarely makes large capital expenditures during an election year, or preceding any meeting of the Federal Reserve. My business seemed to mirror any government hiccup affecting the economy. My income was based solely on large industrial purchases. Strike one, baby. Your entire income is measured by the economic stability coming out of Washington. Shit, this guy is still trying to prove that he has no distinguishing marks on his genitalia. Industrial updating averages twenty-four months from purchase order to payday. That's two years from the time I make a sale until the time I get paid. That's also two years to cancel the deal. Five years ago, we had run our credit cards to well over $50,000 in debt. There were no dinners out. There were no vacations. We came very close to splitting up. I did not want to lose my family because I could not afford to support them. Denise watched as I became obsessed with my business. I continued to build our debt because my business requires a tremendous amount of travel. We began to fight constantly about the time I was gone and the lack of results. I was increasingly difficult to live with. Money doesn't buy happiness. Bullshit. Money gives you choices. Money gives you the time to pontificate on talk shows about the misdirection of those without money. Fuck those self-righteous zealots. They all find the direction after the ship docks. You were there, Garett. Starting over at forty. Cold-calling strangers and asking for money. Did you ever get up in the morning, miserable, Garett? Miserable because you couldn't stand the sight of yourself. Randolf's timing couldn't have been any better. It's like he waited until the time was right. Without any money, there are very few choices. Denise wanted me home more. She wanted me to share the kids because I would never get that time again. I was useless. Some women don't understand that mortgages and homes are not a right of spring. We needed to clear $100,000 per year to break even. My 1995 W-2, showed an income of $13,000. Regression is not the adhesive bond that brings families together. We could have sold our home and down-sized our entire lifestyle. We could have moved to that dirty log cabin in the mountains and been happy because we were all together. It's back to choices. Fairy tales and fables sell books." Jim Shane spit high into the air and watched it christen the water. There was no eye contact with Garett. Jim seemed to be speaking to himself.

"Jimbo, you better start makin some sense."

"Here we go. Last fall, I get a call from this guy at 3-M. We had done some business together on a number of occasions. I helped design the last hot melt system installed in their Milwaukee plant. This guy gives me a lead on some used equipment. A company called Nagr, Industries, out of Hong Kong, was looking to open a diaper plant in Chicago. They needed an agent to facilitate the acquisition of some capital equipment from 3-M. I would arrange the purchase and supervise the move. This was a great lead. The purchase was for five million dollars and Nagr was willing to put the money up front. This is a great hit. At 5%, I'm lookin' at a quarter of a million dollars. My first meeting with Nagr takes place at the Four Seasons Hotel in Chicago. An Asian man is there to greet me with an entourage worthy of most world leaders. Business is conducted and they are thrilled to find someone local and qualified to handle this transaction. After two subsequent meetings at Gibson's Restaurant, five million dollars is wired to an escrow account at the First National Bank of Chicago. The contract signed with 3-M was designed to be finalized after the equipment was dismantled. Any problems after that point would not result in a refund. No firm will initiate a massive project as in the dismantling of   complex equipment without guaranteed money. You follow me, so far?"

"I'm listening. Give me a fucking clue as to what this has to do with Denise and Lindsay."

"The head of Nagr, Industries is a man named Park Huu Chau. The same smack merchant from Saigon. This prick made a fortune during the war and took ten years off. He reappeared in Hong Kong and Bogota, Columbia with a distribution network for his contraband. After my meeting with his representative in Chicago, I did some research on Mr. Park Huu Chau. The general consensus in the industry was clear. The son of a bitch was using a network of diaper plants to route drugs throughout the world. I think he must have enjoyed the irony." Jim stood up and covered his face for a moment. "Man, I'm losing it, Garett. I can't even look at you. I can say this shit, but I can't even look at you."

"Don't stop, Jim. You can't pull out of this now."

"I should have pulled out of this a long time ago." Jim walked back towards the shore and headed for the empty boathouse. The moorings creaked as Flathead Lake took a breath. "So much shit came back to me after learning that I was dealing with this prick. His life had been one wealthy ride. Homes in Southeast Asia were bought and paid for. No mortgages. A few thousand people from his own country had to die. Six and seven year old kids were used as couriers to help line his pockets during the war. Chau taught them to dispense justice for him. It was simple to teach a child how to pull the pin from a grenade. The child had to die, but they were usually able to get close to their target undetected. Thousands of Americans returned home as junkies, but at least they were numb from the needles. Shit, half of them ended up dead. This was my new link in business. I met a soft, fleshy man wrapped in expensive silk suits smiling at the parasites paid to wipe his ass. Fuck him. I sat across the table from Jeong Chan Seo, Mr. Park Huu Chau's associate. I couldn't help but picture one of my kids eating a grenade to settle a debt for Mr. Chau. He used the street kids of Saigon. Orphans, nobody missed. I could never look my own kids in the eye if I didn't try to bring this guy down. Nothing, I have ever done, felt so right." Jim fumbled with a pack of Marlboros. He lit a cigarette and watched the smoke linger in the air. He started to drift. "Man, look at this place. There isn't an artist in the world that could paint something this beautiful. Make sure my kids stay here, Garett."

"Jim, you're losin' me. Don't start with that fading retrospective bullshit. I want to know about the shooting. I want to know about Brian and Jake." Garett stood up and faced Jim. "Finish this, god damnit!"

"Man, you know what scared me the most in my life?"

"No."

"Can you believe we're over forty years old? Do you remember how old that sounded not too long ago? Man, forty fucking years old. I like it, Garett. I like being forty years old. I don't want to be a kid again. Age doesn't scare me, Garett. Eighteen, fuck that. Twenty-five with a little knowledge. Experience in itself is over-rated. Lessons are mistakes without any tangible consequences. If you died today, how many things would you have done differently? Shit, I'd change my whole fucking life. I may not change the players, but the list ends there. Most people spend their entire lives wishing they could do something completely different. There's a legacy to leave behind, right? We go to funerals and mourn the passing of a friend. A half hour later, everyone is at a luncheon, pissed off because the waiter hasn't brought enough bread. Imagine the legacy that guy left. We're taught to live our lives in preparation of our demise. Man, Huu Chau brought a purpose back into my life." Jim had turned and was watching the house. He could see the kids playing in the great room. He put the cigarette out on the bottom of his boot and closed his fist around the butt. "I notified 3-M that Huu Chau was having problems securing the property in Chicago. Huu Chau's people had me involved with the real estate people from the outset. The dimensions

241

of the structure would be designed around the equipment purchased. Huu Chau purchased land on the West Side and would build the plant from the ground up. The Alderman and the Mayor's office had given tentative approval for a virtual tax-free ride during the first ten years of operation. Huu Chau's problems began when the city received some information concerning Park Huu Chau's past. All permits were frozen until the Mayor could review and substantiate the information he had received. The investigation into Nagr, Industries and it's President, was enough for Huu Chau to postpone any plans to operate out of Chicago. A representative from Nagr contacted me about the canceled project. They contacted 3-M. The cancellation was effective immediately and the five million was to be returned to the bank of origin. Trouble was, 3-M didn't have the money. I did. The money was not wired to an escrow account for 3-M. It was wired to an account for verification. Upon verification and consummation of the contracts, the funds would be placed in the 3-M escrow account. The verification account was in the name of PDS, Inc. That was my company. The funds never left that account. I sent Nagr the 3-M contracts. They were to be signed and returned to PDS, Inc. with the funds. As far as 3-M knew, the deal was still tentative pending the land deal. They never had a claim on the funds. I wanted to bring Huu Chau out. To get the money back, they would have to justify it's origin. I informed Huu Chau's people during our last meeting that the DEA and the FBI would be interested in whether these funds were dirty. Nagr, Industries informed me that they would concede the amount of my commission or a quarter of a million dollars as compensation for PDS, Inc. The remaining $4.75 million would be wired back to their account at the Bank of Hong Kong. I informed Nagr, Industries that compensation of one million dollars would be required to release the balance. This last exchange took place just after the first of the year. I did not hear back from them and the money remained with me. Then came the shooting at the United Center. They killed Denise, Garett. I never knew it was them, Garett. I never knew until Brian and Jake were attacked. The destruction of the graves at home after the shooting. The vandalism at the Flathead. It just didn't fit. If they wanted me, I wasn't hard to find."

"They almost killed Lindsay, you son of a bitch!" Garett jumped up, screaming. He froze and stared at the house. "They almost killed Brian and Jake." Garett spoke through his teeth. "Where's this gonna stop? How could you do that to your family? How could do that to my family? You fucking blackmailed some international drug lord and exactly, what did you expect him to do?" Garett was frenetic. "No wonder you jumped at the chance to load up on Trexon. You were sitting on five million dollars. What about the two guys responsible for the shooting? The police found them dead. It was gang related. They were positive."

"They were wrong."

242

"Just like that?"

"Didn't Cortez tell us that they found twenty thousand dollars where these guys lived. The police couldn't really explain that money. It had to be from Huu Chau."

"You are fucking telling me that it never crossed your mind that while you were blackmailing someone for one million dollars, your wife was killed and you never connected the two?"

"I connected them a thousand times, but it didn't make sense. Why didn't they contact me after the shooting? Why play this game? I figured the money was dirty and they were not about to drag it through any kind of an investigation."

"So you did think about the connection? Did you ever think to mention it to me or the police?"

"The police confirmed that the shooting was gang related. When they found the car and the shooters, I pushed the connection out my mind. Christ, Garett. Denise had just been killed. At night after the kids went to bed, I could hear Jasmine or Justine crying. What do you say to your daughter when she asks about dying? What do you say when she wants to die so she can see her mother? It wasn't there, man. You told me that Cortez confirmed the shooters."

"Why didn't you ever say anything to me about Huu Chau or the money?"

"It wasn't over, Garett. I knew they would contact me about the money. Every time the phone rang, that was my first thought. A month passed. Nothing. Two months. I never connected the cemetery rampage with this. They wrecked over one hundred headstones. After we moved, nothing. Maybe it was over. Chau could've conceded the five million dollars because I threatened to go to the DEA. Maybe that kind of money is not worth the risk to him. So, I kept everything from you. I didn't want to get you involved."

"You have to be fucking kidding me. You were living with us. Your children and my children were sleeping in the same house, but you didn't want to get us involved? What is that?" Garett was trying desperately to rationalize something in this exchange. "I share my home and my business with you. My wife is raising your kids as if they were our own. I'm trying to make some sense out of this, but it ain't there. How are you so sure, now?"

"It was him."

"Just like that?"

"Hagan knew."

"Man, this is unfuckingbelievable. You tell me eight months after the fact that you created the circumstances surrounding the death of your wife

243

and the two month torture that Lindsay went through. These same circumstances almost get our sons killed. Jim, how much money is your family worth? Was Denise worth a million bucks? Could you get another million for Brian? I guess my family doesn't bring too much."

"Fuck you, man. Spare me the sanctimonious wisdom you inherited with your Montana wealth. There is nothing more repugnant than a morality lesson from a man who was cold-calling seniors and widows a year ago. Everyone is not blessed with your good fortune to pull them out of harm's way. You know god damn well that I would never intentionally put my family in jeopardy."

"Where does it end, Jim? We have seven kids between us that may have something to worry about."

"I'll end it in Chicago. I'll set up a meeting in Chicago with Chau's people. It will end there."

"Are you going to return the money?"

"If that's what it takes."

"You're not going to return the money, are you? You're going to kill him. Is that what this is about?"

"No."

"Yes it is. This is now the Jim Shane formula for retribution. Right? It's time for you to act. Right? No one else does what they're fucking supposed to do. Right? Man, you have been preaching about how fucked up this country is because no one takes any responsibility for their own actions. I've listened to this Armageddon bull shit for twenty years. Do as I say, Jim, not as I do. Is that what you teach your kids. If you take him out, you'll leave your children without any parents. When do you take some fucking responsibility? When you don't have any left. "

"I'm not going to argue with you, Garett. Chau won't show in Chicago. He knows the DEA would grab him in a minute. I'll be back in Montana as soon as it's over." Jim Shane began walking towards the house. He stopped. "I can't see them now. Take care of my kids, Garett. I can't change what has already happened, but I can put an end to it. Trust me. " Jim headed for the Ram truck in the drive.

"I know you, man. You're going to find him. If you take him out, Jim, don't come back here." Garett yelled. He started up the hill after Jim. The doors to the deck slid open. Garett stopped. Christopher and Jasmine came running out of the house. They were laughing. Jasmine was chasing Christopher. He had snagged the last cookie. They didn't notice the truck backing out of the drive.

* * *

CHAPTER THIRTY-THREE

Joe Cortez fumbled through some files on his desk. Taxman was on vacation and the organization of their partnership seemed to be disintegrating daily. Joe would be testifying that evening concerning a gang related homicide. He couldn't find the file. Joe cursed his missing partner for the fourth time, while not connecting on the raging Johnny Walker morning. Autumn in Chicago teased the city with it's perennial Indian summers.. Warm breezes washed Lake Shore Drive and brought all of the Ivy League sweaters back to Michigan Avenue. The woman at Jilly's on Rush last night teased like the early days of October and bit like the haunches of December. Jilly's provided an adult option to the club scene in Chicago. Molded in the image of Sinatra, Jilly's brought fifteen hundred square feet to life. Oversized martinis and the piano player sounding like a dead ringer for the man himself while belting out a spirited rendition of " I Get A Kick Out Of You. " Rush Street in Chicago had been reborn since the early days of Mr. Kelly's and the strip joints of the seventies. Friday night began with a promising encounter shortly after he arrived at Jilly's. Joe was off on Friday, but rarely ventured out before 10:00 p.m. After ordering a Red Label, rocks with a splash, he noticed a woman enter the bar. Drop dead gorgeous just walked in alone and sat next to the cop sipping his scotch. Not big on names, she was a striking brunette, mid-thirties, bedroom eyes, and legs up to her neck. The bartender was never a stranger. An unexpected farewell at 3:00 a.m. left Joe Cortez as cold as hell. Bring on the wind chill in Chicago and the twenty-two below zero. The temperature had just plunged. Joe hated the wind chill. He wondered whatever happened to the temperature. Now, it was wind chill and heat index. All he wanted to know was the fucking temperature.

Friday night still on his mind, Joe was late for roll call in the morning. His car wouldn't start. It was only early fall, but Joe could see the gray Chicago morning painting a petrified landscape dotted only with the rising smoke from each building, the belching exhaust pipes from the vehicles that managed to start, and the painful breath of those forced to traverse the cold. Shit, if his car didn't start in this weather, he thought, what would happen in two months. It was days like this, that made Cortez think about working the mayor's detail. The phone rang. It was Sheriff Jack Hagan of the Flathead County Sheriff's Office, Kalispell, Montana.

"Cortez, Twelfth TAC Unit."

"Officer Cortez, my name is Jack Hagan. I head up the Sheriff's Department in Flathead County Montana. You ever been to Montana, Officer?"

"Nope. I'm more in the market for a warmer climate."

"Hell, it couldn't be that cold, yet?"

"Colder than you think, Sheriff."

"I'm calling about two men, who recently moved to this area from Chicago. Garett Baine and Jim Shane. Do you know these men?"

"Sheriff, you wouldn't be calling me if I didn't know these men. Listen, I'd love to chat about the wide open spaces, but unfortunately, I work in a fucked up city and I'm sporting the scotch flu bug this morning. I don't mean to be disrespectful, but cut to the chase, Sheriff."

"I'm sorry if I have disturbed you. I have one officer dead, two boys were almost beaten to death, and the two men responsible for this are knockin' on Heaven's Door. Did I mention that these men are from Chicago? The officer they killed worked for my department. The boys they attacked belonged to Jim Shane and Garett Baine. Mr. Shane found them before we did. His attempt to save the county any expense fell just short, but I applaud the effort. We did some checking on everybody. What turns up is confusing. Our new residents, Mr. Baine and Mr. Shane were involved in a shooting earlier this year in Chicago. Mrs Shane was killed and Mrs. Baine was also shot. The families relocate to Montana. Makes sense to me. I had to get the hell out of Los Angeles more than a decade ago. Trouble is, they don't run away from any of that violence. It follows them to Montana. Perhaps you can shed some light on some of this. My research informed me that you were involved with the United Center shooting and that you were involved with closing the case."

"My partner and I zipped the bags on the shooters. Big mouths turned into dead mouths. Bragging still doesn't get you anywhere. We confirmed these guys as the shooters, but this case seemed to linger. Not long after we shut the door on this shooting, I get into a steeplechase with Jesse Owens. Son of a bitch disappears in my own back yard. His vehicle is clean except for a couple of plane tickets to Kalispell, Montana. Seems like your new friends were expecting company. We followed the tickets back to a firm called Nagr Industries, Inc. This firm had been searching for land in Chicago to build a diaper plant."

246

"A diaper plant?" Sheriff Hagan repeated.

"A diaper plant. The little white things that babies wear. The deal fell through due to some untimely reports concerning the President of Nagr Industries. Seems like Nagr's diaper plants were dispensing more than diapers. Mr.Shane, it appears, had business with Nagr Industries. He brokered the deal for the equipment Nagr would be purchasing. When the deal fell apart, Mr. Shane's company was in possession of a substantial sum of money that had been put up by Nagr in advance of the actual equipment sale. Frankly, we don't give a shit if Nagr loses any money. This firm seems to be peddling products from Bogota to Hong Kong with a great deal of protection. My guess is that Jim Shane dabbled where he shouldn't have dabbled. When the deal collapsed, nary a nickel was returned. Jim Shane decided to up his commission. Nagr wants their money back and has gone gang shopping to become an equal opportunity employer. The link is weak and we haven't been able to prove anything. The shooters from the United Center incident had no traceable link to Nagr or it's President. The only link was twenty thousand dollars found in their possession after they died. Where they got it is unclear. Our guess, now, is Nagr. They were not the type to diversify for retirement. Exactly, how can I help you?"

"The enigma in this case seems to be Mr. Shane. He's walking a very fine line. I've had to redefine my own agenda concerning this case. I have to condemn his efforts, yet I applaud the results. Do you believe the shooting at the United Center was random?"

"No."

"When the problems followed him to Montana, he decided to deal with it on his terms. We did some checking. Jim Shane is an ex-Marine bad ass. I'm an ex-Air Force pilot and Shane is the guy you want covering your back side. Two decorated terms in Vietnam will harden anyone. After the service, we traced him to Texas. The state police remembered an incident around the mid-seventies where a biker was beaten to death, but no charges were filed. That fine line, again. These guys were sent to Montana to shake up Mr. Shane. They beat up his oldest boy pretty good. They threw in a beating on Jake Baine for free. If this was an attempt to scare Jim Shane, it failed. Shane somehow tracked these men to a town just south of Kalispell. When we got there, the para-medics had to glue the pieces together. Garett Baine called me yesterday. He suggested that I call you. Mr. Shane has decided to set up a meeting with Nagr's representative, Mr. Jeong Chan Seo, in Chicago. Mr. Baine is concerned that his friend is going to make matters worse during this meeting. Mr. Baine felt that there may be a chance you could convince him otherwise. His mother in law still resides in his Libertyville residence. Mr. Baine

THE FLATHEAD SALOON AND CATHOUSE

assured me that Jim Shane will return to this address at some point during this stop in Chicago. He wants to make things right with his mother in law. He wants her to be a part of his children's life. Baine knows that Jim Shane will not do anything until he is certain that his children will regain their grandmother. I am simply passing on some information. Mr. Shane is not a fugitive. My department would like to thank him for what he did to a couple of cop killers. I'd like to see him back in Montana without a warrant for murder. So would his family."

"I'll see what I can do, Sheriff. I met Jim Shane on the night his wife died. I'll see what I can do."

*   *   *

CHAPTER THIRTY-FOUR

Libertyville used to hold that middle ground between the city of Chicago and a small rural community grasping to retain the character of it's origin. Linked by metro trains and tollways, Chicago was a long commute, but a small price to pay for many. Jim Shane had come back home in Montana. He missed Georgia, but not the cosmopolitan spread of Atlanta. Texas seemed like an out of body experience during some other lifetime. Libertyville once held bits of both during his search for a home to raise his family. He searched diligently for the right place to raise his family. Returning to this community from Montana gave northern Illinois a different perspective. The quaint downtown district had given way to the endless string of car dealerships and strip malls. The farms and space which seemed so vast a few months ago, now appeared to be small roadblocks in the path of new construction.

The house seemed remarkably unchanged from the place they left almost a year ago. Jim walked slowly through the living room stopping to stare at the shelves he and Denise built together along the fireplace. He remembered working on those shelves and debating with his wife about the purpose of a living room. Jim never could swallow the concept of the shrine living room. Why create a room, a major room in the house, where the family is forbidden from using it? They may pass through it occasionally, but never entertain any thoughts about camping there. He walked slowly through the house, reaching up to bang the copper pots hanging from the overhead iron rack. This country kitchen was home to many nights where Denise and Jim would sit on the counters after the kids had gone to bed. An open bottle of Pinot Grigio, a couple of Molsons, and the clock disappeared. Denise loved hanging out in the kitchen. The pictures of the kids still hung on the refrigerator door. Two drawings from Justine remained taped to the freezer door. A bright yellow sun bathed the two stick figures with smiling faces and long hair. The figure at the lower left was either the cat or the dog. Justine's answer changed from time to time. Justine had etched a message on the top of the page. Shane smiled as he read them. 'mommy and me'. His hand reached up to cover the figure of his wife. He didn't want her staring back in judgment. It could have been a mirror.

Jim Shane moved upstairs on this slow motion tour. The house had become a documentary in his mind. Scenes left untouched from the past. He knew that he lived there once, but this was a catatonic glide through the recurring nightmare he created. Their bedroom still smelled like Denise. The vanity table, the dressers, and the Victorian poster bed were filled with Denise. Jim could see her body on the bed. Sensual and at home. They made love in the afternoon all the time. He could see her face against a bevy of plaid pillows. Her eyelids would close slowly and a soft smile would curl her lips as their bodies locked together. This was her house. After she had been gone for months, it was still her house. A dead ringer for a New England bed and breakfast postcard, Jim peered through the picture window overlooking the back of their property. Jim sat on the bed. He could see the play station he built for the kids. His engineering background produced an incredibly sophisticated set of swings, slides, platforms, and multi-level tree houses. The Shane back yard was a popular place for the neighborhood kids. Jim picked up the pillows from the bed they shared. He brought them to his face. Damn, she was still there.

"I left it the way it was." A small voice came from the doorway. Barbara Pendleton was a small woman. At seventy-one years old, she had no health problems. She appeared frail and thinner. It was not her health. It was her heart. She had lost her husband and her daughter. She hadn't seen her grandchildren for more than six months. Sadness filled every waking moment of her life. "It was your home, Jim. I was only a visitor."

"You were never a visitor to this house, Barbara." Jim stood up and walked toward the woman he had come to see. He stopped just short of the doorway. Jim knew that he had experienced in this first trip back, what Barbara had been feeling for the past seven or eight months.

"Did you bring the kids, Jim?"

"No, I couldn't this trip."

"Well, I know you didn't come back to see me."

"I came back for a couple of reasons. First, I wanted to tell you that I have contacted the cemetery and told them that Denise will be staying next to her father, permanently. I was so wrong to ever consider taking her away from there. I hope you can forgive me."

"There's nothing to forgive. It wasn't my call, but I tried to make it anyway."

"It was the right call, regardless."

"Maybe?"

"My company, PDS, has some unfinished business. It may require some travel. I will know in a day or two. It is important that I wrap this up as soon as possible. I'm not sure exactly how long this will take. Garett and Lindsay are watching the kids, but they are busy as hell with their kids and the restaurant. That doesn't give you much time to pack." He handed her an envelope. "Our kids need you. I need you." Barbara opened the envelope and took out a one way ticket to Kalispell, Montana. "This isn't something I care to discuss or debate. Justine, Jasmine, Brian and I are going to be staying in Montana, permanently. We have found, however, one glaring deficiency in our move to the Northwest. Your flight leaves the day after tomorrow. Pack what you need for a couple weeks. I'll arrange to ship the rest. I've got to call the kids. What do I tell them?"

Barbara Pendleton hadn't heard many things that made her happy recently. Her arms reached for the only other man her daughter loved. Christ, she missed those kids as much as she missed her own daughter. "You know, I don't remember living anywhere else in my life. My family dictated where I lived and we always lived here. When Denise's father died, you begin to mark the years you may have left. I never imagined that my time left would be spent alone. Denise and the kids lived so close. You were constantly traveling, so Denise and I became even closer after you got married. We had no other grandchildren, but these three filled my life with the same love that raising my own children gave me. My friends wanted me to take cruises with them. They all said I should see the world. For what? So I can bring back some God awful trinkets from Alaska. Do I need to spend two weeks looking at some glaciers? Some of my friends spent six weeks in Australia. They said it was beautiful. I asked them what they did for six weeks. They went sight-seeing. Trust me Jim, there are only so many kangaroos or Kuala Bears I could look at. I laughed at the invitations, but they were flattering. When Denise died and you took the kids to Montana, my life expired the same as my daughter's. The difference was simple. I had to look at this empty life every day. I tried one trip with the girls, but turned around at the airport. I did not want to be there. I wanted to be with Brian, Jasmine, and Justine. I wanted to be with your family, Jim. You want to know what to tell the kids?" Her words migaretted the favorite expression of her son-in-law. "Love to."

Jim Shane took Barbara Pendleton to O'hare International Airport the next morning. Jim, then returned to Libertyville. His office in the basement had remained unchanged. The computer was quiet. Gone were the endless programs spinning from data base projections fed to him daily from Ford, Proctor and Gamble, Kimberly-Clark, General Motors, and more than a dozen industrial customers or potential customers. Jim recalled the scratches at the office door from his girls. Denise would hustle downstairs and remind the girls that Daddy was working. He often stared at the door for long stretches. He remembered wishing for an office away from home, so he could accomplish more. The office door was quiet, now. Denise had told him on many occasions to be careful with those wishes, they may come true. The telephone shattered the deafening silence.

"Jim Shane, please."

"Speaking."

"Jim, this Joe Cortez from the 12th Police District in Chicago. I met you last winter on the night of the shooting at the United Center."

"I remember. What can I do for you, Detective?" Jim asked, expecting the call.

"Actually, I'm not a Detective. Tac Unit officers do not have gold shields. Pity, most of us are better cops."

"My apologies. What can I do for you, Officer? You wouldn't be calling if Hagan had issued a warrant. You'd be at my door. "

"No warrant. Hagan has no desire to prosecute you."

"Who called? Garett or Hagan?"

"Hagan."

"Garett must have called Hagan after I left."

"Let it go, here."

"Let what go?"

"Chau."

"What do you think I'm here for?"

"The shooting at the United Center last January never seemed to go away. We know about your connection to Nagr, Industries and Park Huu Chau. The DEA and the State Department have been after this guy for years. You connect with Nagr last year. The deal goes south and Nagr is out five million dollars. The DEA doesn't care about the money. Apparently, Mr. Chau doesn't feel the same way. Retribution seems to be your path of choice. It worked in Montana, Jim. It won't work in Chicago."

"The DEA and the State Department have not been able to place a sighting on this guy for over ten years. I'm a fucking salesman from suburban Chicago. Assuming that I want to, exactly how do you think I'm going to get to this guy?"

"He got to you."

"We were in the fucking phone book."

"Why did you come back to Chicago?"

"I came back to help my mother-in-law move to Montana. I came back to put the house up for rent. Did Garett Baine tell you that I came back to kill Park Huu Chau?"

"There is some concern. They want you back."

"Chau would never show himself in the states. Hell, he hasn't been seen, period, for the last few years. Shit, for all we know he's already dead. Tell me, how am I going to kill Mr. Chau in Chicago if he is not here?"

"Mr. Shane, wrap up your business here and get back to your family. That's all they want."

"That's exactly what I intend to do." Jim Shane hung up the phone. He reached for the card file at edge of the desk. The file spun slowly until the number appeared. Jim dialed the number.

"Lappin/Sigman Properties."

"Ira Lappin, please."

"Ira Lappin's office, may I help you?"

"Ira Lappin, please."

"Who's calling?"

"Jim Shane."

*   *   *

CHAPTER THIRTY-FIVE

Barbara Pendleton had been in Montana for two weeks. The joy and exhilaration associated with seeing her grandchildren was tempered by the first sight of her oldest grandchild. Brian's injuries had improved, but they were not gone. Garett carefully explained the accident to Barbara, taking her through every step of the morning they got hurt. Garett described the fall and the loose gravel near the guard rail. They were not allowed to go beyond those rails, but boys never listen. Garett drove Barbara to the location of the fall. Barbara gasped at the ferocity of the rock face the boys rode to the ravine floor. Garett Baine made a point to walk Barbara Pendleton past the injury to Brian and Jake. The kids were so happy to see her. He did not want her to know that their boys were attacked. She would find out in time, but not until everything played it's course. Jim Shane had been gone for three weeks. He had called three times to speak to his kids. The kids knew that he had to stay in Chicago to rent their house and wrap up some business matters. Garett and Lindsay decided that their children would not be told what happened to Brian and Jake. Jasmine and Justine were under their care, therefore, they would not be told of the attack. The boys were schooled in the story of their accident. They had been walking to the intersection where the bus stopped. On this particular day, they strayed from the road while trying to follow a group of deer at the base of the ravine. The ground gave at the wrong time. Both boys fell down a very steep grade of the ravine. Garett knew that Barbara would eventually learn what happened. The story had past the local television coverage and was out of the newspapers. However, as soon as Barbara began discovering the community, she would learn about the attack.

Barbara Pendleton loved Montana. Past her knee-jerk reaction to Brian's injuries, Barbara Pendleton found color in her cheeks, energy in her eyes, and a particular desire to embrace each day. On her flight to Montana, Barbara wondered how the girls would react to her. Would she simply bring the pain back from losing their mother. After all, wouldn't she be the link to Denise that could trigger that trauma all over again. Barbara began to wonder about her own needs. Was she putting her own needs ahead of the kids? Could a selfish grandmother use the emotions of three children as a brace for her loss? The flight became a literal guilt trip. The change over in Salt Lake City, nearly resulted in a trip back to Chicago. What made her continue is unclear, but her fears were mistaken. Her presence filled such a void for Jasmine and Justine. The girls loved her and missed her in a separate way from the feelings they held for their mother. Barbara brought the numbers back. When Denise died, the girls lost. When they moved to Montana and their Nana stayed in Chicago, they lost again. Nana's back and one loss was erased. The compound on Flathead Lake waited for Jim to return.

The holiday season in Flathead County would bring some activity to the area. Late fall was quiet. Many residents tried to convince Garett to close the Flathead Saloon from October through March. At least, they said, shut it down from January through March. Garett was not going to shut the place down during the first year. Hours would change, but The Flathead Saloon and Cathouse would stay open through the winter. Garett began arriving home earlier at night as autumn crept along. Without Jim to share some of the closing hours, Garett was relegated to closing on a nightly basis. The restaurant business has many aphorisms. Among them, the quality of service generally declines with a decline in business. Adults whine more than children. The restaurant business seems to be the only business where customers gain the knowledge to operate the business simply by frequenting the establishment. Never plan to close early. There will always be one party arriving minutes before closing. They plan to take their time and are not offended or hurried by bright lights, by turning off the music, by placing the chairs on the tables, or dropping the check with the meal. Garett made it home before midnight on most nights during the past four weeks.

Lindsay never considered taking care of the kids as a chore or an incredible work load. Barbara's arrival proved to be the window of time that had been shut since they arrived in Montana. Lindsay's responsibilities had changed only slightly when Jim left. Jim and Garett were, for the most part, wart hogs in a crystal shop when it came to accomplishing the daily tasks of child rearing. Barbara Pendleton cut Lindsay's tasks in half and gave her some time to herself, something she hadn't sought, but savored all the same. Lindsay could wait for Jim to get home on most nights without falling asleep. It was late fall in Flathead County, the kids were in bed. Jake still had trouble falling asleep. The fire in the great room grew to fill the fireplace. Garett arrived at 11:30 p.m. Lindsay wore a red flannel oversized robe. She curled her feet up under her legs and poured two glasses of a California Merlot. Garett leaned over and kissed her. His Nocona's hit the table as he tasted the wine.

"How was business, tonight?" she asked, not caring.

"We had more employees than customers."

"It's only going to get worse after the holidays."

"We've been through this before. Let's see what the holidays bring. Kids, O.K?"

"They're fine. Jake wants to go back to school."

"What does the doctor think?"

"Physically, he could handle it."

"But.."

"But, he's still having trouble falling asleep. I know that morning still scares him. I wonder how the kids he barely knew will treat him?"

"I'll talk to him in the morning. I think if he wants to go back, we should let him. He could have gone the other way. He could have buried himself at home and pulled the shades. Let's try to go with him on this."

"Well, at least, talk to him in the morning. Explain to him that it could be rough."

"Done."

"Jim called today. I didn't talk to him. He talked to Barbara and the girls. Barbara said he expects a deal on the house within the week."

"Did he mention coming back?"

"I don't know. I guess we are all assuming that he will come back as soon as the house is rented. Garett, Jim hasn't talked to Brian since he left. He hasn't talked to you since he left. There was a message on the machine yesterday from Joe Cortez. I assume you called him back or he got in touch with you at the restaurant. We've been married for fifteen years, I know when you're keeping something from me. Something happened between you and Jim. I haven't said anything, but something is going on. What did Cortez want?"

"The two guys who attacked the boys are being arraigned next Monday. Their physical condition has improved enough to bring them before a grand jury. They are from Chicago, so Hagan has contacted Cortez about some of the background information on these guys. Nothing is going on between Jim and I. I don't think he'll be back in town before the trial. Everyone knows he was responsible for the condition of the two men when they were arrested. The State's Attorney has decided to charge them with first degree murder for killing one of Hagan's officers. They will stand trial on these charges before they address the attack on Brian and Jake. Hagan may have told him to stay out of town for awhile. I think he's concerned about dealing with a court appointed defense attorney, bent on making their condition at the time of the arrest, an issue. Jim's absence would make it difficult to exploit the issue. No local judge is going to delay the trial to search for Jim. No judge will grant a change of venue, so the trial should proceed quickly."

"Why hasn't he talked to you about this?"

"I'm sure he feels that the less contact we have with him at this point, the less involved we will be with any fallout from this case."

"That's it?"

"That's my guess. I think Jim knows what he is doing. Let's just wait and see. Are the kids asleep?"

"Why, what's on your mind?"

"Nice robe."

"Thanks." Lindsay moved a little closer to Garett. She stretched her leg out along the faded jeans of her husband. "Don't you want to know how my day went?"

"No." Garett pulled the belt from Lindsay's robe. The loose knot opened easily. Garett could see the white skin beneath the flannel. His hand reached inside the robe, moving slowly from her hips to her breast. She wore nothing under the robe. "The wine, the fire, what kind of a guy do you think I am? "

"I don't know. Let's find out." Lindsay leaned over and kissed Garett hard on the mouth. Her teeth gently bit his tongue as it slid inside her mouth. Her left hand began to pull the silver belt buckle she gave Garett on his 40th birthday. She slowly pulled the band collar shirt from his jeans and undid each button. They rose together standing in front of the fire. The fireplace crackled with fresh wood, painting the cathedral ceiling with orange shadows while mixing with the sporadic sheaths of moonlight darting from the lake. The flannel robe fell to the floor. His arms, thick with definition, pulled her closer. She guided him to the floor and slowly placed him inside her. Garett looked up at the silhouette above him. Perfection traced night lines of movement.

The bottle of Merlot was empty. That flannel robe covered them against the fireplace. Lindsay kissed him on his cheek. Garett smiled and lit a cigarette. He smoked only at night and never in front of the kids. It didn't bother her.

"Do you love me?" she asked coyly.

"Sporadically." Garett mumbled. Lindsay began to pull the hairs on his chest. "O.K., O.K., constantly."

"Forever?" she continued.

"Of course. " he answered on cue. Garett smiled while his head fell back against the bottom cushions of the couch. They were still sitting on the floor wrapped only in the flannel robe. Lindsay nestled under Garett's chin.. Long fingers continued to make circles on his chest. Her body profile followed along his side.

"Do you ever regret the decision to move to Montana?" Lindsay asked.

"Absolutely not. Obviously, the question leads me to believe that you have had some doubts? Separate yourself from the incident with the boys. That could have happened anywhere."

"I can't separate myself from what happened to the boys. The kids are still afraid to go to school. We have been driving Brian to the main entrance at school and picking him up at the same spot since the boys were attacked. We are not going to allow Jake to catch the bus when he goes back. How long do you think this will continue? My stomach is in knots every day as I wait for Maggie to walk out of the school door. I barely let Christopher and Conner out of my sight during the day. Didn't we leave Chicago to get away from this?"

"We left Chicago to improve the quality of our lives. We left to give our kids a chance to grow up where the focus of their lives is not what they have, but who they are. Unfortunately, beautiful scenery, alone, cannot instill those values. We didn't leave Chicago in a protective bubble. That bubble does not exist, anywhere. The men in jail for attacking the boys were not from this area. Even if they were, Chicago doesn't possess a monopoly on senseless behavior. We've had more than our share of lessons on human nature lately, but we can't run from them. Don't let one isolated incident distort the decisions we've made."

"One incident in Chicago and we move. One incident here, and we should simply get past it? Explain the difference." Lindsay was not trying to create friction, but these questions had been lingering.

"Lindsay, I didn't run from an incident in Chicago. There are no borders that screen bad people. We left Chicago because we had an opportunity to live our own lives. Didn't we decide to withdraw from that neurotic race to Bloomingdale's? Didn't we decide that insanity was the installation of metal detectors at school to limit the number of armed students? Think back a year. We saw each other briefly, in the evenings. Our communication level consisted of an occasional sneer when the television channel was changed. I don't want to go back there. We don't control what happens to us, ultimately. Shit, someone went to a lot of trouble to teach us that. My grandfather left me a notebook full of his philosophical tidbits. Most of them could fall under the category of cynical dribble. A few stood out. One made particular sense. He wrote, ' Stop looking for excuses to explain everything that happens in your life. They don't exist. Isn't it odd, that the most courageous people on this planet have endured the most pain?' Lindsay, he wrote that fifty years ago."

"Do you find that providential?" She asked ,feeling a bit more convinced.

"Absolutely."

"I'm sorry. I guess I'm just tired of being nervous."

"With kids, I'm not sure that will ever change."

"Tell me what happened with Jim." The fingers stopped making circles. Garett sat up and looked at his wife.

*   *   *

CHAPTER THIRTY-SIX

Chicago is a city famous for restaurants, where legends are born from perception. Time becomes an hourglass, changing players as it shifts from decade to decade. The seventies and eighties crowned the son of a delicatessen owner as the undisputed king of diversity in Chicago. Rich Melman, founder of The Lettuce Entertain You Restaurant Group, developed concepts that included the fine dining of Ambria or The Pump Room to the marketable concepts of Ed Debevics, Maggiano's, and the Corner Bakery. Lettuce grossed more than 100 million dollars for the sale of those concepts.

In 1989, a new king was born at the corner of State and Rush. Gibson's Steakhouse became the collaboration of Steve Lombardo and Hugo Ralli. Lombardo had previously been involved at the same location with a restaurant called Sweetwater. His partners included a combination of prominent local business executives and former Chicago professional athletes.. Hugo Ralli came to Chicago looking to open his own restaurant. Born in London, Hugo trained at the Hotel School in Lousanne, Switzerland. That three year course took him through the age of twenty-one. From there, Hugo traveled Europe, working in some of the most prestigious restaurants in the world. The kitchens at the St. Moritz in Paris and Quaglino's in London, became the background that brought Hugo to the United States. In 1978, he took over the re-opening of Tavern on the Green in New York City as Managing Director. An ambitious man, Hugo returned to Europe as part of an International Restaurant Group, that eventually fired him, after his attempt to purchase the Group failed. The restaurant opportunities of Chicago had not eluded him over the years. Eventually, Hugo came to Chicago, in search of his own legacy. When a restaurant broker showed him Sweetwater, Hugo met Steve Lombardo. Steve knew little about the restaurant business, but he knew everyone who was anyone in the city. Hugo knew the business, but didn't know a sole. They signed an agreement on the back of an envelope. Gibson's Steakhouse opened in 1989. Sales, currently exceed ten million dollars per year from one location. Gibson's incorporates only 8500 square feet, making the gross sales numbers even more remarkable. The business serves dinner only. The jobs at Gibson's, are the most coveted restaurant positions in the city. Waiters will net more than seventy thousand dollars per year. Bartenders would earn in excess of one-hundred thousand dollars per year if they were allowed to work more than three shifts per week. The intensity of the shift necessitates a strict limit on the hours worked. The twelve hour shift does not allow for breaks while the bar is wall to wall from it's three o'clock opening until last call at 1:30 a.m. Gibson's has become the power broker home of the city. From the mayor to almost every visiting celebrity and sports team, Gibson's is a must see and must be seen stop for anyone with a taste for crowds. Dinner is a collection of over-sized prime aged steaks. Seafood portions are no smaller. Lobster tails weigh in at two to three pounds. The staff collaborates for a masculine demonstration of excess that includes the initial presentation of the menu to the flaming desserts that could feed a small orphanage. It simply works to perfection. On any given night, Paul Sorvino can be heard singing Opera at the piano bar. Mandy Patinkin might be offering his own version of " Over the Rainbow," for an overflow crowd. Dennis Rodman holding court with a cigar and a trio of Gibson's finest female regulars. When Ira Lappin called Nagr Industries, requesting a meeting between Jeong Chan Seo and Jim Shane, the reply was short. Seo would meet Shane at Gibsons. Jim Shane called Nagr to confirm. Shane's message was clear. He would be returning the five million dollars, but needed some assurances that there would be no more misfortune befalling his family. By meeting at Gibson's, Seo knew that there would be little chance of giving Jim Shane any thoughts of retribution.

As Park Huu Chau's spokesman, Jeong Chan Seo had become accustomed to traveling in style. Airport meetings were never scheduled. Meetings took place in five star hotels. They were scheduled at the finest restaurants in the world. Rarely, were the meetings private. Seo, seemingly, flaunted the shield Nagr enjoyed. The meeting with Jim Shane would take place in the main dining room at Gibson's. The reservation was for 8:00 p.m. Jeong Chan Seo would arrive well in advance. Seo was a man whose age was hard to determine. Jeong Chan Seo stood five feet, five inches tall. He weighed 177 pounds. Seo wore expensive European suits accented with silk scarfs and matching silk handkerchiefs. The white gloves were always evident. He never took them off. The skin was tight on his bald head. It was shaved twice daily. Age appeared in the lines around his eyes. These eyes were small and although his age was far from evident, he was soft, puffy, almost frail in physique. Hugo Ralli greeted Mr. Seo and his group near the hostess stand. Jeong Chan Seo enjoyed the brief conversation with Chicago's most prominent restaurant owner.

"Nice to see you, again." Hugo exclaimed, having no recollection of these men.

"We never miss Gibson's on our visits to this city."

"Thank you. Let me, personally, check on your reservation. Was it under your name?" Hugo Ralli knew this would produce the desired response.

"Yes, Seo... say-ow." He responded on cue. "It's for eight o'clock. We are early."

"That's fine. Would you like to sit down, now?"

"Yes."

"Robin, please show Mr. Seo to table twelve. Let Jarrard have this table." Hugo Ralli turned back to his customers. "Enjoy your dinner. Jarrad is our head waiter. He will take excellent care of your group. If there is anything I can do, please let me know."

"Thank, you." The group of three followed an attractive young lady to a booth in the middle of the room. Seo and one of his associates settled in the booth. The third member of the group turned and headed back to the bar. Seo ordered drinks, comfortable with the recognition he coveted. Apparently, his generosity on previous visits had been appreciated.

Hugo Ralli reached to greet the following group. He did not know Jeong Chan Seo from the Dahli Llama.

Jim Shane had just finished his second Sam Adams at the Brasserie Bellevue. The restaurant occupied the first floor of the Sutton Place Hotel at the corner of Rush and Bellevue, directly across the street from Gibson's. Owned by a Canadian firm, Sutton Place offers 246 rooms on 22 floors with prices beginning at $250.00 per night. Sutton Place is a European style hotel built three blocks north of Chicago's famous hotel row hugging Michigan Avenue at the start of the Magnificent Mile. Since the emergence of Gibson's as the city's most desired eating establishment, Sutton Place critics have disappeared. Business is brisk Jim looked at his watch and reached for his coat. He swallowed the last of his beer and left a five dollar bill on the bar. He was watching the valets scurry amidst the Mercedes, the BMW's, and the limos pulling up in front of Gibson's. Jim kissed the Asian-American woman he had been sitting with at the Brasserie Bellevue and walked across Rush Street to the revolving door entrance at Gibson's. The sidewalk in front of Gibson's was teaming with the arriving Armani army. Once inside, the coat check and cigar counter were located to the immediate left. The dark walnut motif was adorned with celebrity photographs dating back to Clark Gable and Humphrey Bogart from the Mister Kelly's days. The photos lined the walls leading upstairs to the washrooms. Restroom attendants doled out fluffy hand towels while patrons wrestled with the forced notion of tipping in the bathroom. Jim asked about Seo's table. The bar was three deep in the main isle. Eating was not on the agenda for most in the bar. Jim, carefully, scanned the lounge from the entrance. The piano player had become accustomed to the inaudible level of his music. The Kettle One poured at a seven dollar clip.

Jim did not check his coat. He reached table twelve at quarter past eight. Jeong Chan Seo stood to greet him.

"Please, Mr. Shane, sit down." Seo motioned for Jim to sit across from him, next to his burly associate. Jim Shane obliged. "I took the liberty of ordering some appetizers. Do you like oysters, Mr. Shane?"

"No. I don't have much of an appetite this evening. I'll just have a scotch." Jim gave his order to their waiter.

"Do you know what I like about this restaurant, Mr. Shane?"

"The sixty-four ounce T-Bone?" Jim answered.

"No, Mr. Shane. My culture doesn't understand the concept of a four pound dinner. I like the energy of this restaurant. It moves efficiently and mistakes are rare."

"I'm glad that you like Gibson's, Mr. Seo. Unfortunately, we did not come here to discuss your culinary reviews. I suggest that you instruct your colleague to join his buddy in the bar."

"Mr. Sang will be staying with us during our discussions."

"Suit yourself." Jim lit a cigarette and tasted the Red Label in front of him. "I want my family left alone."

"Mr. Shane, I was sent here to discuss the unfortunate confusion regarding the funds transferred by Nagr Industries. With the abrupt demise of our Chicago ventures, these funds have not been sent back to their bank of origin. I believe Nagr had conceded the commission on this deal. To date, Mr. Chau has not been advised that these funds have been returned." At that point, Mr. Seo turned to his colleague and spoke in his native language. "Mr. Shane, Mr. Sang is going to check for a wire, now. If our conversation is to continue, this must not present a problem for you."

"Suit yourself." Jim calmly replied. He opened his jacket and held his arms apart. The brief search garnered some attention from the adjacent tables.

"Are you prepared to return the money to Nagr, Industries, Mr. Shane?" Seo was direct, satisfied that their conversations were not being recorded.

"Well, this presents a couple of problems."

"Such as?"

"Such as, how do I know that there will be no more incidents with my family or my friends?"

"Mr. Shane, Nagr is interested in securing the funds we lost. Beyond that, our involvement will cease."

"Your word, Mr. Seo, is not the assurance I was looking for."

"Mr. Shane, you are not in a position to be demanding much. Mr. Chau has been patient and agreed to this meeting, but he did not send me here to negotiate with you, Mr. Shane. Your choice is very simple. Transfer the funds back to their bank of origin and the misfortune that has plagued your family will cease. Anything short of those terms is unacceptable, Mr. Shane."

"I am going to repeat myself. This may present a couple of problems." Jim responded, swallowing hard and staring back at Jeong Chan Seo. "When do we address Mr. Chau's patience? My wife was killed in January. Was this an example of Mr. Chau's patience?"

"Mr. Chau had nothing to do with your wife's death. Police reports confirmed the shooting to be gang related. Their case is closed."

"Is that a fact?"

"Here is a fact, Mr. Shane." Seo was growing annoyed with the direction of Jim Shane's rhetoric. "I am going to repeat myself. You are not in a position to dictate much of anything. Either you are prepared to return the money or you are not. This may be the shortest meeting that I have ever attended. Mr. Chau expects one answer. Anything short of that will be considered a failure on your part to live up to the terms of this particular transaction." Seo was avoiding eye contact with Jim Shane. He preferred to page through a small notebook on the table, making some notations as they spoke.

Jim Shane turned towards the main dining room. The activity was pronounced. Food runners moved swiftly through the maze of tables. Balanced high over their heads were mammoth trays stacked with over-sized meals. Cigar smoke trickled into the dining room providing a flavor of tobacco in the non-smoking sections. Gibson's embraced the over indulgent businessman and his guests. Appetizers and bottles of wine were consumed with little regard for the cost. Waiters became accustomed to the unabashed spending of the presiding clientele. Lost in this sea of big egos and big checks, were the anniversary couples or those celebrating a special occasion. Suburban couples opted to split the Herculean portions and preferred the house wine over the wine list. Their scarlet letters became undeniably evident with the arrival of the entire wait staff to sing a thirty second rendition of Happy Anniversary or Happy Birthday. Whatever fantasies of blending were brought to Gibson's, disappeared following the serenade. The wait staff dispersed as quickly as it assembled, leaving a timid couple with their hands clasped under the table wondering if they could blow out the sparkler that accompanied a two pound slice of German Chocolate cake. The room was ablaze for the eighth time of the evening.

"We spent some considerable time together over the past year. The meetings we participated in concerning the plant proposal gave us an opportunity to cover many topics of discussion." Jim Shane appeared to be wandering. Seo put the notebook down. He wanted to know where this one was going. Jim continued. "If I recall correctly, you were educated in the states. California, if I'm correct?"

"Stanford." Seo replied.

"Right, Stanford. Great school. When I was in school, they required some courses on philosophy. I suspect the undergrads at Stanford were expected to sample the same. These courses really weren't good for much. Maybe the opportunity to discuss intellectual evolution with a gorgeous girl that was impressed with your desire to explore reality. The desire had to do with reality, but not the categorical life forces explored by the text. The reality that concerned me, was sliding that tight sweater over her head and removing the jeans that hugged her hips.. Psychology courses were better than bars."

"Mr. Shane, I am not particularly interested in your fornicating habits as a college student."

"I didn't think you were, Mr. Seo. Aside from my primary purpose in school, I managed to absorb some of what the courses were intended for. Guilt, Mr. Seo, seems to be an American obsession spawning in the latter half of this century. In this country, we learn to blame everybody else for the misfortune in our lives, but when it becomes self-serving, we lament about the things we could have done."

"Mr. Shane, can we address the purpose of this meeting?" Seo's eyes moved back and forth from his body guard stuffed into the booth next to Jim Shane.

"Your friend sitting next to me, whose suit is about to burst across his back, will not help you now." Jim turned to eliminate any questions for Mr. Sang. "Guilt appears to be a sentiment that Mr. Seo is not familiar with."

"Mr. Shane, my patience is not limitless."

"Unlike, Mr. Park Huu Chau's?"

"The money, Mr. Shane? The Money?"

"My wife was killed in January as a result of some circumstances that I created. Of course, I never intended that to happen. Hell, I never imagined her death to be a possibility. It wasn't until months later, that I connected her death to our transaction. I held more guilt for her death than any person on this planet. I wanted to die. I wanted to change places with her and if I couldn't do that, I wanted to join her. I wanted to take the fucking easy way out, because it was all my fault. Well, you know what? It wasn't all my fault. I didn't kill her, Mr. Seo. You did."

"Mr. Sang, I think it may be time for Mr. Shane to leave. I would like to enjoy my dinner before I have to inform Mr. Chau that this meeting was not successful."

"I want you to look past me to the hostess stand. There is a man standing in the doorway with a black mustache and wearing a suede jacket. His name is Joe Cortez and he is a TAC Unit officer with the Chicago Police Department. The man next to him is an agent with the DEA. There are three other DEA agents sitting in the bar watching the third member of your entourage. There is a table across the room with four members of the Narcotics Division of the Chicago Police Department." Jim turned to Mr. Sang. "Take a walk, Tiny. Go join your friend in the bar. Mr. Seo and I have a discussion to finish, alone."

Seo nodded. Mr. Sang walked slowly to the lounge. Jim Shane returned to his seat. Neither man spoke. Seo scanned the room. Was Shane bluffing? If he was, why? If these men were with the police and the DEA, Shane was the one guilty of embezzling funds.

"Mr. Shane, exactly what is the nature of your threats? You have five million dollars from Nagr Industries. How does that translate into the Drug Enforcement Agency and the Chicago Police Department? I find it hard to believe that you would be foolish enough to risk what remains of your family. You are playing a dangerous game." Seo broke the silence. "This is not about you or your family. This is business."

"If this is a game, Mr. Seo, then it is time for you to play." Jim Shane stood up and motioned to Joe Cortez, who waited patiently for Jim's signal. Cortez disappeared into the front lobby. Jim Shane stood waiting. Cortez and an Asian woman walked into the dining room. She spoke briefly to Joe Cortez, then headed to table twelve. She appeared to be in her late thirties. Her skin was smooth and her long black hair showed no trace of gray. She wore black slacks with a camel hair sport coat covering a white cashmere sweater. Black alligator boots were hidden beneath the long slacks. Her brown eyes pierced the walnut haze of the restaurant. They glimmered like blue sapphires in a sea of white. It didn't take long for the male clientele to notice the woman walking through the dining room. The years bred grace amid natural beauty. Jim remained standing. Jeong Chan Seo was confused. The woman reached the table and took her place next to Jim Shane. Three people remained silent for a brief moment. Seo could only stare at the woman across from him.

"Hello, Daddy." The beautiful almond eyes spoke first. Jeong Chan Seo was frozen. "It's been almost twenty-seven years."

"I want you to meet someone, Mr. Seo." Jim rescued the stunned gentleman from Vietnam. His silence had been anticipated. "This is Sanya Tu Lee. She goes by the name Sunny. I met Sunny when I was stationed in Saigon with the United States Marine Corps. She was nineteen years old. I had been assigned to the crew of the transport choppers that were to evacuate the United States Embassy compound in late April, 1975. Sunny was one of the last people pulled from the roof of the Embassy. She was hard to ignore. There was chaos in the compound. It was a bizarre scene. Thousands of refugees trying to scale the gates, hundreds trying to ascend to the roof, and too few Marines available to assemble the order of evacuation. When I asked for her name, she stared up silent and angry. The most beautiful eyes I had ever seen, had been stripped of trust. At that moment, I assumed that she was just another living casualty of the war. I gave her my headset. She was wearing some type of clearance badge that must have gotten her into the compound. It was yours, Mr. Seo, overlooked during one of your visits. I told Sanya to lose the badge once the chopper was airborne. The noise was deafening. Our CH-46 was escorted by AH-1J Cobras to the decks of the Hancock. The chaos and confusion on each helicopter was amplified by the constant pounding of the chopper engines and the escorting Cobras. On the Hancock, the refugees were agitated and scared. Food was scarce. I took care of Sunny. I stayed with Sunny during that trip. I had fallen in love with this girl from the first moment I looked down and saw her on the roof of the Embassy. My life changed that day. We talked for hours. She had been alone since the age of twelve. She told me about her father. She knew he was an important man in Saigon. Her father always had money and talked about the wealth that he had accumulated. This important man and her mother were not married, but he came to visit every week. Sunny knew why he came, but at least he came. On most visits, he would bring gifts. Trinkets, crap. The time he gave his daughter was short. He would speak about California and the oceanfront property he had purchased. I'm sorry, Mr. Seo. This is probably very repetitious for you. After all, you were there."

"This is fascinating Mr. Shane, but my colleagues and I will be leaving. This meeting is over." Mr. Seo had regained a sense of his surroundings.

"Sit still, Mr. Seo." Jim Shane ordered. "Let's begin again. Shall we?"

"This meeting is over." Seo began to slide out of the booth. He kept his head down, avoiding any more eye contact with the woman across from him.

"You might want to reconsider. " Jim Shane injected. " There are four DEA agents, a number of Chicago Police Narcotics Officers, and some scattered Chicago Patrol Officers that would be thrilled to know that I was meeting with Park Huu Chau. There are law enforcement agencies around the country that would revel in the knowledge I possess. I believe that

267

your partners with Nagr Industries would be interested in knowing about the salaries and wealth accumulated by Jeong Chan Seo. Over the past twelve years, Mr. Park Huu Chau has been in hiding. International warrants would have made travel extremely difficult. Chau disappears for the past decade. Enter Jeong Chan Seo. Bordering on brilliant, Park Huu Chau can easily alter his appearance and create another individual. Jeong Chan Seo is born. Chau verifies his credentials to Nagr. Seo begins representing Nagr and reporting directly to Chau. Both men draw large salaries from Nagr. Seo attains wealth and great notoriety in a decade as Nagr's front man. All the while, Park Huu Chau continues to collect as a partner. Seo purchases a Malibu estate from a land trust. The land trust was owned by Park Huu Chau. The purchase price was one dollar. All on record. A search of California coastline transactions involving property valued over five million dollars turned up Seo's name. Security Systems, Inc. was contracted to patrol the property. Their records indicated absentee ownership with contact through a legal firm in Saigon. Bottom line is simple. Jeong Chan Seo and Park Huu Chau are the same person. Of course, you know that. Your mistake was an incredible coincidental meeting aboard a CH-46 chopper in 1975. I met your daughter on that day, Mr. Chau. I fell in love with your daughter, Mr. Chau. She spoke about her father many times. The gifts he brought. The California estate he would someday bring them to. She spoke about her mother. When your visits stopped and California never came, Ms. Lee tried to find you. She told her daughter about how busy this important man must be. They would all still go to California together. Sunny's mother finally went to look for you. Sunny never saw her mother after that. Did she find you, Mr. Chau? Of course she did." Jim Shane did not wait for any response from Chau. He continued the pace. Sunny waited patiently, carefully watching the response from her father. "I brought Sunny to Texas with me after I returned from Vietnam. I knew the man she spoke about as her father was the same man responsible for half of the smack trade in Saigon. Your name was infamous in the military. After nearly two years together, Sunny left. I was difficult to live with and Sunny had decided to avoid what her mother had endured. We lost touch after a few months. Twenty years later, I find myself dealing with a company headed by Park Huu Chau. I tracked Sunny down after my first meeting with Nagr. We spoke for hours about where we had been for twenty years. We spoke about her father and California, again. I let it go when my wife was killed. I did not connect the two. The game changed Mr. Chau, after the boys were attacked in Montana. I contacted a friend from the Marines. He works as a robbery detective for the Los Angeles Police Department. I asked him to look at the ownership records for oceanfront estates from Long Beach to Santa Barbara. He was looking for the name Park Huu Chau or any absentee ownership from overseas. Sale records are public. Home security firm records could be used to track some contact for the property. Rental property on the coast often signals foreign investors or absentee ownership. The only estate with these connections was registered to Jeong Chan Seo. The same man representing Nagr Industries. I called Sunny and asked her if she knew the name Jeong Chan Seo. She did not. She told me to send her a picture of this man. The United States Department of State had retained records on Mr. Chau. The United States Department of Immigration had issued a Resident Alien card for Jeong Chan Seo. The Los Angeles Police Department pulled both photos. After sending the pictures to Texas, Sunny contacted me with some startling information. Sit down, Mr. Chau. The police are here as a precaution for me. They believe that Park Huu Chau may be planning to join Jeong Chan Seo in the United States for this meetings. I pulled them in as protection for myself. One word from me, and you'll be working as a butt ranger at the Chicago Metropolitan Correctional Center."

"What happened to my mother?" Sunny asked. Her eyes were difficult to hide from.

"Where's the wire Ms. Lee?"

"There is no wire. I came here for myself and my mother." Sunny answered without deference. She slid to the end of the booth and stood up. Sunny removed the camel hair sportcoat and laid it on the booth next to her. She slowly unbuttoned the white cashmere sweater until the sweater hung open. Sunny leaned over towards Park Huu Chau and grabbed both sides of the sweater, pulling it wide open. A white lace bra wrapped her small breasts. Her upper body was lean and the room began to discover booth twelve. "Put your hands around me, Mr. Chau. There is no wire."

"That won't be necessary, Ms. Lee." Chau did not welcome the commotion.

"What happened to my mother?" Sunny repeated as she buttoned the sweater and returned to her seat.

"I don't know." Chau's response validated everything. Chau knew that success was measured by crisis. Some of the best business decisions are knowing when to back out. Shut the doors and move on. "Saigon was a mess during those years. I never saw your mother after I stopped visiting her home."

"You're lying."

"I'm not lying. Sun Ja Lee never came to see me. If she had, I would have sent her away. There were many others." He was lying.

"You have a grandson."

269

"I'm sure I have many. I do not know how many children I may have produced in my own country."

"Produced? It is difficult to imagine that you could be more despicable than I envisioned. Please, don't add confusion to the years of complete abomination that have precipitated any thoughts of you."

"You're very articulate. Impressive. I did not seek to make babies. My women knew what relationship to expect from a person in my position. Many sought more. They were disappointed. They were not misled."

"What about California? Bringing both of us to California?"

"That was not from me. I may have spoken about property that I owned in different places, but there was no mention of traveling together. I'm sorry. I may have produced children, but I am not a father. I don't apologize for any circumstance that I did not seek. Delusion is the demise of the poor. Sun Ja Lee had it bad. Mr. Shane, I suggest that we conclude this evening." Chau was outwardly agitated. It was time to leave.

"This is what I waited more than twenty years for?" Sunny had not finished. "The only delusion that my mother was under, came from you. She was a beautiful woman with the soul of an angel. Life gave her nothing. She gave her heart to a man without one. Your visits over the years were extended by empty promises. She was used like a whore, stripped of any self-respect and trained like a sea lion. A couple of drinks, a fuck, and you were gone. The only thing quicker than your exits was your performance. End your meeting, Jim. As I learned more about my mother over the years, taking her must have been God's way to end her pain. Honestly, the saddest part for me is knowing that the degrading years my mother spent in this relationship were the only years of hope that she ever had. Sun Ja Lee had no life. After meeting you again, one thing is certain. I am the product of one parent regardless of the biological possibilities. I will wait for you outside." Sunny turned to Jim Shane. "I'm feeling ill." Sunny never looked at Chau as she left the table. Joe Cortez met her at the entrance to the lobby. Together, they walked toward the front doors and out of view.

"That went well." Shane's sarcasm elicited little emotion from Chau.

"Nagr Industries will still expect the return of the five million dollars regardless of the outcome of this meeting." Chau had already forgotten about Sanya Tu Lee.

"You don't get it, do you?" Jim Shane shook his head and looked up at the ceiling. The fans turned slowly while massaging the cigar smoke along the lattice structures overhead. "Age is age. I do not know how old you are. I would guess no younger than sixty. That still leaves plenty of time. You can choose to spend that time at home or in prison. At home, you will continue to enjoy whatever lifestyle you have grown accustomed to. In prison, they'll eat you alive. Hundreds of men will split you like a grapefruit. If you are unable to take your own life, AIDS will wither your body away very slowly. You'll become the personal property of men who cuddle to the backside of soft white new inmates. When the sores and lesions from the disease cover your entire body, they'll leave you alone. That'll take a good five years. The Chicago cops are here because they were asked to back up the DEA. The DEA agents are focused on finding Chau. If they do, you'll disappear in the system. There will be no claims of diplomatic genocide. You'll never crawl out of the cracks in this justice system."

"How do I know that the woman has not given me up?"

"Because you're still sitting here."

"I'm listening, Mr. Shane."

"You own the property at 27450 Pacific Coast Highway on Paradise Cove Beach, just west of Los Angeles. The property is owned outright. There is no mortgage. The Santa Fe style estate sits on 3.5 acres. There is a guest house, a guard house, and a generator house. You own one hundred and fifty feet of beachfront, a lap pool and a full gym. The main house has five levels with seven bedrooms, nine bathrooms, four fireplaces, and a twelve seat theater. The last known appraisal was for 7.5 million dollars." Jim Shane reached into his jacket pocket and pulled out some papers. "This is an irrevocable trust agreement. You will sign the title to this property over to Jason Sun Ja Lee, your grandson. The title will be placed in the irrevocable trust in his name. Ownership will transfer as soon as the paperwork is filed. You will have thirty days to vacate any personal items. Jason Lee can sell the property, live there, rent it, or tear it down. All the taxes will be your responsibility for the next ten years. Money will be prepaid to a California escrow account set up for the tax obligations of this property The tax agreement and the trust are ironclad. Sign them and you can walk."

"You are crazy, Mr. Shane. First, you steal five million dollars from my company. Now, you expect me to sign over the title to an estate worth close to ten million dollars. Your simplicity, Mr. Shane, will destroy you."

"Anything happens to me, Mr. Chau, and your story lands on every desk in the State Department, the FBI, and the DEA. Nagr Industries and the Vietnamese Government will receive the same story. I expect that they will not appreciate the deception."

"What about the five million dollars? Someone will have to answer for that money."

"The money will be transferred back to the account of origin."

"What assurance do I have that I will be allowed to walk out of this restaurant?"

271

"You have no assurance other than my word. This would be the same assurance that you were prepared to give me and my family. Choices, Mr. Chau. Life is about choices. Make yours now, Mr. Chau."

"What do you want out of this, Mr. Shane? I am not ignorant."

"Your grandson, Jason Lee, is my son."

"Give me the papers, Mr. Shane. The California coastline has become too unpredictable, anyway. The mudslides and brush fires could take the place at any time. The hell with it." Chau signed the papers without reading them. It didn't matter and he knew it. Jim Shane folded the contracts and slid them back into his coat. He rose quickly from the table.

"There is a price to pay for the promises we don't keep, Mr. Chau." Shane turned and walked to the front of the restaurant. He reached Joe Cortez and stopped. Park Huu Chau had not moved from his seat at booth twelve.

"Where's Sunny?" Shane asked Cortez.

"She's waiting for you outside. She's alright."

"Did you get the tape?"

"Yes. She was perfect. We heard everything and got it recorded. Did you tell her to take off the sweater?"

"No."

"She diverted all the attention away from the mike. Her Timex just kept on ticking."

"He hasn't moved." Jim Shane stared at Park Huu Chau. "He knows."

"You think so?"

"Absolutely." Three DEA agents were arriving at booth number twelve in the main dining room at Gibson's. The two large men in the lounge were arrested for firearms violations. They would be deported after the arraignment. Jim Shane walked outside. Sunny was waiting on Rush Street. Jim lit a cigarette. The windy city exhibited little wind on this night. The smoke trickled up alongside the streetlight, a gas replica from the 1940's. Sunny leaned against the streetlight and asked Jim for a cigarette. They stood still in the night lights of Chicago. Jim's Stetson hat hung across his eyes, but belonged somewhere else. Jim Shane had not been with a woman since Denise died. A small night breeze kicked the perfume from her neck and brought Jim back twenty years. They looked remarkably good together after all those years.

"How come you never told me about Jason?"

"Because, you would have come back."

"Does he know about me?"

"He knows we split up. That's all I told him for years. Before I came to Chicago, I told him about you and why I was going to Chicago. He's nineteen."

"Who does he look like?"

"You."

"My mother told me that if I wasn't good as a kid, my own children would have funny heads."

"Were you good?"

"What do you think?"

"She must have been bluffing. Your other kids are precious. Trust me, Jason doesn't have a funny head, either."

"What's he like?"

"You."

"Is that good?"

"That's good, Jimmy." Sunny smiled. "He's with me. He's waiting across the street at the hotel. Do you want to meet him?"

"Absolutely. " Jim Shane never hesitated.

"What are you going to say to him?" Sunny asked as they headed across the street.

"I don't know. I might start by asking him if he likes California."

"What?"

*   *   *

CHAPTER THIRTY-SEVEN

Three weeks later, the Wednesday before Thanksgiving, 1996.

Interstate 90 rose up from Wyoming and crossed into Montana at the Crow Indian Reservation below Billings. The highway split the Little Bighorn Battlefield before it turned west at Billings. Jim Shane was going home. What awaited him was unclear. The Ram pick-up had been on the road for the better part of a week. Jim was traveling alone and drove no more than ten hours per day. The early winter had made travel slow. Thirty-five miles per hour between Billings and Butte, extended the state beyond the imagination. When Jim turned north on Highway 93 at Missoula, the drifting ceased. The road cleared for his final ascent into Lakeside. Jim had rehearsed dozens of scenarios concerning his arrival. The drive took Jim through Elmo, Montana. He thought about the woman at the Elmo Depot and couldn't remember her name. There had been no word on the fate of the men convicted of beating the boys. The telephone calls to the kids did not broach the subject. Brian did not offer, either. In fact, Brian had very little to say during any of Jim's calls. Garett would assure Jim that Brian was fine. Quiet, but fine. Garett and Jim never discussed the conversations at the lake after Jim left. Jim Shane was determined to allow his family and Garett's family time to absorb the details of that evening and accept the outcome. His long absence had been justified in his mind as time to cope for his family and friends. They would need time if there was any possible forgiveness for the consequences of his actions. Consequences that cost Denise her life. Jim envisioned the girls as the most forgiving. Age would be Jim's ally. Brian may never forgive him. Barbara Pendleton would return to Chicago. The confrontations played out over and over again in his mind. Lindsay had insisted that Jim and the children accompany them to Montana. Now, she knew that his actions precipitated the shooting. Could anyone have that much capacity for forgiveness?

Jim Shane drove through Lakeside. At the last moment, his plans changed. It was after ten o'clock. The night sky around Flathead Lake was clear. The moon danced off the snow capped peaks guarding the western shores of the lake. Driving north on 93, the road narrowed while tracing the shoreline of Flathead Lake. The Ram slowed to withstand the steep descent preceding the Flathead Saloon and Cathouse. This was the Wednesday before Thanksgiving. Many in the hospitality industry experienced their biggest night of the year. It was the night where many college students returned home for the first time. This was the first large influx of tourists since Labor Day. The California migration began early in the week. Even in Flathead County, this was a night to be out. This evening signified the start of the holiday season. For the next six weeks, the Flathead Saloon would gross more than the entire first four months of 1997. The pick-ups, four-wheelers, and snowmobiles lined the gravel parking lots surrounding the Flathead Saloon. The activity at the Flathead Saloon lit up the Continental Divide on a clear November night.

Jim Shane pulled his truck around the rear of the building. He parked behind Garett's Blazer. It was just after ten. The music could be heard from the lower level bar as Jim approached the Flathead. The night sky drew unobstructed clarity throughout the stars while highlighting an endless montage of constellations. Thick wooden railings lined the stone walkways leading to the restaurant. Flathead Lake appeared frozen and perfectly still. It wasn't. The seasonally warm water had melted the snow as it fell. Tranquility feigned the canvas of an artist searching for nature's best. The Flathead Saloon stood anchored in the November fallout from an early snow storm. The imposing pine trees struggled to hold the weight of the snow. The outside deck wrapped around the restaurant like a white sash, frozen out of season with the tables still in place. The Flathead was busy. The crowd was well oiled as Jim Shane pulled open the door to the lounge. A bottle broke in the back of the room. Alex, Jim's favorite cocktail waitress, hoisted a full load of Rolling Rocks and Jagermeister shots. The ivory banging from eight pool tables filled the room.

"Jimbo!" yelled one of the burly bartenders stationed at the main bar.

"Perry, what's going on here?" Shane pulled his friend over the bar and they embraced with a bear hug.

"My following has arrived. Pretty impressive, huh?" Perry Coles, a native of Kalispell, smiled at his friend and boss. "You back to work?"

"Can't you handle this? Don't crumble on me, now. I just pulled in from driving four days straight. Man, I don't care if I ever see Chicago, again. Where's Garett?"

"I'm not sure. Try upstairs. I think he's up there closing down the dining room."

"Thanks."

The noise level subsided as Jim climbed the over-sized staircase leading to the main dining room. The hostess stand was empty at this late hour and the kitchen had been closed for almost thirty minutes. Three tables remained at some stage of their dinner. Two busboys cris-crossed the room clearing tables and folding linen napkins. The mammoth stone fireplace crackled with a fading fire. Sparks shot across the floor with each burst of wood. Garett Baine stood huddled over the computer station with one remaining waitress. Jim waited by the stairway. Garett was completing the last staff check-out. He decided to wait for Garett at the bar downstairs. A cold one might go down just fine. Before Jim could reach the stairs, Perry Coles stuck his head up the stairwell and yelled. In any bar, there are certain tones that are not ignored.

"Garett, you up there? Traylor's got a problem with one of the customers at the back bar. I think you need to see this."

Garett Baine moved quickly but within his own reactions. Frantic always meant scared. Bar owners were not supposed to act scared or frantic. It fueled most alcohol induced predicaments. Garett moved swiftly down the stairway. He didn't notice Jim Shane standing by the hostess stand. Jim kept silent. He wasn't hiding, but simply allowed Garett to address the more pressing issue. Jim Shane followed Garett down the stairway. Perry Coles was leading him to the back bar. A large crowd gathered at the back bar. This particular bar was not used during the majority of the year. Garett found it necessary to open the back bar on sporadic weekends during the summer. Most often, he would work the bar himself if the business needed it. Tonight, something was causing quite a commotion. When Garett reached the bar, he had to stop and regroup for a moment. What he encountered was undeniably unique. Standing at the bar, was the fullback and captain of the University of Montana Rugby Team. The team was in route to a rugby tournament in Whitefish over the holiday weekend. The Flathead Saloon and Cathouse had been playing host to the team since they arrived shortly after 5:00 p.m. Rugby defined men. The fullback defined the team. This team had been drinking from their boots for the past hour. The epitomy of this team, stood erect at the bar. His neck was short and thick. The shoulders and arms blended into a barrel. He sported a premature receding hairline at the age of twenty. Black hair covered his arms and shoulders, continuing on his back. At six feet one, he packed two hundred and thirty five pounds into a sleek one piece, red, woman's bathing suit. The thighs were cut up over the waist. The back dipped to the buttocks. The gentleman's manhood poured out over the narrow crotch leaving nothing to the imagination. A couple of employees had suggested that the man get dressed. Those suggestions were ignored and the swim suit clad patron did not appear to be inclined to change. Thirteen members of the same team were not about to spoil the fun. Garett looked at the muscular man in the red bathing suit. A rather large appendage was hanging out of the suit. Prohibition had it's good points.

"As impressive as this may seem, I'm afraid you need to get dressed." Garett uttered the words knowing the response.

"I need to get another fucking pitcher. In fact, this whole team needs to get another round of pitchers. In fact, you can buy us these pitchers. Now, that sounds like a good idea, my friend?"

"Bad idea, my friend. Get dressed before I puke." Garett always lacked a little diplomacy. Before either one of them could respond, someone else stepped out of the crowd.

"Hey, fat fuck! You, the fat fuck in the red suit." Jim Shane moved between Garett and the rugby mountain. "I believe the owner of this establishment asked you to get dressed. I think the rest of us are bored looking at your balls." Garett Baine smiled at the sight of his friend. It was apparent that age had forgotten about Jim Shane.

"Your wife never was." The rugby man took the wrong route. He continued. "Tell you what. You buy us a round and I'll stop calling your wife. She'll be disappointed, cowboy, but four pitchers might get it done." The rugby captain in the red suit, the toughest man on a tough team, turned to bask in his vociferous triumph, certain of his opponent's imminent capitulation. Jim Shane was done speaking. He grabbed the man's testicles with the vice-like grip of a forty-two year old ex-Marine. The force of his grip paralyzed the young man. In the same split second, Jim grabbed what was left of the man's thinning hair and slammed his head backwards. With the heel of his size twelve Tony Llamas, Jim crushed the left instep of the man in the red suit. His foot shattered. The breaking sounds were unmistakable. In less than ten seconds, the problem resolved itself. Jim stood over the man wreathing in pain. His teammates were less than enthusiastic about following their leader. Shane leaned over the man he continued to hold against the bar. He whispered without relinquishing his grip on either hand.

"I don't think my wife would have liked you at all." Jim released his grip and the young man crumbled to the floor. Jim Shane turned to Garett. "You call this running a business?" A smile stretched across his face.

"That's something you would have done." Garett ran his hand through his hair as a rugby team rushed to aid their fullback.

"No fucking way. Red is definitely not my color."

"Get this guy out of here." Garett instructed the team. "Nice timing." he muttered as he approached Jim Shane and the two embraced hard. "We missed you, man."

Three members of the rugby team had a long drive to reach Kalispell Regional Hospital. One would be missing the holiday tournament. Garett and Jim watched as the room returned to normal. Jim got caught up with some of the staff, while Garett finished the check out in the dining room. They agreed to meet in the office in fifteen minutes.

Jim was waiting in the office when Garett made it back downstairs. Jim Shane had a cigarette and a two Genuine Drafts.

"I got you a beer."

"Have you been to the house, yet?" Garett asked while reaching for the Genuine Draft on his desk.

"No. I drove in from Chicago over the past four days. I intended to immediately go to the house and see the kids. Something changed when I got to Lakeside. I came here first. I wanted to talk to you, but got sidetracked by the swimsuit competition at your pageant."

"Your judging techniques are somewhat unorthodox, yet remarkably effective. Thanks for taking the wind out of those sails."

"What is it they say? Timing is everything. Garett, what should I expect at the house? Call Lindsay and tell her I'm in town. If this is too soon, I'll understand." Jim Shane did not wear timid well.

"I got a letter from Joe Cortez, last week. It was a short note telling me about your visit to Chicago. He sent along a newspaper article. The article detailed the arrest of Park Huu Chau at Gibson's. The paper described Chau as an international drug operative, masquerading under a different identity for years in this country. Chau and the company you told me about, Nagr Industries, built a network of diaper plants all over the world to front massive shipments of heroin and cocaine. The whereabouts of Chau's confinement will not be released. Seems as though his ten year absence from the human race may have exhausted a number of diplomatic channels. If convicted on all charges, Chau will reside in prison for the remainder of his life. The paper, also, mentioned the bank accounts seized at the time of the arrest. Mr. Chau was able to accumulate millions of dollars under two names in a number of foreign bank accounts."

"There will be no more threats to anyone. Chau's put away. His people won't know where he is. Since the government in Vietnam never co-operated with the United States in extraditing Chau, the State Department will make Mr. Chau disappear. Chau's assets will be returned to the Vietnamese government. That way, both governments can continue the channels of recognition without Nagr making noise. The amount seized far exceeds the five million that Nagr was seeking. The State Department swallows Chau in a series of drug related charges. He faces prison terms in Florida, New York, California, and Washington D.C."

"So, this thing is over?" Garett asked.

"This thing is over." Jim Shane was looking straight ahead into the eyes of his friend. Garett remained still for a moment, then picked up the phone and buzzed the main bar.

"Perry, have Alex bring a couple of MGD's to the office." Garett put the phone down. "Jim, I got a call from Spencer Dryden on Monday. I haven't talked to him since the night of the shooting. We never had any contact after Trexon hit the motherload. No one knew what the SEC investigation would reveal. Turns out, they found nothing illegal or improper. They may have suspected the unusual, but nothing they chose to pursue. Spencer called to ask for the Social Security numbers for my kids. He informed me that there were ten accounts set up at Dean Witter through an attorney named Richard Nilsson. Seven accounts were set up as trusts with Jim Shane as the trustee. The accounts are for Justine, Jasmine, and Brian Shane. Conner, Christopher, Maggie, and Jake Baine. Two other accounts were set up in the name Jason Sun Ja Lee and Sanya Tu Lee. Each account exceeded $250,000. The disbursement of the money would take place over a ten year period beginning when each child reached the age of twenty-three. The account for Sanya Tu Lee is a standard brokerage account. This account was funded with one million dollars. Ms. Lee would have access to that account from day one. Spencer explained the accounts as long term goals with investments in blue chip stocks, conservative equity mutual funds, municipal bonds and laddered CD's.. These accounts should be substantially more by the time these children reach the age of disbursement. Jim, this will set these children up for life. What about the money? The legalities? The risks?"

"The risks, Garett? They took Denise. I'm not about to put the rest of my family at risk, again. I went back to Chicago for the purpose of eliminating any further risk. Cortez, the DEA, and the State Department wanted Chau. Hell, they hadn't seen him in twelve years. I agreed to produce Chau under the strict provision that the money Nagr forfeited was a business transaction. No indictments or claims would be made on the funds. My attorney, Richard Nilsson, has the affidavits signed by the Justice Department. A sizable portion of these funds will be claimed by the Internal Revenue Service. The balance was put into these accounts."

"There is an account for the Flathead Saloon and Cathouse. A quarter million dollars in money market. The account is in my name."

"It's your place. We always talked about the winter. No one knew what kind of business the winter would bring. This should help if it tanks."

"Jim, we could close for the winter if we wanted to."

"That's the point, Garett. You have the choice."

"How did Cortez get involved in a Federal investigation? He is a TAC Unit officer in the 12th District."

"I know you contacted Cortez after I left. He relayed your concern that I would go after Chau. I never intended to physically harm Chau, although, God knows, I wanted to. I met with Cortez and told him that I could produce Chau. The DEA got Chau. That's what they cared about. The feds did seize

Chau's accounts. There would be no way to determine the origin of every dollar. Cortez leaked the amount to the papers. The leak included a DEA statement concerning a five million dollar deposit that had been funneled through an escrow account in Chicago. In return for the leaks, I gave them Chau. Nagr's missing five million is now accounted for."

"How can you be sure they won't come after you, again?"

"Garett, they're not going to issue a written guarantee."

"Who is Sanya Lee and Jason Lee?"

"Jason is my son. It's a long story. Do you remember a girl named Sunny Lee?"

"Sure. She was the girl from Texas after you got back from Vietnam. I never met her."

"Sunny is Sanya Tu Lee. She was pregnant when we split up in Texas. I never knew. I met them both in Chicago. I'll give you the details later. I want to go see my kids. I know Brian's up. I'm sure Jake's with him. We haven't talked about that night at the lake. All these weeks, I was afraid to ask about the fallout. I can't blame Lindsay if she never speaks to me, again."

"Jim, don't expect fallout from Lindsay. Accountability is not about blame."

"No? Garett, accountability is blame. It is the assignment of responsibility. To renounce. To condemn. No matter what I do for the rest of my life, no matter how good it gets, or how much I accomplish, I will always wake up knowing that I would trade every single day of my life to give Denise one more. Will there ever be a morning when I don't think about her? No. If I am able to raise three great kids and these kids are fortunate enough to bring families of their own into the world, I will still regret every day since Denise died."

"Self pity doesn't suit you at all." Garett commented.

"Garett, I love you, but spare me the rhetorical analysis. I have overdosed on the incredible appetite in this country for call-in hypocrisy. Move on with your life, begin a new chapter, or get past it, are all terrific talk- radio slogans for the Wal-Mart shrinks paid to advise the megabytes generation. Honesty is inside. You can't get rid of it or hide from it. All the catch phrases in the world won't change it. It's always there."

"I know you've been honest with me. I just want you to understand something. That's enough. That's all I ever asked for."

"I want to go look at my girls, Garett. I know they're sleeping. I don't care. I need to go talk to Brian. I'm not giving up my relationship with my son. If it takes twenty years for him to understand, I want it to start now. Call for me, Garett. I owe Lindsay the courtesy of calling. Shit, that doesn't even begin to scratch the surface of what I owe her. Will she see me?"

"I think so."

"Could you call her?"

"That's not necessary."

"Man, just call her. I can't imagine that my involvement with the shooting was accepted blindly."

"It wasn't accepted at all. " Garett pulled the remainder of his Genuine Draft. " I never told them."

*   *   *

CHAPTER THIRTY-EIGHT

The lights framed the entrance to the Lakeside Boulevard compound. It was nearly midnight when Jim's truck pulled down the gravel drive. The two houses were quiet but not dark. Through the main house, Jim could see the kitchen lights and the television glaring from the great room overlooking the lake. He knew Brian and Jake were still up. Lindsay and the other children had most likely gone to sleep. Brian and Jake often fell asleep in front of the television. There would always be the excuse of waiting up for Garett and Jim. Barbara Pendleton kept many lights on all night. She was raised in an era where safety was not an issue at bedtime. It was now. Jim Shane would leave his luggage in the truck. He and Brian would pull it out in the morning. Jim walked slowly through the shed examining the tools hung in specific order. Perfect. The bows were tight and the axes were sharp. Brian maintained the order he was taught. The flagstone walkway crackled in the winter air. Jim walked to the north side of the property where the guest house was located. Jasmine and Justine would be sound asleep. They slept like black bears in the winter Rockies. Outside of thunder, those girls could sleep through a bull ride at a Montana rodeo. Jim unlocked the deadbolt and pushed the front door open. The house was immaculate. Pictures of the kids lined the mantle over the fireplace. The kitchen lights cast a yellow glow throughout the front room. An over-sized Scottish plaid sofa was flanked by the stone fireplace and the corduroy easy chair. The kitchen sparkled with flavor of dinner still in the air. Colorful drawings adorned the refrigerator. Jim reached the hallway. The bedroom doors were pulled, but not shut. Barbara slept in the first room. Jim peeked in Barbara's room. She slept in a single bed. Through the white hair and age, the image of her daughter was all too evident. Jasmine and Justine's room was located at the back of the hall. Jim's eyes fell upon two angels in the night. He kissed each one of his daughters. They smelled of somber innocence, a mixture of children's shampoo and Vapo-rub. Jasmine never slept under the covers. A tattered blanket was curled up under her chin. Justine was burrowed under two blankets and a comforter.

The baseboard heat toasted the room. Jim sat for nearly five minutes. He wondered why the children made him feel safe. He thought about the morning and two little girls tugging at his neck.

Brian and Jake were parked in the great room of the main house. They dozed through the cable channels, while a half eaten bowl of popcorn would provide Juneau with a midnight snack. The lake and the mountains painted the windows in reflections along the rear of the main house. The lighthouse brushed the deck with dim efforts from a fading beacon. Garett had meant to change those lights for the past week. The dog was aroused by the sporadic wildlife darting through the property. Brian watched as the dog became agitated and paced the length of the back windows.

"Relax, tough guy. Do you want to go out?" Brian groaned as he rose to open the door for the eighth time of the evening. Before he reached the doors, a reflection in the window startled him. He noticed a red truck in the glass reflecting from the back of the house. Brian turned and hurried through the kitchen to the back door. The Ram pick-up sat at the top of the drive.

"Dad!"

Jim Shane was halfway across the property. The lawn between the guest house and the main house covered one hundred and fifty feet. The snow was marked by the activity of the afternoon. Three sleds carved their tracks into the early season powder. The kids rode the soft slope to the frozen edges of Flathead Lake. Jim stopped to gather a glove, forgotten and wet. A translucent moon traced the Mission Range mountains while casting long shadows across the water. He saw Brian pulling at the glass doors. Jim stood up to watch his son. The small boat was barely visible at two hundred feet from the shore. Red laser dots danced through the snow. Two shots pierced the solitude of Flathead Lake.

*   *   *